# MENTALLY ORGANIZED BUSINESS

RICH CAMACHO

NOTEBOOK
PUBLISHING

First published in 2019 by Notebook Publishing,
20–22 Wenlock Road, London, N1 7GU.

www.notebookpublishing.co

ISBN: 9780993589843

A CIP catalogue record for this book is available
from the British Library.

Typeset by Notebook Publishing.

To Mom & Dad: We're going to Disney World!
But not before we make a trip to the bookstore :)

In Memory of Adrie Thom and Raymond Edwards:

Brothers,
You both played vital roles in my life, and at different junctures, respectively, your very presence paid dividends. You were two of the best men I've ever known, and I learned so much from both of you. I will always keep your memories alive within me. I miss you and I love you both dearly. I hope I've made you proud.

—Rich

# ACCLAIMS

"I find it amazing how a writer is even allowed to publish these disgusting words under the Literature category. I am appalled!"

—Random white woman

"Fascinating."

—Older black guy from Harlem

"There's no way you could put this book down: it flows freely from the beginning to the end. There is something about Rich Camacho's writing style that keeps you stuck to the edge of your seat. This guy is awesome!"

—The INquirer

"How anybody could say this is great writing, I'll never understand. They should be hung. As a matter of fact, I think I'll partake in said hanging right now... Honey, where's the noose?"

—Stupid Racist from God-Knows-Where

"Camacho has done it again! (Although I do believe this is his first book, so I'm not sure how he's done it again, but...) Read this book ASAP!"

—Impulsive Reader from Barnes & Noble


"What is this guy sniffing? Is he on crack cocaine? Blue magic? Angel dust? Whatever he's doing, I want in!"

—Stonehead Society


"Amazing story; wonderfully written; comedic God! I don't approve of all the profanity, though..."

—Rich Camacho's mom


"This guy fuckin' rules! Where the fuck are the chimichangas at?"

—Deadpool


"I want this guy arrested! He should not be walking the streets, claiming that this book is worth more than 79 cents at a flea market! T.R.A.S.H.—to the fifth power!"

—Random man at flea market who only had 78 cents in his pocket.

"Incredible!"

"Kiss my ass! You know I've been trying to fuck you since elementary school, but you fucked my sister! Fuck you, Ice Cube! Oops, I mean, fuck you, Rich Camacho! I hope you rot in hell! Great book, but you're still a piece of shit!"

"This is not supposed to have a happy ending: the streets are negative. This book is just like a horror movie... It's supposed to end horribly!"

"That's my boy! Where does he even find the time to do this? With his wife and all them damn kids... Hell! And them two dogs! Oh, yeah, Rich, the Mets suck this year..."

"The fact this idiot can call himself a published author is insane to me; the guy can hardly spell his name correctly! I mean, c'mon! The guy has two middle initials, and one of them is a number! He is a menace to society, and should be blackballed from all of entertainment—period!"

"I believe this guy is an absolute genius! (Can you please put the gun down now, Mr. Camacho?)"

—A frightened critic who was asked nicely to review the book

"I can't wait for the next book! I hope this is the start of a series! I want to hear more about Frederick Linguini and Alexandria the Grape!"

—The Food Network

# FOREWORD I

S O, WHERE TO BEGIN after more than thirty years of brotherhood? I guess you start at Irvington Little League in New Jersey. At that point, I didn't know I would have a brother from another mother, but that's exactly what I have—and, before we had ever even played a game against one another, his dad, Ordonez, was telling me to stay in line during our baseball parade in Irvington Center. From that very moment, from that first game until now, we have been in each other's lives constantly.

Rich has always been that friend I had the most in common with, from sports, to losing our virginities after most of our other friends, to loving our families and always trying to do the right thing, always. We have both made a lot of mistakes in our lives and—in essence, anyway—, but he has been my twin in so many ways.

When Rich first told me that he was writing this book about our family, I kind of laughed to myself: I didn't think our story was able to be told in such a large capacity, but after he explained how he was doing it, I realized all the possibilities it could bring. "That's going to be a very different type of book," I'd pointed out. The more he told me how our childhood M.O.B. aliases were being portrayed and how he was approaching it, I felt much more compelled to want to read such a novel and see how he would bring us all to life from his creative and humorous perspective.

Rich is the only one I know who could write this book of our family and do it justice—not because he is the only creative one amongst us, but because he is, to me, the most versatile person in our family. I believe that, with his talent and excitement for this book, he will turn the volume way up on these real-life adaptations and personas of the people who were closest to him when we were growing up.

With family, you're going to go through tough times, but I can't think of one moment when I was upset or created any bad memories with my brother... well, unless we're counting the fact that he sucked his high school senior year at baseball! We played on the same great teams and performed on the biggest stages together, but none of that ever took precedence over the brotherhood we have.

All jokes aside, I love this guy, and I can't wait to read this book. I know we will be celebrating the greatness of what we're all about to experience.

Thank you, big brother. I love you.

Talib Winston

# FOREWORD II

WHEN I WAS INITIALLY approached about this book being made, my first thought was, *It's been done: Rich wrote this book chronicling our legendary movement many moons ago,* containing the names, bios, events, and history of our new families. However, it had never been done quite like this.

Never has a story of destiny, fate, and happenstance ever been told in this capacity. When I think back on this thing of ours we have created, only one word comes to mind: family.

See, I was never really close with my immediate family: I never had a brother or a sister, and as much as I had lots of cousins, most of them were either too old or too young to hang with. I never really had an issue with making friends, but I always thought how funny it was how God (or whatever you believe) moves certain chess pieces into place.

Who knew our obsession with the mafia and its influence on hip-hop culture at the time (remember Wu-Gambinos?) would manifest into me having an extended family for life. We (Rich, Sam, and I) literally created these crazy names based off various personalities, mobster figures, and our very unique and crude humor. It was shortly thereafter that we provided similar names to some of our closest friends—and, considering we were pretty popular, these didn't take long to catch on. However, this was an extreme understatement: what started as a group of three grew to thirty, which then quickly grew to fifty and, before long, more than we could count. What had started as a joke became something we would take far more seriously than anticipated: we were littered with power, respect, and loyalty. What started as a crew became a family I had always prayed for—a family that would love me unconditionally and hold one another down the moment we need each other. What started as a friendship grew into a bond that blossomed into an unparalleled lifetime of love. What started as an idea became life as we know it and would change our worlds forever.

This thing that we started all those years ago hasn't finished, and it's etched in the hearts and minds of us all.

So, in conclusion, I repeat, this book has been done before—but never, ever quite like this!

Cory Davis

# PROLOGUE

"**P**ENNY, COULD YOU PLEASE worry about the job at hand and stop looking at the dude over in the corner with the Reebok pumps on?" Pudgee cried out. "I mean, really; Reebok pumps? They don't even have the *orange* pump on them. *What* are *those*? This guy's a *loser!*"

"Oh my God, I'm just *looking*," Penny huffed. "Besides, I think he's kinda cute. I be seeing him over there every now and then, and I know he's seen me checking him out. Can you blame the kid?" She playfully tossed some hair over her shoulder. "I'm pretty cute myself, if you ask me."

"Nobody asked you, girl!"

"Yo, you're tripping," Penny replied.

"I'm trippin'? Kinda cute! This fool look like a bag of ass juice had a baby with the lead zombie from *The Walking Dead* and"—she clapped her hands together for emphasis—*"Boom*, out came this nigga!"

"Damn! Don't you think that's a little harsh? Ass juice?"

"Yes! Ass juice!" Pudgee insisted. "Now, bring ya little self over here... you know my brother is gonna be on our asses if we don't take care of this the way he wanted. We wanna graduate, right?"

"Okay, sis, damn... calm the fuck down. I *got* this. Don't I always?"

Penny and Pudgee were the little sisters of two of Ghost Town's leaders, the former being the Inspector Deck (of Wu-Tang Clan fame) of our crew: she would sit and watch you play yourself for hours on end and then, just when the time was right, *bam*, she'd go in for the kill. She'd always had a maniacal approach, cooler than Freddie Jackson sipping a milkshake in... well, whatever that song was. She was smooth as a baby's ass on Sunday morning— although I'm not quite sure why it can't be Tuesday or Thursday morning. Nevertheless, she'd get the job done discreetly.

Pudgee Da Phat Escobar had always been the direct one, the one who never bit her tongue for anything or anyone; the one who, regardless of her size, would talk shit to the biggest of men. She took a lot after our aunt, Myrtle Escobar—God rest her soul—, who once intentionally threw her beloved husband out of a fifth-floor window.

Pudgee was also the one who knew everybody's business but could never mind her own, which is probably why everyone always went to her when they needed some information on the daily happenings or the newest rumor in town. "Ask Pudgee," they'd say, "she knows everything."

Her nickname was The Star-Ledger, which was our town's city newspaper—a rather fitting nickname.

The duo spent their days trying to impress us and move up in the family rankings. They were the cutest things walking, but also deceivingly dangerous—more dangerous than a motherfucker: when it came down to it, they followed through with whatever we needed them to do. They weren't necessarily the "killers", but more of the ones who used their beauty and smarts to lure in the newest dummy—hence making room for the actual killers.

My name is PR Escobar, a.k.a., Delayno Floyd, a.k.a., Paul Hardcastle, and if I told you what else I'm known as, I'd have to kill you. I am one of the original three members of MentallyOrganizedBusiness, and I created this atrocity of personalities alongside my longtime compadres, my boys, my homies, my testicles, my booboos—more notably, my brothers Don Corione and Sam Luciano. What started as a joke in the living room of brother Luciano's crib grew into this immense conglomerate that reigned supreme over the entire East Coast. New Jersey was our original stomping grounds, although we eventually grew to Boston, New York, Connecticut, Delaware, Pennsylvania, North Carolina, Georgia, Alabama, and Florida.

Business was executed internationally, as well as when Sam Luciano and Hak Hennesey went on a special assignment together for a few years, sacrificing themselves and their time with their respective families for the betterment of the business. Led by Harry Horrendous, a few of our henchmen later joined them on some overseas excursions that benefitted us greatly in the years to come. Members also eventually popped up in Chicago, Detroit, and even California and Las Vegas.

MentallyOrganizedBusiness was exactly that: a faction of cerebral assassins; a collective unit that would make you want to commit suicide upon realizing you couldn't do anything better than us. You weren't as cool as us, you didn't dress in the same clothing as us, you didn't have the best athletes or musicians in the state. We got all the girls—and hell, even our leading ladies had all the guys drooling over them. I guess it's safe to say we were incredibly popular.

How can I get into the business, you may ask? Do I have to know someone? Is there an initiation process? Do I have to kill someone to prove myself? Indeed, there were many misconceptions on how you became a member of the family.

All in all, we had a lengthy run—some would say a Godly run. Of course, there were always others who would pretend not to care and shrug, "They weren't shit." Chances are, those people are now probably somewhere asking Jimmy Hoffa to move over because there's "not enough room in here for all of us".

In other words, people didn't fuck with us—or, in layman's terms, we weren't to be fucked with, period. So now, I think it's time for you to just lay back, put your lube away (you nasty motherfucker), kick your feet up, and experience the legendary MentallyOrganizedBusiness crew. This book is priceless, so don't talk shit about how much it cost: "I know these motherfuckers... Why didn't I get a free copy?" Simple: because I spent months on end creating this entertaining shit, and somebody has to pay for the carpal tunnel surgery in the end!

Now shut the fuck up and enjoy yourself—and promise me you'll tell someone to buy their own copy. I strongly suggest you not let someone borrow yours because we might kill... well, just don't do it. Thanks in advance.

# CHAPTER 1

"Yo! You fuckin' Tony Danza, jean jacket-wearing ass nigga! I'm telling you now, if you get any mud on my new carpet, I'm fuckin' you up, right where you stand." Tony Victor sniffed. "Matter fact, where the fuck is my Tupac tape I let you hold, like, eight years ago? I don't care what other album you keep, but my 'Pac album? Nah, son... I'm 'a have to put this size fourteen up ya ass!"

"Ahh, relax, you Jack Tripper, ankle socks-wearin' ass nigga!" yelled Al Gebra. "Niggas came over with 40s and blunts and I ain't know..."

"Nigga! That ain't got shit to do with my tape!" Tony said.

"I'll buy you four more 'Pac tapes," Al shrugged.

I can't tell you the amount of these comedic back-and-forths we had with on another; we could probably write an entire book just on those verbal spats alone.

"So, what the fuck's up? I got a chick waiting for me in two of my rooms right now so this better be fucking good!"

"Escobar said we got an emergency meeting at The House of Nesbit in twenty-five minutes," Al responded. "He said he tried calling you, but you didn't answer—and you know he don't call twice, so hurry the fuck up and get your two-point-seven minutes in with these chicks. I'll be waiting in the whip with Celo for you."

"Man, fuck outta here!" Tony exclaimed, exasperated. "That ain't *nowhere* near the time I need: tell Escobar he gotta give me an hour at least, or I ain't coming."

"Yeah, aight. I ain't telling him shit. Either you come downstairs, or you face the consequences, and I don't think you want that. I'll see you in a few minutes." Al turned on his heel and left.

Tony Victor was our lead henchmen, the guy with the no-nonsense demeanor, the guy who looked like he wanted to slap the shit out of your grandmother every time he walked into a room. He was the muscle, the call you made when you were in trouble. The *Schwartzaniggah*, if you will: the Kronus from *God of War*. Plus, I'm pretty sure he had twenty-seven other aliases, and I didn't want to fuck with any of them son-of-a-bitches. Nonetheless, we had a very sound and mutual respect, and when one came calling, the other responded.

Tony decided to engage in a quickie with the lesser looking of the chicks by bending her over his new custom designed recliner—courtesy of the good folks at Diakonos Designs. After reaching his climax, he sent her home in a taxicab—the Uber of the past—before fleeing downstairs, peeking his head into the so-called bachelor room and asking the other woman to wait there till he got back. He admired her nakedness, spread out on his sheets, looking like a chocolate goddess. He hurried to put on his signature army hat and black Timberlands before locking his front door, leaving just enough time for them to get to The House of Nesbit.

"Damn, son, that was quicker than I thought," Al commented. "I didn't *actually* mean two-point-seven minutes—you could've stayed for at least three. You're the worst." He shook his head in mock disapproval and started the car. "You're getting old, man. Maybe you need to try that Viagra shit that just hit the market. We could stop at Rite-Aid on the way?"

"Man, shut the fuck up and drive before I rip your dick out'ya throat and feed it to the pigeons!"

Celo sat shotgun in the '91 Acura and simply shook his head. Celo didn't talk much, but when he did, everyone listened—and this just happened to be a time where I guess he didn't see it fit to say anything. Instead, he chuckled at Al and Tony. He was probably wondering how they hadn't killed each other yet—but then again, who knows what goes on in the mind of Celo Gaston? He was an honest man, a man who had lived a not-so-easy life but still came out on top—and that alone was worth applauding.

Celo cracked his window in hopes of the wind making just enough noise that it'd drown out the constant bantering between the other two: you'd think they were sponsored by the LGBTQ+ community or some shit, the way they went at each other.

Being honest, I wasn't sure how successful he thought he'd be: despite the fact that they were driving on a residential block and it was around seventeen degrees that night—to the point where he couldn't exactly put the window all the way down without freezing his nipples off—he was pretty damn hopeful.

# CHAPTER 2

*Location: Tasty's Chicken Shack; 7:37 pm*

"I SWEAR TO GOD, if there's onions on this cheesesteak, I'm reaching around this window and ripping your mustache right off your face."

Frederick Linguini did not give one fuck: not half a fuck, or a quarter of a fuck, even. He often spent his time trying to figure out why anyone was left breathing who didn't understand that a cheesesteak had no business having onions on it—he just couldn't understand the logic behind it.

He was a killer, a shoot first, ask questions last kind of guy. Although he always talked about becoming a chef of some sort, he could never leave the business alone. I had always thought the culinary world would've done him good: it probably would've been exactly what he needed to bring some satisfaction to his life. Believe it or not, Frederick Linguini made the best damn cheesecake I'd ever had—but don't tell my momma that. Outside of the fact that he was a great cook, he had never exactly met a meal he didn't like. He was a large individual, the kind of guy who I assumed the toilet paper companies probably tried recruiting to be a spokesperson for.

Now, he sat down at the table and took a big-ass bite from his sandwich. It was then that his phone rang—and it wasn't his normal *Please, Hammer, Don't Hurt 'Em* ringtone: it was *the* ringtone, the one that made him take a deep exhale and smirk devilishly simultaneously. He picked up, all he could initially hear being the sounds of the legendary rapper Cheef Bali playing in the background.

"Fred? Fred, can you hear me?"

*Yeah, if you turn the damn music down,* Frederick thought.

"Frederick! It's Sam Luciano."

"Brother Samuel! What's shaking?" Frederick said, grinning. "I was just about to indulge myself in one of our favorite cheesesteaks—you know, the one with everything but onions and extra mayo? I'll bring you one after I'm finished fucking this one up, if you like?"

"No, thank you, Fred. Although I appreciate the offer, I'm calling you for an impromptu emergency meeting taking place. Call Snugglez and tell him he needs to be there as well." Sam's tone was serious. "I need you to round up Muscles Montana, Blues Holloway, and the rest of the henchmen. Meet me O3 at The House of Nesbit, tonight at eight. Exact. Don't let me down—there'll be a handsome reward for you once this situation concludes. Got it?"

"Got it, boss," Frederick replied.

Frederick Linguini couldn't not pass up his meal, so he immediately began calculating how long he had to eat his sandwich, pick up the henchmen, and get to The House of Nesbit in the next half hour. After thinking long and hard about all this—and even contemplating being late—, he got up, slid his chair rather forcefully under the shack's table, and threw his sandwich in the garbage. He would not be rushed eating, nor could he drive while eating. Besides, after threatening the cook and the time it took talking to Luciano, the damn sandwich was already cold.

"Son-of-a-bitch," he muttered under his breath.

# CHAPTER 3

SARA SAFEBREAKA AND WHISH Johannsen were very close friends—sandbox buddies, if you will. They finished each other's sentences and borrowed each other's clothes: after all, that's what sisters did. Although unfortunately, they weren't the "stay at home and play with dolls" kind of chicks growing up: these women were bosses. Alongside fellow boss Mula Madison, who ran the Spanish division of the business on the outskirts of North Newark to Queens, NYC, these women would spit in your face and make you believe you liked it—plus, they were trained by O3, so they were the Omega to their Alpha.

Since they were little girls, they'd figured out ways to steal the subs from Kathy's Corner Deli and the candy from the front shelves at C-Town, the local supermarket. They weren't exactly the typical "can't wait to take you to meet my mother" girlfriends, either—although I guess it depends on who you're speaking with. A lot of guys in the neighborhood loved them, and the girls wanted to be them—because of their attractive exterior, yes, but also because of the attitudes that came with them. They were sexy, according to most of the guys.

Married to Sara Safebreaka, Al Gebra had known she was The One back in Elementary School—but then again, he had also thought she would change her maiden name after walking down that aisle. Safe to say, she didn't: she just didn't like how Sara Gebra sounded, or even the ever-so-popular hyphenated surname of Safebreaka-Gebra.

"It doesn't roll off the tongue smoothly," she had ever-so-eloquently stated, shrugging—and that had been it: she'd refused to lose Safebreaka if it meant potentially losing the legacy she'd created along with it.

After receiving their orders, they walked past a couple arguing about some fat-ass the guy had looked at the other night, or something of that nature. That was usually a way to get your girl to slap the taste buds out of your mouth—or at least to warrant a swift kick to the family juelz santanas.

"Excuse me," muttered the lady disparagingly, "are you two going to act like I didn't just see you checking out my man?"

Whish and Sara looked behind them and then back at each other.

"Is she talking to you?"

"Nah, she can't be talking to you, and she's not talking to me... so I don't understand. Who could she be talking to in that disrespectful tone?"

"Yeah, bitches, I'm talking to the both of you!" the lady continued, her voice laced with rage.

Sara turned to Whish. "Will you hold my purse real quick?"

Whish obliged and, just when the crazy woman's threats grew even more vulgar and she tried to reach for Sara's hair, *blast*, Whish shot a bullet through her temple.

Just like that.

The lady dripped to the floor like excess paint from a wall. Both wearing heels and ignoring the girl's boyfriend, Whish and Sara stepped over the corpse's body.

"Come on, girl!" Whish continued. "How could you get strawberry icing on the necklace I sto—bought for you? I swear to Mother Nature herself, you can't keep nothing nice." (Note that the MentallyOrganizedBusiness women felt that God was indeed a woman, and Mother Nature was her name.) "You keep this up, and Al won't be buying nothing lavish for you anymore."

"*Shit*, girl, if he wants this pussy, he gon' get me anything I tell him to get me," Sara shot back. "Besides, my requests are automatic; we're married, for God's sake!"

"Alright, girl," Whish shrugged. "If you say so. Hey, have you spoken to Mula recently? I heard she's been teaching her little brother Gwop Madison the tricks of the trade. That little boy is eight years *old*; why she doing that to that little boy?"

They both laughed while Sara's phone beeped. She looked at it and sighed.

"I just got a two-way message from Don Corione: he needs us at The House of Nesbit by eight. Business as usual, I guess," she huffed. "Well, duty calls. I can't even appreciate my strawberry sundae with these stupid-ass hoes lurking throughout town. I'm telling you, Whish, I'm thinking about moving to Canada. At least that country treats their people like they mean something, you know?"

"Girl, I ain't talking no damn politics and civil rights with you right now; we gotta let Mula know—and the rest of the Feline Council."

"Feline Council?"

"You like the name?" Whish grinned. "I've been trying to come up with a slick but sexy name for the other ladies in our family, so I came up with that. Well, do you like it?"

"Whish," Sara whispered gently, "I like it as much as I like gettin' fucked in the ass with a blowtorch." Whish snorted. "I like it almost as much as I like scrotum sweat spread on my pancakes in the morning." Whish whacked her sister on the arm. "That name sucks left titties. We'll come up with a better one, *together*. Now, who in the hell is gonna clean this mess up? Does Dairy Queen have a janitor on-site?"

# CHAPTER 4

*Location: 18th Avenue; Livingston, NJ; 7:41 pm*

AN ALBUM BY RAEKWON the Chef blasted out of Jay BaDouche's trunk as he waited for Hak Hennesey to finish getting dressed. Salawicious Dough—blood brother of Hak Hennesey—never had the patience to wait for Hak: he'd take eight years to get dressed to go somewhere. Talk about annoying. Dough was probably at the meeting already, devising an evil plan to take over the world by using three rubber bands, a Jake "The Snake" Roberts DDT, and a smidgen of mustard. Jay, on the other hand, had the patience of a catfish sucking on the inner glass of a fish tank. He'd just sit there all damn day.

The Douchebag Bros, as they were so lovingly known as, were the epitome of bad influence: cool, good-looking guys, but not the guys you wanted teaching young men to value their women. They were gangsters and comedians a hundred percent of the time: I often didn't know if I should fear for my life or grab a tissue to wipe my tears from laughing so damn much when I was with them. Nevertheless, they were loyal, and I could count on them for literally anything.

"Jay!" called Hak. "Whaddup, fool! I ain't even know you was out here!"

"Nigga, get in the fuckin' car! I called you when I got here," Jay retorted.

"But that was over an *hour* ago."

"Yeah, I know, and I've been waiting for your slow ass since then."

"Damn, Jay, you're a loyal man," Hak grinned. "A man of integrity. An honest man. But since we're being honest, I wouldn't wait three minutes for you—although I feel bad now. Next time when we go through the Wendy's drive-thru, I got you—but don't fuckin' order no super-sized shit. I gotta save my coins for the trip to Jacksonville."

"Trip to Jacksonville? Hot-ass Florida? I *hate* that fuckin' state," Jay frowned. "And what trip you talkin' 'bout? I ain't know nothing about a trip out there."

"The one I'm taking ya moms to!" Hak responded. "You know, she been buggin' me to show her the naked beaches out there!"

Jay shook his head. "You asshole. I hate your bitchass. Literally hate the very essence of you. I hate everyone you know just 'cuz they know you."

They traveled up Springfield Avenue on the way to meet the rest of the crew at The House of Nesbit. They quickly saw fellow crew member Joseph Stylez on foot as he crossed Nye Avenue.

"Yo! Your car outta the shop yet?" Hak asked through the passenger window. Stylez eyed them: they knew full well he'd never had a car.

"Yeah, motherfucker, it's still in the shop where ya mom's at, giving out 'complete vehicle inspections' and asking niggas to 'change her oil'." Stylez rolled his eyes. "Open the fuckin' door, man; it's hotter than a devil's kneecap out here."

"Get in, nigga! We almost late."

"We good. We'll be there in five minutes, if that," Stylez shrugged. "Yo, turn the music down for a second. Matter of fact, turn that shit *off*." Hak obliged. "What happened the other night when I left the house? You know, with the chick who wanted me to blow her back out?"

Jay looked over to Hak; Hak looked over to Jay; and they both looked at Joseph Stylez with concerned expressions. Jay took a stick of yellow juicy fruit gum from out of the center console and asked, "You wanna take this young grasshopper, or shall I?"

Hak proceeded by explaining in the only way he knew how to. "Well, Joseph, if you must know, she was distraught that you were unable to insert your fine self—as she said—inside her Snapple circle due to your musical commitments. She just could not understand how you'd rather go somewhere with a bunch of other dudes to record some nursery rhymes— again, as she called it—and not want to be there going in and out of her, and in and out of her, and in and out of her, and in and—"

"Holy *shit*, I *get* it, dammit! Just finish the damn story!"

Hak was shaking with silent laughter. "So, we did what any genuine brothers would've done."

"Yeah, and what was that?" Joseph's expression was pure resentment.

"We sent her on the Amtrak."

Stylez looked puzzled. "You sent her home via railroad transportation? Wait a minute, doesn't she live, like, five minutes away, in Maplewood?" He shook his head. "Why would you make her take the train?"

"Oh, ain't nobody said nothing about sending her away." Hak's eyes glittered. "We ever-so-gently ran a hard-fought train on said vagina holder—because we felt bad for her, you know. You had a hook or some adlibs or some shit that you had to do, so we took turns wiping our penises on the curtain—ala Kool G. Rap."

Joseph Stylez looked on, —disgusted at the mere fact that he was even associated with these guys.

"You pieces of shit," Stylez muttered. "Did you at least take her home afterward?"

"Take her home?" Jay asked with the most perturbed look on his face. "The bitch is in the trunk right now!"

# CHAPTER 5

*Location: The House of Nesbit; Short Hills, NJ; 8:00 pm*

**M**ULTIPLE CARS PULLED UP at the precise time of 8pm: time was always of the essence, and it was as precious as a woman's vagina to Escobar, Corione, and Luciano.

Both wings of the beautifully gold-plated residence—located in the desirable city of Short Hills, NJ—all shined to the brims. There stood a gold statue of Velma the Goddess in the far-left corner of the East Wing, who just so happened to be the birthmother of Celo Gaston and the second mother to us all. Long ago, she'd opened her home to us all and showed us how to never let this world take advantage of you—and, as much as her approach may not have been the most popular one by some people's standards, it was the most respected one, and that resonated with us all deeply. Corione had paid for the statue: $35,000 in cash. Luciano paid for her grandkids to go to college, while I covered the rest of the mortgage on the house—which ironically only had just under $35,000 left on it. Celo was always grateful for the respect and genuine love we had for his family, and I know he knew how much we loved her.

Everyone who was supposed to be there was on time—as were a few passersby who seemed to think they'd been invited. However, they were stopped at the door by a couple stiff ones to the chin, courtesy of Snugglez McPherson and Muscles Montana. Hopefully they didn't leave any stains on the pavement: I didn't really feel like spending the money to have it cleaned. After all, the amount I'd had to spend getting shit professionally cleaned out of rugs, carpets, or whatever else, all while trying to avoid ongoing questions by the cleaning guy/girl/ authoritative figure that "just so happened to be in the neighborhood", was ridiculous.

As the seats filled, I gathered Corione and Luciano up.

"How in the blue hell are we going to tell them this?" I demanded. "What exactly do we say? What's the plan of action?"

After a few moments passed and some tears were shed, we rounded ourselves up and headed to the stage area. This was probably going to be the hardest thing we'd ever had to announce.

I chose to speak first.

"As many of you know, I just recently had my divorce finalized." I swallowed, hard. "It was heart wrenching, but a process that needed to be fulfilled nonetheless: my heart and soul were never fully connected with that woman. I know some of you weren't exactly happy about it because it would mean her excavation from MentallyOrganizedBusiness, and although that may be true, we have all made a pact to never harm her or her family." I sighed. "Now that I've shared that, this meeting was supposed to have been a happy one, one in which I could share my newfound happiness with you. A meeting to introduce you to my new queen, Tanyell Escobar, otherwise known as Yelly."

My new wife strutted her undeniable beauty to the stage to share in the announcement, and most—if not all— were elated for our newfound union: lots of the crew already knew and approved of her, something that filled me with ecstasy. However, this happiness was destined to be short-lived.

"Thank you. Thank you to everyone for their blessings, but I need silence right now. Because we've unfortunately brought you here for another reason, too."

The crowd looked around at each other in confusion, searching for some clarity. I walked over to Don and asked him to share with the family from this point, who obliged, quickly rising from his seat and walking over to the podium with me. It was probably the hardest announcement he was ever going to make.

"Ladies and gentlemen," he began, his throat catching, "it brings me great sadness to have to tell you that we lost one of our own late last night." Don grabbed his handkerchief and kept it in his right hand, as if he knew he'd probably be using it a few more times before the meeting was over. A ripple of shock passed over the crowd and all began looking around again, this time to see who wasn't in attendance.

After an uncomfortable few moments of silence, a voice laced with panic yelled out, "Remington! Remington's seat is empty. Where is he?" It was Mula Madison.

"He's probably late, or just leaving a different chick's house. You know how that fool do!" Joseph Stylez said quickly.

All the guys in the front row started high-fiving and talking some bravado and machismo stuff, singing Remington's praise.

"Yo! No more disrespect, family. We must let Don continue," shouted Sam Luciano. For some reason, something seemed to click with the crowd upon hearing Sam's words: suddenly, this was very real.

"I'm afraid Mula is correct in her assessment, family," Don announced. "Yes, Remington's chair is empty. And it will remain empty from this day forward."

The crowd was utterly silent. Everyone suddenly seemed in shock.

"It's true. Remington Steele is—"

"*No!*" a voice—cracked, broken, strangled—screamed out. "This can't be life! Anybody but him." It was Stylez. His exclamation was quickly followed with the sound of smashing glass: he had thrown his glass of wine against the wall. "How could this be? Take me to the fuckers and I'll kill them with my bare hands!"

"He was killed in a car accident late last night," explained Don. "Although the details are hazy at this point, there is no reason to believe that there was any foul play involved." He bit his lip and his eyes glistened, his whole body stiff as he tried to restrain his emotion. "This is a very sad day for the family and for our business as a whole. I want you all to reflect on the beautiful times we've shared with Brother Steele and remember him for who he was. We love our brother, and we will miss him terribly. We must continue moving to make sure that we take care of his family." His breath shuddered as he exhaled. "Meeting adjourned."

A deafening silence filled the air: it was literally as though God himself had pressed the Mute button on the big controller in the sky. At that point, all the bosses could feel what the other bosses were thinking, and everything suddenly felt extremely surreal: we were the untouchable MentallyOrganizedBusiness crew, the crew that never lost. We looked in the eye of Death and whooped its ass.

But not this time. This time had called for results we were not used to, results none of us really knew how to fathom. Sure, we'd seen Death before—usually on the other end of a smoking barrel—, but we'd never *felt* Death. This was different.

After a few moments, there were various rumblings, conversations filled up with everything from pure sadness to revenge plots toward anyone breathing or walking near them at that time of heartbreak and anguish. There was not a dry eye in the building.

Remington Steele was one of the most genuine souls we all knew, and, in a lot of ways, he was the glue that kept a lot of us together: he'd taught us how to juggle multiple chicks at once, how to dress and look crispy. He'd only owned about 10,000 button-up shirts. Hell, the man had literally taught me how to drive. He was the epitome of a hustler, using his car for any odd jobs to make extra cash around town. I remember taking a drive with him to Willow Brook Mall to see a chick when he was supposed to be delivering a pizza to someone in Totowa.

"Would I get fired if I delivered a pair of panties to the house this pizza is going to? You know, spread out on the pizza like a topping?" Remington had asked innocently.

"I'm pretty sure that level of adolescent behavior would be encouraged; in fact, if you delivered that pizza with panty topping to my house, I'd give you a triple tip," I'd responded.

We had both laughed uncontrollably.

If I'd known then how his loss would've affected a few of us, maybe, just maybe, we'd still be in business today— well, the flourishing business we once were, rather.

The greatest thing about life is that you never know what it's going to throw at you. To some people, that's nerve-wracking; to others, that's exciting. Either way, when life steps on the mound and throws you the proverbial curveball—positive or negative—, you must learn how to adapt. Everyone wants to win that first–place prize. Why wouldn't you?

Saying that, there was this one time I learned from a runner-up during a post-show. The interviewer asked, "How does it feel to not have won the race after all the months of preparation?"

The runner had simply responded, "Sir, I didn't lose. I learned."

I only wish some of us had done just that.

# CHAPTER 6

*Location: The Henchmen HQ; The Next Night; 9:30 pm*

"**V**EHICULAR HOMICIDE! I'M *TELLING* you, it was vehicular homicide!" cried out Al Gebra.

Al was always a believer in conspiracy theories, and refused to believe what appeared to be on the surface. True to his nature, he was now convinced that someone had set Remington up to lose his life in that car.

"You don't know that," said Celo. "Besides, O3 already said it didn't appear to have been foul play, so..."

"Exactly! It didn't *appear*, which means they don't actually *know*." He sniffed for emphasis. "I smell a rat."

"Or your ass," Celo said softly, tone devoid of humor.

"Or my what? You wanna speak up so I could hear you, son?" yelled Al.

"Or your *ass*, motherfucker! Did I stutter?" He was smiling now. "Have you *washed* your ass today? Or any day this week, for that matter?"

All the fellow henchmen laughed.

A few minutes passes, and Snugglez McPherson got up from his chair and walked over to the window. He peeled the curtain over his shoulder—reminiscent of the classic Malcolm X *By Any Means Necessary* photo—and took out the revolver he had tucked under his jacket, placing it on the edge of the table bedore sitting back down, sipping a fifth of black straight. He was a loyal henchman—and a talented one at that. He was always told he could make it as a singer if he were to truly pursue it, but, alas, this life as an unforgiving, cold, calculating MentallyOrganizedBusiness hitman was a very enduring career, and he was always paid handsomely to "get the job done". Along with cohorts Blues, Muscles Montana, and a few other guys, he was pretty much second in command to Tony Victor—outside of The Great 8, anyway. He was also a very intelligent guy, and often saw the good in somebody till they proved themselves wrong.

He also did not believe Remington's death was a homicide, and he said so now. "You know, for the first time in probably over ten years, I don't get that feeling."

"What feeling's that?" Blues asked apprehensively.

"The feeling I usually get when I know what direction I need to go in to pop a nigga. It's a very settling and confident feeling, and I think I've got a ninety-nine percent success ratio in this: I always know who to get, who to go after. Who to kill." He shook his head. "But *this*, this right here? This is different. The feeling I get in the pit of my stomach is a very calm one, a peaceful one. I'm telling you, fellas, Remington's passing was of the Lord's calling. This was not a street-oriented demise."

Blues Holloway walked over to join Snugglez by the fireplace, where they would often meet. It was a peaceful environment, the tall, crisp flames that trampled one another being a soothing sight to see. That mantel at the HQ was built by Tony Victor himself. It was no short feat.

"I don't like when you get like this, Snuggz," Al muttered.

"Don't call me Snuggz."

"My bad, Snuggz," Al said, holding his hands up. "I just hate when you get like this: when you have a by-yourself-meeting at this juncture, you're usually right."

"I thought I just told you not to call me Snuggz? You want this semi pointing at your lower back area?" The revolver was in his hand. "I know I got a little gut, so the gat sits tough, but don't get it twisted."

"Twisted? Me? Snuggz, I believe you forgot, I'm a G8 Guy, so you can't touch me."

Snugglez McPheerson got up and thought about back-smacking Al Gebra so hard that he'd remember what he ate for breakfast six years ago—but then decided against it. He got up from the couch and ignored Al completely, instead looking over to Celo and nodding at him. According to him, it was just Remington's time.

The other fellas got up and joined hands in a circle, where Celo led them in prayer. Everyone felt some slight closure dawn upon them in that moment, one that appeared to convince Al that Snugglez was right.

But then again, there goes that word "appeared" again.

# CHAPTER 7

A FTER REMINGTON STEELE'S FUNERAL, we were all still very much in a state of shock. Some of us handled it better than others, but nevertheless, it was business as usual.

Three weeks had passed when the time for Mula Madison and I to meet up. We met outside The Castle movie theatre, a hole in the wall that somehow got a permit to show movies. It would've been better if it were a lab that contained mice being studied to find the cure for whack rappers.

Mula and I were very close; for some reason, we just got each other, and we quickly built a bond that would last forever. Don't get it twisted, though: it was more of a sister/brother bond, if you will.

On this day, I wanted to meet with her to see how business was doing on the North side of Brick City.

"Brother, I hate this," she sighed.

"Hate what?"

"That I'm *so* damn good at what I do. Toma!"

She then proceeded to throw a bag full of dead presidents in front of me, but not before removing her cut.

"Now, motherfucker, who's your top bi-atch now! Huh? huh?" Her voice had climbed to a high-pitched shriek.

"Oh, that's easy: Lil' Kim from Junior Mafia," I replied jokingly.

"You asshole. Could you be serious for a minute? For *sixty seconds*? For the love of *God*, that's all I ask of you."

"Okay, okay," I conceded. "Yes, you are my HBIC. You deserve all the accolades coming to you, and you've done well. Although I understand you've been teaching Lil' Gwop Madison a thing or two prematurely, yes?"

"Oh, yeah? Says who?" she challenged.

"A little birdie. Named Whish."

She huffed. "I *told* that girl not to say nothing. She can't keep her big mouth shut."

"Well, that's a trait all women have, I'm afraid." For that I received a death stare and around seventeen smackdowns on the back of the head and with that, she got into her $47,000 Mustang and jetted down Springfield Avenue.

Anyone will tell you I'm an easy-going guy. I believe in always—or maybe selectively—telling the truth. Tell the truth, and you'll never have to remember a thing for a single day of your life. Most people love that about me, and others hate it. If you ask me what I think about how "they" feel, you'll quickly find I don't really give a fuck. And that's that.

I stepped into Jezifs—directly next-door—for a two-piece with a biscuit snack box. Jezifs was a bootleg version of Tasty's, but the dude always hooked me up with an extra biscuit—really a punk-ass dinner roll. This time, I invited him to my birthday party.

His eyes lit up with gratitude, when in fact, I'd been inviting all kinds of people to my birthday party—essentially anyone who seemed to have a genuine and gracious soul. The list had been growing for ten years now, so when I finally decide to throw the damn thing, it's gonna be super diverse and cultural. It'll be *outstanding*.

I finished up my box and grabbed the bag that Mula had thrown at me—in a very loving manner, I might add. It was as I walked out the chicken spot that I saw a few shadowy silhouettes, looking like they were approaching the corner nearest to me. It was dark out, there, and I realized with irritation that my car was around that same corner. Those bullshit cops ticket you for parking in front of The Castle like there's no tomorrow.

I tried to react quickly but, before I could turn around, *wham*, a barrage of fisticuffs were sharing equal time on my face and ribs. I felt like I was at an ECW wrestling show in Philadelphia.

The next few moments were a complete blur to me; even now, I have zero clue what happened or how fast it happened. I had no idea how many people were pouncing on me, or what I even got hit with: all I knew was that I hit a fire hydrant on the way down and felt the sickening crack of my skull opening. The entire thing was like an out-of-body experience: I had, albeit surprisingly, never been "jumped" before in my entire life.

As this event was unfurling, while I was somewhat in shock, I knew one thing in my gut: this was not an innocent bystander type of robbery: it was premeditated, planned. I had been watched. I had gotten too comfortable in my own 'hood that I had let my guard down to an embarrassing extent.

*Note to self: Don't invite these assholes to your birthday party.*

The only thing I knew after the whole ordeal was that Luciano, Corione, and my wife Yelly were there when I woke up in the hospital two days later. It was while I was in my sanatorium that Sam said that, for the last two or three hours, I'd been talking in my sleep. He said he had initially ignored it, until he managed to figure out that I was trying to tell him who did this to me. I apparently mentioned something about the Vailsburg Clan, but he couldn't figure out why I kept saying something in Creole.

"Motherfuckers!" Don yelled out. "I knew it, I fuckin' *knew* it! They're coming after us! I figured it out!"

"Who's coming after us?" Sam returned, perplexed.

"The fuckin Haitians from Vailsburg." There wasn't a trace of uncertainty in Don's voice.

"Who? Fame up in Prospect?" Sam said, frowning. "Nah, that's my nigga. Love wouldn't disrespect."

"Sam, what the fuck's the matter wit' you? Snap out of it. Our brother is laying in a fuckin' hospital bed, and you wanna quote a Biggie lyric in this time of crisis?"

"My bad, Don. It's a force of habit,' Sam shrugged. "This hip-hop shit got me fucked up. It destroyed my life. We do know somebody on Prospect now, don't we?"

"Polo Pasé!" they both yelled out simultaneously.

It was then that our sister Cocoa Butta walked in to check on me.

"Hey brothers, sister," she greeted. "How's he doing? Has he awoken at all?"

"Yeah, he's in and outta sleep right now," Sam responded. "The doctor said it might be a few days before he regains full conscien— Wait a minute," he stalled, frowning, "how'd you know we was even here? We didn't announce nothing to the family: we wanted to receive positive news before saying anything. There's no way anybody would've been able to handle this after we lost Remington."

"Well, Cocoa?" Yelly challenged, not missing a beat. "Sam asked you a question, so I suggest you give him an answer before your face has a conversation with my fist."

Cocoa stepped back, holding her hands up. Apprehension was written across her face: she didn't want to share what she knew.

A few moments passed and Sam stepped forward. "Today, Cocoa, I'm a very impatient man—especially when I see my brother laying half dead on this gurney."

She began wringing her hands. "Umm... I just want to apologize before—"

"Apologize for what...?"

Sam and Don's faces contorted in confusion.

"I just wanted to apologize... I wanted to say I'm so sorry for this." Her voice trembled violently and she quickly broke down, starting to cry profusely. Don, taking a breath, went to over to console her.

"It's okay, honey. It's not your fault."

"No Don, you don't understand," she hiccupped. "It *is* my fault."

"What are you talking about?" asked Sam.

Cocoa cried a little more on Don Corione's shirt before excusing herself to the bathroom, grabbing some tissues to wipe her tears away. As she did so, she went over and over again in her head what and how she was going to say what she knew about the situation. She was stalling, filled with anxiety. She asked for a cup of water from the nurse on-duty.

When she finally returned, Yelly was, to say the least, extremely on edge.

Cocoa Butta took a deep breath and began to speak. "The reason I knew Escobar was in this hospital bed is because I'm the one who put him there. I ordered the hit."

# CHAPTER 8

*Location: Overlook Hospital Parking Lot; Summit, NJ;*
*March 8; 3:16 am*

DON HAD A LOT of the nurses on payroll—or 'weekend personal favors roll', as I'd call it. Don had a thing for nurses, as we all should: I believe they were all registrars who worked on different floors and had no idea the others even existed. I used to refer to the one he'd see on Friday as Friday Night Lights—well, until he showed me a picture of her. After that, I started calling her Friday the 13th: she had a fat ass, but looked like Jason had his way with her on the outskirts of Camp Crystal Lake prior to her becoming a registered nurse.

Anyway, he made sure Friday the 13th gave me special attention, as well as an extra pillow, if needed. He then proceeded to meet Luciano and Yelly in the parking lot, where they stood interrogating Cocoa regarding what she'd said in my hospital room.

"I didn't want to make a scene in the hospital, because you might've ended up in the next room to my husband," Yelly growled. "You wanna tell me exactly what the hell you meant by saying you put him in there, Cocoa?" She glanced at her wrist. "You got three minutes and not a second past to explain yourself."

Cocoa circled in place repeatedly, wracked with nerves—understandable, if you ask me. She then started to pace back and forth when Don said, "Two minutes."

"Okay, okay!" she exploded, visibly shaking. "I ordered the hit, but it was not supposed to be on Escobar! You know I love him as dearly as I do the three of you." Her eyes began to fill again. "I was having some trouble with one of the Spanish drug lords over in the Neck"—the Neck was a fonder name for the Spanish section of downtown Brick City, where Mula reigned supreme—"and so I told my cousins, and they asked me for a description of the guy..."

"So, these stupid motherfuckers believed Escobar was that guy?" Sam's voice was laced with venom.

"Yeah, what exactly did you say?" Don added, incredulous. "He was light-skinned, had a mustache since he was twelve, and loved black women? That would've probably narrowed it down to eighty percent of Downtown Brick *City*."

"No, no, no," she said, shaking her head rigorously. "I gave them a very detailed description, and the guy doesn't remotely look like Escobar—not in the least. This is all just very confusing to me. I don't know how this happened." She sighed. "I'm so angry at myself and my cousins for doing this. I don't know what came over them."

In that moment, Yelly couldn't stand the sight of Cocoa. She stormed back into the hospital to see me in my room, while Don and Sam sat down on the bench facing the IHOP on River Road. Cocoa was still a nervous wreck; in her mind, she was good as dead—which, all things considered, probably was a fair assumption. After all, she was responsible for putting one of the biggest bosses in the country in hospital.

She sat down, Indian squat-style, in front of the bench Sam and Don were sitting on. Minutes passed, each feeling like an hour, and over and over, Cocoa kept thinking to herself: *How did this happen? Why would they do this? They know Escobar is family, they know he is my family.*

She began to silently plead for forgiveness when Don decided to speak.

"Cocoa, clearly someone has to pay for this," he whispered to her, "and they're going to have to pay for it with their life. No, better yet: with their *lives*. If you said you didn't order it on Escobar directly, then we believe you. After all, we're family, right?"

Cocoa nodded her head and exhaled heavily, the weight of the world seeming to slip off her shoulders.

"So, what you're going to do now for us and our sister Yelly is show us pictures of these cousins who decided to go into business for themselves," Don continued. "We need these visual references as backups in case you fail."

Cocoa was silent for a second, already tearing up again.

"Don, I don't understand," she blubbered. "I know you guys are beyond upset with me and this whole ordeal, and I really appreciate you guys for not offing me right off the bat—but you seriously want me to point out my own flesh and blood, so you can... so you can..." She couldn't finish her sentence, her voice was threaded with so much emotion.

"No, Cocoa, that's silly," Don said. "*You're* going to kill them. One by one."

# CHAPTER 9

*Prospect Street & 40<sup>th</sup> Street; Ghost Town; March 8; 4:17 pm*

TONY VICTOR HAD A specific target: Polo Pasé, leader of The Haitian Squadron—the people who had terrorized certain parts of Ghost Town for years. Polo was one of the coolest guys you could meet—well, until you crossed him. Then he'd have you eating through a straw for life—and that's if he even let you live. He once caught a guy who was looking at his young niece as bait and took him down to his basement, where his men stripped him naked and blindfolded him after tying him to the ceiling fan. They took turns throwing darts at the naked man's body, the sensory deprivation of the blindfold adding a whole new horrifying edge to the whole experience. This was happening while a mean game of Dominos was taking place just five feet away. Come to think of it, he was my kind of guy.

Anyway, we never had a problem with them: they'd never given us a reason to. Until now, that is.

Tony walked down the street with his 45-cocked back in an arm sling—a disguise, of course. Linguini and Snugglez were right behind him, hiding by the bushes. He spotted his prey standing on the porch of his crib; after all, we knew better than to roll up on Polo Pasé, so this had to look discreet. Tony thought about catching him off-guard, but quickly changed his mind: he figured he'd just roll right up to him directly.

"Polo! Polo!" Tony yelled out.

Polo was a little stocky dude, and now, he turned around in his leather jacket jet black, with the signature black eight-ball logo. "Who's asking?"

"I'm not askin'. I know who you are, so don't front, nigga. I'm Tony Victor, but you already knew that, too, so save the bullshit questionnaire."

Polo was unimpressed.

"Polo, I got one question for you, and I'm not gonna ask twice: considering we let you live throughout these parts because we respected your gangsters, how could you let ya squadron out on Escobar?" Tony asked.

"Escobar?" Polo scoffed. "You honestly think I'm the man one who put him in that hospital bed?" He shrugged casually. "I mean, I've probably thought about it a time or two, but I've never actually gone through with it. Although I think I dreamt about putting Luciano in one. Some of my guys think he's a little disrespectful. In over his head, you might say."

"In over his head?" Tony repeated. "In over his *head*? Nigga, MentallyOrganizedBusiness has run this motherfucker since the beginning of time. Camp Town"—the name given to Ghost Town some years ago—"was owned by the great Adam 'Copeland' Escobar alongside his cousins Sean Michael Corione and Austin Luciano III." Tony shook his head in disbelief. "Them niggas owned this city for decades—we just took it to a higher level. So if anybody's in over his head, it might very well be *you*, patna."

Polo took a few steps back: maybe Tony Victor was standing a little too close for him. He decided he'd explain a few things to Tony himself, even if it meant just getting rid of this guy, goddammit.

"Listen, dude, I appreciate the history lesson and all, but I ain't' got time for this shit right now," he said. "Accusations. Pointing the finger without any real evidence. That's for the cops. You a FED now or something?" He smirked to himself. "I'll tell you this: if I had the audacity to go after one of the lead dudes of your organization—and I do, don't get me wrong—, then everyone would know it, without a doubt. Polo don't hide. Polo don't mask himself. But Polo also lives by one degree: respect. And I've *always* respected them niggas. Why you think Luciano still walking?" Tony remained silent. "'Cuz I put a stop to my guys that wanted that nigga handled. So, you see? No harm has been brought to your precious leaders. Not by me, at least."

Tony Victor was not someone who appreciated arrogance from anyone, and if Polo was anything, it was arrogant. Tony began circling in motion for what seemed like forever, each step intensifying as it fell to the ground. It seemed as if he was trying to see if he believed what Polo was saying, but couldn't come to a decision. Polo walked up to him and put his hand on Tony's left shoulder—the one not in the sling.

"Homie, I got one last thing to say, one last thing to ask you, since we're talking about history: I was talking to an uncle of mine the other day, and he said that his great uncle 'Crazy' Jack St. Pierre used to have all kinds of trysts with Safebreaka and Victor women from Camp Town when they served on the board of trustees for the city. So, I can't help but wonder... Dawg, you think you might be Haitian ya'self?"

Polo's voice dripped with sarcasm, and Tony still didn't say a word. As Polo started to walk away, Tony, seething, thought, *This motherfucker been breathing for too long.* He took the gun from the sling but, unfortunately for Polo and the '74 Nova he was walking towards, someone else had the same idea.

The moment Polo opened the driver's door to his baby, there was instant pyro and the loudest blast heard on this side of town since the infamous Brick City riots in the sixties. With that, Tony and the henchmen ran as quickly as they could to the getaway car—before any authorities showed up.

Polo landed across the street on the lawn of the Church of Latter-Day Saints. The blast had been impactful: his precious car looked like a Lego set engulfed in flames.

Within minutes, most of the town had emerged to see what had happened. At that point, there was no telling if Polo had survived the blast.

The town's residents were screaming for the violence to stop, for all the nonsense to end—seemingly forgetting this town was literally *built* on violence, on respect, by warriors who wouldn't take no for an answer. Indeed, Camp Town had later been dubbed Ghost Town because there were so many areas that were left for dead. Abandonment was regularity. The smell of death in the air reeked for decades. This was no ordinary town, not by any stretch of the imagination.

When the wailing sirens approached the horrific scene, one townsman cried out, "Is that an arm? Oh my God, his arm was blown clean off from the blast!"

The ambulance driver approached the victim and checked for a pulse: at first, nothing, but then, something. At least then, the medics were hopeful.

\*

"Hello? *Hello!*"

Tony frantically tried answering his phone while operating the vehicle he, McPherson, and Linguini sped off in.

"*Boom!* Yeah, motherfuckers! So, how'd you like it? Did I do a good job? Was it loud enough? I worked hard on this; really, I did! Tony? Tony! Can you hear me? It's me... Sal. Salawicious Dough. Tony?"

# CHAPTER 10

"IS THIS THING FUCKIN' working? I mean, really, I can put a bomb together, but can't manage to figure out a way to speak to someone on the phone clearly? What a crock of shit this is."

Sal slammed the phone on the table before leaning down to Blues.

"Blues. Blues, wake up, man. I can't believe you slept through the explosion. Our plan was *perfect*."

Salawicious Dough turned the music up high, grinning.

"Huh? Whose range got towed? They double-parked by a hydrant!" were the confused words Blues muttered as he woke up. Clearly, he was dreaming about rap: he did this often. He blearily opened his eyes. "Son, are you serious? I was busy having a meeting with my thoughts in the deepest, darkest, corner of my mind."

"Oh, excuse me, sleeping beast," Sal hissed. "I didn't mean to wake you. Now shut the hell up and listen to me, man: the plan worked!"

"*Word*?" he said, sitting up. "That's good news. So, how did it look?"

"See for yourself. Press play," Sal told him. On the foldout table stood video footage on the big computer screen of the entire thing and, after he had watched it for the first time, Blues kept rewinding it and playing it back, over and over again, repetitively muttering "*wonderful*" to himself.

In the attic of a three-bedroomed family house directly across the street from where the explosion took place stood Blues Holloway and Salawicious Dough. They didn't often work together: sure, they had a love for maniacal behavior, bombs, and death, but that's where their similarities ended. Salawicious Dough was an absolute asshole, a member of The Great 8, so he had rank to pull off a stunt like this. Blues, on the other hand, was certifiably insane: a great mind, but legitimately off his rocker. With these two, think House of Pain meets Souls of Mischief.

Clearly, Salawicious Dough had asked for some help from Blues to pull this off: after all, Blues was an absolute genius with computers. Don't get it twisted, Sal wasn't any slouch with technology, but this was something way past his caliber of talent.

"So, did you speak to Tony or what? What did he think? I need to know," Blues asked Sal, finally pausing the footage.

"I haven't spoken to him," Sal responded. "I tried calling him, and in a matter of seconds, the call dropped. Maybe bad reception. I don't really know. You know this new cellphone shit isn't exactly reliable. I wonder if they'll even last."

Fifteen minutes went by when the sound of Sal's phone sounded, interrupting the Sabu versus Tazz match he was watching.

"Yo, this is Dough," Sal answered.

"Dough! Dough!"

"Yeah, this is Dough—who the fuck is this?" Sal asked, miffed. The most he knew was that it was a G8 family member: no one had this line but G8 members.

"Dough, it's Tony!"

"Ahh, Tony, I've been trying to reach you. How'd you like the—"

"Sal, you stupid son-of-a-bitch! You just tried to kill one of the biggest bosses in Ghost Town!" Tony's voice was shaking. "I normally don't give a fuck who you off, but *this* motherfucker? Me and the henchmen had this. I went to talk to him to see if I could get any information from him."

"Tony, relax. I *know*, I heard everything: me and Blues have had Polo bugged for the last few weeks." He grinned devilishly. "As soon as we heard what happened to Escobar, we put a plan in motion. You know big-butt Tonya from Grove Street? We paid her to seduce him and plant a bug on the inner part of his jacket. You know he don't go nowhere without that jacket, so we knew if he was going to spill anything to his Haitian squadron, we were going to have him dead to rights." Sal paused. "Anyway, I was paying close attention to your conversation: I was listening to and watching the whole thing from the window at the hideout across the street. I saw him put his hand on your shoulder and tell you that bullshit about your ancestors. You gotta admit, that was pretty funny." He chuckled lightly. "Either way, when he started to walk away, I saw you start to take the gun out of your arm sling, and I thought, well, he's about to kill him, so I might as well do it with class. That way, no one could say they saw you attempt to kill him or anything. Me and Blues planted that bomb on that shitty-ass Nova he loves so much at around three this morning. Nobody saw us, I can guarantee that. He been in that house since. Plus, I didn't know you were going to be there: it just sort of panned out that way."

"But Dough, why *Polo*?" Tony asked, exasperated. "Why not see what's up with him first, like me and the henchmen did? He's owed at least that, considering his status."

"Tony, let me tell you again, we're *good*. We know Polo was the guy who wanted Escobar dead. Chill out, son."

"And how in the blue fuck do you *know* that?" Tony seethed.

"Because Cocoa told us a month ago."

# CHAPTER 11

YELLY WAS, AND STILL is, my queen: that woman just does something to me that no other woman ever came close to doing. There was an aura about her: she lit up any room she walked into with style and grace—allowing me to lace these lyrical douches in her bushes, or something like that. *Notorious B.I.G.,'94.*

There was just something about her that I couldn't put my finger on, but after a while, I stopped trying to figure it out. We've been together for almost twenty years now, and anything you could think of, we've been through together. Key word: *through.* That's what makes us whole, special, the power couple that we are today. She once challenged me to a basketball game—she was a college basketball star at Seton Hall University in her heyday—, where the winner had to be the other's slave for an entire week: cooking, cleaning, sex... Whatever the demand was had to be fulfilled. I took her up on the offer, and to this day, a winner has yet to be declared: we were tied 7-7 when the cats and dogs came down from the clouds. To this day, she still reminds me that our game is tied. Sometimes I want to take her back out to see who's would win, but I kind of like not knowing.

I'd been thinking about who the guilty party was that had tried to end my life. Cocoa was the sweetest thing walking, and I didn't believe for one minute that she did this to me directly. Plan gone wrong? Yes. But that plan intentionally put in place to end me? Nah, that's a negative.

Polo Pasé? Yes, he's got the gall and the means to do something of this magnitude—but then again, it wasn't his style. I was in the hospital for over two and a half weeks, and I heard Polo was also having surgery over in East Wing due to his "accident". Either way, it just didn't make sense to me.

I called Don and told him to set up a Mental—a meeting—at The House of Nesbit this coming Friday night to discuss our upcoming plans for revenge—as well as to figure out how we were going to clean up any potential bad circumstances the family may have put us in. I told him to fill Luciano in on everything and to make sure he was there. Sure enough, this was beginning to become a massive mess my family had started to create—although I was touched by the level of love they'd shown me and proven to me, the depths they'd gone to in order to avenge my suffering.

I finally got up from my recliner that I'd used to read one of the many entries in my personal library. It was after I got off the phone with Don that I plopped myself down to read for another forty-five minutes. I'd always been an avid reader: usually biographies, but I could always enjoy a book by James Patterson, or one of my new favorites, The Cunning Linguist. A great name for an author, if you ask me. Anyone from NJ must take the time out to read his books *The Jersey Wars, 30 Stories to Tell*, and, my favorite, *Lunacy*. That guy is a mix between Stephen King and the rapper Scarface. If you're a literary nut, then this maniac is for you.

Anyway, I went over to my music collection—which was obviously second to none—and pulled out a mixtape from a local group called Necessary Ruffness. There was a cut on there I loved: *We All Crew*, featuring another group called Krome 45. The hook was sick and was the embodiment of my family. It always hit a special place in my Grinch-like heart—you know, the one that was two sizes too small.

I'd always loved music—rap music more so—, and I always thought that if I made enough money—which I probably did a decade ago—that I'd get out of the business and start a record label. Corione and Luciano always shared my sentiment, but alas, the streets kept calling.

This song was on a mixtape one of the town's peddlers had been selling on the market a few months before—I think it was DJ Ron G. I had needed some new kicks from Dr. J's, and on my way back to the car, I'd bought a copy.

These kids had talent—*real* talent. Most of the cuts on it were dope. A little rough around the edges, maybe, but I just knew we could finetune their abilities.

As I turned the volume up to listen again, I came across a vinyl from Tina Turner. That woman's legs were to die for: I looked at those legs for probably three minutes straight. It was then it happened: the thing I'd been waiting weeks for. *Damn, Tina, you did it again!* Thirty seconds later, I heard my wife call me.

"Babe, did you need anything else? I think I'm gonna go catch a movie with my mom. The kids are tucked asleep in their rooms."

"Come in here real quick, honey," I responded. "Hurry up, get in here!"

"What's wrong, babe? You okay?" Yelly responded quickly, running into the room.

"Look, babe! Look!"

I pointed down to good ol' Space Mountain—as I always affectionately referenced my love package. Her eyes lit up.

"Babe, is that what I think it is?" she asked rhetorically.

"It sure as hell ain't a stick of dynamite. Well, not in the literal sense." I grinned. Since my ass-whooping, I hadn't been able to get an erection. We'd thought there might've been something wrong, but we'd wanted to let healing time commence before checking me out.

She came close to me to cop a feel and said, "Well, maybe we should see how that's working later."

I frowned. "Maybe we should see how that's working *now*."

I pulled her half-worn sweater off and threw it down on the swivel chair she loved using. I picked my queen up clean off the floor with a little pain in my ribs and proceeded to take her into our humble haven of love. I don't think I need to tell you that there was no movie seen that night—but there *was* a cinematic feature for us. I could only hope my mother in-law wasn't too upset with me. I'm sure Yelly told her it was my fault.

# CHAPTER 12

*The Black Box Night Club; Miller Street; Brick City; April 7; 10 pm*

"WHISH, WHEN YOU GON' let me hit that?"

Whish looked Luciano up and down and shrugged, "When you make a car ride without wheels, motherfucker." Whish was a no-jokes kind of chick, and anyone could tell you she held no punches. In other words, she was perfect for Luciano.

"Why you always gotta make me work for it, girl?" he cried out. "You know I've been trying to chase you down since high school. I was the one who elected you to become one of the original females in MentallyOrganizedBusiness. So, where's my love, eh?" He stood back and held out his arms. "I demand my love and I demand it right now."

Whish walked over to him, batting her eyelashes, and began circling him—a statuesque, calculating vulture. Sighing, she stopped and signaled him to meet her in the backroom behind the pool table before stalking off.

Sam could hardly contain his excitement: he threw back the last of his drink and threw a few more dollars at the strippers in front of him, loosening his tie. The time was upon him, the time he'd been waiting for for well over a decade.

He wiped the sweat off his forehead and walked over to the room where Whish was waiting for him. Pulling himself together, he opened the door.

There stood Whish in an open fur coat, sky-clad, in nothing but cucumbers covering her nipples and vagina. Sam Luciano couldn't believe his eyes, and it was all he could do to just let his jaw drop to the cherrywood floor and watch, dumbstruck, as Whish walked toward him and kicked the door behind him shut. As she reached around to make sure it was locked, Luciano's mind began racing: his dreams were about to come true.

I still ask Sam from time to time what happened between them that night, but he won't tell: it's like this big government secret he has, as if he'll instantly self-destruct or some shit if he tells anyone. We used to tell each other all kinds of details about our female triumphs, but this one, he refused to share. Rat bastard. He literally once told me, "I'd like to keep this one special."

I'd looked at him and said, "Whish probably told you she'd chop your dick off, dip it in salsa, and force feed it to you on family game night if you told anybody what happened."

Sure enough, he didn't deny it, so I've basically gone with that explanation ever since. They were the only two leaders of the business who were not involved with anyone, and they deserved loving too. I was just glad Whish finally cracked, because it was getting annoying hearing him beg.

"Escobar! We brought you out here to celebrate your birthday and recovery," came Hak Hennesey's voice.

Notably, this was not the birthday party I'd been inviting people to for the last ten years: that'll probably be reserved for my fortieth, or something.

"My fellow douchebag brother Jay is rounding us up some drinks," he continued. "Jay, hurry the fuck up, man, Escobar is waiting."

"Yo, if you rush me one more time, I'm gonna stick this Captain Morgan up ya ass!"

Smirking, he shot back, "Wait, the whole Captain? You mean, like, the man himself? You're going to try to protrude an entire man up my rectum, here in this nightclub?"

"Niggas..." Jay muttered while walking away, shaking his head back and forth.

"Escobar, here's ya drink. It's hard"—a drink placed in my hand—"and you need it, so drink up and enjoy, buddy! It's on us."

I sat back and laughed, listening to these two argue like they were a married couple. I'm telling you, I don't know any two fools funnier than these guys.

"Jay, look at this chick on the stage," Hak said, nudging him in the side. "How does she *do* that? Is she human? I mean, how can a woman stuff an entire Corona bottle in her pussy? And look at this one: is that a cigarette? This bitch has a *cigarette* in her *vaginal passage!*"

Hak's voice had risen to a shriek, and my stomach began to hurt from holding in my laughter. Meanwhile, Jay BaDouche just sat there in amazement: it often looked like he was riding off on a pony or some shit when he was looking at a fine woman. On one end, he saw a woman literally laying on the stage with a bottle inside her pussy—and, in all fairness, even I must admit that the motion of her gyrating hips pouring out liquor into the cups sitting below her on the stage steps was rather... hypnotic—, and on the opposite end, there was a chick making her VaJayJay—as my wife calls it—smoke a cancer stick. We were three fools stuck in a trance, a trance that only the devil could muster. Yelly could appreciate a beautiful woman and a fat ass too, but she had to slap me on the back of my head to snap me back to reality.

Accompanied by Mula Madison, Padlock Penny, my sister Pudgee, Alexandria the Grape, and Laura Longleggs, Al Gebra and Sara Safebreaka joined the party.

"Escobar, I'm happy to see you," Al said warmly. "We all are. Alive and well! Who would've thought, after that little episode?"

Sara then asked politely, "So, when does the killing barrage begin? There's clearly a war going on outside. No man is safe."

"*Oh*, good one, Sara. That's Prodigy from Mobb Deep. I like what you did with that," Alexandria giggled.

Sara looked at Alex, confused. "Who the hell is Prodigy? Mobb Deep? What is that, another local faction trying to take our spots?"

"Oh, come on, Sara, even I know who Mobb Deep is!" yelled out Celo Gaston as he walked into the room. Of course, Celo did not like to be bested, so behind him stood the 6'4" frame of MentallyOrganizedBusiness alumni, Reeeno Nevada—naturally.

"Reeeno! We haven't seen you since that day we ran up in them niggas house off Weequiac."

*

For a bit of side story: Reeeno Nevada was a special dude—a genuine dude. A guy who would give you the shirt off his back or put your back on the opposite side of your shirt if you fucked with him or his family.

Although a gangster at heart, he was a true entertainer: he and Celo were once known as the greatest steppers—stepping having been made famous by collegiate fraternities and sororities throughout the country—in NJ history. Ironically, a lot of us had been part of this as well: I remember those days, traveling up and down the East Coast as part of a Jr. Division of a Larger Frat. We'd been popular, yet defiant; so loved, yet hated. In a sense, that time served as the seed that sowed the group you know today as MentallyOrganizedBusiness.

We'd been ordered—not advised but ordered—not to perform at a particular show because of its negative connotations, for fear of putting a blemish in the Frats' eyes. The president of our division had been an upstanding citizen and a mentor to most of us, but he could be a stickler about a lot of things—and, safe to say, he was not a fan of hip-hop culture.

So, to make a long story short, we'd basically been asked to be the intermission entertainment for a show at Symphony Hall in Brick City. It was actually a music concert headlined by the likes of Naughty By Nature, Whitney Houston, Total, Monica, Missy Elliott, and a young upstart named Gina Thompson.

As a matter of fact, there was one day where we were in the basement practicing our show when this beautiful young lady walked by us. Celo Gaston always thought he was a charmer, and so asked the young lady where the lunchroom for the talent was. He also made a fool of himself by asking what time her shift started—basically insinuating that she just got there and didn't know where the room with the food was. She politely smiled and said, "Sure, it's right over there: fist door to your left after you go around the corner of the hallway."

"Thanks, Miss. I appreciate it," Celo had uttered. As he'd walked back toward all of us, we were all silent, our eyes wide open.

"What's the matter with yaw? You never seen a pretty girl before?"

"No, you stupid fuck," I muttered to him. "You just asked Gina Thompson if she worked here and then asked her where the lunchroom was!"

Celo was dumbfounded. "That was Gina Thompson? That bitch looked good as hell!"

Moving forward, we had proceeded to do the show and been kicked out of the Jr. Frat Division because of it: it was hard to ask a bunch of teenagers to not do a show in front of thousands of people, to not share a locker room with national—and even some international—music stars, and to not be treated like the stars we'd known we were destined to be. We'd been told we were acting like petulant little children, and that we did not deserve to be a part of the Frat. So we'd said fuck it, we'd create our own frat—or, better yet, we'd create our own division. Actually, we'd create our own *organization*, one that would adhere to our mentality and follow our ways of handling business. A mob of some sort, a collective unit that saw, thought, and lived life the same way. A unit that understood that greatness is not given, but taken. So, shortly thereafter, MentallyOrganizedBusiness was born, and the rest is history.

*

"Remember when we ran up to some dude and tied him up to a chair in his own living room, and took turns punching the shit outta him?" Al was saying. "It gets me mad to this day: that fool's blood got on my new crispy white T-shirt, and I couldn't get that bitch off."

Frederick Linguini chimed in, "Shit, that was one of my favorite times ever. I believe that was the time when he decided to kill, like, a whole neighborhood, right? Just spray that whole bitch up!" He started laughing. "Yeah, that was the time when Victor, Dough, Corione, and Swindel got jumped, and it seemed like all of Brick City was out to see it unfold. A *hell* of a sight to behold. I don't know who was mouthing off or what exactly started it, but I know that we finished that shit." He thought for a moment. "Matter fact, where the fuck is Swindel at? That nigga owes me one-dollar-twenty-five!"

Everyone laughed, reminiscing about the crazy, fun times we'd endured together.

"*Holy* shit, where the hell have you been?" yelled out Al, addressing Reeeno.

"Family, family, it's a long story, and we'll have time for that later. I needed to come to town to make sure Escobar was okay from the apparent pummeling he took." Reeeno shrugged. "I needed to see him with my own two eyes."

"Reeeno, thank you for coming; and Celo, thank you for bringing him," I said. "I'm sure that was a hell of a flight from Alabama. Did you have the time to insert your penis in a stewardess?"

"A gentleman doesn't kiss and tell, Escobar," Reeeno sniggered. "*So*, considering I didn't kiss any of them bitches: *hell* yeah! I fucked the lead stewardess! Exchange student from Australia. Bad as hell." He bent over clutching his stomach, laughing hysterically.

"Did I hear Australia? They got bad bitches in *Australia*? I didn't even know that was a real place," Jay BaDouche asked.

Shaking his head, Hak Hennesey put his arm around his friend and walked away from the table in disgust. "Hey, Don," Hak said as he walked past Corione down the entrance hallway. "Just taking this dumb motherfucker back to the crib. He's had enough for one night. I'll catch you over the weekend."

Don told Hak to take Jay out the backway and to take his limo—he'd fill him in later. Hak obliged.

Don had just arrived at The Black Box Night Club and, besides the fact he had just pulled off the vaginal heist of the century by engaging in a triple-threat match with Friday the 13th, Saturday Night Fever (the Saturday bitch), and Any Given Sunday (the Sunday bitch), his high didn't last very long. Grabbing his handkerchief from his lapel to wipe the corner of his mouth, Don went in.

"Yo, yo, yo! We got some trouble outside. One of them Haitian niggas just snuck me, and Luciano is out there trying to shoot the fair one with all of them!"

Apparently, Sam had taken a smoke break outside after his rendezvous with Whish: I guess he was in recovery mode. He overheard Don talking some shit with somebody and, before he knew it, Don caught a right one to the chin.

Sam stepped in and told him to go inside and tell the family what was gettin' ready to pop off. In a chorus of safety switches, everyone's guns were drawn in a matter of seconds. Swindel miraculously appeared with Johnny Sliver from under the dress of a fat chick in the cut, and Tony Victor and the henchmen were ready on standby. Salawicious Dough was fucking some broad on-stage but got up once he heard Don's voice. Joseph

Stylez was "getting his Johnson powdered" by celebrity guest host and world-renowned porn star Cherokee—who's awesome, by the way.

Sara, Mula, and Whish were asked to stay inside the club: this was not a scene that a lady should be a part of.

"*Fuck* me!" Laura Longleggs shouted out. "We never have a chance to be part of the real fun!"

She walked off in a tantrum while continuously shrugging her shoulders. I told her to punch the first stripper she saw walk by her so she'd feel better.

Pudgee and Padlock Penny climbed the fire escape of the club and hopped on the roof. As usual, they always found themselves in the middle of something; after all, they were nosy as hell. As Penny would say, "We not nosy, we training."

We bust open the French doors of the club to the outside, guns out and ready for whatever. It was there that we saw Luciano getting in a few shots on this little Haitian nigga who couldn't be more than 5'7". The dude caught Sam a few times but never hurt him.

It was a bit of a surreal scene: there stood The Haitian Squadron—probably around twenty of them—, while adjacent to them stood the MentallyOrganizedBusiness crew—at least twenty-five of us. And that wasn't even the most impressive sight: the most impressive was the fact that all these gangsters, their guns drawn, decided to allow their representatives to fight it out one-on-one. This was virtually unheard of in Ghost Town: people never settled their differences with their fists. That was old-school, the longer route to achieve a goal. Some looked at it as an unnecessary, cheap way out of the inevitable.

The art of fisticuffs was exactly the opposite: it was a way to settle a dispute between two men; a way to toughen each other's manhood; the ultimate and definitive manner to determine the bigger man. The fact was that it was honorable—but then again, if my memory serves me correctly, the old adage said there was no honor amongst thieves.

"Let them fight. Let them represent each other's family," said a voice in the back of the crowd—somewhat of a familiar voice. Almost stoic. I didn't recognize it instantly.

"*No!*" yelled out Cocoa. Cocoa, who had kind of been at the epicenter of all this, literally ran in-between her Haitian brethren and Luciano, almost catching a right hook in her efforts. "Please, just *stop*. Stop all of this now! I can't take this any longer. You heard my brother, and now I ask that you hear me: please stop this madness. *Please*."

*Your brother?* I thought. And then it hit me. *You gotta be fuckin kidding me!* That was the voice I thought was familiar a few minutes ago, a voice I'd heard many times over since grade school. The voice of a man who I respected, who I knew for quite some time and had traveled many miles with.

"We're all your brothers, Cocoa," Sam yelled out to her.

"No, Sam. My *blood* brother."

"Wait, now hold the fuck up!" Sam shouted back. "I know all these Haitian punks out here, and I know ain't none of these dudes your blood brother."

It was then that the shadow of a man walked through the now-sectionalized group of the Haitian Squadron like a rehearsed dance line.

He was surprisingly formal and very well-spoken.

"Now, now, now, Luciano. I believe it's Sam Luciano, right?"

"And who the hell are you?"

"Calm down, homie. Relax," he said gently. "There's no need for disrespect. Let's ease on back from the obvious tension in the air, shall we? It's nice to meet you."

"Again, who in the rats' ass are you?" Sam barked.

"I'm Cocoa Butta's brother... blood brother, as she said," the man said.

"Blood brother?"

"Yes, Sam," Cocoa said. She then motioned to the rest of us. "Brothers, sisters, this is..."

"Vein. Poppa Vein, to be exact. Good to meet you all."

Sam Luciano nodded his head up northward to acknowledge Poppa Vein.

"Tell me something, Sam," Poppa Vein continued, "when ya mother gave you your name, did she spell it with one or two *M*'s?"

# CHAPTER 13

*Location: Don's Diner; Lincoln Place & Nye Avenue; Apri 8; 2:30 am*

POPPA VEIN, POLO PASÉ, and his number-one hitman, Jake Solomon, sat at the far end of a long table in the back of the diner; and across from them sat me, Don Corione, and Sam Luciano: six of the most powerful men on the East Coast, unsure if they should continue letting the other three breathe or break bread with them equally.

Polo, still nursing a missing arm from the horrific explosion a few weeks back, was adapting nicely to the prosthetic replacement he'd received during his emergency surgery: the story goes that he took off the fake arm and beat the living shit out of the male nurse on-staff when he came to and was made aware of what happened. Although it provided him with instant relief, he was served with papers the following day, stating that the Chairman of the Hospital was suing him for every penny Polo was worth: turns out the guy who Polo beat down was the Chairman's son. What a stroke of bad luck. *Good job, Polo.*

Don's chick—Saturday Night Fever—was the one who told him what had happened. In turn, Don told me. I instantly knew how to use this situation to my advantage, and how to have The Haitian Squadron eating out of our hands and not trying to kill us in whole for what's transpired. I decided to hold my "Get Out of Jail Free" card till the time was right.

"Now, let's cut to the chase, gentlemen," Poppa Vein announced. "I'm going to assume there is a mutual respect here and each other's family grind—yes? So, even with the finest respect, there is still a line that must never be crossed, and I believe it's clear that that line has indeed been crossed—not just once, but several times." He paused to survey everyone. "And, most recently, with my brother here having to lose a vital limb for his troubles, can anybody here tell me why I shouldn't stop your hearts from beating right at this moment?"

Sam jumped across the table and almost snatched Poppa Veins' fedora from his head, but I quickly restrained him. Sam had just met

Poppa, but he'd already decided he didn't like him: he felt he was smug, and Luciano didn't like that kind of quality in anybody.

"Calm *down!*" I hissed at Sam. "Chill out, I got this. We got this."

Me and Poppa go back a couple decades, and I was sure neither of us were happy about what'd been going on for the last few months between our families.

"I don't know who's going first, but somebody better tell me which one of you motherfuckers is paying for my medical bills," Polo growled, slamming his only real fist on the table.

"Polo, relax. I heard my Saturday bitch thinks it's cute," Don said, sniggering slightly. "She said if you played ya cards right, she'll let you finger her with your real fingers and then pop her in the other hole with the other set. She said she heard the prosthetic fingers feel: dildo-like, you know?"

Jack let out a sudden burst of laughter but quickly resorted back to his usual gully face when Polo gave him his death stare.

"Besides, we know you're getting ready to be broke, and ya Poppa over here is going to have to move you into his mansion soon," Don continued, not letting up. "You'll have to get a job as the head cashier at The Sweet Shop on Mill Road."

To break the tension, I turned to Vein. "So... buddy. How's it goin'?" I smiled delicately. "How's this beautiful life treating you? Shot any clubs up lately? No? How about any drive-bys, huh? I know how you like drive-bys." I pretended to think for a second. "Oh, no, that's not it: you've been busy sending ya little hooligans to come and get me, to assassinate me, to murder the kid. *That's* it. Right?" I cocked my head to the side. "Your sister—whom I adore—told us I was not the intended target. Don didn't believe her at first, nor did Luciano, but we ultimately concluded she didn't do this. So, what do you have to say for yourself regarding this matter Vein? Huh?"

"Nothing," Vein answered coolly. "There is legitimately nothing for me to say, because we didn't do it."

I pursed my lips, holding back what I truly wanted to let out. All I wanted was a confession, the truth—and if I'd got that, we straight-up could have quashed it right there. I knew they did this, but I couldn't understand why—well, I didn't *know* per se: I just had a gut feeling. I could've been wrong. Or not.

"Escobar," Poppa Vein gently responded, "with God as my witness, I did not do this—nor did any of us. As you said earlier, we're old friends, and if I'd had a problem with you, I would've come to you directly. You know this." He paused as he watched my expression change: I *did* know this. "Honestly, I'm a bit annoyed that you'd think I'd go through all of this and not be up-front. If I'm one thing, it's direct. The fact your family believes we did this to you is one thing, but *you*?" He swallowed. "That's hurtful, man."

After thinking for a few moments, I realized he was right. There had been a time before MentallyOrganizedBusiness when Vein and I were going to start a click called Brand X: a group of street dudes shunned by their peers, left out because we were different. We went ridin' on a few niggas in Ill Town, all the way down to Charm City, Maryland. Ultimately, we decided to part ways: we just wanted different things. Regardless of the reasons, we separated with nothing but respect, with the promise we'd look out for one another.

For twenty years, we'd kept our respective families clear from hurting each other—or, even worse, killing each other. These past couple months had been stressful: if I hadn't been in hospital, there was no way Salawicious Dough would've planted that bomb, and Polo would still have his arm. Or maybe not: I don't know. Don and Sam didn't stop it. But then again, they weren't invested in Poppa Vein in the same way I was, and maybe just didn't give a fuck about stopping it. Their brother was in a hospital, half-dead and unconscious for several days. I got it. Of *course*, I got it.

Through my peripheral vision, I could see both my brothers were getting antsy: I was sure Sam wanted to blow one of these niggas' heads off right in the diner. For a quick second, I also thought Don had had enough and was grabbing his pistol when he reached in his inner pocket, but he only pulled out his nasal spray: he'd been under the weather lately. Actually, I didn't think I'd ever seen him without the damn thing. Maybe he was addicted, or maybe he'd found a way to liquidate weed and put it in the spray bottle. Who the fuck knows?

"Listen, you look me square in my eyes and tell me you didn't do this," I said to Poppa. "Right now. Stand up and face me, man to man, and tell me you didn't do this."

Vein looked at his men, put his head down, and rose from his chair, walking over to me and tipping his fedora up so I could get a clear look of his face. With the softest voice, he proceeded, "Escobar. I *did not do this.*"

I believed him.

Just at that moment, Luciano got up and started walking toward the exit, and Jake Solomon, who'd been quiet for most of our sit-down, was quiet no more: in the most fluid of actions and without a word, he stood from his seat.

*Boom!* In a matter of three seconds, without warning, Jake Solomon shot Sam Luciano right in the neck.

All our eyes popped from our heads in disbelief. It was reminiscent of when Rollins turned his back on his brothers Reigns and Ambrose in the classic movie *The Shield.*

"Escobar," Jake uttered, "Vein is right. He didn't do this to you. We didn't do this to you. *I* did this to you."

Jake surveyed his Haitian brothers and took the backway out of the diner, driving off in his Celica. Vein and I made eye contact but didn't say a word, and Polo stayed seated. Don was the first to spring to action: he rushed to the counter and called 911 as the waitress wrapped her apron around Luciano's neck to stop the bleeding.

The shock continued well into the night.

# CHAPTER 14

*Location: Jake Solomon's House; 3:45 am*

*T*HE LOOK ON THEIR *faces was priceless,* Jake thought to himself as he walked into his house from the diner. *No more will these fuckers take Jake Solomon lightly. No more will I be disrespected.*

"I should've smoked Don's little ass too," he said aloud. "He was ripe for the killing at that table." *Nah, I'll take care of his little ass soon enough.*

Jake took his jacket off and sat it on the couch. For the last ten years, he'd done everything Polo Pasé had asked him to—and yet he still lived in a two-bedroom duplex in the not-so-flattering Felicia Village Complex in Ghost Town. He also still drove a 1987 Toyota Celica, and, although his refrigerator was full and he always looked fly, he never understood why he was not treated like a boss, why he was not given more respect. After all, Jake probably had about two hundred bodies on the same .38 he'd shot Luciano with.

He was always the Hitman of choice, Polo Pasé's number-one guy, the man who always got the call when a "situation" needed to be handled. He was their Tony Victor, their hothead: no other way to describe him.

At least Tony was calculated. Jake, as we've seen, literally just shot a man inside of a crowded diner and in front of witnesses and bosses that would have him and his family dead by sundown.

Why would he do that? What was his motive? Was he that stupid to think that there wouldn't be immediate retribution? Imminent death in less than a days' grace? This man had *DEAD* written all over him the second he left that scene. Was this all just to prove a point? All to show his comrades and peers in business that he could "hang" with us, too? Was the fact that he was going to pay for his transgressions with his life *worth* it? There were just too many questions without answers—and, judging by the looks of things, they weren't stopping.

"Yo, did you make dinner?" called Jake. "I'm starving—and I'm gonna need some of that gooshy stuff in-between your legs. I had to catch a body tonight, baby. You know that makes me horny."

The woman he addressed flew around the corner. "Are you fuckin' serious? No, I didn't make dinner: it's four in the damn *morning!*" She shook her head. "Didn't you just come from a diner? You know, the one you just shot *Luciano* at? For Christ Sakes, Jake, what the *fuck's* wrong with you?"

"Damn, how the hell do you even know that? It just happened, like, twenty minutes ago."

"Never mind how I know. You do know you're a marked man, right?" Her voice shook with anger. "And you expect for me to give you some *pussy*? You're a crazy son-of-a-bitch. I can't even believe you right now. I can't believe I ever loved you." She began to walk away. "I will *not* be made to stand in the middle of the crossfire coming to you."

Right at that moment, Jake snuck up from behind her as she walked and wrapped his monstrous hand around her mouth. With the same gun he'd shot Luciano with minutes before, he nudged her on the side of her left temple with it, massage-like.

He put his lips to her ear, then sucked on it and kissed it. He then bit on it—hard—, and whispered, "Bitch, when I say I want some pussy, you gon' give me dat pussy, you understand me?" The woman was whimpering in his arms. *"Do you understand me?"* he repeated.

She nodded her head up and down, trembling: it was clear she was now officially terrified of Jake.

"Now, make me my fuckin' dinner, and get that pussy ready for me. I want it nice and wet. Matter fact, strip down now—and I mean *now!* I want to see you cook my food naked."

With tears rushing down her face and her dignity ripped from her, she took her clothes off and took the pots and pans out of the cabinet. Cocoa Butta had never seen this coming.

# CHAPTER 15

*Location: The House of Nesbit; Front Lawn; 6:30 pm*

AFTER RECEIVING WORD THAT Luciano was in ICU the morning after the shooting, Don and I gathered at The House of Nesbit. A normal family would've spent hours crying before trying to continue on as normal, but not this family: we were not cut from that kind of cloth. We didn't exactly believe in self-pity; it just wasn't our style.

Celo Gaston and Al Gebra were out front discussing the Knicks and Bulls rivalry—as if there was any chance Jordan was going to let Ewing ever get a ring. Negative. Anyway, Tony Victor and Salawicious Dough were setting up a game of chess on the terrace when we pulled up.

"So, what's the plan, fellas?" asked Dough. "If you want, Blues and I can make another bomb and blow that motherfucker up to smithereens. We could have it done in as little as two hours if you want." He thought for a moment. "In fact, I can get in touch with Brilliant Bobby Bushetta out in Colorado, and he could probably send an atomic version with a more powerful, faster and intricate process."

"No, fool!" I returned, exasperated. "You're part of the reason we're *in* this mess right now." I shook my head. "*Really*, Dough? A car bomb that you didn't even run past me, let alone get my approval?"

"Whoa, whoa, whoa!" he said, putting his hands up. "Since when did I need approval from any of you to do what I wanted? I'm a Great 8 member, and I got rights."

"Since the last time you did some crazy shit like this," I snapped. "Remember some time ago when we were at Woodbridge Mall, and I saw my girl at the time with another dude at the pretzel stand?"

"Yeah...?"

"So, we saw the chick, and I told you and Don to distract the dude so I could go wrap this broad up right quick. You strongarm the dude out of the line and position him in the corner—which I appreciated—, but that was the last I saw of you for two hours! Two *hours*, Dough! Where were you? At the end of the other side of the mall, hanging the guy from his dick off the second floor!"

"Proceed; I'm still waiting for the bad part of the story."

"Dough," I growled, "you were hanging the man from his *dick*. From the top floor of a shopping mall!"

"It was partially Don's fault! He dared me," Sal said.

"Oh, so now it's Don's fault? Because when we got back to the house, you were boasting about all of your doings to all of the family!"

"Chill, son," Don piped up. "Leave me out of this: I didn't think you'd do it. That's worse than the time I gave rubbing alcohol to Escobar to drink."

"Did you really have to bring that up, Don?" I sighed, rolling my eyes.

"Moving on," Don continued, turning to Dough. "I'm with Escobar on this one. I mean, c'mon man, from his *dick*? His Johnson? His shlong? His lovemaker?"

"Since when have you not thought that a certifiable maniac like Salawicious Dough would *not* do something as stupid as that?" I said. "The man is insane. If he wasn't Hak Hennessey's brother and fell into the business by default, I probably would have denied his entry into MentallyOrganizedBusiness. He's a loon."

"Well, *that's* hurtful," Sal sniffed. "Matter fact, I'm so hurt right now, I think I'm just gonna get in the thunderbird, drive up Springfield Avenue, and find me a chick to fuck, in the ass, on purpose."

I couldn't help from laughing: the man was Joker-crazy, just the man you wanted at a time like this. He just needed a little supervision sometimes, that was all.

"Sal, hold up," I backtracked. "Don't go nowhere. I didn't mean that. I'm stressed the fuck out: we just lost Remington a couple months ago, I'm not even fully recovered myself from my attack, and now this shit with Luciano got us all fucked up."

"It's fine, Sir," Sal said respectfully. "So, if we're not bombing this asshole, are we at least hanging him from his dick? Maybe off a twelve-story building, like this motherfucker?"

I didn't even dignify his question with an answer.

At that moment, Tony Victor walked up to Don Corione and told him he was madder than Pigleg in an ass-kicking contest. Don leaned in and nodded his head in understanding, almost divulging in the plan until frowning and saying, "Wait, madder than who?"

"Pigleg. You know, the legend," Tony whispered, grinning.

"Yo, why are you whispering?" Don muttered. "I love you, man, but we ain't *that* close."

Tony shook his head. "I don't wanna say his name too loud; a lot of people don't believe in him, and some of us won't even admit they've seen him at all."

"You said 'him', so it's a man," Don pondered. "Dressed up as a pig?"

"*No*, man, listen: it's a man with a pig's leg in place of his own leg. He got from some war from back in the day after his leg blew off in combat, so he asked the doctors and nurses on-staff if there were any limbs available from the dead. After they checked, the coroner on-duty said they only had a dead pig from the field with both its legs." He began grinning. "So, the man said, 'Sew me up!' It's a true tale of a man's courage, a real man's plight to finish what he started. So, ever since then, the man has been called Pigleg. He walks like this."

The hilarity that ensued proved to be just what we all needed: a good laugh. And what a gut-wrenching laugh it was.

Tony Victor proceeded to mimic the funniest thing we'd ever seen and, while we were whooping and hollering from his walk impersonation, Tony didn't find anything funny.

"Yo, da fucks wrong with yaw niggas? The man has a pig's leg sewn into him and ya'll are *laughing*?" Tony shook his head in disgust. "That's the last time I'm gonna mention Pigleg around any of you again. The fact that—"

"Pigleg! *Pigleg*?" hollered Jay BaDouche who heard the commotion from the house. "Nigga, don't start with that shit. Fuckin' *Pigleg*? Pigleg! A man with a leg from a pig? *That's* what you want me to believe? With all your heart and soul? Huh?" Jay shook his head. "I'm sorry, family, I can't. I just can't, and I won't." And he walked right back into the house.

Meanwhile, in the West Wing Kitchen, Sara grabbed a recipe from the top cabinet. This wasn't any recipe: this was *the* recipe, the one for Peachy the Great's biscuits. Those things were to die for.

Peachy the Great was Celo Gaston's grandmother, and— yep, you guessed it—everyone's grandmother. The wisdom that woman spoke made us all become honest men and women—well, almost. She planted the seed, at least. Rarely does a parent outlive their child, but it always seemed like Peachy was going to outlive us all: she was—and is, to this day—remarkable.

"The biscuits are done. Bring ya'll assess inside before they get cold," yelled out Sara Safebreaka.

Whish Johanssen was inside already, obvious concern plastered on her face. "I think someone is in *love*," Sara taunted.

"Girl, ain't' nobody in love," Whish shot back. "So chill wit dat shit! Besides, I'm too gangster to use that word. Love is overrated."

"That's why you circled the spoon on your plate around the same part about thirteen times and haven't even taken a bite," Sara responded.

"I'm not hungry."

"Bitch, do you know who you talking to? I will stomp a mudhole in ya ass and walk it dry! You know you can't lie to me!" Sara arched an eyebrow. "You played hard to get with that man for well over a decade, so *obviously* you were interested, and when you finally succumbed to his advances, it's been clear that you've been glowing since then. So, I don't wanna hear anything else but the truth now. Ya dig?"

"You make me sick," Whish snapped. "Why do you always have to be so *maternal*? You pregnant, or something? Got baby fever?" She shook her head. "I can't call it with you sometimes: you think you know everything. Well, this time—" she grinned devilishly— "you're right, as usual. I think I love him."

And with that, Whish sat down on the corner stool by the breakfast bar and cried. Sara sighed and went over to her sister, rubbing her on her back.

"It's okay, sister. We're all worried about Sam. He's a motherfucker, though. He'll pull through. He has to."

*

Meanwhile, Celo Gaston sat on the swimming pool deck by himself, awaiting the day's' plan. He often found himself out there: it was where he could be alone with his thoughts.

The more he thought, the more he started to believe maybe he was better off getting away from all of the craziness that was the life of MentallyOrganizedBusiness: after all, with the passing of Velma the Goddess a few years back, he had never really been the same. Don't get me wrong, he's still one of the greatest men I know, but a loss like that can puncture a man in a way that can't truly be understood by anybody besides those who have been through the same thing.

He had been dealing with that as well as the separation from his first love, Sester, for quite some time: Sester was Don Corione's sister, and they were childhood sweethearts. He hadn't seen her in years, but knew she was alive and well. If not for the child they shared, chances were very high he wouldn't have talked to her again. They were the proverbial oil and water: it looked good on paper, but it was not good in real life. His daughter had migrated down South with Sester, and he never got to see her as often as he wanted to: he was lucky if it was a month's total out of a calendar year.

He'd then found himself in another relationship that seemed to be doomed from the beginning: from domestic violence to court appearances, it was not a healthy situation. He had asked Whish and Sara to escort that last "situation" into the Hudson River, but he'd changed his mind at the last minute. After that, he'd found himself at a crossroads, unsure with what to make of life. After a few more sips of his drink, he put his glass down on the patio table and took a deep breath.

*I wonder what North Carolina is like in the winter.*

\*

Mula Madison walked in and sat down at the table, swiftly applying her eyeliner on and brushing her hair back into a ponytail. You could see on her face how disturbed she was about the news regarding Luciano: the two of them were closer than a Pig and his leg—a tasteless example, but you get the picture—, and she was not happy.

Sam had been there for her when she'd gone through a bad breakup with Evander Highwaters: he'd been on the high school football team because of his size, not his talent, and safe to say he'd been a corny motherfucker, looking like Eazy-E's long-lost cousin from North Dakota or some shit. Nevertheless, she'd loved him, so we'd accepted him; but when he did her wrong, she came to us and said she'd had enough. She'd wanted him out of the picture, so, naturally, we'd done what we thought would be best: we got him at his safe haven: The Gridiron.

Sam and I had caught him slipping—literally—after practice one evening. The rest of the team was already gone, and he'd just gotten out of the shower—and, to his surprise, Sam and I were standing there in three-piece suits when he stepped out. With no room for talking—I've always been uncomfortable talking to a naked man—, we ran toward him. However, before we could even touch him, he slipped on the water on the floor while trying to run from us, hitting his head on the ice tub. Sam and I had looked at each other for what seemed like hours.

"Well, *that* sucks," I'd finally said. "We didn't even break a sweat. I'm a little disappointed."

"As you should be: we wasted these perfect suits for this occasion, and we didn't even get any blood on them. I'm not exactly sure how I feel about that."

"Well, considering that it looks like our job is done here, I think I'm gonna go have sex with somebody's daughter," I shrugged. "Hopefully someone who's so good I'll actually remember her name afterwards."

Sam had then told me he'd catch up with me later: he'd looked at Evander and a lightbulb had gone off. Armed with his new great idea, he had decided to put Evander in the team equipment bag, and, all by himself, Sam Luciano pushed that damn thing onto the football field. That bag had been heavy as all hell and, by this time, he'd called Swindel, Johnny Sliver, and Frederick Linguini for some assistance.

They'd promptly met him on the field and proceeded to tie Evander up to the goal post, butt-naked besides a helmet. They'd painted two black stripes under his eyes, and glued—yes, glued—a jockstrap to his penis. They'd taken a picture and made copies of it, which they had later posted throughout town. By the next morning, Evander Highwaters was more popular than he ever could have made himself to be. We never checked on him: I'm not even sure if he lived. Oh, well.

"Don, what in the fuck is everybody doing just sitting around?" Mula demanded. "Our brother is in the ICU and we're not out there exacting revenge on a motherfucker? What's going on around here? You know you don't catch me around here a lot because I'm busy running Spanish Brickz, but this is unacceptable. Where's Escobar?"

"I'm right here, Mula," I said as I closed the front door behind her. "I'm glad you made it: you were the last person we were waiting for. Have a seat."

In the corridors of the Family Room, as we liked to call it, stood The Great 8—minus Luciano, of course—and our Sister Leaders. The smell of revenge was in the air, a stench that resonated within the small oxygen space we had to use in the tight-knit room.

I walked over to Don. "This meeting is mine; I got this. Kick back and relax."

Don stepped back to allow me to walk past him to the front of the room. I had been thinking long and hard about our level of retaliation and decided this was the moment to let the family in on it.

"Family!" I began. "Tonight, we are going to commit a murder—a good old-fashioned homicide. Now, I don't want everybody going crazy here—because I know how fuckin' crazy you all are." The group snickered. "Because of who the recipient is going to be, I will not—I repeat, will not— have this publicized or done in typical family style. No; Don and I have already gone over the plan and what everybody's role is going to be. It will go as follows."

Just as Don and I were preparing to provide the family with instructions, a long Bentley Limo pulled up to the front of The House of Nesbit. Al Gebra happened to notice it first, and Hak Hennesey and Tony Victor immediately reacted with a couple of Glocks in hand. Celo walked over and peeked through the draped curtain, me following. I looked back at everyone wordlessly, but my expression asked by itself: *Does anybody recognize this?*

The expressions on their faces answered that question clearly: this was a vehicle no one had ever seen before. Not too many people could even *afford* a ride like that—and perhaps most confusing of all, nobody even knew about this place but us. Who in the hell was in that thing?

The back door suddenly swung open, suicide-style, and Poppa Vein hopped out.

Guns off safety, I told everyone to hold fire: don't do anything unless me or Don give you the word. Poppa Vein walked directly toward us both.

"Escobar; Corione. Cocoa is in trouble: that son-of-a-bitch I once called my family has my sister. If I know you, as I can see you here with your family, you're already plotting to take his life. If I may, I'd like to be the one to do it for you."

# CHAPTER 16

THE DOUCHEBAG BROS HAD been brothers longer than a set of testicles; longer than a prostitute's vagina after 101 customers, male and female; longer than the time it took for Bill Clinton to tell the truth about his sexual relations with that woman.

The reason they'd moved in together was because of a shootout we'd been involved in a couple years back, in Linden: after that night, they'd felt they'd be better to stay in the same spot.

We'd been celebrating Salawicious Dough's College Graduation (don't ask me how that maniac managed to graduate from college; I'm pretty sure he threatened the Dean's mom, or some shit), a celebration a childhood friend of his was throwing at his home—which just so happened to be located right by Jay's mom's house.

That party had sucked ass—until we'd arrived, of course. Every woman there had stopped what they were doing to throw themselves all over us—us being me, Al Gebra, Jay BaDouche, Hak Hennesey, Harry Horrendous, and Sam Luciano.

You know how Ray Charles had Georgia on his mind? Well, we'd had pussy on our mind—although I suppose that was nothing out of the ordinary. Within the first ten minutes from walking into that party, we'd had all the girls on us. None of us had actually smashed any of those chicks; after all, it had been a school graduation atmosphere. Saying that, Dough may have slipped his Vale-dick-torian into some chick's diploma. But who knows?

After the party, we'd hung outside the house for a little while, just talking shit, as we do. It was when we'd started walking toward Jay's mom's house to get some food that a little red Ford Escort had come riding down the block.

It had slowed; then gotten slower; and slower. The driver's side window had rolled down, the driver leaning out towards us.

"Which one of you lil' niggas been fuckin' with Charlene?"

We'd all looked at each other, stupefied: no one knew who he was.

Al Gebra had walked up to the window—probably not the smartest move, in retrospect—and leaned on the dude's car. "Yo, my nigga, don't none of us know no damn Charlene. Now we ain't gon' tell you twice, so get movin', son!"

I'd heard this whole conversation before: Al had created a diversion so Jay and Hak could walk around the other side of the car and blow his fuckin' brains out—what you get for stepping to us in that manner. Unfortunately, it didn't exactly go like that: we'd had the dudes—I believe it was four of them stuffed in that little ass escort—dead to rights. The plan was executed perfectly until one of the dudes in the backseat saw Jay come up empty. He'd then reached for the revolver he usually had tucked and told the driver, "They bluffin'! They bluffin'! Shoot these niggas!"

At that moment, Jay knew he'd fucked up: he'd left his gun inside the house because he didn't want to scare anybody at a house so close to his mother's home—or at a college graduation party, at that.

Al, his whole body tensing, had yelled, "Run! He's got a gun!"

Al had apparently seen it on the guy's lap when he'd approached the vehicle, thinking he was safe because the henchmen had been right there. Boy, was he wrong about that.

Anyone who saw us five motherfuckers running that day would have thought we were all track stars, trying to figure out who was Bruce and who was Caitlyn.

We'd hauled ass, to say the least, hurdling over fallen trash cans, dodging other people who'd been running as a result of the gunshots that had gone off. I believe Harry Horrendous had almost gotten hit by a truck during the whole ordeal.

Far down the block, I'd happened to see Hak jump over the fence, but that was it. We'd all eventually made it safely to Jay's mom's house—all except, we noticed quickly, for Hak Hennesey.

We'd immediately gone back outside to retaliate, but the Ford Escort gang had been nowhere to be found—and neither was Hak. We'd searched to see if he'd gotten hit, a pit of worry sitting in my stomach at the thought of my brother bleeding out somewhere.

Our search being in vain, we'd had no choice but to go back to Jay's mom's crib after two hours of looking throughout the neighborhood. When Jay had opened the front door, there was Hak, beating his mom and sister in a game of cards.

"What the *fuck*?" Jay exploded. "Where you *been*, nigga? We been out looking for you for the last couple of hours."

"Really?" Hak asked, raising his eyebrows. "Well, I ran down the opposite way of the shots, hopped the fence of the bad Polish chick's house, got some ass, ate a sandwich, got some more ass, and then walked over here. Your mom said all of you was okay, so I challenged her to a game of rummy." Hak grinned lazily.

We'd all just shaken our heads and walked away, Jay calling good-naturedly over his shoulder, "You fuckin' douchebag!"

Still one of my favorite stories to tell.

\*

Jay walked into the dining room area of their house with a pink suit in his left hand and a green suit in his other.

"Yo, which one?"

With a twisted look on his face, Hak responded, "For what occasion? You going to the Diarrhea Charity Gala again? Or you auditioning for the Pepto Bismol awards?"

"*No*, motherfucker, to wear to Jake Solomon's funeral," Jay shot back. "Are we killing him today, tomorrow? What the hell's goin' on? Have you heard from O3 or any of your Great 8 cohorts?"

"Today was originally going to be that pussy's expiration date, but now, I'm not so sure; earlier this morning—when Poppa Vein pulled up to Escobar—, they spoke a few words and then fled the scene together with Corione. All we gotta do is stay ready." Hak leaned back in his chair. "So, whether it's today or next week, as long as we wrap this nigga Solomon up, I'm good. If we ain't busy today, we'll make ourselves busy. Matter of fact, my dark-skinned brother, I'm 'bout to hit that hot Brazilian chick I met earlier this week. I want some ass. We got these Jackie Chan Bootleg joints over here and maybe, just maybe, if we're lucky, she'll bring her camel-toe friend."

"Damn, my nigga. Camel-toe?" Jay echoed, shaking his head. "You gon' set me up with her friend who face look like a camel's toe? That's some bullshit right there."

"No, you dumbass," Hak screamed out, cackling. "Her friend's pussy so thick it look like a camel toe! You never heard that before?"

Before Jay could respond, a shattering sound came from the back of the house. Hak and Jay quickly grabbed their Glocks and walked into the kitchen: their window was broken and an iron lay on the floor, a note attached to it:

*Dear, Assholes,*

*I understand that you guys are known as The Douchebag Bros around town. Cute!*

*This letter is to inform the both of you that neither of you are as smart as you think you are, as tough as you think you are, nor are you as prepared as you think you are. Chances are very high that by the time this letter finds you— and I hope it finds you well—, one of your brothers will be dead.*

*You've been so kind to read this letter till the end. THX—it shows you care :)*

*—The Curse*

Hak Hennesey and Jay BaDouche couldn't believe it.

"What in the fuck is this?" Hak muttered. "And who or what the fuck is The Curse?"

Jay didn't respond, lost for words.

After a few minutes, Jay suddenly spoke. "Yo, you think he's going after Dough?"

Hak frowned. "Why do you ask that?"

"Because he said one of our brothers will be dead."

"But what makes you think it's Dough?" Hak demanded. "We're all brothers. It could be any of us."

"My brother been locked up in Statesville for years, so this Curse asshole ain't got no access to him."

Hak had a very disturbing look on his face. *I mean, at the end of the day, it could be any of us,* he thought uneasily. *Whoever this is better not lay a hand on my baby brother's head, or they're dead! Two times over!*

# CHAPTER 17

POPPA VEIN SAT DOWN at the back table at his brother's shop, constantly mulling over what his sister had told him the other night.

After Jake Solomon had his way with her, he'd quickly gone to sleep—after which she'd tiptoed to the bathroom and called her brother to tell him what had just happened: she had been repeatedly held against her will and forced to perform sexual acts on Jake—acts she no longer had an interest in doing ever again. They'd been together for a while now, but Poppa Vein had never known of any serious problems in their relationship: from what he'd seen and heard, Jake always treated her with respect. Now, it seemed he had a death wish Poppa Vein did not mind fulfilling.

Vein took another bite out of his beef, sausage, cheese, and egg sandwich, waiting patiently for Polo Pasé to arrive. The day was as dark as the mood, dark clouds hanging around like the guy you didn't want in your clique.

Vein looked at his watch and realized Polo was ten minutes late to their meeting. It was when he started to get up and walk outside that Polo beat him to the punch, walking in toward the table in a hurry.

"My apologies for being late, Vein. The traffic from downtown at this hour is brutal," he apologized, shrugging off his jacket.

"What the hell were you doing downtown on a random Tuesday morning?"

"I went to see a lawyer about my case," Polo responded. "You know, the one I caught for beating the holy shit outta that male nurse when I was in the hospital a while back."

"Yet another hothead move of yours. Good job, Polo," Vein sighed. "Listen, speaking of that case: in terms of the parties who put you in hospital, there will be no retaliation. Do you understand me? None. Zero."

"Are you fuckin' crazy, yo?" Polo protested. "Those motherfuckers are responsible for my losing an *arm*! My arm, Vein! And you want me to just crawl over to the corner and die?"

"Figuratively, yes," Vein said simply.

"And why the fuck would I do that?"

"Because we got bigger shit to deal with."

Polo's eyes looked like they were going to pop out of their sockets. "Bigger shit to deal with? Bigger than a limb? Bigger than a vital part of my body? Bigger than—"

"Jake raped Cocoa."

Polo stopped in his tracks and leaned forward toward Vein. "What the fuck did you just say?"

"You heard me." Vein's jaw was set and he seemed to have zoned out. "It's too damn painful for me to say again." He snapped out of his trance and met Polo's eye contact. "Jake Solomon, our once-brother, our lead hitman, your righthand man, raped my sister. And and that is the motherfucker who's going to pay today. Slowly."

Polo shot up in total disbelief: he could not fathom this being true. He just couldn't believe it.

He grabbed an iced tea from the shop fridge and pulled out a Cuban cigar. The prosthetic arm helped him do multiple things, but it did not feel like the real thing; still, he was grateful that the option was there to use it. He took a few puffs and sat back down with his brother at arms.

"Vein, I can't imagine how you feel right now," he began delicately. "My deepest apologies to you and for this man's behavior. It's beyond unacceptable. I was the one who brought him on a couple years back, and I'm the one responsible for my men. You know I love Cocoa like my own flesh and blood, but right now, I want Jake Solomon dead." He took a deep breath. "My only question to you is, why isn't he in a ditch somewhere already? How in the fuck are you just sitting here stuffing your face and not ending this nigga's life?"

Poppa Vein grabbed his jacket and tossed it onto his left shoulder. "Polo, when something like this happens, something that hits this close to home, it's human nature to want to retaliate and get vengeance as quickly as possible; that's what most people do. But I haven't been in business for as long as I have by reacting without thinking, without a plan. Yes, he hurt and disrespected my sister; yes, he hurt my family; so, yes, Jake Solomon's days amongst the living are numbered—and those days will be ones of suffering, loss, betrayal, and death, all before he meets his own demise. Trust me on this, my brother, all in due time. I'll be in touch soon."

Poppa then started walking toward the front door. "Oh, I forgot," he said, turning to Polo, "you might wanna play nice with Tony Victor."

"Play nice?" he echoed, frowning. "I don't *like* that nigga. He thinks he can't be touched."

"Well, you better put your differences aside, because for the next few days, you'll be working with him."

# CHAPTER 18

*Location: Twisted Sins Bunny Ranch; Brooklyn, NYC;*
*April 9; 8:00 am*

*I*F THERE AIN'T A *hole I can't fill, that bitch ain't real!*

That was the end of the promotional commercial Qurtis Jenkins ran on the local TV networks for his Porno shop, *Qurtis Jenkins presents: The Glowing Midgets.* Apparently the 'midget' portion of the title was metaphorical for all the 'small' parts on a woman that makes a man's privates 'glow". It took me about ten years to figure that out.

Qurtis Jenkins and I had been friends for a long time, but him and Salawicious Dough had been in competition for just as long.

"I can't believe he's doing it again!" yelled Sal Dough to his secretary. "Can you believe it? He's advertising on *television* now. I can't compete with that! *And* he's got midgets! *Glowing* midgets, that son-of-a-bitch! He's always trying to one-up me. I'll show him, that rat bastard! I'll get titties, big ol' titties that not only glow, but *sing. And* I'll sell Vagina in a Can behind the counter!" his face was flushing with excitement. "I'm gonna whoop his ass in sales this year!"

Salawicious Dough was not only a suicidal, homicidal, genocidal maniac, but he also took his Great 8 earnings and invested in a sex-romping, fantasy-fulfilling ranch in the countryside of Brooklyn, USA. Little did he know that Qurtis Jenkins was a god in that territory. Indeed, when Sal found out about it a few years back, I was pretty sure he was going to murder him—death by castrated penis to the throat, stuffed. Thankfully, I'd happened to be at the right place at the right time and was ultimately able to save my friend's life: he'd actually plotted to kill Qurtis at the GM Headquarters—really a back room at The Glowing Midgets Porn Shop where people went to get "head" exclusively— while Qurtis was sampling his own goods.

The story goes that Dough went in there to confront Qurtis one day, only to find ol' QJ himself enjoying a delicious schlong slurpee—

administered by one of his employees with a pair of lips that would put Angelina Jolie's pair to shame.

"*So*, playing around while on the clock, I see?" Sal had grinned. Q had jumped up and pushed the girl back, fumbling with the zipper on his pants.

"What the *fuck*, dude! How'd you get in here?! Matter of fact, who the fuck even are you?"

"Relax, relax, man," Sal had returned, holding his hands up. "I'm just here to advise you on a few things, that's all—a few instructions, if you like, that you're going to follow. Okay?"

He'd cocked his head to the side and smiled; Q had remained silent.

"What you're going to do is close this piece-of-shit establishment you got here—for good—, and you're then going to forward me that big lip server you just pushed away to my bunny ranch in Brooklyn. I'm pretty sure I could make great use of her."

Q had looked at Salawicious Dough like he'd just stepped out of a fuckin' DeLorean created by a guy named Doc.

"You wanna repeat ya'self, youngblood?" Q responded, his tone menacing.

"No, not really," Sal shrugged. "I was hoping you'd just go quietly into the night like a good little bitch, but it appears like you're not going to do that. Apologies, but I'm gonna have to gaffle you."

"*Gaffle* me?" Q spat. "Motherfucker, I'll gaffle your neck with this entire penis I just took from this chick's mouth and backslap the shit outta you with it! Who the *fuck* do you think you are, coming in my place of business and makin' threats you ain't gon' follow up on?" Q walked to the door. "You know what? I got somethin' for you. You wait right here, buddy."

And all Sal could do was watch this guy walk down the hallway, opening door after door. Sal was mildly irritated: he easily could have put a hole in this nigga, but he'd admittedly found himself interested in what the guy apparently had for him.

Two minutes elapsed and Q returned, unsurprisingly and slightly anticlimactically with a Harper Ferry shotgun in hand—the shit Davy Crocket used on niggas back in the day. He aimed at Sal.

"Any last words before I shoot your balls right off?"

Sal had taken a step back to observe the situation, but in that moment decided to lean into the barrel of the gun.

"Nigga, you ain't got the heart to use that on me," he said gently. "Not here, not now, not anywhere. Not in a box, not with a fox, not in—"

"You really quoting Dr. Seuss right now, nigga?"

Sal had thought for a moment. "I suppose I am."

It was then that I'd entered. Opening the front door, I yelled out, "Q! It's time to go get them chicks that we met at Newport last week." A pause. "Where the fuck you at?"

I'd heard footsteps coming toward me and, before I could say anything else: "Escobar?"

"*Dough*?"

"What in the blue fuck is goin' on here?" Q demanded, lowering his barrel. "You two know each other?"

I'd shook my head in confusion. "Hold the fuck up." My head has started to pang as I took in the scene before me. "Sal, what are you doing here—and Q, why do you have a fucking gun in your hand?"

Q proceeded to tell me what had happened, and the more talking he did, the more I side-eyed Dough in disapproval. I then assured Q he wouldn't have any more trouble from us that day forward.

I'd then escorted Dough out of Qurtis Jenkins' business and smacked him multiple times as we walked toward the '89 Oldsmobile Cutlass Supreme I'd been pushing back then.

"What's the matter with you, man?" I'd demanded. "That man is untouchable, not to mention one of my oldest friends! He's not to be fucked with, ya hear me?!"

"But he's detrimental to my *ranch*!" he'd shouted back, reminiscent— as I'd thought at the time—of a toddler throwing a tantrum. "He's costing me money!"

"I don't give a flying *fuck* what he's costing you," I snapped back. "If that man—or any man, for that matter—is in your pockets, you need to go back and see what you've done wrong; you don't just start trying to kill everybody in sight because you think someone is stepping on your toes!"

"But, Escobar, that's what you, Don, and Sam have been doing for the last decade," he pointed out. "If someone's in the way, you move them. Simple."

He'd had a point, but my pride had prevented me from admitting it.

Instead, I said, "Your last name is Dough; you understand that, right? If there's anything you know how to do, it's making money. There's nothing but money out here!" He surveyed me steadily as I spoke. I pressed on. "So I refuse to believe what you're sayin' right now; it's your personal issue, and I frankly don't wanna hear shit about it right now. I know you, and I don't want no more bullshit excuses. I just want you to assure me that you will leave this man and his family alone. You got it?"

"Alright, Escobar," he muttered. "I don't like it, but I respect your wishes."

Dough will still tell you to this day that Qurtis Jenkins was only still breathing because he allowed him to, as per my request. And so he did.

After this whole ordeal, Sal entered one of the so-called Bunny Holes—the rooms where they serve a customer's desires—to see if business was picking up. A customer had walked in five hours before and hadn't emerged. He *had* paid for a threesome fantasy with Tasha Banks and Licky Bella, but five *hours*?

Don't get it twisted, these were Sal's biggest moneymakers, and they would have a man's toes curl up for hours like a weightlifter. Saying this, something seemed off; he could feel it in the air. He took a swig of his Infamous Smirnoff liquor he'd invested in a decade before and put the bottle down on the island counter, then walking past a picture from long ago hanging on the wall of him leaning against his Jeep Wrangler. That was the one his father had given to him, and Alexandria the Grape—his old flame—was sitting in the driver's seat in the image.

He began to reminisce the good times they used to have, the silly mistakes they'd made together. They'd been high school sweethearts who'd met through mutual friends, and an interesting couple, to say the least. It was as they got older that it hadn't worked out, but they were thankfully able to not allow the split to affect family business. Sure enough, there was still a respect and demand of being cordial with one another when family business is in tow.

He shook those memories loose and continued to walk toward the room his client had entered earlier, leading ladies in tow.

He knocked: once; twice. *Could they actually be asleep?*

The door was locked, so he proceeded to take his skeleton key from his pocket and turn it into the keyhole. The door obediently swung open to show the room: devoid of people.

Upon exploration, Sal found a note on top of the pillow.

*Dear Sal (if I may call you that),*

*This is a pretty nice place of work you got going on here. Too bad no one works here anymore—well, at least, no one with a vagina. You see, those two ladies (if you can call them that) that you had in here earlier... well, they're on timeout right now. I have a few things I need for them to take care of for me. Also, could you do a better job with your inventory, please? You're out of lambskin condoms. Oh, and that poor schmuck you overcharged? He's out. Actually, come to think of it, he's in—in the stove, I mean. You might want to turn the gas off now, unless you like extra crispy fat white guy as an entrée.*

*—The Curse*

# CHAPTER 19

THE MORNING DEW SNUCK its way into Don's house as he opened the back door to his deck, and Any Given Sunday similarly penetrated the place, could walking through the house in her birthday suit.

At this point, I'm not sure if he even knew the name her momma had given her—although I'm not sure how important that was, considering she did whatever he asked her to. Plus, her ass was so fat—so fat it'd make a grown man drive all the way to his mother's house, slap his momma, get back in the car, and drive home.

He grabbed his bong to join him outside, where he also had his music playing. He took a seat on the far side of the patio table as he listened to HeMe through his speakers—quite possibly the greatest hype man of all time. If he ever felt like it, he could've been one of the dopest artists out himself: you could often find him on tracks with $A^2$ and Cheif. Man. Don turned the volume all the way up.

Don was a heavy marijuana smoker: in fact, he and his cousin Brilliant Bobby Bushetta made most of their millions in the weed business. Brilliant Bobby was a masterful computer whiz.

He and Blues could have made millions together in that business, but they usually didn't see eye-to-eye; thus, they (wisely) kept their relationship non-business.

Brilliant Bobby moved out to Colorado when marijuana became legal to sell in that state, and Don put up the money for Brilliant Bobby to run the business out of a Greenhouse in Colorado faster than you could say, "Girl, bring that ass to me"—and, ever since then, Don had been delivered an abundance of packages of different shades and strengths of weed. He'd been a happy man for a long time—that is, until recent events had transpired throughout the family in the last couple months.

With the death of Remington Steele, my near-death experience, and the shooting of Luciano, Don almost felt guilty—guilty for dodging what most promised to undergo in this kind of business: a gruesome demise.

Don was a son-of-a-bitch, an asshole, a sarcastic, arrogant prick—in other words, pretty much a dark-skinned version of me. Whenever he'd introduce himself to people, he'd say he was Don Corione, and I was him when he got angry.

He found himself questioning why these crazy things were happening to those closest around him, but not to him directly: was he not good enough to kill, to blow up, to be run down by a limo by a guy with a Rikishi mask? Indeed, even in pre-death, he was arrogant—but he's one of my very best friends, one who, despite his faults, I have always been able to count on. A man who has a heart of gold but a mind of question.

Don was never one to exactly think positively all the time: as a matter of fact, he was a bit of a skeptic about pretty much everything.

After a few moments of mental silence, his phone rang. He turned the music down.

"Yo."

Joseph Stylez's voice emerged from the other line. "Yo Don. You fully awake right now?"

Don sighed. "No, this is actually a timed recording meant to fuck with you every time you call me."

Don could hear the smile in Sylez's voice as he spoke. "In that case, tell ya moms I'll be over later: she's got a few holes that need filling."

"I told you to leave my moms out of this, you motherfucker."

"*And I* told you to answer the damn phone like you got some sense, but did you listen?"

Don rolled his eyes to himself. "What do ya want, Joe? I'm busy rolling up a fat-ass blunt with hash, and one of my days of the week is fingering herself on my living room couch."

"Well, that's always good," Stylez responded. "Take a pic for me?"

"You got it."

A few moments of silence elapsed before Stylez spoke again, his tone more serious now. "Listen, family, the rest of the fellas are getting antsy. What do we do? Just sit and wait to roll on these niggas who've hurt us?" Another pause. "This is unlike us. Luciano's in the ICU, Escobar's not even fully recovered yet from his attack, and we lost Remington a few months back, and we all feel like we've just patted the enemy on the back of his hand, like some 'now run along and play nicely with your friends' kind of shit."

Don exhaled. "Joseph, I need you to listen closely—*very* closely. Do you hear that?"

"Hear what? I don't hear shit."

"The moaning," Don said. "The groaning. There it is again!"

"Don, what the *fuck* are you saying?"

Don's stomach hurt from trying not to laugh. "No, the question is what *position* am I gonna put this chick in? I swear to *God*, after this last blunt, I'm out!"

"Can you be serious *ever*?" Stylez's tone was exasperated yet amused.

"I *am* being serious," Don insisted. "I'm always serious."

*Beep:* another call clicked through on Don's phone.

"Hold on, Stylez," Don said quickly, "I got another call coming through." He switched the line and answered the caller. "Hello?"

No response arrived: instead, the line crackled with heavy breathing.

"Hello?" Don repeated. "Listen, man, I can't hear you."

It was then that a voice came through: deep, menacing, raspy—and apparently absolutely hilarious to Don. "I'm gon' kill you, motherfucker," it seethed.

Don just laughed. "Faye?"

"I'ma kill you, you skinny motherfucker," the voice responded.

Don nodded to himself. "Yeah, okay, brother—you and a hundred other motherfuckers. Get to the back of the line, nigga."

Unfazed, Don then clicked back over to Joseph Stylez. "Yo, Stylez! You there?"

"Yeah, I'm here," Stylez responded. "So, what we doin'?"

"In all seriousness, Escobar and I got a plan of all plans to wrap this Jake Solomon nigga up," Don responded. "But it ain't gon' be how we usually do it: instead, we gon' take this nigga down from the inside. We gon' use his own people against him while some of you take care of some of his peoples on the outside." He grinned to himself. "We're not going just for his flesh: we're going for that nigga's very existence."

"Okay. I like that," Stylez mused.

"But you're not to do anything till you hear from us," Don said firmly. "I've already told the fellas, and I suggest you reiterate it to them again: this cannot go unplanned. Jake Solomon is a dangerous man, and he cannot be taken lightly."

"True, true," Stylez responded. "So just wait to hear from either you or Escobar directly?"

"Unless the directions come from a higher-up—as in, a G8 member. So, if Tony Victor or Hak Hennesey give you and the other henchmen instructions, you follow them."

"Got it."

"Now, is there anything else you need from my life, my nigga?" Don asked. "I'm pretty sure Any Given Sunday is getting frustrated waiting for good ol' ST's dick to climb up her chimney."

Stylez chuckled. "We good, Don."

Don hung up the phone and promptly proceeded to put his blunt down. For a brief second, he felt something like unease as he reflected on the "life threat" call: he received many on the daily, and yet this one felt a little realer than usual.

Saying this, Don wasn't one to worry about something he couldn't control, so he rose from his chair and undid his robe, exposing his full erection. He opened his deck door and there was Any Given Sunday, right there to pull him in by his natural extension.

# CHAPTER 20

**M**ULA MADISON, SARA SAFEBREAKA, Yelly, Whish Johannsen, and Pudgee da Fat Escobar were all greeted by Padlock Penny and fellow family member Dixie Domae at the nail salon. They literally took up every spa chair in the place, receiving all their pedicures in succession. It was while halfway through their session that Pudgee passed Penny a note, telling her to give it to Sara after they left.

"Why can't I give it to her now?" Penny asked.

"Because I don't know what to make of it."

"But why don't you just tell everybody that? We're all here; we can clear it all up real quick!"

"Be *quiet*," Pudgee snapped. "And no, I can't do that."

"Well, why the hell not? It's the perfect opportunity!" Penny insisted.

"Because..." Pudgee started fidgeting in her seat, looking around aimlessly. "Because... I stole it from her." Penny's eyebrow arched and Pudgee panicked. "Well, not really: when we got here, I rode in the car behind her, and I saw this envelope fall out of her purse. As I went to pick it up and tell her she dropped it, I noticed it was addressed to my brother. So... naturally, I felt compelled to know why Sara would be walking around with an envelope addressed to my brother. So I opened it."

"You did *what*?" Penny hissed. "You fool! My sister will whoop your ass for going through her things."

"I know, I know," Pidge whispered, "but that's why I need you to give it to her!" She sighed. "Listen, I didn't read it: I was *going* to, but there were too many eyes on me at the time. And now I just want to get rid of it." She shrugged. "I don't know what the hell's going on, but I just wanna give it back to her without her knowing anything."

"And how in the hell do you expect me to pull this off? You ripped the *envelope*!"

Penny couldn't believe Pudgee had even put her in this predicament: now she'd have to lie to her sister—and fast, before she realized the letter was missing.

It was at that moment that a young man entered and sat beside Penny. He was tall and handsome, and Penny could tell he kept himself well-groomed.

It was while she was staring at him that she fell into a bit of a trance, gazing into his eyes. Only a few moments of such heaven were endured before Pudgee mushed her in the back of her neck.

"Yo, your sister is up gettin' her eyebrows done and her purse is on her seat. This is your chance!" she hissed.

The man forgotten, Penny hopped out of the chair with one of her feet still halfway through its treatment, speeding past Mula and Yelly—who were engrossed in their conversation—and stuffing the letter into her sister's bag. She didn't know what she was going to do about the missing envelope, but she figured that was her sister's problem. She then slid back into her chair to resume her service.

Meanwhile, Yelly and Mula were still talking. "So, when are you going home?" Mula asked, wriggling her freshly painted toes. "We've been out all day; I'm sure Escobar is awaiting his queen."

"Of course he is," Yelly shrugged. "He ain't got no choice with all this chocolate; he can't resist."

The women laughed heartily. Beside them were, Whish and Dixie, who were receiving manicures.

"How do you get a Leading Lady role in our family, Whish?" Dixie enquired. "I'm assuming there's a wealth of space available at the top."

"Well, you have a point, young lady," Whish responded. "Sara, Mula and I are the original ladies of MentallyOrganizedBusiness, so we've been here since its inception. We've seen it all, been through it all. There's a certain amount of class you must exhibit while still being as ruthless as the guys." She paused. "So I guess there isn't exactly a specific way to become one: it just materialized that way. Although O3 have something to do with finalizing that, so I've heard."

"So how exactly did Yelly shoot all the way up the rankings?" Dixie demanded. "She fucked an O3 member and boom, to the top she goes?"

Whish sighed. "Did you just ask me that? Really?"

"Yeah, Dixie," Yelly retorted, walking past. "Did you just ask her that? Why don't you ask me that directly, huh?"

Dixie blushed. "Yelly, I'm sorry; I didn't mean no disrespect. It came out wrong."

"Listen, little girl," Yelly said, leaning against the wall. "I've been a made bitch for quite some time: I ran parts of Jersey over by the Hudson for almost a decade and have been stompin' bitches out for longer than that. When I was twelve, my mother walked in on me reciting NWA lyrics to my little niece—which probably wasn't the most responsible thing to do in hindsight, but then again, I was twelve and didn't know any better: all I knew was that I liked it.

"I went to college with Al Gebra and crossed paths with Escobar a few times when he'd come to visit Al, but didn't really know who he was at the time. I also heard of MentallyOrganizedBusiness during those times but didn't bother with looking into it further." She examined a nail. "Fast forward seven years and I'm in a meeting with this financial company: the street family I was dealing with at the time had suggested I took a different route to life—you know, earning an honest living like a pretty young lady should." She grinned. "I thought about it and decided to do it—especially since a year before that, I had been jumped in the street by three guys at that, one of those assholes hitting me in the back of my head with a pipe. I was in the hospital for a few months after that before I gained full use of my legs again. To this day, my short-term memory sucks.

"So anyway, I'm in this company presentation, and who do I see? PR Escobar himself, walking from one of the corner offices; apparently, he was there doing some business with one of the agents. Well, I shot him a stare. All he did was stare back, but it felt strange—like we were meant to be.

"Two weeks later, we were madly in love, and have been inseparable since then."

Dixie's face was still flushed and, once Yelly had finished, she said again, "My apologies, Yelly; I was out of line."

"We all good, girl," Yelly responded, offering a smile. "Just be careful with how you approach things out here: even in family territory, you could get ya ass handed to you, and fast." Dixie nodded. "I wasn't given anything in my life: sure, I was made a Leading Lady to our family here rather fast, but Sara, Whish, and Mula will all attest that I would've been one without

Escobar if I'd been recruited earlier. My marrying into the family just made an inevitable situation happen quicker—that's all."

And with that, Yelly went back to her seat. Once her treatment was complete, Dixie Domae walked away knowing she'd fully put her foot in her mouth, yet again. She often reacted without thinking, and that got her in a lot of trouble.

A lot of people said she was jealous of Yelly Escobar's quick ascent to the top, that she felt she had taken her spot. Back in high school, she'd dated Don Corione, but that was in the family's very early days: there really weren't any rankings in place at that time for any ladies outside of the original three. Twenty years later and it still seemed like she couldn't get over it.

"Sara, are you coming out of there today?" Whish yelled out. "All of us would like to get our eyebrows done at *some* point today! *And* I wanna go see Luciano in the hospital before visiting hours are up."

There was no response.

"Girl, go get your sister," Whish said to Penny. "She don't want me to go down there!"

With that, Penny raced down the stairs and into the basement, where the salon ladies wax and thread brows.

A bloodcurdling scream sounded from below: Penny. Her sister was rapidly drowning in her own blood.

"Oh my *God!*" Penny screamed, hyperventilating. "Oh my *God!* Oh my *God!*"

Mula, Whish, and Yelly all ran down the stairs in their flip flops: indeed, there was a little old Chinese lady slumped over the bottom railing beside their sister, who had blood oozing from the side of her head.

Everything happened quickly from there: the salon owner dialed 911, Yelly called me, and the place was filled with screams of terror: not just from the Leading Ladies, but from the rest of the salon's customers, who its employees desperately tried to calm down.

As soon as I'd heard my phone ringing, I'd picked up. "Yo, hon. What's up?"

To my horror, my wife's voice was trembling with both fear and adrenaline. "Babe, somebody tried to kill Sara in the nail salon!" She began sobbing. "She's on the floor right now with blood coming from the top of her head. I don't know how nobody heard anything. We were just one floor up. Can you get down here?"

"I'm on my way."

# CHAPTER 21

*Location: Breathless Gentlemen's Club; Rahway, NJ;
Two Hours Before*

AL GEBRA, TONY VICTOR and I were regulars at Breathless: the bouncers all knew us, and the ladies loved us. We were legends—but you should already know that by now. There were faces and asses we could recognize from hundreds of feet away.

We often held up the upper right-hand corner of the stage, left of the runway: it was our spot. There was this one occasion when someone was sitting in our area and Tony asked them to move: Ugly Guy #2 (as they'd all been an eyesore) got up and told Tony to eat a dick. Tony looked over to me, gave me the *wait till they get a load of me* smile, and told the guy that he was sorry and that he'd sit somewhere else.

Just when the guy let his guard down and sat back in his chair, Tony came up from behind him and, within two seconds flat, *snap*, the fool's neck was broken.

No one ever sat in that area again—even when we weren't there, as the staff attested.

We decided to meet each other for lunch: I ordered a corona with lemon pepper wings, Al had the chicken cobb salad (he liked to throw the croutons at the strippers), and Tony would always order the biggest fuckin' burger in the joint. He was a big motherfucker, and he needed his angus.

Just as we received our food, the head bouncer approached our area—a cool dude.

"When you guys gonna buy stock in this place?" he said, grinning. "I would think you owned it already." he

"Yeah, you're right, I should buy this motherfucker right now," I mused. "How much you think it's worth? Nine hundred thousand? Ten?"

"The current owner said it's worth over one-and-a-half million," the bouncer responded, "and that he wasn't even going to entertain anything lower."

We all nodded in approval. *Who knows, maybe we'd each put up some cash and buy this place too*, I thought. It'd be my greatest acquisition ever—if I somehow managed to pull it off, that is.

At this moment, the Brazilian woman and the Russian woman were doing aa double-shower scene on-stage. All the men looked like hound dogs waiting for their master to provide them with a well-deserved treat; indeed, while Russian women don't exactly have the greatest bodies, there is something incredibly sensual about them. The way she licked the Brazilian's areola and then laid her down on the stage, licking and kissing around her vagina, was a work of art, to say the least. These women work hard, and they deserved a raise.

Meanwhile, Tony Victor could be seen in the corner rolling dollar bills into small balls and throwing them at the girls, trying to hit their vaginas like he was Bird hittin' a 3 from the corner. The women at this club were exotic and incredibly beautiful: you had your rainy-day specials (read: chicks who were only on the brink of being smashable), but the majority of women there were undeniable goddesses. Some had been there for as long as we'd been going—the Breathless Legends. They automatically got respect from the door just because of the time they'd put into those performances.

Al Gebra found himself in the champagne room receiving a few lap dances: what started as "let me just get one" ended with about five and a stiff penis. He was a married man, after all: he didn't engage in actual sex with these chicks—or any other chicks for that matter—and same with me. My wife is black: she'd cut me if I did.

After an hour or so, there was an import from Scandinavia being introduced. She was bouncing that thing all over the place to the sounds of a DJ mix of Uncle Luke and his 2Live Crew. She was insanely gorgeous.

Meanwhile, Al was back at it in the champagne room. We couldn't blame him: it's a great room, after all.

When Tony and I were ready to leave, that's when I received the call from my hysterical wife. I'd hung up and turned to my crew, heart pounding.

"Yo, yo, we all gotta go *now!*"

"Chill, son," Al had giggled—fucking *giggled*. "Can't you see I'm a little busy here?"

"Family, we gotta go now," I repeated. "Like, right at this moment. It's your wife, and it's not looking good."

# CHAPTER 22

*Location: Jake Solomon's House; April 10; 2:20 pm*

THE DOORBELL RANG: ONCE; twice; thrice. Jake, sighing, put his half-bitten cheese and chicken roll down on his plate, wiping his hands on his pants as he approached the front door.

He opened the door to the girl and, without greeting, demanded, "Well, did you get that bitch? She's dead, right? The dark-skinned one?'"

The girl tossed her hair over her shoulder. "Oh, yeah; and the little Chinese eggroll, too. She was just in the way." She shrugged. "I didn't mean to, but she saw me kill her, so I had to do her—" She then halted mid-sentence, freezing. "Wait a minute, did you say the *dark*-skinned one? I thought you said we wanted the chick *with* the dark-skinned?"

Jake felt the color drain from his face in rage. "Are you *kidding* me? You are kidding, right?"

The girl didn't answer.

"I wanted Whish Johannsen dead," he pressed on, eyes bulging. "She's the dark-skinned one, the one who killed your sister at Dairy Queen a few months back." The girl remained mute, shuffling her feet anxiously. "You stupid bitch!"

The girl's expression contorted into anger. "Who you callin' a bitch? So I killed the wrong hoe." She shrugged. "Well, fuck it; they both gotta go, then. It's no big deal. I'll find Whish in the 'hood somewhere later in the evening and—"

*Pop! Pop! Pop!*

Jake had lodged three shells right between the girl's eyes. His shadow loomed over her carcass. *How could you go to avenge your sister's death and you kill the wrong person?* he thought. *I'm telling you, people are fuckin' dumb these days.*

Jake grabbed the young lady's limp body and threw it over his shoulder, walking towards the back door. It was right when he was about to open it that he froze: a new thought had popped into his head. She'd only been dead for a few minutes. *I'm sure that thang is still warm and tight.*

Changing plans, he brought the woman's body into his bedroom.

Meanwhile, Cocoa Butter was in the basement, locked away so no one could find her: it had only been a few days since he'd shot Luciano in cold blood, so no one would think she was seriously missing. Saying that, I'm sure Poppa Vein would've been looking for him at this point—which would have been for naught, considering no one knew about this particular hideaway but Cocoa Butter. Jake didn't have anything to worry about.

On occasion, he'd go and check on her. It had been the night before that he'd wanted to have sex with her, but she was being visited by her old pal Aunt Flo—or, as I like to call it, Satan's Waterfalls.

Now, he stared at the woman's dead body he'd just thrown onto his bed, admiring that curvaceous shape. He ripped her top off with his teeth, exposing the swell of her breasts: she didn't have a bra on. He then slid her skirt and panties off, leaving only the tall hooker-like boots she had on.

Inhaling deeply, he slowly inserted three fingers inside of her and, for five minutes straight, he pushed in and out of her. Perhaps he thought she could still produce natural juices in a perished state. Either way, you couldn't tell him he wasn't enjoying it: he quickly proceeded to take his own clothes off and, for a second, he considered asking Cocoa to join them. Then again, she probably wouldn't see the joy in it; plus, she hadn't really been very submissive in the last few days anyway, and he didn't feel like arguing with her about anything—especially not now he had a piece of ass he'd been trying to fuck for a long time now naked and on his bed. Granted, she was dead; but she was still naked, wasn't she?

*There's no greater time than the present*, he thought, and, cupping his erection, rammed himself into the dead woman's body in one full thrust.

Jake was a sick man—although if you'd asked him about his current mental health, he would've denied it being anything other than normal. I suppose some may agree with him, depending on their stance on things; after all, his sole reason for fucking a corpse was because his girlfriend—who he was holding hostage, don't forget—was on her period. Jake was a swell guy—even if it was only in his deranged mind.

# CHAPTER 23

Al Gebra could be found in the hospital waiting room pacing back and forth—as he had been for hours. The entire family was there, awaiting the results for Sara Safebreaka's condition.

The whole ride there had been chaotic: Mula had hit every guardrail and curb on the way to the emergency room, and Padlock Penny had taken her sweater off and, along with some towels from the salon, wrapped her sister's head up to hold the pressure and delay the bleeding during the ride.

Upon arrival, Mula and Whish had slapped the shit out of two nurses—deserved, if you ask me, as they were responding as though they were dealing with someone with a common cold.

"Bitch, don't you see my sister is bleeding from her *head*?" Whish had cried out. She then turned to the rest of the bustling room, filled with visitors, doctors, nurses, and patients. "I *demand* a doctor right now, or you gon' have a waiting room full of new patients!"

Sure enough, in a matter of moments, a gurney was being brought in by one of the staff members, on which Mula placed Sara.

"We'll take good care of her, ma'am, don't worry," the woman said to Whish, "but right now, I need you all to remain calm. We'll let you know what the score is as soon as we find out ourselves."

My sisters and my wife regarded one another in utter bewilderment: this had happened right under their noses.

"How the fuck did we let this happen?" Mula whispered, echoing everyone else's thoughts. "I can't believe this: first Escobar, then Luciano, and now Sara. We slippin'."

"Chill, we ain't slippin'," Yelly responded loudly, blinking back tears. "It's just the opposition getting a little smarter, that's all. They know not to fuck with us straight up, so they have to keep sneaking up from behind to attack us. She rubbed Mula's shoulder. "It won't happen again."

I headed to the payphone and paid the $0.50 deal for unlimited minutes. It's a good job I did, as the phone rang five times before Poppa Vein bothered to answer.

"Yo, Vein: Sara got knocked over the head with God-knows-what just a little while ago. Do you know anything about this?"

"Nah Escobar. I'm sorry to hear that," Vein responded apologetically. "I know she's a pivotal part of your family. I've been busy with my contribution toward our plan to destroy Jake Solomon."

It was then I heard a voice in the background: a little girl trying to get Vein's attention.

"I'm on the phone, girl... my apologies, man: my niece is bugging me," Vein said. "She's been trying to get my attention since you—*what*, girl?"

The signal cleared and the little girl's voice on the other end was crystal clear. "Jake just sent a fax over of a naked lady! With a *note*!"

My blood froze.

A pause. "Gimme that," Vein ordered quietly. "Escobar, I'm sorry, hold on for me a second."

"Sure, no problem."

Poppa Vein had taken the papers from his niece to get a closer look—to find, to his horror, that he recognized the girl in the photo.

It only took a matter of moments for him to put the pieces together: he now knew what had happened to Sara Safebreaka.

At the bottom of the image, the note read:

*Vein,*
*I always knew this bitch would be a good piece of ass. Remember when we used to try to holla at her and her sister when their brother came around the way to try to get down with the team? She was hot, but talked too damn much, so I had to wait till she was dead to experience it. It wasn't bad at all.*
*By the way, your sister's fine—fine as hell! Oh, and tell your new buddies Escobar and Corione I said hello.*
*P.S. POLO is a dead man walking.*
*Thx.*

Poppa Vein shook his head in disbelief: he didn't know if he was angry or happy that Jake sent him this. Probably depends on how you look at it: on one hand, he never would have wanted to see that disgusting picture; but on the other, Jake had helped us out with his location, as Vein could trace the sending fax machine.

Vein picked up the phone again. "Escobar, what hospital are you guys at right now?"

"Mountainside," I answered. "Why?"

I could hear the smile in Vein's voice. "Would you believe me if I told you that stupid motherfucker practically just gave us his whereabouts? I'm starting to wonder if this nigga *wants* to be found." He paused. "Or if he's just really stupid. I'm on my way."

# CHAPTER 24

*Location: Summit Overlook; 6:45 pm*

WHISH JOHANNSEN KNEW SHE had to go see Luciano; she was just struggling with the decision to leave Sara. There had still been no news on her condition when Whish finally decided to head to Summit Overlook to check in on her new beau.

She walked in and, as soon as she saw Luciano was still not breathing on his own, instantly teared up, small tears gradually turning into much bigger ones until they were streaming down her face relentlessly. For the first time in her adult life, she felt lost—like some kind of big-ass bowl of chocolate pudding, sitting there without any idea what to do next.

She felt wracked with guilt and disgust toward herself: she allowed something like this to happen to Sara—and she'd failed in protecting Luciano, too.

Don't get me wrong, MentallyOrganizedBusiness has probably made hundreds of enemies over the last few decades, but for some reason, this felt a lot more personal: she just couldn't put her finger on why.

Whish sat by Luciano's bedside and grabbed his hand, beginning to tell him what he'd missed over the last few days. She then started telling him how much she missed him, that she was a mess, that she couldn't wait to have him back to normal.

This was a place of vulnerability Whish usually didn't visit, let alone show for anyone who might happen to walk in to see. And yet she couldn't help it: she felt completely helpless, adrift, useless—usually foreign feelings.

Thirty minutes elapsed before, overtaken with exhaustion, she drifted to sleep on top of Luciano's chest. Shortly after, a nurse walked in and tapped Whish on her right shoulder.

"Ma'am, he's not breathing on his own, so you may want to get off of his chest," she said gently.

Whish started and looked up, apologizing groggily and muttering in agreement to her obvious assessment.

"Is there any news on his recovery?" Whish asked, rubbing her eyes.

The nurse shook her head apologetically. "You're more than welcome to stay if you wish, though; it may do him some good."

Whish Johannsen obliged, mentally promising herself that she would come here as often as possible during his recovery.

Whish opened her purse, pulling out her lipstick and walking over to the bathroom mirror, where she quickly applied it before settling back next to Sam's bed. She gazed upon him and caressed his left cheek: she should've given in to his advances years ago. Perhaps he wouldn't be in this predicament right now: she could have kept him off these streets, away from this life.

I used to always tell her she was the only one that could set him straight; indeed, I thought from the get-go she was perfect for him.

And now, she felt overwhelmed with regret: for waiting for so long; for putting her pride before her heart.

She bent down and kissed him on his forehead, leaving a perfect imprint of her lips on his skin. She wondered if he would still feel her presence after she'd left his side.

# CHAPTER 25

*Location: Mountainside Hospital's Lobby; 6:55 pm*

VEIN, AS PROMISED, CAME down to the hospital as soon as he hung up, fax in hand. My blood ran cold upon looking at it, disgusted but not surprised, and I called Corione, Yelly and Mula Madison over to listen in.

"This is what my niece was bugging me about over the phone earlier," Vein explained. "My apologies for hanging up abruptly, but I knew I needed to show you this and tell you what I believe happened to Sara."

"You know what happened to my wife?" Al demanded, pushing through the crowd roughly.

"Yeah, I believe so," Vein said, sounding apologetic. "The woman in the photo is the sister of the woman that Whish put a bullet in a few months back at the Dairy Queen on Stuyvesant Avenue. I know the majority of you weren't there, but consequences come back to haunt us.

"Regardless, I'm assuming Jake decided to get in touch with the woman's sister to see if she was interested in seeking revenge on her sister's killer; however, there was obviously some form of miscommunication on their end, as the woman tried to kill Sara—not Whish." Vein bit his lip. "Why she's dead and laying naked in this picture, I have no idea—but I'm no longer interested in trying to figure out how Jake Solomon operates. I believe this is what happened. I know her because I know of the family, and I truly believe this is the person who put your queen in that room over there, Al.

"The fact Jake sent me this fax tells me a lot: he really doesn't care about dying. The man has legitimately gained more enemies in the last week than he has in his whole life, and he's not even trying to cover shit up. He is blatantly doing this and showing off that it's him. So, for what it's worth, I believe we need to push our plan a little sooner— maybe a lot sooner. For now, you can't exactly try to avenge Sara's hospital stay; the person who tried to kill her is already dead."

"Yeah, but Jake's still living," Al hissed, his expression menacing. "And that's the problem. I think I'll change that status amongst the living for him right about now."

And with that, Al Gebra stormed out the hospital, striding past security and the various people in the Emergency Room lobby. Blinded by his own rage, he knocked over several plants and other décor items on his warpath: he was a man on a mission.

He hopped into his car and sped off faster than a Russian racehorse, juking and jiving through every car in traffic. He didn't care if it were residential or highway: he didn't do less than 60 miles per hour.

He had one thing in mind, and one thing only: search for Jake Solomon, find him, and kill him. The man had a plan—a simple and concise one.

Believe it or not, we tried to stop him, but I'm sure you don't need me to break down to you the success ratio of stopping a husband from trying to destroy someone who hurt his wife.

# CHAPTER 26

*Location: Horrendously Fun Party Store; 8:10pm*

"DID THE GHOST FACE masks come in today?" Harry asked his cashier as he walked past.

"I think so," the young girl responded. "Look on the back shelf, next to the ballerina outfits and leprechaun hats."

"You *think* so?" Harry echoed. "You're supposed to *know* so!" He shook his head. "We're closing in about forty-five minutes and this place looks like six pounds of shit stuffed into a two-pound bag. Why don't you ever *know* anything?"

The girl's face drained of colour.

"Matter of fact, I've had enough," Harry resolved. "Get the fuck outta here; you're fired!"

The girl remained mute and still: she seemed to have gone into shock.

"Why are you still standing there?" Harry exploded. "Get the fuck outta here! Now!"

Snapping out of her trance, the young girl nodded and left the store, shaking and with tears rolling down her cheeks.

Harry Horrendous had left Sam Luciano's side early that morning before checking on Sara Safebreaka's condition directly afterward. He had stayed in the lobby with the rest of the family, learning about the fax and the dead girl's identity. However, he also had a business to run, and hadn't been at his store for most of the day; thus, he'd had to leave the hospital and make sure things were okay before he headed home for the night.

Now, he closed shop and hopped into his Chevy Trailblazer. He couldn't help but feel like he and some of the other henchmen weren't quite doing their part in all of this: he wanted to do more, to impress his higher-ups.

So what did he do? He called his righthand Lexington Arms—otherwise known as Swindel.

"Yo Harry!" Swindel greeted upon picking up the receiver. "What's poppin', fool? I just got in from the hospital; 'bout to see what's up with my girl right quick. You good?"

Nah, man, I ain't good," Harry responded honestly. "This is some bullshit; too much shit goin' on around these parts and not enough action."

"I feel you. So, what you thinkin'?"

Harry paused. "I'm not sure right now, but I know I gotta do something. You in?"

"Of course," Swindel answered, not missing a beat. "In like the holiday."

"In like the *holiday*?" Harry repeated. "That's whack, yo..."

"You the *last* person to say somethin' is whack, nigga," Swindel guffawed. "No one laughs at your jokes. *Ever*."

"Damn, the *last*? Really?"

Swindel thought for a moment. "Well, maybe not the *last*: Celo Gaston's jokes are pretty horrible."

"Glad to hear you've not completely lost your mind," Harry sighed. "Can you meet me at the crib off Grove Street in, say, two hours?"

"Yeah, I think that's enough time for me to get some ass and get there."

Good man," Harry said. "Check you, then."

Harry Horrendous could always count on Swindel to get his hands dirty, although he figured he needed one more person to at least be a lookout—or even a viable piece to the plan he was thinking about.

With that, he turned on the radio—HOT97, of course, where Funkmaster Flex was currently spinning at The Tunnel that night. He then remembered one of our brothers was playing live there tonight, too: Billy Drumsticks.

Billy Drumsticks was a talented musician who often played on the road—which was clearly his day job "in the metaphorical sense". The negro was crazy.

About twenty years ago, we were at a charity basketball event—a way to give back to the community; ironically the same community that had made us into mobsters. Or monsters, depending on who you spoke to.

The day was a beautiful one: 78 degrees and not a cloud in the sky. Momma cooked the breakfast with no hog, the Lakers beat the Supersonics, and none of us even had to use our A.K.'s. It was a good day indeed.

That is, until Sticks Morano walked toward us and declared his "appreciation" for the ride home that Hak Hennesey had given him the night before. Sticks was an arrogant motherfucker that no one liked, and Hak had only given the guy a lift the other night because he was hoping he'd see his sister, who was hot and red boned—but to no avail.

The following five minutes were one of the funniest verbal transactions you've ever heard.

"I said *thank you* for the other night, Hak," Sticks was saying.

Hak Hennessey had simply looked passed Sticks and brushed his hands in front of him."Ya sister home, yo?"

Sticks frowned. "I don't know. But anyway, I said thank you for the other nigh—"

"Yeah, yeah, just tell me when ya sister gon' be home," Hak said impatiently. "I wanna fuck her, dude."

Sticks had looked like someone had just slapped him in the face. "What the hell did you just say to me?"

Hak annunciated every letter: "*Tell me when your sister is going to be home, Sticks. I want to fuck her.*"

Hak then made a circle with his left thumb and pointer finger and pushed his right pointer finger it in and out of it—just to drive the point home.

Sticks hadn't found this so amusing. "You're a disrespectful motherfucker, you know that? Here I am, trying to—"

"Tryin' to what, stick your dick in Hak's ass again?" Jay chipped in. "Sticks, why don't you just admit it? Admit to us all, right here, in front of this crowd of sixty-three: you like penis in your asshole. Go ahead, we'll wait."

We'd all looked over at Sticks Morano like we were watching an episode of *Days Of Our Lives*: this shit was getting good, and, as much as we wanted to leave the conversation, alone and let them have their lovers' tiff, we physically couldn't: me, Don, and Sam were laughing our asses off.

Sticks snapped his head to Don. "I don't know what the fuck *you're* laughin' at with your metrosexual purse-carrying ass."

"Whoa, whoa, whoa, I'll have you know this is a fanny pack, personally gifted to me by your mother."

Jay piped up again: "Sticks, we're still waitin' for you to admit that every now and then you enjoy a big ol' hard salami up your rectal cavity." He shrugged. "I know it; he knows it"—nodding his head toward Hak— "and your momma knows it. Heck," he laughed, "the girl that wanted you to fuck her quickly realized you were gayer than the driven snow knows it. *Everybody* knows it but you!"

Sticks Morano was visibly fuming; for a second, I literally thought I saw smoke coming out from his ears—although, on second thought, it could've been dried-up sperm from who-knows-how-long-ago trying to peel itself off his lobes.

Sticks then seemed to pull himself together. "I'm not gonna stoop to your levels," he said calmly. "I'm better than all of you: I dress better; I smell better; and I get way more girls than all of you put together."

We couldn't help it: we all simultaneously burst out laughing at the ridiculousness of it. However, Sticks pressed on.

"I don't give a fuck what any of you say: you can all kiss my ass. From the inside!"

"From the inside?" Hak enquired, cocking his head to the side. This sent us into peals of laughter yet again. "But how? How does one do that?"

Jay shouldered Hak, sniggering. "Chill, dude; you're making him blush. Plus, you don't wanna give him hope by asking for the details."

Hak nodded. "Point taken."

"Jay, I can't stand you," Sticks hissed. "I wish you'd go to hell and leave your bitch-ass there."

Jay rolled his eyes. "Just shut up and lick the line dividing my testicles like a good boy, why don't you?"

Sticks then turned to me. "Escobar!"

I dried my tears of laughter. "*What*? I didn't say shit to you."

Sticks just shrugged. "I just expected more from you. And Don—you little fuckin tadpole—, I will hurt you. Keep talkin' that shit you keep talkin' and somebody gon' end up fucking you up."

"Oh, I'd love a man to fuck me up in any direction." The man was relentless. "Up, down, sideways... anyways. Would you like to oblige?"

"I fucking hate you," Sticks fumed. "I wish all of you would fall off the face of the earth."

"I'll see what I can do about that, buddy," responded Don, clapping Sticks on the shoulder. "Now run along and go find a tight ass to play with."

Giving up, Sticks Morano stomped off the court and stalked down Lyons Avenue, all on his lonesome.

Billy Drumsticks turned to us all. "Damn, what's that guy's problem? What a major pain in the ass."

Don thought for a moment. "Yeah, he is. Kill him; I want him dead."

Billy froze. "For real?"

Don shrugged. "His sister's fine, but he's just a waste of air."

*

One week later, we were at Chancellor Avenue, playing a game of 21. Sam Luciano and I had just met Tony Victor and his cousin Mone "The Groan" Slone for the first time, the former of which we knew wanted to kill us: we kept hiking on him and his cousin throughout the whole game.

"Yo, you can't D me!" I yelled at him at one point. "Look at this nigga: his hairline look like the Wu-Tang symbol!"

"He look like he got the whole Australian swim team on his back, he so slumped over," Sam joined in, this time referring to Slone.

Tony, for some unusual reason, not only let us keep breathing, but also let us continue in our taunts. Indeed, as much as he looked like he was a serious hothead, every time he seemed to want to punch the shit out of one—or both—of us, we made him laugh.

Of course, our fun had to be interrupted by Sticks Morano, who came walking toward us again—with a cast on his right arm.

Don raised his eyebrows. "The fuck happened to you?" he said as way of greeting. "Been trying to fist too many tight assholes?"

Sticks' eyes darkened. "I've never met a more pompous son-of-a-bitch. You really just going to stand there and act like you don't know what's happened here?"

Don frowned. "I don't know what you're talking about, dude. You sound like Tupac at Quad Studios."

"I got shot," Sticks hissed. "Right in my shoulder. Almost lost my whole fuckin' arm."

"Word?" Don responded. "That's dope, man, but I didn't do it, so better luck next time!"

"The *fuck* you didn't!" The man was shaking with anger. "You better watch your back; you ain't safe out here no more."

Don cocked his head to the side: cool, calculating. "Are you honestly coming on our grounds and threatening me?"

"I wouldn't give a fuck if you were Jesus fucking Christ Superstar!"

"What exactly is it you think I did?"

"You sent your little goon to come and get me," Sticks responded simply. "Real cool, dude. I'll be seeing you around, you can count on that."

"What little goon exactly?"

"That fat motherfucker; I didn't ask him for a business card. The guy who plays the instruments."

*Billy?* Don thought. Had he thought he was serious the week before?

Despite his inner panic, Don feigned cluelessness. "I don't know who or what the fuck you're talking 'bout, but I suggest you get your fruit roll-up ass outta here before I send the real goons."

Sticks Morano didn't need telling twice: he swept away, leaving Don looking stumped. We continued with our little rendezvous before heading to the Thunderbird we'd rolled up in. Hak, who we'd arrived with, also came shortly after, once he'd finish his game with some of the other fellas.

We all set off and, after fifteen minutes or so, we'd dropped Don off at The House of Nesbit. Don had quickly rushed in and dialed for Billy.

"Hello? Who's this?" came Billy's voice.

"Is that how you answer the phone? All scared and shit?"

"Corione?" Billy said stupidly.

"*Yes*, you fool," Don responded. "What's good? You alright?"

"Yeah, I'm straight. I've been waiting to hear from you."

"Oh yeah?" Don said. "And why's that?"

"Well, why'd you call me?"

Don sighed. "Okay, Billy: I gotta ask you a question, and you need to answer me truthfully and without hesitation, okay?"

"Cool, no problem. Ask away."

A pause. "Did you shoot Sticks Morano?"

Billy's voice was proud. "Absolutely! It was cool as fuck; you should've been there! I'll start from the begin—"

"*What*?" Don interrupted. "Why the *fuck* would you do that? You don't even know him!"

There was a long pause. "But... but you said..."

"I don't even wanna hear it! Are you serious, Billy? You actually shot this Homo-the-Clown lookalike nigga?"

"But *you* said to!"

Don was absolutely flabbergasted: he couldn't fathom the fact that Billy had done this. He was mostly angry, but a small part of him was also flattered that he'd obeyed without hesitation.

"Billy, I didn't mean it," Don said gently. "I was joking."

Billy's confusion grew wider on the other line. The guy had been clueless.

"And besides," he continued, "you didn't even get the job done: Sticks Morano just left me, alive and well. Where'd you take your shot classes? At Stevie and Ray's school for 20/20 vision?"

Billy's voice was wracked with embarrassment: "I... I just wanted to impress you, boss."

Don sighed. "Well, that you did, young grasshopper, that you did."

One thing was for certain: the influence we had over people back then was absolutely mind-blowing. We just couldn't believe the shit we got away with sometimes.

And maybe now you understand why Harry Horrendous felt Billy Drumsticks was the perfect guy. Or maybe you think that Harry Horrendous is an idiot and shouldn't be leading any group of guys into anything. I don't know, you pick.

# CHAPTER 27

A L GEBRA HAD BEEN driving for what seemed like days: it had been two or three hours since he'd left the hospital, and was now driving throughout the 'hood, looking to see if he could catch the slightest glimpse of Jake Solomon—to no avail: there was not a Haitian in sight that remotely resembled him.

Al was at his wits' end, his mind starting to go in different directions trying to figure out why someone would do this to his lovely wife: she hadn't ever hurt a soul—well, not on purpose or for personal gain, at least. Sara Safebreaka was one tough son-of-a-bitch, and he knew it. That's why he loved her so much.

They had been through a lot to be together: they'd had a rather on-again, off-again relationship starting a few decades back. As a matter of fact, there had even been a time when Sara and Celo Gaston had been an item. They had admittedly been cute together, but the everlasting love between Al and Sara was undeniable and could not be delayed any further.

Al and Celo had been friends since the beginning of time, so it was naturally a little awkward when Sara and Al reunited: those guys would play basketball against one another into the wee hours of the morning, the rest of us sometimes joining and continuing till 2am.

You could say Al and Celo fell victim to the classic "girl is mine" mantra, the whole ordeal even bringing them to a point in their lives where they didn't want to be around one another at all. However, in the end, time heals all, and genuine love and respect always win out. There's something about the love between brothers that can't exactly be recited, and this was—thankfully—one of those instances.

Al started driving back toward the hospital, stopping when he got off the 78W ramp at the 7-11 just down the block to get a pack of Peanut M&Ms. It was when he emerged from the car that he found his front left tire was completely deflated.

"How the *fuck*? Can this day get any worse?" he muttered to himself.

"Say, youngblood, if you're wondering how that happened just now, look no further."

Al snapped his head up and turned to the voice. It was a homeless man outside the store. He was pointing toward the Valley Fair parking lot where, sure enough, he could make out a silhouette of a man running away.

"Oh, you good man," Al said gratefully, fishing in his pocket. "Here's a hundred dollars for the info."

And, with that, Al became Jesse Owens as he chased down the dude that had burst his tire, dodging an Acura truck in traffic and barreling himself over a '92 Honda Civic hatchback in the process of trying to gain ground on the perp.

It was after a few minutes of this chase that he saw him bank a sharp left around the back of the shopping plaza.

*Bang!*

That stopped Al dead in his tracks. Most would run at this point, forgetting the flat tire, but the mobster in Al told him to proceed. As he crept along slowly, there was a large silhouette of a man coming toward him.

Without thinking, Al pulled out his 45 and cocked it back, waiting for the man to come around the corner so he could lodge a bullet right between his eyes.

"Holy *shit!*" came a familiar voice.

"Hak?"

"Al?"

"What the fuck are you doing here, man?"

Hak Hennesey had just laid the running man down to rest—but for a whole other reason.

"I just had to pop this nigga; he never does what I ask him," Hak responded. "He does the same shit to Tony, too. I've been trying to help these little jokers out on the block and give them a couple dollars here and there to wash my car and take care of my tires, but *this* little motherfucker"—he nodded to the general area where he'd fired the bullet—"broke the valve stem on my low-profile wheel, so the shit started leaking." He shrugged. "I told him, 'If you don't go find me one in the next five minutes, I'll put a cap in your ass'".

"He brought you one and yet you still laid this nigga down? Real nice, Hak."

"Yeah, well, mine got the silver caps, and he brought me a black one." He paused. "Hold up, why are you here again?"

"Because, you fuckin' Bill-Cartwright-mustache-havin' motherfucker, that shit came off my car!"

With that, both of them laughed off the whole situation, Hak Hennesey throwing his arm around Al.

"Brother, I just want you to know I don't you worrying 'bout nothing. I bet Jay's mom your queen will be fine."

"His entire mom?" Al asked.

"His entire mom," Hak echoed. "I'm taking her to a naked beach in a few days, so I'll have immediate access to her, if I have to give her to you."

Hak helped Al put his spare on and they both then heading their separate ways to check on their family members; Al went to see his wife, and Hak to see Luciano. Hopefully there was some good news in store: the family desperately needed some.

# CHAPTER 28

MULA AND YELLY—WHO were, ironically, dressed up as security guards—, stood outside the charter school off Lyons Avenue, the students of which having just been let out. Word around town is that someone there knew something about Sara's attack.

"Did you see the little skinny lady and the chick with the glasses?" Mula asked, staring them down. "Petite little thangs, ain't they?"

"Yeah. I don't know how they keep their husbands satisfied," Yelly responded, tossing a lock of her over her shoulder. "No ass, no tits... Do you reckon they're trannies?"

"No, girl; I'm assuming it's the money they make here. I heard they'll pay you almost sixty thousand at these charter schools to be a manager." Mula paused. "I mean, I know we make that in a month, but for the average woman, you've got to admit that's pretty good."

"Anybody could do that shit," Yelly said firmly. "That's not impressive. We should leave the business and work at schools like this, take over those roles."

Mula Madison thought it over and said, "Nah, no one would ever believe we were genuine. As soon as a kid acts up, we're liable to whoop their little ass, call their parents, and then whoop *their* ass even harder when they pick them up."

Yelly grinned.

"Besides," Mula continued, "that's a career you have to devote your life to, and we wouldn't last two weeks there. I'm all for potentially getting out of the business—it's getting hot in these streets—, but working at a *school*? That ain't happening."

"Maybe you're right," Yelly conceded. "They wouldn't see our 'vision' or approach to 'strive' in a... less conventional manner."

"That's life."

The kids were all emerging in their little bunches, Yelly and Mula promptly making their way into the school building. They were given a lead by an informant on the streets to go see a teacher by the name of Jordache Blu; Miss Blu had apparently been asking about the usual whereabouts of Sara Safebreaka for some time now. Yelly and Mula exchanged a look: she had something to do with Sara's attack, regardless of the actual perp being killed by Jake Solomon.

They made their way up to the fourth floor and found Jordache Blu in her classroom by herself.

"I could take her out from here?" Mula whispered at the doorway.

"You crazy, girl?" Yelly hissed. "You ain't stupid now, are you? We're in a school, remember?"

"Oh yeah," Mula mumbled. "Well, you know I'm a shoot first, ask questions last type of chick."

"Just follow my lead," Yelly sighed. "I don't trust you Latina chicks; y'all some crazy motherfuckers." Her tone was lighthearted, but Mula did as she asked regardless.

Yelly pushed open the door. "Miss Blu?"

The woman's head snapped up. "Yes? I'm sorry for staying longer than usual, ladies; I'll be out of your way in two minutes."

"Oh no, sit," Yelly reassured. "You have plenty of time. In fact, you got all the time in the world."

Mula swiftly locked the classroom door behind her, and Yelly smiled at Jordache Blu: all teeth.

Miss Blu frowned. "Excuse me, ma'am? I don't follow."

Yelly turned to Mula. "Miss Madison?'"

"Yes, Mrs. Escobar?"

"I believe Miss Blu here doesn't know why we've come to see her. Or maybe she's playing like she doesn't know who we are?"

"Well, that's not nice, is it?" Mula sighed tantalizingly. JBlu had suddenly frozen. "I think you owe us an apology, Miss Blu."

"Ladies, I believe you have me mistaken for someone else," she countered. "And I don't mean any disrespect, but neither of your names ring a bell, either. How am I supposed to know you?"

Mula cocked her head to the side and approached Miss Blu, a tiger on the prowl. She leaned into the woman and whispered, "Because we're the bitches your momma told you to steer clear from. Oh, and we're also here to kill you... or not."

From there, Yelly quickly covered her mouth, muffling the teacher's cries for help.

"Considering we've now told you who we are," she said, "I think you should be courteous enough to now tell us who you actually are." She smiled that vicious smile again. "We'll give you a minute to get over the shock of what's happening right now. We understand how it can be."

Mula, however, was impatient. After approximately ten seconds, she burst out, "You better start talking right about now."

The woman shook her head, trembling. "I don't know what you want from me. I'm sorry, but I can't help you! I don't—"

"We're not repeating ourselves," Yelly interjected coolly. "You either tell us what you know about Sara Safebreaka's attack or you won't be making it home tonight."

JBlu paused. "Safebreaka?" she echoed. "The nice little lady whose son goes to my nephew's private school?"

Yelly and Mula exchanged a look of confusion.

"What are you talking about, lady?" Mula demanded.

"Wait... didn't you say your name was Escobar?"

Yelly frowned. "What about it?"

"I gave Safebreaka an envelope with a copy of the kid's hockey schedule at the parent-teacher conference a few days ago," she said slowly. "My sister was unable to attend, so I went in her place. Sara asked me to get her another copy for her brother and write *PR Escobar* on it. It seemed he couldn't make it that night, either."

Yelly took a seat on a small desk, glancing at Mula, who looked troubled: she knew they'd fucked up.

"Ma'am, Mr. Escobar is my husband," Yelly said, "and that hockey schedule would indeed be for my son—our son. I want to apologize for the inconvenience we've caused you today and would like to ask you for your forgiveness."

JBlu just shook her head, now blinking back tears. "I'm just so confused. What's even going on here?"

Yelly exhaled. "You fit the perfect description of an alleged accomplice who helped put our sister in hospital. We misread the situation and apologize profusely." She rose from the desk. "We'll be leaving now."

"Don't be getting no ideas though, lady," Mula warned. "No pressing charges or shit like that. I mean, the police are on our payroll anyway, but do you know the amount of paperwork involved when someone presses charges?"

"Mula, just shut up," Yelly muttered.

"Miss Madison?" JBlu said delicately. "I think you're a nice young lady. Maybe just misunderstood, in the wrong crowd, perhaps."

Mula shot the woman daggers. "Did I ask your opinion?"

Yelly quickly interjected before this escalated: they needed to go. "Miss Blu, here's your purse I was thinking about taking. I guess you could keep it as an apology." She grabbed Mula by the wrist. "We'll be on our way now. Be safe out here on these streets; there's some crazy people out there!"

*

Neither would admit it, but both women felt rather shaken after that experience: they hadn't been that wrong in a *long* time. As a result of this, they hardly spoke a word to each other on their way back to The House of Nesbit, also switching positions in a sense: Yelly kept dozing off at the wheel and, because she didn't feel like dying that night, Mula insisted they switched steering wheel maestros.

The ride up RT 24 West through Hillside, Union, Morristown and Livingston was, indeed, a somber one; it's not like they were upset with one another or anything, but pride can really make someone sit on their ass—hard. After all, they both knew their suspicions had been dead off-base.

Yelly kept thinking to herself, *Why Jordache Blu? Why were we pointed in her direction?*

Mula, on the other hand, was less troubled and suddenly remembered that she left the stove on. *Dammit, the stove!*

# CHAPTER 29

COCOA BUTTER HAD BEEN having a rough couple of days: she'd had no contact with the outside world for 72 hours now and had no idea what the score was on Sam Luciano's condition, nor did she have any idea on what happened to Sara Safebreaka. She hadn't spoken to her brother either, and she wondered what was taking him so long to murder Jake Solomon. He was clearly still alive: she heard him talking through the walls every goddamn day.

Sickeningly, she'd also heard the horrific endeavor with that young girl. She'd pretended to be asleep the entire time, squeezing her eyes shut and trying to zone out from the grunting from the other side of the basement.

Now, it was Thursday evening, and she'd last spoke with her brother Vein on Monday night. She'd been trying to figure out why Jake was even still living; after all, she knew her brother, and she also knew her equally insane MentallyOrganizedBusiness brothers and sisters. Quite frankly, there were a lot of things that just didn't add up. Perhaps this was some kind of punishment by Corione after she'd orchestrated the hit on myself a few months back?

There was only one thing she was certain of: there was something much deeper going on around here, and she did not appreciate being out the loop. Even if the business family had been feeling some type of way about her, why would Vein, her own brother, be dragging his feet? Something wasn't right.

Cocoa had to reuse her clothes to soak up the blood she was producing from her menstrual cycle; thankfully she'd been wearing two shirts the day Jake had locked her up in the basement. She'd at least been able to somewhat preserve the other one.

She stunk and was cold and hungry: she hadn't brushed her teeth or hair in what seemed like forever. She just felt straight-up *nasty* all over, and the fact that she was even *in* this predicament was mind-boggling to her. She knew she'd made a lot of mistakes in her life—particularly the one that had got me hospitalized—, but generally speaking, she was able to take care of herself.

What's funny about this whole situation is that Mula, a few days after I'd met with Cocoa, had a brief run-in with a guy that wasn't paying her on-time. She'd told him that the next time he came up short, she'd take him out, right there. I never knew—and, to this day, have never known—Mula to lie a day in her life, so, when the next day came and the guy inevitably fell short again, Mula Madison smoked his ass.

The reason I'm even sharing this with you is because it turned out that this was the same guy that was giving Cocoa Butter trouble back in February—the same guy that she had indicated for her cousins to get rid of. However, those cousins of hers had clearly possessed a different agenda—one that was spearheaded by Jake Solomon. We found this out that night at Don's Diner, when Sam Luciano was shot and this whole shitshow got even worse.

It's just funny how shit turns out sometimes, how they come full-circle. The guy ended up dead—by the hands of one of us, notably. All Cocoa had to do was tell Mula Madison, and it would've been taken care of immediately. Instead, Cocoa chose another route, which unfortunately led to me getting hurt in the process. But that's water under the bridge right now.

Cocoa had briefly drifted off to sleep when she suddenly heard a loud thud come from the other side of the basement. The sound scared the hell out of her: after the past few days' occurrences, she had now come to fear any sudden noises.

She initially crawled into a ball onto the couch she was using as a bed, her own bubble of protection. She then heard what sounded like pieces of shattered glass falling to the floor—before she heard the very last sound she expected to.

"Cocoa, you in there?"

She almost sobbed. "Tony?"

"Yeah, baby, I got you," Tony Victor said. "We came to get you the fuck outta here."

"We?" Her heart was pounding.

"Yes, we," came a second voice.

"*Polo?*"

"That's right, little sis," Polo responded warmly.

"Oh my God," Cocoa whispered. Everything was now coming to the surface, and she rapidly dissolved into tears. Their voices were coming from outside the broken window.

"Don't worry," came Tony's voice, "we'll get you to my place and all cleaned up. Are you strong enough to climb through the window?"

Wiping her eyes, she mustered enough strength to leap and scramble through the window, being careful to avoid the jagged shards of glass running along its edge. The two muscled men then pulled her up and through it. Cocoa felt herself tearing up again: at the familiar faces before her; and being able to smell fresh air again.

Polo wasted no time. "Let's go; we still got a few things to put in place here. Well," he reconsidered, "not us, but our other family members. Jake'll be coming back at around seven, too; I know his hustle."

Cocoa seemed to snap out of her emotive state for a second to smirk. "I kinda want to stay and see the look on his face when he realizes I'm gone."

Tony grinned. "I think that could be arranged."

# CHAPTER 30

*Location: Poppa Vein's House; Saddlebrook, NJ; 6:00 pm*

THE TIME WAS UPON us.

Don Corione and I met up with Poppa Vein at his house, Snugglez and Harry Horrendous in tow. Tony Victor, Joseph Stylez, and Polo Pasé were meeting us there, too, and, before long, all the members from both families began showing up in sequence. We had already received word that Cocoa was safe and sound with Whish Johannsen and Mula Madison at Tony Victor's crib.

Now, Vein walked up to me to thank me for allowing him to contribute to this elaborate plan we'd concocted.

"You made me see things a bit clearer out here," he was saying. "I had been so comfortable in these streets that I made a mistake—but that's okay. Polo here has always been a major player in my organization, and I'm thankful for him. I know you needed Jake dead." He bit his lip. "Not only did he have you beaten within an inch of your life, but he tried to kill one of your partners in cold blood, right in front of us. Retribution is undeniable. But when you and Don allowed me into the scheme of things, I was greatly touched. I'll never forget this."

"Vein, your sister was raped," I responded simply. "There's no way you *weren't* going to join in on the fun. She's your blood, and our inheritance through sweat and tears; she's our connection, and why our families have joined together. Better circumstances would have been preferred, of course, but at the end of the day, it's better for us all when we're not at odds."

"Yo Vein," Don interjected, "you ready?"

Vein grinned. "I've never been readier for anything in my life. Has your cousin tuned into Jake's house yet?

"Let me go check."

Don whipped out his phone and dialed for Brilliant Bobby Bushetta out in Colorado, who answered with the first ring.

"Bobby! You in?"

"Yo, fam! I'm here," Bobby responded. "Quick question, though: is this Jake character tall and skinny?"

"Yeah, he is. So you got him?"

"I think so," Bobby affirmed, "but I thought you said he was Haitian?"

"He *is*! What the fuck's going on, bruh?"

"The nigga I got on camera right now is Caucasian! Whiter than a motherfucker."

Don was losing more and more patience by the second. "Well you're clearly in the wrong house, dumbass. So why haven't you zoomed into the correct one?"

"Well I wasn't really sure 'til a moment ago, but he's in there, fuckin' this big-booty chick."

"You motherfucker. Yo, save that footage for me later, would you?" Don added, attempting to be quiet so we wouldn't hear. Then, louder, "If you don't stop fuckin' around and get to the right house, we'll be having a problem."

"Listen, dude, the address I got for Jake Solomon is 781 Avon Avenue."

Don looked like he could punch someone. "It's *187* Avon Avenue, you dyslexic bastard!"

Bobby sighed. "Well, that'll be why I can't see him, won't it? Good job, Don."

"Just call me when you're in there," Don snapped, massaging his temples. He then hung up the phone and turned to face us all.

For the last week or so, Vein, Don and I had been funding this new invention Dough and Blues told us about, where you could zoom in on anybody's property from a satellite high up in the sky. In order to gain access to its signal, one would have to be wealthy enough and know a hell of a lot of people in very high places—and, fortunately for us, all three of us held those titles.

Hak Hennesey still had close connections with people overseas he and Sam Luciano had struck deals with during their military days, and it had been a couple of days ago that he'd gave them a call to tell them what was transpiring—and, of course, what he would need to complete our desired goal.

His contact was, sure enough, happy to help—for $1.2 million. With a slight pang of irritation, we paid the amount and, just like that, we had access to the signal.

However, we still needed someone brilliant enough to figure out how to use it and have it functioning the level we needed it to be. The first port of call was Don's cousin, and that's where we were now.

"Dough, is it?" Vein asked respectfully.

"Yeah, that's me. Good to meet you."

"Likewise," Vein responded. "I have someone I'd like for you to meet."

"Oh? I hope she's got a fat ass." Dough's eyes had lit up. However, they were rapidly replaced with panic. Vein smirked.

"Polo. Polo Pasé," he mumbled. "What's up, man? How are you?"

"Who are you?" Polo responded shortly, regarding Dough like a slug on his shoe. "I don't believe we've met."

I had never seen Dough look so uncomfortable. "Uh..."

Vein cocked his head to the side, eyes dancing. "Go ahead, Dough; sounds to me like you've needed to do this for a *long* time."

Dough's cheeks blazed. "I'm Salawicious Dough. I'm kind of the guy responsible for—"

"Responsible for what?" Polo snapped. It didn't take long, however, for dark realization to dawn. "Hold up, Vein: is this the motherfucker who blew my fucking arm off?"

Vein took a deep breath. "Calm down Polo. He's here to make amends."

"I am?" Dough said stupidly.

I shot him a look. "Yes, you are. Now could you stop bullshitting and apologize to the man before I call Qurtis Jenkins over here to make fun of you sweatin'?"

"I'm not sweatin'," Dough muttered, wiping some perspiration from his forehead. "I'm just a little parched. Can you get me some water?"

"No, motherfucker! Get on with it!"

"Okay, okay." Dough turned to Polo, whose expression was dark with rage. "From the bottom of my bottomless heart, I'm sorry for blowing your stinkin' arm the fuck off."

Everyone started holding their breaths, bracing for impact. What the fuck did Dough think he was doing?

Polo sidled up to Dough so they were practically chest-to-chest, the size difference between the two being borderline humorous. Indeed, a couple of us did laugh nervously: Polo towered over Dough.

"What the fuck did you just say to me, homie?" he said gently, voice dripping with venom.

The rest of us couldn't help it: we started to snigger. You could have cut the tension with a knife.

"I said I was sorry." Dough had never looked so small.

"I don't think that's how you said it, punk." He turned to Vein. "I'm gonna hurt this little nigga."

"Chill, Polo," he shrugged, slapping his friend on the shoulder. "Everybody calm down. I believe he's ready now."

Dough, you on some bullshit," I muttered to him. "I'm calling Qurtis right now."

"Okay, okay!" he burst out. I grinned. "Yo, word up: Polo, my apologies. Cocoa told us you wanted Escobar dead a few months back, so me and my cohorts were just waiting for the perfect excuse to take you out before you tried to do the same to our man Escobar. Simple." He shrugged. "Obviously he was hospitalized, and you were the primary suspect. There wasn't much talking that we felt needed to go down once that happened."

"I'm gonna kill that girl!" Polo fumed. Vein shot him a look. "Well, not literally."

"You better watch yourself, homie," he said, his tone half-serious, half-lighthearted.

Polo continued. "We had a conversation at the beginning of the year about the Ghost Town bosses and how long they've been in their respective roles. We were at the crib, drinking and smoking that good-good Vein imported from Cali. We ended up deciding to play truth or dare."

"How very elementary school," Dough muttered, thankfully too low for Polo to hear.

"So," Polo was saying, "Cocoa asked me who I would kill first out of the three M.O.B. Bosses, as she likes to call them. So, 'cuz I'm an ugly motherfucker myself, I chose Escobar. I couldn't *stand* that nigga." I almost laughed at this. "Every time I saw him, I thought, 'here goes this pretty motherfucker again, with his nice hair and shit'. Can you believe they use to call him Koochie Kurls in high school?"

The other guys turned to me to snigger. *Real nice, man*, I thought.

"I told her if I ever had to, I'd enjoy killing him off, just based off of that—but that was until I met him through Vein and truly got to know him. I can now say that that's my dude." He scanned the rest of us. "I don't know about you other niggas, though."

I grin. "You still ugly as hell, but you better call me if you ever in trouble. Matter of fact—here." I handed him a business card. "Take this card and call this guy: he'll help you with the case of the missing arm stuck up a nurse's ass. Guaranteed."

"Attorney Edward Smooth?" Polo read. "An attorney that would go all around the world for you? Damn, that's really nice of you."

"Well, I'm a nice guy."

"Hold up, Polo," Dough chimed in. "How does this explain what Cocoa said about you wanting Escobar dead?"

Polo just shrugged. "When you mix drugs and alcohol together, you should be prepared for some unforeseen circumstances. It's very possible she misconstrued my words when I was answering her question at that time. You'd have to ask her directly, though."

"Ain't that a bitch?" Dough sighed. "I blew your fuckin' arm off for something that was probably not even true! I'm really sorry about that, man." This time, he seemed genuinely apologetic: the gravity of what he'd done suddenly seemed to crash down on him. 'Truce?'

Polo paused. "You mean that?"

Dough grinned. "Nah. Where the bitches at?"

We still had some time to spare before the show began at Jake's house, and we were just elapsing into more conversation when my phone rang: Celo Gaston. He was really late—and that was unlike him.

"Celo?" I answered. "Where you at? You okay?"

"Yo! I just wanted to extend a courtesy call to O3, to you specifically."

"What do you mean?" I responded impatiently. "We can talk when you get here. Let's go!"

"Fam, I'm not coming."

My jaw quite literally dropped open. "Excuse me?"

"I'm not coming," he repeated. "I've thought about this long and hard, and..." There was a long pause. The man's voice was wracked with emotion. "Well, the fact of the matter is, I'm just not cut out for this life no more. I've ran these streets; I've been in jail; I've been married and divorced. I have a daughter that I never see, and it's just time for a change."

I didn't speak for what felt like a long time: I was completely lost for words. "Wow," I said finally. "Okay. I didn't see this coming."

Celo was quiet for a few moments; the man seemed deep in thought. "I know it's a lot to take in right now, but I needed to tell you this directly," he said slowly. "I stopped by your house to tell you face to face, but your big-head wife"—I chuckled—"said you left already. You know I didn't want to do this over the phone."

"Do what?" I asked. "Street life ain't for everyone, but we'll still be annoying your ass for a while."

Another pause. His silence felt packed with meaning.

"Celo, I feel like there's something else you're not telling me."

"I'm leaving, Escobar."

I frowned. "Leaving?" I echoed. "Like, on vacation?"

"No," Celo murmured. "I'm leaving—permanently. I'm moving."

"*Moving*?" My heart sank. "Moving where?"

"Raleigh."

"Fucking North Cackalacky?"

"I've already made up my mind, Escobar," he said. He sounded sorry. "Just signed the deed and I'm moving into my house this weekend."

I couldn't help it: I felt hurt. "Why am I just finding this out now?"

"You've been in way bigger issues lately. I get it; you're needed. You're one of three major bosses for a conglomerate business, an empire we all helped build. It's not easy for you to pay attention to the little details."

I was a little choked up. "You're my brother and I love you, man. You're not 'little details'."

"I know, I know. But there are so many things going on here that no one can fix but you. Don is up for the job and you'll need his help, considering Luciano is incapacitated at the moment." He paused. "But me? I feel like I'm being called for something different. I'm not sure what that is right now, but I know I'll discover it and take heed to it soon. I don't mean to get all religious on you, but I just feel like God is telling me to do this." He exhaled shakily. "So, listen: I'll call you once I get there. You be safe, and keep every one of our family members safe, too. I love you, man."

I smiled weakly. "Love you too, baby boy."

Celo hung up the line and, just like that, one of my closest friends to date had left.

You haven't heard a lot about the relationship Celo and I harbored. It's probably the most genuine one I've ever been a part of—outside of the one I have with my wife and my god, of course. Indeed, we'd always had a very special bond—one we established post-sandbox days. We literally played Little League Baseball together.

So, when he told me he was leaving, it felt like a chapter of my favorite book had been ripped out and the book replaced on the library shelf, ready to be rented out to the next reader. There was a void in my personal life—one I ultimately felt in the business and, more importantly, throughout the family.

Celo Gaston may not have been part of O3, but he was a Great 8 Member—which was, in a lot of ways, equally respected and revered amongst our peers and members alike. He was not naturally violent: as a matter of fact, he was the opposite—although don't get it twisted, he could still handle his business when a situation called for it. He'd been taught how to survive.

I mentioned earlier that he didn't have the most appealing upbringing, and, indeed, whether it was drugs or crime, he had seen it and lived it through his parents, as well as various other family members. You'd never know it if you knew him, though: he kept that part of his life under wraps.

As a result of such events, he was forced to become an adult at a very early age. He had always been closer to his mom, and I tell you, that woman loved us like we were her own: Velma the Goddess. Her life could be a piece of literature by itself: her struggle, and her overcoming of that struggle.

Our relationship had always been built on trust and loyalty; indeed, that is the code of MentallyOrganizedBusiness, but it always seemed like there was a higher level of that between him and I—for me, anyway. There was always this silent understanding between us: we never ever let anyone speak negatively about the other, and we vowed to always have each other's best interest at heart.

Over the course of the last couple of decades, I've been blessed to be part of quite a few of those kinds of relationships: I have it with Don Corione—my original O3 brethren—and I have it with Qurtis Jenkins. I like to think I have great personal relationships with all my family members, and that authenticity plays a big part in that. I hope I've made them as proud as they've made me.

I know I've gone off on a bit of a tangent here, but it feels as if this needed sharing for some context. My point is, Celo had the ability to tap into the deeper realms of a person's heart and to make them realize the greatness life has to offer.

To this day, he'd tell you, his life is an open book—not to mention an inspiration to most he comes across. But I'll get to those specifics soon enough. For now, it's back to business as usual.

# CHAPTER 31

*Location: Everywhere and Anywhere*

*I* REALLY CAN'T BELIEVE *these dumbasses can't figure out who I am; from Dough to Hennessey and BaDouche. I guess they really are as dumb as they look. Is this really such a hard code to crack?*

*I thought I made myself clear when I told them shit is real out here, that life is a puzzle, a geometry equation. I'm always gonna hit them from multiple angles at once.*

*I've been fuckin' with Don Corione for a long time; I can't even begin to tell you how many encounters we've had together. I've probably enjoyed this life with him more than anybody and, for some reason, I feel like it's either easier with him, or if it's just more fun because of the level of trust he has in me.*

*I don't think I care. I'm just having the time of my life with these idiots.*

*I think I'll maybe take a little vacay somewhere; perhaps to an unexpected place. I'll meet with unexpected people who will never see the unexpected coming.*

*See you soon.*

*—The Curse*

# CHAPTER 32

*Location: Vein's Front Porch; 6:45 pm*

SNUGGLEZ McPHERSON WAS OUTSIDE with Harry Horrendous, choppin' it up and looking a bit irritated by this whole thing. Because he could tell he'd been drinking a little too much, Harry offered to take him home—that is, if he wasn't feeling up to what the night would be bringing.

Snugglez swiftly declined the offer. "I'm good, yo! Where's the action at, though?"

"It'll be here soon. Believe me."

"Good, 'cuz this waiting around shit is for the birds," he huffed. "I'm ready to put that work in—right fukin' now! Ya heard?"

Harry discarded his cigarette down the side of the brick layout of Poppa Vein's home. "I feel you, bruh," he sympathized. "I feel like I've been waiting my whole life for this moment right here, and I'm *not* gonna squander it."

Just at that moment, Poppa Vein arrived.

"Gentlemen!" he greeted. "I'm glad I bumped into you: I wanted to ask you guys a few questions regarding the skills you've acquired over the years. You mind sharing that information? I got a couple young members of my family that could probably use your tutelage."

Harry frowned. "Well, they gotta be serious out here, Vein; niggas can't be on some bullshit; these streets ain't no joke, and this gun game is real. If they 'bout it, we 'bout it." Vein nodded. "I'll tell Linguini about it; he'll be happy to teach your new pups the ropes."

At that moment—6:50pm—my informant reached out to me: Jake Solomon was roughly ten minutes away from his home. Quicker than I could think, I ran outside to tell Vein and the others. In retrospect, I really wish I hadn't.

"Yo, showtime in ten minutes or less!" I called. Let's get inside and get shit crackin', family!"

Vein grinned. "Sounds like beautiful music to me. Let's go!"

"Whoa, whoa, whoa, hold the fuck up," Snugglez interjected. "Who are you to tell me—to tell us—matter when or how to move?"

For a second, I was stumped—as were, it seemed, Harry and Vein. "Excuse me?"

"Yo, Snugglez, chill out, son!" Harry said, a line forming between his eyebrows. "The fuck you smokin'? That's Escobar you talkin' to like that!"

"I know who the fuck I'm talkin' to, nigga," Snugglez snapped. He eyed me with disdain. "PR 'Bitchass' Escobar, the one and only. One of the Original Three." He waved his hands in mock admiration. "How impressive!"

"Chill out, right now," Harry ordered, visibly losing patience. "Let me get you outta here and—"

"I ain't goin' nowhere! This motherfucker right here—" nodding towards me—"needs to hear what I gotta say, godammit!"

It was at that moment that I realized one of our lead henchmen was drunk out of his mind—and, as much as I knew not to take whatever he was saying to heart, I also knew alcohol usually brings out a person's hidden truth.

It was then that Snugglez stepped up to my face, practically nose-to-nose, and proceeded to curse me to living hell. It took everything in me to not retaliate: after all, he was my brother, and I knew he wasn't in his right mind. Saying this, I couldn't help but wonder what was real and what was the alcohol.

The whole time, I prayed for one thing: that he wouldn't put his hands on me. It would destroy our whole operation and, most importantly, potentially our brotherly relationship.

Thankfully, it didn't come to that; instead, Snugglez just continued with his little rant. Yo! "Fuck you, Escobar! Fuck you, straight up. Thinking you better than all of us... Nigga, you ain't better than *any* of us! You ain't *shit*! And if Vein was a smart dude, he'd recognize you for the bitch-ass nigga you are."

"That's enough," Harry intervened, physically pulling him away. My jaw was set. "This shit is getting out of hand. Escobar, I'm gonna get him outta here. It's clear he ain't in his right mind."

"Thanks, Harry. I appreciate that. Make sure he gets home safely."

"I will."

Both men left and Vein turned to me. "You mind telling me what that was about?" he demanded.

"I wish I could tell you, Vein," I responded honestly. "Clearly there's something that needs resolving there. But that's for another time."

Vein nodded, accepting my words. "He made it seem like you two needed to settle something, and that it just couldn't wait. That's why I didn't get involved."

"You may be right about that, man," I said simply. "I just wish I could've been warned."

Meanwhile, Harry Horrendous escorted Snugglez over to the car parked on the long driveway at Vein's house.

"Get in the car," he instructed impatiently. "I'll be right there; I just had to make a quick call."

With that, hee shut the door and walked away, pulling out his phone dialing. The receiver picked up pretty much immediately.

"Yo, Swindel!"

"What's up, man? We ready?" Swindel asked, cutting to the chase.

"Nah, not yet." Harry paused. "Some shit came up; I'll explain later. Just hit up Drumsticks and tell him the plan is still on; I just gotta push it back maybe an hour or so. I'll hit you when I'm done."

"Copy that."

As Harry hung up and made his way back to the car, he saw Snugglez had settled down into the driver's seat. He opened the door. "The fuck do you think you doing, son? Scoot over. You ain't driving."

"Nigga, I'm *good*," Snugglez slurred. "I ain't drunk. I've driven home in *way* worse conditions."

"And that's something you're proud of, I suppose?" Harry snapped. "You're trippin' tonight, nigga. But I'll let you handle it if you say you got it."

A poor decision, clearly.

Harry proceeded to push the recliner all the way back, after which he checked to see if he had any messages. He left the driver's side, slid into the passenger seat, and buckled up.

The second his buckle had clipped in, Snugglez McPherson sped off Poppa Vein's block, taking a sharp left turn at the end of the road. The highway was exactly thirty seconds away once you made that left and, from there, it was a straight shot back to Ghost Town.

Unfortunately, they never made it.

Not five minutes after making it onto the highway, Snugglez realized, his stomach dropping, that he was not exactly as good as he thought he was.

Trying to convince himself otherwise, he yelled out to Harry, "Nigga, I'm nice right now. I feel *great*! I feel untouchable!"

"Focus on driving then, so we know we both good! I ain't never seen you trippin' like this."

"I don't even *remember* what I said to Escobar, man." To Harry's surprise, he started laughing. "Wait, it was Escobar I spoke to, right?"

Harry felt panic seize him. "Pull this bitch over, Snugglez. Now. I'm serious."

"You don't trust me, nigga?" Snugglez responded, eyes widening. "I told you I got this."

As he said this, he began drifting to the other lane on the highway, almost colliding with another vehicle. Harry leaned over and took control of the wheel, his heart in his mouth. The guy they'd nearly crashed into leaned on his horn and Snugglez jumped, clearly only just realizing what had nearly happened.

Once the car was back on-track, Snugglez grabbed the wheel again. "I told you I got this, dude!" he protested.

Harry continued to lean over. "You fuckin' kidding me? We could've died back there!"

Harry clung onto the wheel and Snugglez, his voice raising to a frenzy—"I got this! I got this!"—seemed more preoccupied with convincing Harry he could drive and fighting him off the wheel than with actually driving.

It was during this struggle that Snugglez, completely delirious, began to lose total control of the car. Harry screamed something unintelligible at Snugglez and tried to reclaim the wheel again, to no avail: the vehicle had already plunged head-first into a divider.

Long story short, Harry Horrendous lost all his front teeth on the dashboard and suffered major cuts and bruises. Snugglez McPherson emerged relatively unscathed—that is, with the exception of his arrest and charge of DWI.

Needless to say, the plan Harry had with Swindel and Billy fell apart—thank the Lord, or it could have blown our entire operation to PoloVille.

Insensitive? Maybe. Accurate? Absolutely.

# CHAPTER 33

COCOA BUTTA HAD JUST emerged from a very well-deserved shower that felt like heaven sprinkling over her body. She had been joined by Mula Madison, Yelly, and Whish Johannsen at Tony Victor's house, and Cocoa set about admiring the art and music collection on the walls of his home: it was rather extensive.

Tony's house was something of a shrine: he was a serious lover of hip-hop music—like the most of us—, but his home looked like the Tupac Amaru Shakur Museum. *Everything* was Tupac. I always believed Tony saw a massive resemblance of 'Pac in himself, and that that's why he gravitated toward him to the extent that he did. Tupac was not only a great artist, but he was a revolutionary—a prophet of sort. He always saw the system for what it was, and not for what it appeared to be—and, indeed, Tony Victor was a lot like that. Neither of them took shit from anybody under any circumstances.

The amount of music that man had made was unbelievable; I believe on *Makaveli, Vol. 28*, he had a song with PigLeg on there. Well, okay maybe not, but I couldn't help it.

"Ladies, I'm pretty sure Jake will be home right around seven," Cocoa said. "Tony said something to me about arranging to see when he got there. Do any of you know anything about that?"

"Nope, we're just sitting around in someone else's home watching this big-ass screen in front of us with the words 'Live Feed' because we're bored." Mula arched an eyebrow.

"I get the feeling you're being sarcastic," Cocoa—naïve, innocent Cocoa—frowned.

Mula sighed. "Affirmative. I would've thought you'd notice if we were zoomed right in on the house you were held captive in for the last nearly five days." Mula indicated to the screen.

"Wait! Are you serious?" Cocoa ran over to the screen, staring at the displayed image with an expression Mula couldn't place. "I really couldn't see that well; I don't have my glasses with me, you know. I know the guys are good, but how in the coochie crunch did they pull this off? This is amazing!"

Unable to resist, Cocoa touched the screen, as if she could control it. I wonder if that kind of technology will exist in the future. Time will tell, I suppose; as long as it's equipped with some kind of Vaginal Application that allows a man to believe he's inside of a vagina when he's not. That would be outstanding.

"My husband, along with Don and your brother, actually put up the funds to a government official," Yelly explained. "He provided them with access to a satellite system in the sky that would enable us to zoom in on anything or anyone in the world, as long as we had the proper coordinates."

"But who's manning the boards?" asked Cocoa. "Blues? Dough?"

"Actually, Don's cousin Brilliant Bobby in Colorado is the genius operating everything—all from the comfort of his own home," Whish responded.

"I can't *believe* it," Cocoa breathed. "This is fuckin' awesome! A dream come true! Is there popcorn in this place?"

"I don't know. We don't live here," Mula snapped.

Cocoa looked hurt at Mula's tone. "Why do I feel like there's hostility between us? Do you have a problem with me?"

"Girl, are you serious?" Mula exploded. "The last two months of our lives have all been a living hell, and you're at the center of it all! Do you not see the problem with that?"

Cocoa was clearly taken aback, but Mula pressed on. "That woman's husband over there—" pointing to Yelly—"almost died because you didn't think something through before trying to execute 'plan of action'." She shook her head incredulously. "Whish's newfound love is still in the ICU because of it, and even though Sara's condition wasn't admittedly a direct fault of yours, I guarantee that if I dig deep enough, I'll find out the ice cream place where Whish laid that chick down was owned by Jake fuckin' Solomon's Great Aunt Mable or some shit."

"Alright, sis, calm down," Whish intervened. "We've all had a shit time these past couple months, but we don't need to start taking it out on each other. Cocoa's already seen the error of her ways, and when things aren't thought out so well, you see the snowball effect it can have. It's the proverbial avalanche of destruction."

"Destruction? Thought out? You put a *bullet* in that woman's head without a second thought and now Sara is suffering because of *you*, Whish! And I'm the only one who makes irrational decisions?" Cocoa's eyes were filling with tears.

Whish turned to Cocoa, clearly unimpressed. "Who are *you* to question my doings?"

Thankfully, Yelly had had enough. "Y'all need to chill with all that shit right now," she shouted. "I think your ex just pulled up."

"Oh, good; got me worked up in here. You sure there's no popcorn?"

# CHAPTER 34

*Location: Denver, Colorado; Saddle Brook, NJ; Brick City, NJ*
*(Simulcast), 7:02 pm*

L IKE CLOCKWORK, WE KNEW Jake Solomon would show up at around
7pm, and, as his old clunker pulled into the driveway, all our feeds
became live in three different places. The target was Jake's house,
but everyone could see what was happening: from Poppa Vein's house,
Tony Victor's crib, and Brilliant Bobby Bushetta on the wheels of steel
from his home in Colorado.

"Showtime, folks!" Vein announced. "Make sure you don't get any
food or drink on my carpet while we're gone; that shit cost me twenty-five-
thousand dollars. Imported from Scandanavia."

"Wait, where in the hell are you three going?" Jay asked.

I laughed. "You didn't honestly think we'd be here to see this unfold,
did you? We set this whole thing up so you guys can observe the fruits of
your labor." I grinned. "Us, on the other hand... We have to be there for
the finale!"

"It's gonna be a doozie!!" Don grinned.

"Polo, I need you to do one thing, and one thing only," Vein said.

"Anything," Polo responded, not missing a beat.

"I need you to lock the door," Vein said simply. "You need to hear the
alarm alert anytime my front door opens; I don't trust these M.O.B. niggas
yet; too many Spanish niggas up in here."

And, with that, we hopped into my '92 Audi S4 and headed to Jake
Solomon's house. It was a beautiful car, but not my every day one. I had
only decided to pull it out today because its standard-size Sedan look
blended in with a lot of the other cars in Brick City. After all, you should
never bring unwanted attention on yourself. Don't get me wrong, we
owned Ghost Town, but Brick City was a bit more prevalent in the crime-
ridden world of cities in NJ. Thus, smart decisions still had to be made.

Meanwhile, the rest of the crew were watching the livestream in their respective places with bated breath. Eventually, Jake appeared on-screen.

"I can't believe that bitch didn't cook again!" he was fuming, wandering throughout the house. "What good is she? I leave her here all fuckin' day and she hasn't cooked or cleaned. Cocoa!"

Hak burst out laughing. "Look at this dumb fuck!" he exclaimed, delighted. "I assume he's forgotten he locked her up in the basement for the last four days so she couldn't take a piss, never mind cook or clean."

Polo shook his head. "Nah, he's just gone right now; probably gettin' high off his own supply. That motherfucker is definitely on some other shit right now. Look at him: he just poured some cereal in the bowl and is looking for the milk in the microwave!"

Tony's eyes twinkled. "This is gonna be better than we thought."

At that moment, Bobby Bushetta's voice rang through. "Are all of you seeing this?" His voice was, sure enough, laced with amusement. "Is the feed clear? Or did this stupid nigga actually look for milk in the microwave?"

"Ha! This is *awesome!*" came Cocoa's voice.

"Oh, we see everything, alright," came Yelly's response.

"Technology is amazing." This was Whish. "Bobby, can you put one of these thingies in my purse?"

"No, Whish, I can't do that—I *won't* do that. It's inhumane. It's against the law."

"Is that a dildo?" Dough chipped in. "If so, that's brilliant. I must have that in my Bunny Ranch."

"*No,* you sick fuck! What's the matter with you?"

"Chill ya'll," said Hak. "He found the milk! Look, on the end table in his living room. That nigga probably left that shit there since this morning!"

"Probably tastes like Sticks Morano's breath after a long night of strudel-hopping," Jay said, scrunching his nose.

Everybody started laughing, which was swiftly shut down by Billy. "Quiet now, family; I think he's trying to say something."

"Well, I wish he'd open the closet door in the pantry so he could see the Douchebag Special we left in there for him!" Jay grinned.

Sure enough, Jake Solomon began speaking again. "Where the fuck did I put that rope at? I think it's time Cocoa finds out Jake Solomon ain't to be fucked with. And if she still bleeding down there in her twat hole, well... she gon' be bleeding elsewhere, too."

The guy ranted and raved like a madman, during which Cocoa seemed to be having a seizure. "Fuckin' *pig*!" she spat. "Oh my God! I *hate* you!"

Yelly swiftly began to calm her down, and Jake, blissfully oblivious, continued.

"Maybe I put it in that closet up front..."

Hak was practically wetting himself with excitement. "Yes, go in there! Let's go!" he urged.

"Actually, no," Jake resolved, stepping away. "I put it in the drawer in the kitchen."

"Oh, for fucks sake!" Jay said, exasperated. "Just open the damn closet already, you fuckin' cunt burglar!"

Jake proceeded to find the rope, after which he went over to the sink to wash his face and wake up some. He'd been in the 'hood all day collecting his percentages and taking a few names; indeed, we had heard of a poor soul's life being taken by the hands of Jake earlier this morning— simply for not having the right colors on. I'm not exactly sure what colors someone's wearing have to do with the only color we should all be concerned about—green, of course---, but hey, I'm just a part of a multimillion dollar trifecta that built a conglomerate of an empire that went out and took what it wanted. What do I know?

Jake took a big spoon of cereal from the bowl he had poured the 'Sticks' milk into—and, predictably, after approximately two seconds, he spat the whole shit up into his kitchen sink. He went to grab a paper towel, to no avail: the holder was empty. He then headed to the closet to get a new role. The show was starting.

As soon as he opened the door, he let out a bloodcurdling scream. "Aunt Mable! What the fuck happened to you?"

Mula almost laughed. "Holy shit, the asshole really does have an aunt named Mable."

Meanwhile, Jay and Hak were busy high-fiving, proud of themselves for their handiwork.

"What did you guys *do* to her?" asked Cocoa.

Jay grinned. "We just took her out of her misery, that's all."

Cocoa audibly gasped down the line. "You killed an innocent woman?"

"*Innocent*?" Hak echoed. "That woman has been stealing from us for the last twelve years! We used to always look out for her on the streets, and how did she repay us? By being Jake's aunt."

"How does that mean she stole from you?"

Hak thought for a moment. "Uh... Jay, tell her how this means she stole from us."

"You motherfucker," Jay sighed, rolling his eyes. "Cocoa, it's simple: Hak and I used to deal to her a long time ago. She was always short on the two-for-five specials, but we let that slide, 'cuz me and Hak were banging her twin nieces. So, we thought it was a fair exchange."

"Indeed, it was," Hak agreed gravely.

"That is," Jay countered, "until her nieces decided to get on their grown woman shit, becoming responsible and getting married and shit. So, we stopped fuckin' with them. You understand now?"

Cocoa clearly didn't. "What in the hell does that have to do with her stealing from you—especially if you let the deals slide on *purpose*?"

"The deals?" Hak repeated. "Oh, you talkin' 'bout her being short on the specials?"

"That is what you *said!*"

"Yeah, but that's not how she stole from us," Jay clarified. "The bitch stole twelve years of twin vagina we can't get back from us, don't forget."

"But... but her nieces made the decision to do that."

Hak shrugged. "Well, she should have been more persuasive, shouldn't she? We found out she was Jake's aunt recently, when Poppa Vein told us, so we went to pay her a visit and voila! Now we're here."

Bobby cut into Hak's little anecdote. "Look what he's doing to her! What the fuck?"

"It had to be those M.O.B. niggas," Solomon was muttering. "They will all die, Aunt Mable! Mark my words!"

As we all looked intently, Jake was visibly crying, holding his aunt's cold body in his arms. It was after a few moments of this seemingly innocent embrace that he started unbuttoning her blouse, opening it up and unclasping her bra to expose her massive breasts. He then laid his head on them, sobbing heavily.

Yelly was the first to speak. "Yeah, this man is completely insane."

"At least he's not trying to fuck her," Cocoa offered. "A couple of days ago, he had sex with a dead woman on the other side of the basement he had me locked up in. He thought I was asleep, but I heard everything." A pause. "I cannot believe I loved this man."

"Dead woman?" came Whish's voice, thoroughly disturbed. "Brothers, is the woman the same one who wanted to kill me, but ended up trying to kill Sara?"

Dough grinned next to us. "Bingo, Whish."

"Ha! Funny how things come around."

Tony Victor then drew our attention back to our screens. "Look, he's moving around now. Looks like he might find Frederick Linguini's surprise next, upstairs on his bed."

Bobby then started speaking, voice filled with what seemed to be panic. "Oh, shit, the feed's signal's going!"

"*No!*" everyone started shouting. Bobby's laughter filled the line. "I'm just fuckin' with you. This is too good."

"Asshole," Mula muttered.

"I love you too, Mula."

"Say, Bobby," Blues piped up, "is the equipment hard to figure out? I mean, all that hardware couldn't have been easy to operate."

"For the normal man, yes," he responded flippantly, "but I had great training from a genius mathematician and software developer for some time, so it took me no time to figure this whole thing out."

Blues sounded impressed. "You got his name?"

Billy paused. "Actually, it was done through the computer," he said hesitantly. "I never actually met him, but what I was being taught was incredible; I knew I'd make millions with this info. And the fact that I have surveillance in all the rooms of Jake's house is insane."

"Wonderful. Just wonderful," Blues breathed.

Breaking into their little bromance, Hak observed, "He's at the top of the steps now. Yo, Fred, bring your ass in here!"

Frederick Linguini's shouted he was coming in the background. Meanwhile, Jake Solomon was walking up the steps to go to his room, unable to believe that his favorite aunt was lying dead on his living room floor. However, what he saw next was even worse: he opened his bedroom door and... "Lou? Denise?"

Padlock Penny's voice came through the line. "Who the hell are those people?"

"I don't know, but this is some crazy shit," Pudgee said. "My brother is nuts."

"Hush!" Frederick hissed, having just tuned in. "You can't mess this moment up for me; you'll ruin a masterpiece."

Jake Solomon walked into his bedroom to see his childhood friend, Lou Morals, and his closest cousin from Pennsylvania, Denise Merchant, in the most gruesome scene he's ever witnessed. They were both dead and stark naked: Denise standing upright by the edge of the bed, her feet in cinderblocks to hold her up straight and a strap-on dildo attached to her; and that same dildo was between Lou Morals' ass cheeks, which were high in the air, face buried in the pillow below it.

Jake walked over toward the scene in a state of utter shock: he was completely numb. There was blood everywhere, but that was secondary to him; he just walked over to them and touched their skin lightly. They were ice cold.

He closed Lou's eyes respectfully, surprising the crew, before smacking Denise's left tit to see if it would jiggle—which it didn't. They had been dead for quite some time.

He sat down on his recliner chair in the corner, trying to absorb what had happened in his very home. He laid his head on the arm of the chair and just stayed in that position for what felt like an eternity.

Frederick was grinning like a mad scientist. "Success!"

"Our brothers are fuckin' maniacs," Mula muttered.

Yelly retorted, "My husband didn't do that, so I don't feel so bad."

Dough looked proud. "You outdid yourself there, Frederick," he commended. "How the hell did you pull that one off all by your lonesome? I'm sure your fans are anxious to hear."

"Oh, I had help," Linguini responded vaguely. "Well, not physical help, but geometric help. Blues helped me figure out what exact angles I had to put the bodies in to have them placed exactly where and how I wanted them to be. We were going for maximum shock-factor."

"That's some bullshit right there, yo," Jay said. "Why didn't we get that assignment?"

"Escobar and Corione thought you'd have too much fun with it and end up fucking it up."

"Are you serious?" Hak demanded. "That's unacceptable."

"Agreed," Jay said.

"But what did you use to get them *in* that state?" Tony asked.

"Well, Tony, I'm glad you asked." Linguini was lapping this up. "I kidnapped them, suffocated them, and then embalmed them both. It was actually pretty easy."

"Suffocation? Well, how do you explain all the blood?"

"Blood? What blood?" That's ketchup, for added drama!"

This seemed to snap everybody out of the shock of what Linguini had done, and all fell about laughing: this was atrocious behavior, and would only ever be dreamt of by this nightmare collective we call M.O.B.

"I love you motherfuckers," said Bobby.

Joseph Stylez then tuned in. "What did I miss?" he asked. "I've been taking a shit for the last twenty minutes."

"We all could hear that, you know," Whish shot back, tone filled with disgust.

"Well, that's what makes us all closer, right?"

"Wrong."

"My apologies ma'am." Stylez then addressed the rest of the group. "What's poppin' out here, though? Anything good? And where the hell is Snugglez and Harry?"

It was at that moment that the home phone rang at Tony Victor's house, where the women were tuned into the livestream. Vaguely irritated, Mula rose from her seat and went to pick up the phone.

"Hi, this is the Victor residence."

"Mula! It's Swindel."

"Swindel, what's up, baby? Why you guys not here? We've been waiting for Harry to get back from dropping Snugglez off home."

Swindel was silent for a moment. "Well, none of that actually happened. Snugglez and Harry got into a car accident on the Garden State Parkway."

Mula's heart sank. "Are you serious? Are they okay?"

Swindel sighed. "Well, depends on how you look at it. Snugglez got locked up for drunk driving, but he escaped with no injuries. Harry, on the other hand... He's going to need some serious dental work. He lost all his front teeth."

Mula felt sick. "Where are they now?"

"Harry's is at UMDNJ, and Snugglez is at a precinct somewhere. I don't know exactly where right now."

"Okay, sit tight. I'll hit you back."

When Mula sat back down with the girls and resumed watching the livestream, Stylez said, "What was up, Mula?"

"Fuckin' Snugglez and Harry have got themselves into trouble again."

"Why, what's happened now?"

"What kind of trouble?" Tony chipped in, evidently concerned.

"Swindel just called and said they got into an accident on the parkway," she explained. She exhaled deeply. "Snugglez got arrested and Harry is at UMDNJ getting looked at by a dental professional because he lost his front teeth."

"What the *fuck*," Hak muttered.

"I can't with this drama right now," Mula continued. It was true: she had some palpitations coming on, and she'd been knocked seriously sick. "As long as we know where they are, we'll get to them soon. We got an asshole to catch on-video first, and our culprit looks like he's leaving the upstairs scene now."

Mula was right: Jake Solomon had finally risen from the edge of the bed. He looked around and caught a familiar whiff while he was blowing his nose from the excess snot and tears he'd acquired over the last twenty minutes, and, upon closer inspection of the blood splattered everywhere, he realized his mistake: this wasn't blood at all.

He smirked a little. It's not like the lack of blood would bring his people back, but it was a humorous touch. He shrugged it off and let out a long exhale, making his way downstairs around the small staircase. He stalked past Aunt Mable, who was still lying on his living room floor, and took a seat on the small couch. He pulled out a cigarette and lit it, and, as he inhaled the thick smoke, it is then that I believe he came to the realization that his time had come. Maybe he was looking for any kind of stress reliever at that time, but little did he know that the best was yet to come.

In good Solomon fashion, he began musing aloud once again. "Since it looks like tonight is probably my last night on this earth, I think I'll go get Cocoa to spread those legs and take some good old-fashioned pipe. If I'm going out, I'm going out in some pussy."

And with that, he extinguished his cigarette on the coffee table beside him and grabbed a wet rag from by his kitchen sink, presumably to clean Cocoa up with.

"But who's going to be downstairs?" Cocoa enquired, suddenly sounding nervous. "As much as I'm enjoying this, please don't tell me one of you killed his momma?"

"No, girl!" Tony said. "Ain't nobody killing nobody momma! Even we have boundaries."

"That's fucked up, Cocoa," Jay cringed. "His mom? That's cold."

"Well, I don't know what to expect from you anymore," she shrugged. "Y'all be doing some crazy shit."

"These niggas are definitely crazy, but watch what your brother and them other niggas have in store for Jake now," Polo smirked.

Jake was still making his way downstairs, wet rag in hand, preparing to wash Cocoa's goodies up before he slid inside her. He was still disoriented and almost missed that second step coming off the stairs in the basement: it was pitch black, and he had to feel his way around the wall as he tried to locate the light switch.

"Cocoa!" he shouted. "Wake up, bitch. Daddy's home!"

He finally found the light and flipped it up, the bright filament blinding him for a moment. When his vision adjusted after a good minute of blinking back black spots, he found the couch Cocoa usually occupied to be empty. Initially assuming the light was still just playing tricks on him, he rubbed them and felt his heart sink at what still lay before him: a seemingly empty room.

Still not convinced that she was gone, he loudly sighed and stalked over to the other side of the basement. "Cocoa! Who the fuck told you to move to the other side? It's off limits to you. I should—"

Vein emerged from behind the couch. "Good evening, Jake. Were you expecting someone else?"

I then sauntered out from behind the door. "Hey, Jake! How you doing, brother? Good, I hope?" I cocked my head to the side, surveying the pathetic man levelly. "Damn, you look like hell. You mind if I sit my gun on this box right here? Thanks."

Don, meanwhile, had been sat in the furthest corner from us. "What's poppin', homie? Everything good with you?"

Despite his attempt to maintain a cool and collected demeanor, Jake was evidently shaken up. He turned to Vein. "So, these guys did this, huh? I'm assuming you saw them down here and waited 'til I got home so we could end their miserable lives together?"

"Sure, Jake," Vein smiled. "Sure. How would you like to handle this?"

"I'm glad you've come to your senses, brother," Jake said, clapping him on the shoulder and ignoring his question. "I was hoping you weren't too mad with me about the shooting in Don's Diner; I wanted to make it up to you by telling you I took care of that stupid bitch from Chancellor Avenue that almost gave us an STD. You remember the one we ran a train on earlier this year?" Vein nodded. "Anyway, turns out her sister was the one that Whish Johannsen killed at the Dairy Queen a couple months back—so I thought I'd capitalize on that situation for all of us. Thanks for your understanding, Vein." He began scanning the room. "Where's Polo? I know I told you he was a dead man walking, but I was mad. Where he at? I wanna tell him I love him." Crocodile tears rose to his eyes. "I just wanted you to know everything that was going on, to keep you in the loop; that's why I faxed you that picture of her dead body. Matter of fact, I killed her right over there."

Vein examined his nails. "Thank you for sharing that with me, Jake; you're a good man. Honorable. A man of integrity."

Jake pretended to wipe his eyes and started to smile with all his teeth. "And now these motherfuckers are dead." He settled his gaze on Don and I. "So, who are we taking out first, Vein? I don't care who it is; just let me have the first crack at him."

Vein nodded. "Anything you say, Jake." He turned to him. "You know what I'm gonna do for you? We're gonna make this easy. I'm gonna sit the both of them down on these chairs, side by side, and you look them both in the eyes and choose which one you want to die first. How's that?"

Jake grinned again, eyes dancing. "Sounds like my kinda plan, boss."

Decision made, Vein turned to us. "Gentlemen, you mind taking a seat?"

"Don't mind if I do," responded Don. I similarly obliged.

"See, Jake? They're not so bad, are they? They're polite and were properly raised by their mommas."

Jake was apparently unaffected by Vein's praise towards us. Instead, he spat, "You know I really hate both of you motherfuckers. If it wasn't for my dumbass cousins from Illtown, you would've been dead, Escobar." I just arched an eyebrow. "Sam Luciano is in the ICU because of me, and I'm damn proud of that: that nigga used to fuck my baby moms a few years back. I tried to end his life then, but I wasn't strong enough in these streets; I had to wait for the right moment. That night at Don's Diner ended up being the most fulfilling moment of my life; I'd do it all over again, too." He shifted his gaze to Don. "As for you... I've been waiting a long time for this. I've always wanted to snatch your little ass up and play hopscotch on your balls—"

"Hopscotch on my *balls*?" Don burst out, laughing. "You been hanging with Sticks Morano again, Jake? I told you, that guy is bad news. He's only going to get you and your dick in trouble!"

"Who the fuck is Sticks Morano?" Jake snapped, unamused. "Shut the fuck up; I'm in control here!"

Vein rested his hand on Jake's shoulder. "No, Jake." His eyes twinkled. "I think you'll find I'm in control."

And with that, Poppa Vein hit Jake across the back of the head with a Louisville Slugger, size 33 ½. Jake Solomon fell like a ton of Lego blocks— or a tall-ass house of cards, depending on how you want to look at it. Vein loomed over his body and cocked his head, circling him like a vulture before kneeling toward his right ear.

"That's for my sister, you sanctimonious son-of-a-bitch. You take advantage of her, I take advantage of your life."

Don and I couldn't stop smiling: the deed was done. "Well done, Vein," I said warmly. "Although I hope you haven't killed him; I would've liked to get a hit in or two. Not to mention the fact that the main event hasn't occurred yet."

"Nah, brother, he's not dead," Vein said firmly. "You know how many times I've knocked someone over the head with this slugger? I know how to take a permanent swing or a temporary one." Sure enough, Jake started stirring. Vein smirked. "See?"

"I suppose not," I conceded.

"It was a nice swing, though," Don offered. "Did you play little league with this guy and Celo Gaston?"

"No; the game itself isn't my cup of tea. But I appreciate the equipment used on the field." Vein then turned to the pathetic mess bundled on the ground. "Get up, motherfucker," he spat. "It ain't over."

Jake remained virtually mute and motionless and, a moment later, Vein and Don exchanged a look I read immediately: time for a phase two.

With that, Don and Vein lifted Jake Solomon and sat him on a chair in the middle of the floor, Don swiftly taking a length of rope from his pocket—as you do—and tying him up tightly. Leaning back and surveying his handiwork, he then lit up a blunt, leaning into Jake and blowing a pint of smoke into his face.

"This ganja ain't bad this time of year," he murmured. "You really should try it, Jake; I think you'd like it."

And with that, Don slipped the blunt into the side of Jake's mouth.

We waited around for about ten minutes after this ordeal, restless and filled with anticipation: we had waited for what felt like way too long for this comeuppance.

Finally, Jake began stirring again, eventually coming to. All our eyes sparked: showtime.

As would probably be expected, Jake's initial words were strung together in a mumbling, bumbling mess. "Vein?" he slurred, squinting his eyes. "Did... did you *hit* me?"

Vein feigned concern. "No, of course not, Jake. That was your Aunt Mabel."

Jake leaned his head against the back of the chair, frowning vaguely. "Oh, okay." He appeared to be lost in thought for a few moments before recognition—dark, fiery recognition—sparked in his eyes. Still restrained in the chair, he lunged forward, eyes bulging. "Aunt Mabel is dead upstairs on my living room floor! What kinda game are you playing here?"

Likely as a result of the adrenaline of the whole situation—or perhaps he genuinely was fearful—, Jake started trembling all over as the gravity of the situation dawned on him, taking in his bound legs and wrists. His enemy was before him in his own house and he was at our mercy, and there was nothing left for him to do. He spat out the blunt Don had given to him and began screaming from the top of his lungs.

"You fuckin' traitor! I'll kill you for this! I thought you had my back! I thought we was family!"

"Family?" Vein repeated. He slowly approached Jake, jaw clenched with fury. "Was that before or after you emotionally abused my sister? Before or after you raped her?"

"*Raped* her?" Jake exploded. "We've been together for years! I don't *need* to rape her! It's always been consensual. If I want some pussy, I just come into the room and—"

Unsurprisingly—and deservedly—, Poppa Vein proceeded to slap the living shit out of Jake.

"Watch your fuckin' *mouth!*" he barked. "Say some shit like that again and it'll be the last thing you say. Now shut up and listen to what that man in front of you has to say."

Vein was referring to me, but Jake's gaze stayed fixed on Vein—perhaps because of the shock, or maybe as an act of defiance.

"Hi, Jake," I cooed, waving. "Over here, buddy."

Reluctantly, Solomon traced his gaze to me.

"That's it! Thanks for finding me." I smiled. "Now, where shall we begin?" I pretended to think for a moment before shrugging. "I think you've waited long enough; it's time for your surprise."

With that, I turned on my heel and walked over to the basement door that led out to the backyard. This was a surprise Jake Solomon would probably be quite familiar with.

From inside the room, Jake's voice was rising with panic. "What the fuck's going on here, man? If you wanna kill me, just get it over with already! I tried to end your life and didn't get the job done, so I get what the score is here. Just get this over with."

I raised an eyebrow and cocked my head to the side. "My, my... That's your problem, Jake: you're always in a rush to get going, and always end up nowhere." I sighed. "We knew you'd be dead the second you tried to take me out; you just expedited the process with everything else you decided to partake in." I paused. "Saying that, I'm not gonna kill you."

Jake hadn't seen that coming. "You're not?"

I smiled. "And Don's not gonna kill you."

"No?"

"Nope," Don chipped in. His face was glowing with excitement.

"And get this: Vein's not gonna kill you."

Jake had had enough. "C'mon, you smug bastards! What is this?"

It was time. "Please say hello to the man who *is* gonna kill you."

Sam Luciano was looking surprisingly good: fresh out the ICU and he was already raring for action.

"Yo, Jake!" he greeted warmly, ambling inside. "What's up now, motherfucker?"

Sam Luciano had .38 special raised—the very same gun Jake had tried to kill him with that night at the Diner. The look on Jake's face, as expected, was absolutely priceless: eyes widened, lips pulled back in horror. He certainly hadn't seen this coming.

Smiling widely, Luciano, gun still raised, approached Jake casually. Wordlessly, he stood right before him and looked him square in the eye, surveying his prey for a few moments before properly taking aim.

"Tell Scott, the bridge is still over," he said simply. He then pulled the trigger and shot Jake Solomon right between the eyes, the bullet making easy shrapnel of his calcium, phosphorus, sodium, and collagen case. Solomon instantly slumped in his chair, a perfect hole rimmed with burnt flesh now in his face.

The sound of the bullet resounded around the place for a few seconds before all elapsed into silence once again. The air stank of burning flesh: Luciano had been standing so close to Solomon when he fired the bullet that the gun's smoke and powder had sizzled his skin alive.

I was the first to speak. "I think you was over to the left a little. How many times we gotta practice that shot?"

Luciano lowered the gun and turned to me, disbelief on his face. "Damn, nigga, give me a break. I've been in ICU for a minute and been outside freezing my balls off for the last fifteen!"

"Balls?" Don repeated, sniggering. "Man, Sticks got *all* of you fucked up around here. I've never heard so much talk about balls."

Luciano frowned and turned to me. "The fuck is this guy's problem?"

"Sticks got his boxers up his ass," I shrugged. "Nigga been paranoid for a few weeks. but I'm sure he'll be all good now that the team is back together."

Vein came over and slapped Sam on the shoulder. "Great work, Luciano. I'll leave you to your family now." He turned to me. "Escobar, I'll call you later on. Gentlemen, it was a pleasure doing business with you."

"The pleasure was mine, Pop," Don said, and with that, Vein left the scene.

"Yo, Don, can you take me to go see Whish? Is she home?"

Luciano's tone was filled with hope and excitement.

"Nah, we had her camped out at Tony Victor's house with the other leading ladies."

Luciano nodded. "How's Sara?"

"I hear she's recovering," Don responded. "Recuperation just seems very slow. I don't know, man; I ain't no doctor.

"Well, let's get up outta here. Escobar, you coming, my nigga?"

I paused. "Ya'll go ahead without me; my wife been blowing up my two-way for the last couple minutes. I think she wants me to meet her at that hotel over by the GW Bridge." I winked. "Time to bless my wife with some lovin'."

Sam responded the only way I expected him to.

"Bussherassniggafuckit!"

# CHAPTER 35

*Location: Denver, Colorado; Saddle Brook, NJ; Brick City, NJ;*
*7:35 pm–8:25 pm*

"WHAT THE FUCK!" WHISH exclaimed, eyes wide. "Did ya'll *see* my man blow that motherfucker to another zip code just now?!"

"Give it a rest, Whish," Mula sighed. "Grow some titties and admit he's your man."

Whish eyed the group coyly. "No comment."

Yelly was glowing with pride. "Be honest, who saw that coming?"

"I wished it, but I didn't think it'd be possible," Mula admitted.

"Sam Luciano is my *nigga*!" Tony Victor proclaimed, quite literally sat on the edge of his seat. "Crazy! I can't believe he checked himself out the hospital for this... Or did he?"

"I don't know," Whish admitted. "I'm just happy to know he's okay."

"We know, Whish."

"It's time to celebrate, bitches!" Jay DaBouche announced. "Tonight, we go to Breathless and have unlimited lap dances, all on Hak!"

"What?" Hak piped up. "Get the fuck outta here, son! I'll pay for unlimited lap dances for one person, and one person only: me!"

"You cheap motherfucker," Jay sighed. "You know, I'm really starting to dislike you. You just always about you, never thinking about no one else but yourself. You're an asshole."

"Just one?" Hak asked, clutching his hand to his chest. "Can't I be a mixture of assorted assholes?"

"Absolutely! All kinds of rectal cubes, mixed ethnicities and all. It's like a Sticks Morano Salad made with just cucumbers and ass liquid. I think they sell it at C-Town."

"Now I know why my husband loves you two fools so much," Yelly sighed, hitting both men over the head. "You remind him of himself."

Bobby was still staring at the now-blank screen, looking damn close to tears. "I can't believe we pulled that off—and without a hitch! This technology is genius!"

"That was the scariest and happiest I've ever been," Cocoa added. "I'm so happy that nigga is out of my life forever! My brothers are *heroes*."

"Wait a minute, what about what *we* did?" Linguini remarked. "What are we, a bologna sandwich on molded bread?"

Cocoa sighed. "I'm sorry, Frederick: that shit you guys did to craze Jake out was amazing. I could've never done anything like that. Thank you to all of you."

Whish exhaled contentedly. "And now we can all be happy."

Stylez frowned. "Well, not all of us."

"Why, what's up?"

Stylez paused. "Nah, man. I need to speak with Don and Sam ASAP; something been fuckin' with me for a long time."

Tony thought for a moment. "So, you don't need to speak with Escobar, too?"

"No."

"Okay," Tony said slowly. "Well, just hit me if you need anything; I'm 'bout to check out these Italian chicks I got on standby."

"Have fun with that. I'm 'bout to be out; I'll catch up with you fools later."

And with that, Stylez rose from his seat and left Poppa Vein's house, his demeanor troubled.

As soon as he was out of earshot, Hak said, "Yo, Tony, what's up with Stylez? Somethin' don't seem right."

"I peeped that," Tony returned. "Something is definitely off with him."

"You know, ever since he came back from Michigan on that special assignment, he ain't really been himself," Dough pointed out. "You guys haven't noticed that?"

"I have," Tony confessed.

"Me, too," Mula seconded. "And that's my boo; you know how I feel about Stylez."

"He got an issue with Escobar?" Jay suggested.

"I don't know. It did feel that way, didn't it?"

"I did sense that," Whish said. "When Tony asked him if he needed to speak with Escobar, he didn't hesitate when saying no. Rather abrupt."

"Yelly, your hubby hasn't said anything to you about this? Anything at all?" Mula asked.

"No, not at all. I'll talk to him about it: I'm 'bout to go meet him now."

"Is it okay if we stay at your house for a little while, Tony?" Mula asked.

"Of course. I believe Don is bringing Sam over there now anyway. Just don't mess up my sheets!"

"Really?" Whish sighed, unimpressed.

"Yes, don't mess up my sheets! They imported like Vein's rugs!"

"Well, I'm really going to Breathless," Jay said, standing. "Who's coming with me?"

# CHAPTER 36

WHISH JOHANNSEN WAITED PATIENTLY for the guys to arrive. Mula had stayed to see her brother and give him a massive hug, but then been alerted about a deal gone wrong in the Soho District down the neck that she had to attend to: when business calls, business calls.

Frederick Linguini drove up to Tony's house, which fairly close to Poppa Vein's, waiting outside until the boys arrived. He didn't want to leave Whish in the house without protection; even though they were out in the boonies, you never know with this world.

After a few minutes, the guys pulled up to Tony Victor's house, only to find Frederick Linguini having a heated argument with somebody over the phone.

"Bitch, I'm telling you, if the lettuce ain't on the Champ Burger, I'm coming down to that motherfucker and shoving each patty horizontally up your ass! You got me?"

After this little rant, Fred glanced up, noticing the rest of the crew.

"Oh, what's up, family!" he greeted as they pulled up closer to him, as though nothing had happened. He then addressed the individual on the other end of the line again. "Bitch, I'll call you later and check in. Don't forget the fuckin' lettuce this time!"

And, with that, he hung up the phone and turned to the rest of the gang.

"Brothers, brothers... Ya'll good? Luciano, you rat bastard, we didn't even fuckin' know you was out the hospital! We were celebrating like the Knicks won the championship!"

"First of all, you know the Knicks are never gonna win the championship so fuck outta here with that," Sam said goodnaturedly. "Secondly, who the fuck was you cursing out on the phone like that? I know it better not have been your wife. Don't make me smack fire out ya ass!"

"Nah, fool. That was one of my employees over at the restaurant."

"It's a fast-food place," Don corrected.

"It's a restaurant, you fuckin' let's-go-to-school lunchbox-carrying motherfucker," Fred shot back.

"It's a goddamn fanny pack!" Don cried out, burying his face in his hands. "Why is it so hard for people to get that? It's a fucking fanny pack!"

Fred turned back to Sam. "Anyway, the broad at my restaurant been fuckin' people's orders up and shit, so I had to tell her what's up, or that's a wrap for her job. Plain and simple."

"I can dig it; that's all I needed to know," Sam shrugged. "Whish good upstairs, yo?"

"Absolutely; she's been waiting for you." He clapped his friend on the shoulder. "Alright, I'm 'bout to be out: going to meet Tony and Jay at Breathless. Gonna be a night of celebration—and hopefully we take a few strippers home."

"Be safe; you know shit is real out here," Sam warned. "Jake's 'hood is probably still hot with what transpired earlier. By the way, excellent work by you and the henchmen: very creative. I liked it. Brilliant Bobby sent me the footage and I saw it on this new phone shit Don just copped. This technology shit is gonna rule the world one day, you watch." He began to walk away, calling over his shoulder, "Be good, unless you have to kill somebody."

Fred saluted and walked away, Sam turning to the rest of the group.

"Is Whish really still here? All the lights are off."

"Is there any way possible that maybe she wanted all the lights off? For you? For the both of you?" Don countered, rolling his eyes.

"I guess anything's possible, dude," Sam murmured, a lump forming in his throat. "I know I had her worried: when you and Escobar came to get me from that hospital bed, I was still in a weakened state, but I knew that I'd come around to see this plan through. Hell, I probably should go back to properly heal."

"Properly heal? My nigga, I can't think of no better healing than what Whish got in store for you." Dough looped an arm around his friend's shoulders. "Let's get your punk ass in the house and let that woman take care of you. Ain't much time you gon' need anyway, right? What, two minutes?"

"Actually, you might be right: the right side of my body still ain't quite up to scratch. I'm just thankful that bullet didn't paralyze the kid, or it wouldn't have been no lovin' for me ever again."

Arm still around his neck, Don helped Luciano walk toward the house. He was recovering well because of this super drug we'd had sent in from Thailand—which wasn't no FDA approval bullshit process. He still needed some assistance getting from place-to-place, but he was overall doing well. We kept his recovery wrapped up: couldn't run the risk of too many people knowing what was going to happen at Jake's house. Besides, that ending was incredible, wasn't it?

Once we'd received word he'd be strong enough to operate, we decided to revise the plan to take out Jake Solomon—the original plan being for me, Don, Vein, and Cocoa to take turns bangin' him in his scrotum sac with a spiked bat until it fell off, looking like a deflated balloon. However, Sam was coming to quicker than we'd expected, and we gathered that would be a lot less messy. So, Plan B was formed and ultimately opted for.

The men had arrived onto the doorstep, Don delicately letting go of his friend and smiling mischievously. "Have fun, my nigga. Just don't fuck up Tony's carpet—or his sheets. And don't take any of his Tupac albums without him knowing—well, unless you want that man to ride on you like he rides on his enemies!"

It was at that moment, just as they were about to part ways, that Don received a call that stopped both him and Sam Luciano in their tracks.

"Hold up, yo; Stylez is calling me. I know he probably calling us to congratulate us and to tell us how incredible we are for taking this nigga Jake out." Don pressed the phone to his ear. Don: Yo! What it do? You like how we rocked that nigga Jake tonight?"

"Yeah, it was cute," came Stylez's response, "but I gotta talk to you and Sam, like, right now. He with you?"

"Yeah, actually. Hold up, let me put him on speakerphone."

"Stylez, what's up, bruh!" Luciano called.

"First off, I'm glad you home. That's real talk."

"Appreciate that. All love, boy!"

"Secondly, we gotta problem." Stylez sounded hesitant.

"Cool, where he at? I'll murder him," Luciano said simply. "Anything for you, man."

"Absolutely; you know it," Don agreed. "Where it at?"

Stylez paused. "Alpine."

"That's my neck of the woods," Don said, grinning. "Well, if a nigga gotta catch a hot one, then these bullets don't care where somebody lay their head."

"True, my nigga," Luciano said. "Let's ride!"

"Wait a minute. What about Whish?" Don reminded Luciano. "She's in the house waiting for you, son."

Luciano thought for a moment. "Let me go upstairs right quick and let her know what's poppin'. I'll be right back down. Give me five minutes."

And with that, Sam Luciano headed up to the front door of Tony's house.

"Yo, Stylez, you got the address?" Don asked down the phone, taking it off speaker."

"No doubt—but I believe his wife might be home. I don't want her to get hurt in any kind of crossfire. She's innocent."

"Noted. So, who we gotta murk?"

Don heard Stylez exhale heavily. "PR Escobar."

# CHAPTER 37

*Location: Club Abyss; Sayreville, NJ; 10:18 pm*

ON'S STOMACH HAD ABSOLUTELY dropped the second Stylez mentioned my name. Unable to speak for a moment, he simply instructed Stylez to meet them at Tony's house, which Stylez swiftly agreed to. Don hung up the phone and, sure enough, Stylez pulled up just as Sam came back downstairs from seeing Whish.

Don rolled himself a fat blunt and gave it to Stylez to enjoy to himself in the back seat. "Yo, hit that. This is some Bob Marley shit right here."

"Good lookin', my nigga," Joseph grinned, taking the blunt graciously.

Don was still in a state of utter shock but seemed to cover it well. Luciano, wincing slightly, was meanwhile clambering into the back of the car.

"I want to roll with you guys to Club Abyss to collect on a business transaction," he said, settling into the seat with one last cringe of discomfort.

"Speaking of," Don countered, "I spoke with Hector Elantra this morning: he told me we could still make that bread from the music investment we made a while back. Remember the money we put on The NOW project? Those young kids from Brick City?"

"Yeah, I like them little niggas. I could dig it."

"So, we gon' go inside and see what's up with the host: I wanna see if she'll let The NOW open up next week for The Bootcamp Clik. If she doesn't, I'll threaten to kill her family, and then they'll be performing anyway. It's a win-win situation, but still needs to be handled professionally."

Don then slid into the car and Stylez pulled out the drive, taking the ten-minute ride out to RT 35 in Sayreville. The club was poppin' already when they got there: there was a line around the corner to get in already.

"Yo, Stylez, stay in the car and enjoy that weed, family. It's good, ain't it?" Don said, unclipping his seatbelt.

"That it is," Stylez agreed, taking another puff.

"We'll be right back, my nigga. Relax, and if you see a fat ass go by, get your ass out the car and don't let it go by."

Having already recognized his cue, Luciano got out the car at the same time as Don, Stylez thankfully being too preoccupied with his blunt to question it. Once they were both well away from the car, Sam turned to Don.

"Yo, what the fuck's goin' on, dawg? I knew you was speakin' in code when you mentioned The Now; them niggas been broke up for *years*."

Don looked like one troubled man. "Yo, I don't even know how to say this," he said honestly. "When you went upstairs to give Whish some love, I asked Stylez who we needed to murk."

"Right?"

Don opened his mouth, but no sound came out: he was truly speechless. *Someone in our very family wanting to hurt Escobar.*

"Well, spit it out, nigga!" Sam snapped impatiently. "Who is it? MC Ren? Spice-1? The lil' nigga that hangs out in front of Fast Break asking for change all the time? The Jewish guy that owns Lord & Taylor in the center?"

"No, asshole," Don shot back, clearly not in good humor. "It's fucking Escobar."

The men were entering the bar, and Sam very nearly froze. "The fuck did you just say to me? I thought you just said *Escobar*. The ICU shit must've got my hearing acting crazy and shit."

"I'm serious, man," Don sighed, sliding onto one of the stools at the bar. "It's Escobar he's after." He shook his head. "No hesitation, no delay, no nothing. He straight-up said our brother's name. I couldn't even believe he said that shit at first."

Sam Luciano looked equal parts devastated and furious. He rose from his stool and began pacing back and forth rapidly, shaking his head in disbelief. He wanted to go out to the car and beat the living shit out of Joseph Stylez with his bare hands. Then again, he couldn't help but also feel curious: how on earth had he even come to the conclusion that that's something he wanted to do?

"We gotta approach him, and we gotta do it now," Sam fretted, still pacing. "This is some bullshit, Don; you know damn well this shit don't make no kind of sense. What could Escobar have done to any of our family members for him to want him dead? Especially a member like Joseph *Stylez*. There's no logic attached to this whatsoever. We gotta—"

The expression on Don's face was enough to make Sam shut up, for Stylez, absolutely high as a kite, had just stumbled into the bar in search of his friends.

"Yo! I'm glad I found the both of you; you said if I see a fat ass to not to let it go passed me, so a white chick with a big-ass booty walked by and I followed her in and said, 'Bitch, why you don't let me get up in that ass right now?'"

"That's cool, dawg," Sam murmured absently, "although I'm not sure if that's how you're supposed to approach a woman. The sentiment was there, though." He paused. "But, word-up, we gotta talk *now*."

"Okay, nigga, calm down." Stylez slumped into a stool next to Don. Luciano stayed standing.

Luciano didn't waste any time. "What's this I hear about you wanting to take Escobar out? The fuck's the matter with you? Are you on crack or some shit?"

"No, I'm not," Stylez said simply, eyes glazed, "but you wanna try this angel dust I got over here, nigga; this shit right here is called Death, and trust me when I tell you niggas that PR Escobar is going to be the death of you."

"Death?" Luciano echoed, shaking his head incredulously.

"Yeah. You wanna try it?"

Sam Luciano just stared at his brother of fifteen years and found he didn't know who he was looking at. Don looked at Sam and gave him a look.

"Nah, son, I'm good," Sam responded. "I'll stick with this weed. Little bong to get me through the rest of the night."

"Suit yourself, nigga," Stylez shrugged. "You don't know what you missin'. What about you, Don? I know you ain't no pussy."

Don Corione seemed to genuinely think on it for a brief second before swiftly declining.

"Nah, you go ahead. Matter of fact, it looks like you're having such a great time that maybe you should see if you can take that big-booty white chick home and get that poppin' tonight." He grinned lazily. "Whatever you wanna talk about regarding Escobar, we can deal with tomorrow. Right now, I think I see shorty over there still grillin' you. She can't keep her eyes off you. You should do something about that. Don't let no opportunity like that slide."

"Yeah, I think you're right," Stylez conceded, following Don's gaze. "That ass is *amazing*. Ya'll be safe tonight! Luciano, I'm glad you home, nigga!"

And with that, he slid off the seat and made his way to the poor woman.

"What the fuck is wrong with this nigga?" Luciano asked, frowning. "Was he really smoking Angel Dust? That's that hallucination shit: makes you feel like you're getting jumped by a gang of Mexicans dressed as leprechauns."

Don looked on at his brother, biting his lip: this whole situation was making him uneasy, to say the least. "At least you're okay," he said, "but this shit right here that Stylez is spouting about Escobar? That shit is crazy. We gotta talk to him and Escobar about this ASAP, or this isn't going to end well."

# CHAPTER 38

*Location: Escobar Residence; April 12;' 11:00 am*

LAST NIGHT WAS AMAZING; nothing short of phenomenal—but that, then again, is what happens when two people are married to the loves of their lives. I met my wife at the five-star Hilton Resort by the GW Bridge, and when I tell you it was a night to remember... Well, I'll leave that between my wife and I.

"Babe, are you up yet? It's eleven," Yelly called. "I'm making breakfast: French toast and beef sausage on the menu. You want coffee, too? I got the French Vanilla creamer you like."

"Hook the kid up; sounds outstanding," I called back. "A man has worked up an appetite."

We'd got in from the hotel around at around 4am that morning before going straight to sleep—the best sleep I'd had for months. Six hours of uninterrupted rest now felt like forever for me.

I couldn't stop thinking about all that had transpired the previous day: we'd conspired to kill a man, as well as multiple people we knew meant the world to him. We broke our brother out of the hospital against doctor's orders because of a miracle drug we'd imported from overseas, and saved our sister from a raping lunatic's basement. My best friend had left me and moved down south, and I'd been cursed to hell by one of my own guys.

Despite all this, I couldn't help but feel like it wasn't over.

Cutting into these thoughts, my phone began to ring with an incoming call: Don.

"Hello?"

"Yo!"

"What's up, family?" I greeted. "What's goin' down?"

"Listen, dude, I need you to sit down. Are you sitting down?"

I frowned, mildly irritated: I don't much like drama. "Nigga, unless you 'bout to tell me my wife is a man with two dicks, or that my kids aren't mine and actually Brad and Angelina's, I'm pretty sure I can take what you getting ready to say standing up."

Don dove right in there. "Joseph Stylez wants you dead."

Suddenly, the room started to spin. I felt my eyes widen and my cheeks begin to burn.

"Yeah, let me sit down."

Around a minute of complete silence ensued. I thought Don had hung up. I wondered for a moment whether Don was just drunk from the night before and didn't know what he was saying. Or perhaps he was just being classic Don: fucking around, trying to wind me up.

Finally, I found my voice again and spoke. "Can you repeat that, buddy? My wife says my hearing is going."

*"Joseph Stylez wants you dead."*

Well, there was no doubting the sobriety in that.

"Not being funny, dude, but do you have any clue whatsoever why this fool wants to end your life?"

"No," I responded. "Do you?"

"Oh, I don't think he wants to kill me, so I haven't really given that much thought..."

I remained silent, not in the mood for jokes.

"No, I don't," he finally sighed. "I think I made that pretty clear when I asked you if you had any earthly idea why he'd want to kill you."

"Well, way to go, buddy. You're on a roll today. Have you had sex today? Matter fact, have you had sex this year?"

"That is a *horrible* question to ask me in this day and age," he retorted. "Why would you ask me something like that? I feel violated."

"You're an asshole."

I could hear the smile in his voice. "I know."

"Honestly, though, this is some bullshit," I commented. "I feel like the kid just stabbed me in the chest." Being honest, I felt a little sick: not at the prospect of someone being after me, but at the prospect of that someone being family. "Why me? How exactly did he come to tell you about this? I mean, this is insane, don't you think?"

"Of course, I do, but do we just wave it off; it's just Stylez on his bullshit again." He paused. "Well, we could take that approach—or do we attack this head-on before something... crazy happens."

"I just can't fathom why he'd have a problem with me to this degree—and not come to me directly about it."

There was a thoughtful pause on Don's end. "Maybe because whatever it is... is true?"

"What?"

Don sighed. "I don't know, yo; you've kind of been on your moral high horse for a while now, and it's kind of annoying."

"Moral high horse?" I repeated incredulously. "Since when do you use words or phrases like that? Nigga, you went to Myrtle Avenue School!"

"So, did you..."

"Yeah, for, like three months."

"What's your point, jackass?"

I paused. "Actually, I don't have one. This whole shit is just frustrating as fuck. I don't even know what to do, or how to even begin handling it."

"I feel you."

We both elapsed into silence before Don spoke again. "Maybe you should just lay low for a while; let me and Luciano figure this shit out. If Stylez wants you out, he ain't stupid enough to come to your house to do it." Another pause. "I mean, obviously there's a huge problem here somewhere that we need to get to the bottom of, but 'til then, I think being home and away from the day-to-day business operations will probably do you just right. Maybe take Yelly and the kids on a nice vacation somewhere; I know they'd appreciate that. It's probably been a long time."

"You're right." Even just at the thought of it, it felt like a physical weight had been lifted from my shoulders. "That's an excellent idea. I do believe I want to go to his house now and kill him right now, though."

"That's understandable," Don reasoned. "You're PR Escobar. When someone desires to hurt you or your family's wellbeing, you have a wire that's tapped internally, sending a signal to destroy. I know; I have the same one."

"Okay. So why am I not doing that, then?"

Don thought for a moment. "Because as much as this has you heated, your love for Stylez outweighs the latter."

The man spoke sense. "Perfectly stated. So, I have your trust that you and Sam will take care of this bullshit?"

"How could you not?"

I can't lie, I felt a sudden rush of love for the guy. "I'll send you a postcard."

I hung up the phone with my brother and contemplated going to see Joseph Stylez directly. However, my wife quickly broke into those thoughts.

"Babe, your food's getting cold!" she yelled up the stairs.

I swung downstairs, trying to shake the news from my head. Instead, I turned to my girl and said, "Hey, how do you feel about London at this time of year?"

She frowned. "Probably beautiful. Why? You gotta go on business?"

"No; we gotta go on vacation, baby! You, me, and the kids. Let's get the fuck outta here."

"Really?! Are you serious?"

And with that, she threw herself into my arms, squealing with excitement.

This situation was eating away at me, but the vacation time with my family was a more attractive devotion of my time. Besides, when I got back home, if this situation wasn't completely taken care of, rest assured I'd take care of it myself.

# CHAPTER 39

## Location: Wherever, However, Whenever

*D*EAR *A*SSHOLES OF *A*MERICA,
*It is with great sadness that I tell you I am the direct reason for dissension within the ranks: I take full blame and am quite happy that my plan is working.*

*You hate me, but I love you, and without me, there is no you. I need you to thrive on, and you need me to do the same. We are Us. We are One. We are America.*

*Graciously and Begrudgingly Yours,*

*—The Curse*

*P.S. I hope you like the style of font I picked: I thought it was cool, elegant. Not brash, but classy and simplistic, all rolled up into one. Contrary to what you may believe, I do care. Hence, why you're still breathing.*

# CHAPTER 40

S INCE RECEIVING THE NEWS that Jake Solomon was dead, Al Gebra had been by the bedside of his wife, who had finally decided to come around: she'd been heavily sedated after the—very last-minute—brain surgery she'd endured.

It had been weeks since her attack, and Al had a choice to make.

It was at that moment that she awoke, joy rapidly filling Al's very being as those beautiful eyes opened once again.

"Hey, honey," he said gently. "It's me. I'm here." He took her left hand and caressed it lovingly.

"Chris?" croaked Sara.

Al frowned. "Chris? Who the hell?" He shook his head. "Baby, it's me, Al. Your husband."

"Chris is *not* my husband!" came her dazed response. "I know who my husband is, silly! But where's Chris? Are you sure you're not him? You're awfully cute. You kinda look like him."

Al didn't know what to make of his wife's words; naturally, as a man, you're a little uneasy upon hearing your wife say another man's name—particularly while half-asleep and in bed. Mind you, this was obviously a very different set of circumstances, and this is what he tried to tell himself: she was likely just completely out of it because of the medication. He'll ask her about "Chris" at a different time.

"It's time to rest, boo," he said instead, drawing the covers back up to her chin. "I'm just glad you can formulate a sentence right now. You scared the living hell out of everybody; I've been holding the family business down and checking on all of your ventures. This new technology Brilliant Bobby used is official! I can't wait to show you what it can do. I've been having a lot of fun." He smiled down warmly at her. "I'll tell you this: if it gets into the wrong hands, the world could be over as we know it; it's truly a game-changer. I've been by your side, mastering this thing, waiting for you to wake up. For a second, I wasn't sure if I'd see those beautiful eyes again."

"I have no idea what you just said, but flattery will get you nowhe ...actually, flattery will get you everywhere, sir." Sara's words were jumbled, slurred. "You're a nice man. If I were a little younger, I'd take you in that other room over there and let you have your way with me. But I'm not, and honestly, I'm not even sure if that is even a room over there. Anyways, I'm sure my husband wouldn't approve of that, so I'll stop before I get us both in trouble, okay?"

"Sure, honey. No problem. Whatever you want. I'm here."

"I do have a request, though."

"Anything."

She snuggled into the bed. "A goddamn Italian Cheeseburger from Tasty's."

"Coming right up!" Al grinned. He just shook his head and laughed at his wife.

# CHAPTER 41

S AM LUCIANO ARRIVED AT The House of Nesbit with Whish Johannsen on his arm and Don Corione by his side. For the first time in its history, only two-thirds of O3 would be conducting a family meeting—incomplete by a long stretch. They decided to let a few weeks blow over before addressing the family; besides, Joseph Stylez hadn't been answering his phone for the last few days. They weren't worried, but it wasn't exactly reassuring to not have spoken with him, either.

This meeting was highly necessary, but it was going to be a bit of a different one—interrogation-style, almost. They knew they had to get to the bottom of this thing between Escobar and Stylez; they just weren't sure what their plan was, or how exactly to execute a discussion as sensitive as this. Indeed, there were two very noticeable empty seats, which managed to throw off a good few people.

"Not again!" cried out Mula as soon as she spotted them. "My heart can't take another loss. Why are we here?"

"I'm not playing around with these niggas out here no more, fellas," Tony Victor declared. "Did somebody take two of our brothers out, or something?"

Dough then mumbled under his breath, "Fuckin' Curse."

Jay BaDouche instantly whipped his head round to where he had heard Dough. "Did you just say *Curse*?"

Dough froze. "No! Shush!"

"What do you know about The Curse, nigga?"

"I don't know shit!"

"Don't you start that lying shit," Jay hissed. "I'll have your brother Hak over here to stick that lie right up your Morano!"

"You're a jackass," Dough responded simply, "and I deny, wholeheartedly, anything going into my anal cavity of exclusive exits."

"Just you wait 'til this meeting's over," Jay muttered.

"Yo! Dough! Jay! You care to enlighten the rest of us about what is so much more important than what we have to share with you?"

"Oh, nah, Don, I'm just tripping," Jay stumbled. "I just asked Dough if he had sex this morning, that's all."

"At least he has an acceptable reason," Don shrugged, not sarcastically.

"Jay, you're disgusting," Whish remarked, wrinkling her nose.

"*I'm* disgusting?" Jay echoed, hand to his chest. "Look whose arm you're holding! I've been through *many* a'train line with Luciano throughout different continents—with Hak, too. I think you'll find Sam Luciano is the epitome of disgust: I remember one time when he had this chick put her entire fist—"

"Jay, what the fuck?" Sam hissed. "That's enough!"

Jay grinned. "Whish, please accept my apology. I'm an asshole, I know—but I can't help it. I'm tryin' to change."

Whish just sighed. "Sam, I don't even know how he's a part of our family."

"Because he makes Escobar laugh. All the time."

"So do I!" Don chimed in.

"Okay, enough of this crazy shit ya'll speaking. Where the hell are Escobar and Stylez at?" Tony demanded.

Don cleared his throat. "Actually, Escobar has been on vacation with his family; he'll be back in about a week or so. In the meantime, however, we have some business to attend to. I'll start with Harry."

Harry Horrendous' ears visibly pricked up. "Yes, schir?"

"How are you? Can you speak clearly?"

Harry smiled apologetically. "I'm mokay. Had'chu get my'chu font teef repwaced wit'dis fake ish—"

"Well, we're just happy you're alive, dude—although I'm not trying to decipher what you have to say, so I'm just going to need you to not say shit else until we can actually understand you."

"Chu' got it, bruva."

"Snugglez McPherson," Don called, turning to the man in question. "Have you seen the error in your ways? You almost killed your brother out there. You know we could've gotten you out in a matter of hours, but O3 thought it be better you sit in that cell for a while to think about what you've done." He cocked his head. "Oh, and don't think we don't know how you acted toward Escobar—which, by the way, is unacceptable, and you will apologize for when he gets back."

"That's all good, bruh. I feel horrible about all that shit." He shrugged. "I hardly remember anything, and that's part of the bigger problem. My sincerest apologies to Harry and to the Escobar family: I was out of line, and I know that."

"Then it's all love, right?"

"That it is," Snugglez affirmed.

"Now that that's settled," Sam countered, "Tony, to answer your question: Stylez is absent on purpose."

"Is that so?" Tony remarked, visibly unimpressed. "What kinda machete to the back shit is that?"

"Just listen, Tony," Don murmured.

"We need to ask everybody here a question, because we need everyone's thoughts and points of view. Don't hesitate to share. Nothing is too little." Sam looked nervous.

"And the first one that has any real information we can use is allowed to fuck Saturday Night Fever," Don declared in good, typical Don fashion. "Or Any Given Sunday. Friday Night Lights is out of the equation: that hole is mine and only mine, family."

"What about the women?" Mula retorted. "Do your girls go both ways? Any lesbian tendencies?"

"Absolutely not!" Don burst out. "That consolation prize is not for any of our ladies."

"What kinda sexist shit is that?" Mula muttered, clearly miffed.

Don shrugged. "The prize for our women is three nights, all expenses paid, to Aruba, sponsored by Qurtis Jenkins and The Glowing Midgets. It'll be a sexcapade of activities with nothing but models licking each other and sucking you dry 'til you can't orgasm anymore."

"Are you serious?" Mula snapped. "That's atrocious!"

Sam cut into the twosome's bickering. "All kidding aside, has anybody noticed anything strange going on with Stylez?"

Tony frowned. "Like what?"

"Like literally anything out of the ordinary."

Hak seemed lost in thought for a moment. "I mean, I've haven't exactly seen him around as much."

"Yeah, me neither, come to think of it," Frederick Linguini seconded.

Alexandria the Grape then chimed in. "I was with him a few weeks ago—in the studio, making some music—, and I do remember him acting a little different. We made our song, but it just didn't feel the same in the air. I didn't know what was going on, but I didn't ask him about it."

"That's interesting," Sam mused. "What about you, Al? I know you've been busy with your queen over there." He then nodded to said queen. "Hey, Sara, you feeling okay?"

"I feel good," she smiled. "Better each day. I was just released a few days ago; apparently, it took me about twenty-four hours or so to snap back to reality. Hubby over here told me I was saying some pretty crazy stuff as I was recovering post-surgery. I missed so much. I'm sure glad to know Cocoa Butta is okay."

"Thank you, big sister," Cocoa responded. "You missed it! Your brothers were amazing! Al, I wish you could've been there."

"I *was* there. Well," he stammered, "in spirit, that is."

"So, what's all this mess I'm hearing about Stylez?" Sara asked. "I don't know what any of this is about, but I know I don't like it."

"Yeah, me neither," Tony muttered. "The other night, he mentioned to a few of us that he wanted to speak with the both of you. I asked him, 'So, you don't need to speak to Escobar as well, because I see you didn't mention him in the equation', and he immediately said no. I thought that was quite cold, if I'm honest, but I didn't put a whole lot of mental real-estate to it."

This seemed to bring something back for Hector Elantra. "Yo, I wasn't gonna mention this, but I seen him at this spot a few months ago; it was right around the time Remington passed. This wasn't necessarily a spot you go to chill and have fun at—well, unless you're participating."

"What do you mean by 'participating'?" Sam asked apprehensively.

"Well, I was there collecting on business. He didn't see me, but I saw him there with a few people I recognized from The Oranges—some music industry folk I've heard could take talent to a higher level. But there was usually a steep price to pay." He paused. "So, there I stood, leaving the establishment in question with a little bit of a shocking discovery."

"Well? What exactly was that?" Sam pressed impatiently.

"Well... I'm pretty sure I seen our brother Stylez smoking."

Don almost laughed. "That ain't news! We *all* smoke."

"*I* don't smoke," Tony retorted. "And neither does Escobar."

"Could you let the man finish explaining and stop interrupting, please?" Whish snapped.

"You heard the woman," Sam shrugged.

Hector sighed. "I'm not exactly sure what I saw, but it sure wasn't being inhaled."

Sam stilled. "Are you insinuating..."

"That our brother is doing some other shit? I think we both know that I'm probably not 'insinuating' anything here—more like stating an obvious fact."

"Fact? A fact of what? Of life?" Don challenged. 'I don't think you know what you're talking about here."

"Don, that was mean," Sara scolded. "Maybe you're having an issue with what he's saying because it's true—and maybe you know it to be true, because maybe you've seen it too!"

"Alright, Yoda, chill out."

"Tony, what do you make of this?" Sam asked. "Al? Hak? Dough?"

Tony thought for a moment. "I think Hector just opened up our eyes to the very real possibility that our brother has strayed away from the family and joined forces with a different kind of giant—one that facilitates to one's ego and, eventually, their wants and needs, until those urges become addictive."

Sam weighed this up for a second. "What are you saying, Tony?"

Tony sighed. "I'm saying that maybe our brother has an addiction problem—and not this weed shit some of ya'll smoke, but a serious one. And I believe Hector right here has nailed it on the head that this new crowd he's surrounded himself with is probably not the one that's going to help his cause."

"Well said, Tony. I think I'm in agreement." Sam turned to his Don. "What do you make of this?"

Don just looked at everyone darkly. "Fuck this, this is bullshit! I've known my brother for almost thirty years, and there ain't no way he's got some kind of addiction problem ya'll yapping about." He stood up and stalked away. "Fuck outta here! I'm out."

And just like that, Don stormed out of the door.

Everyone sat in shocked silence until Mula finally spoke. "I'll go talk to him..."

"Nah, sis, leave him," Sam ordered. "He's got to deal with this alone—just like we have to deal with this ourselves. I won't sleep on this—*we* will not sleep on this. But perhaps Don needs to: he's on overload with a mental drug he's experiencing right now."

"And what's that?"

"Denial. And it's very powerful."

# CHAPTER 42

*Location: East Corridors of The House of Nesbit;*
*25 Minutes Later*

"I CAN'T BELIEVE I'M going to say this, but that trip to Aruba sounds amazing," Dough murmured to himself, heading toward the back patio of the house. "Maybe Qurtis Jenkins isn't the worst thing walking on God's green earth—although I actually still wouldn't pass up the chance to kill him."

"Wait, wait, wait," came a voice behind him: Jay BaDouche. "Where in the double-twat-muffins do you think you're going? You ain't going back in there until you answer our questions!"

Hak quickly followed suit with the interrogation. "Bro, what do you know about it?"

Dough turned on his heel to face them both. "About what?"

"Yo, stop actin' stupid," Hak snapped impatiently. "You know what we talkin' about."

"Deluxe apartments in the sky? Cards attached that say *thank you for being a friend*? Taxis that you'd rather smell later?"

"And you call *me* an asshole?" Jay retorted humorlessly. "I kinda like your style, though. I think you'll make a perfect third member to The Douchebag Bros."

"Really?"

"No," Jay responded drily. "Now hurry the fuck up and tell us what you know about The Curse, or I'm gonna pick your brother Hak up and beat the shit outta you with him!"

"That's uncalled for, Jay," Dough sighed, leaning against the wall and examining a nail. "Seriously, you need help."

"You see why I don't deal with my little brother like that?" Hak asked. "He's annoying. I love him, and I'll kill anybody for him, but I can't chill with him for too long."

"Why you so hostile with him, though?" Jay queried. "Why you always so mad? You always trying to fuck somebody up; why don't you try lovin' somebody?"

"Because once your mom proved her disloyalty, I was scarred. It's been downhill since then."

"Don't start your shit today, nigga," Jay sighed. "I was having a good day 'til you said that dumb shit."

"Can I go now? Considering the two of you clearly have some unresolved issues?" Dough cut in.

"No, you fuckin' Ali-boom tanktop-wearin' motherfucker! We asked you about The Curse, .so answer the question, dammit!"

Jay clearly wasn't messing around today.

"Okay, okay, but I don't know much!" Dough warned. "I was at my bunny ranch a little while back, and I went to go check on a client. A lot more time passed than what he actually paid for, but I didn't notice it immediately. Anyway, I went to put an end to his session when I found a note from The Curse."

"And? What did it say?"

Dough shrugged. "Just some bullshit about my two highest-paid workers and the fat guy in the stove."

"Fat guy in the stove?" Hak repeated. "My client was in the fuckin' stove in my kitchen area—burnt to a fuckin' crisp—and I've yet to see my two moneymakers since then."

"Interesting," Jay commented. "Fucked up, but interesting."

"Why is it interesting? You seen him?" Dough asked.

"Nah, we ain't seen him," Hak shrugged, "but that nigga left a note with us, too."

Dough was visibly surprised. "And here I was thinking I was the only one. What was yours about?"

"Apparently he wanted you and/or Jay's brother dead. We don't know why, but it was like some kind of warning, or some shit."

"Yeah, well, he ain't shit," Jay muttered.

"Maybe so," Hak conceded, "but if you keep letting them small things slide, you'll be a failure."

"Didn't Prodigy say that?"

"I don't know what you're talking about."

"Well, regardless," Dough cut in again, "whether he ain't shit or not, he's real. The question is: what the fuck are we going to do about it? And do we tell Don and Sam about it?'

Right on cue, Sam walked into the porch, frowning upon hearing his name. "Tell Don and Sam about what?"

Dough froze. "Uh... That we saw a Sir-Mix-Alot mixtape on broad and market. Can you *believe* that shit? I didn't know he had more than one song, even."

"Stop with the bullshit, Dough," Sam snapped. "Really? You couldn't come up with a better lie than that? I should suplex you onto the back of my pickup truck! Now what the hell's actually going on?"

Hak sighed. "We each got a mysterious note from somebody named The Curse."

"The *Curse*?" Sam parroted, eyes widening. "Wait. Are you fuckin' serious?"

Jay frowned. "Wait. You know him?"

"Do I *know* him? I practically raised his ass!"

"What in the hollowed fuck are you saying?" Hak demanded.

"Dick Felt!" Sam exclaimed. "He was a college buddy of mine; he grew up getting bullied because of his actual government name. He was a monster halfback for our football team, and used to tell us that he was cursed for having such a horrible name—so, naturally, we started calling him The Curse on the field—Dick 'The Curse' Felt." It was as though he couldn't speak quick enough as more memories poured into his mind, triggered by the name. "It was funny, because as soon as we started calling him that, his production went through the roof: he got drafted to the NFL, as well. Man, I'd love to see him—but I guess my question is why in the hell would you get letters from him? He doesn't even know any of you."

"I'm assuming because they're not the same person, Sam," Dough sighed. "I heard of him, and I'm pretty sure he passed away a while ago: I was making fun of his name when they announced his passing on ESPN."

Sam audibly gasped. "Are you serious? Old Dick *died*? Where the fuck have I been?"

"Running a conglomerate, perhaps?" Hak offered. "Killing people? Getting shot? You know, the usual."

"I guess you have a point there," Sam admitted. "Damn, that sucks."

"So, who the fuck is this Curse guy or gal, then?" Jay said. "This note-leaving business got *chick* written all over it."

"Do you have the notes with you now?" Sam asked.

"Actually, yeah." Hak fished in his pocket. "I folded it up and put it in my wallet, just in case."

"Good idea, Hak," Sam praised. "See, Hak's not all brawn. He's got brains, too!"

"Hak performs fellatio behind closed doors," Jay muttered.

Sam almost laughed. "Jay, how in the land of assless chaps did you come up with that?"

"It's okay, Sam," Hak shrugged. "You know how long I've been dealing with this fuckin' guy?" He turned to Jay. "The fact that we live together and you don't know that I do this tells me you don't pay enough attention to us. This is unacceptable—and, frankly, I'm not gonna take it anymore. I'm moving out."

Jay clutched his chest in mock heartache. "But who will I call when Sticks Morano comes to the house asking for a free popsicle rub-down? You know he doesn't like chocolate; he's a butter pecan kinda guy."

"I'm sure you'll think of something. For now, I'll move in with my baby brother over here at the Twisted Sins bunny ranch; I'm sure I'll find respect over there."

"Well, just remember you still have half of the rent to pay for the next fourteen months. We signed a lease agreement, and I ain't paying your obligations."

"Oh, c'mon, dawg! That's not fair!"

"How is it not if you're moving out and reneging on our agreement?"

"Because your mom is there now and, because I'm practically your stepfather, you gotta continue taking care of the family!"

I can't stand you motherfuckers," Sam grinned.

"Ya'll on some crazy shit right now," Dough finally piped up. "The meeting's been over for thirty minutes now, and all you jackasses wanna do is talk shit and chill—and I ain't *tryin'* to chill: I'm trying to get my dick felt."

"You are of equal assholedom Dough," Sam sighed.

"What the fuck else is there to do on this exquisite day of this newly acquired drama our family has created?" Jay pointed out.

"Well, I'm legitimately going to get my dick felt: I got auditions at the bunny ranch for new talent. I gotta replace my two stars; there's been no sign of either of them."

"So, what's happened to Banks and Bella?" Sam asked, echoing everyone else's thoughts.

"I don't know, brother," Dough shrugged. "I assigned them to a client, and a few hours later, they were gone—and I had a fat ass Irishmen in my stove."

"What the fuck?"

"*In my stove,*" Dough repeated for emphasis. "It took me and the helpers I hired over by the Home Depot, like, thirty hours to get that motherfucker out—and to relieve the stench he left in my kitchen."

Hak frowned. "You actually got him out of the stove?"

"*Hell* no! We picked that son-of-a-bitch up, put him and the stove on a truck, and dumped his ass over in the Passaic river!"

A stunned silence ensued. "Well, *that's* different," Sam muttered under his breath. "Good job, Dough. You wouldn't happen to have the note he or she left for you as well?"

"Nah, but I could have my assistant bring it to you later today."

"Alright, that's peace," Sam nodded. "Make sure you do that. Even after being in ICU just a few weeks back, I clearly still gotta be the one to overexert my brain cells to figure this one out." He sighed. "Who knows when Escobar is coming back? And Don is somewhere trying to figure out what to think about Stylez. It's a very delicate time right now in our family, and we'll have to tread lightly on all of this."

"No doubt," Hak agreed. "Just let me and this asshole know what you need from us; in the meantime, I think I'll go join my brother over here and help with his 'auditions'." He smiled slimily." At least there'll be some kind of highlight to this day."

"That's a good idea, Hak," Dough responded. "We'll have some brother time. I *miss* that. It feels like it's been—"

"Nigga, I said I'm going to your ranch to feel on some ass and get my dick felt; I didn't say we was going to reminisce about family shit."

"Damn, Hak. That's cold." Jay raised an eyebrow. "Apologize to your brother, right now."

"Do I have to?"

"*Yes*, you pompous son-of-a-bitch!"

Hak sighed and addressed Dough. "Lil' bro, my bad: I shouldn't have said that. You're right: it's been a while since we've spent time together. Let's use this time to be as productive as possible."

"Okay, I could live with that," Dough shrugged. "For a minute, I thought I was going to slice you with this machete I stole off Qurtis Jenkins' wall at his shop."

"Anyways, I'll check ya'll fools out tomorrow," Sam said by way of goodbye, turning from the group.

"Cool. I'm hopping in the Wrangler with my brother. I'll see you at the crib, Jay."

"Hold up, Hak; you riding with Dough?" Jay frowned. "You know, ever since you and Sticks was in that back seat... Nah, let me stop!"

# CHAPTER 43

THE LOOK OUTSIDE WAS a calming one, almost giving Don a sense of life: there was something about the air and the clarity of it in Alpine, NJ, that he truly appreciated.

Since a couple of nights before, when he'd walked out on the family, he'd locked himself in the house and decided to devote his time to business. He'd been in talks regarding creating a new business venture ever since Qurtis Jenkins had been inducted into the family a few years back. Indeed, he told me about one at one point—although, of course, I thought he was bullshitting. However, as time came and went, I started to realize that maybe he was being truthful.

I kid you not, the man literally wanted to produce porno films. For about five years, we all thought it was the funniest thing ever: to this day, we still give each other porno names and provide them with the title to our newest flick. It's actually been quite enjoyable creating all these inventory ideas for his characters and their... plotlines, if you will. Although I'm not exactly sure how much of a plot there can be with these types of "films".

Anyways, he finished the paperwork on what appeared to be his first production entitled *We Aim to Please*—a cumshot extravaganza. Apparently, Blues Holloway will be directing it—which, to be honest, is a good look for Blues: he's an interesting character, and for some reason, I feel like his love for technology and the conspiracy-driven mindset he already has would make him a great porn director. I've yet to find out what the qualifications are for that position, but hey, since we're funding it, who gives a fuck?

The ink was barely dry when he received a call from the Camp Flemington Camp Counselor.

"How the hell are you, Don?" the Chief Counselor asked warmly the second Don pressed the phone to his ear. "I've left numerous messages on

Escobar's voicemail, and I haven't been able to reach Sam Luciano, either. It's that time of year again."

What the chief was referring to was the annual Sponsor-A-Scout camp program we usually did charity work for: this camp held a special place in our hearts as, believe it or not, alongside Don, Sam, Whish, Mula, Sara, and my ex-girlfriend Shadeene, we were all Jr. Camp Counselors when we were kids. Don't ask me how or why we did this, but we had a talent show the camp was putting together, and they asked us to do something separate with the elementary boys and girls.

To make a long story short, we didn't know what to do immediately, so we told the boys that we were counseling to run around the woods for a classic game of hide-and-seek. Because of the open landscape, it made the potential prospect of the game being fun that much more enticing—but, of course, we're natural assholes, and we told them all we'd give them a long head-start before we found them.

They all went running in excitement toward the open fields and tremendously tall trees, and what did we do? We went to the bathroom and took a shit, a three-part harmony shit. Three stalls, right next to each other. While the kids were on a wild goose chase—chasing themselves, mind—, we were sharing an intimate moment together as men.

"You good over there, Sam?" Don had asked from one of the neighboring stalls.

"Oh, I'm great. Yo, Escobar, you alright?"

"I'm currently engaged in quite possibly a Top 5 shit," I'd responded swiftly. "I'd say I'm *more* than alright. But thanks for asking, buddy!"

"Yo, what are we gonna do with these little kids at the talent show?" Don asked. "There's, like, thirty of them. I don't have the mental capacity to try to create something for each of them."

"Yeah, that's not happening," I reassured. "I only wanted to come to camp to try to smash some of the other Camp Counselors from the other schools."

"I was successful in doing so, thank you very much," Don boasted.

"Good man."

"I got it!" Sam suddenly burst out. "Why don't we all go out there and lip sync to *Protect Ya Neck* by the Wu-Tang Clan?"

"That's *genius*," I laughed.

"I'm in. Let's do it." Don paused. "But before we do that, can someone please throw me a roll of toilet tissue? These little bastards used up the last bit in this stall...."

After that, we'd proceeded to do the talent show, performing with the kids on stage to one of the greatest songs ever created. Those kids were jumping around and acting like Ghost, ODB, RZA, METH, RAE, and all the rest of the clan. It was classic, a truly iconic moment. I'm pretty sure you could hear a roach pissing on cotton when it was over—probably because the camp officials were in absolute shock. But fuck it: we killed it.

Now, all these memories came flooding back as Don spoke through the phone. "Chief! How are you on this fine day we're having?" He leaned against the wall. "I'm sorry we haven't exactly been communicating as effectively as we are known for doing: we've been having to deal with some family issues, but all is good in Mobville." Don tried his best to sound convincing.

"I'm fine, Don; thanks for asking. I'm sorry to hear that there's been a bit of turmoil: that's the last thing I want to hear, considering your legendary status here at Camp Flemington." The guy had a very earnest voice; you couldn't help but warm to him. "You know, I still get people who ask about that show you guys put on with those kids so long ago. It was unlike anything we've ever experienced. I do hope all is well as you stated. Should I come around to the office to pick up this years' donation, or will you be mailing it in?"

"I appreciate that trip down Memory Lane, sir; I wasn't sure if we were going to be banned for life, or honored for years to come." Don grinned. "Judging by our long-lasting relationship, I'd say we're good to go."

"You most certainly are."

"You're more than welcomed to drop by; if I'm not here, my assistant will have the donation ready for you."

"Thank you very much," the Chief said warmly. "Send my best to Luciano and Escobar!" And with that, he hung up the line.

Don pulled the phone away from his ear and remembered the innocence of what once had been—when things were so much simpler. He and Stylez had run the streets of 18th Avenue and fought out of more bad situations than they could count. They were very close; the initial terrible twosome before Sam and I had entered the scene. This had been way before MentallyOrganizedBusiness had been established, but there was always something special between us four: we were inseparable, always finishing each other's thoughts and sentences, often sharing our goals and dreams to one another.

Thus, the fact that Joseph Stylez now apparently wanted me dead was just so beyond mind-boggling, to the point where there was no way this could just be "handled": there had to be something so totally off-base here for Stylez to want my head, so to speak. None of us could make any true sense of it—and it's not like this was the only conflict we were dealing with: Don had also just found out about The Curse from Sam Luciano.

Don had no idea what to make about this Curse character: being honest, it sounded like someone was out to give us all our final demise as a collective unit. In all fairness, it felt impossible to count the number of lives we'd ruined, or how much blood we'd spilled on the concrete. In turn, it was also impossible to count the number of people that want us all dead. I believe I stopped counting after the Weequahic brawl—i.e., the same brawl I made reference to earlier in this story. That was the night where my manhood was questioned by a lot of people, my integrity compromised, the night where I became unworthy of being an O3 member. Even though we were kids. Measly teenagers.

For a while, I was made fun of for "running away" when the shit hit the fan that night. However, I've been in many a-fight in my day, so that wasn't my main concern that night: it was protecting my baby sister Pudgee—who was with me that night—no matter what. Without going into any drawn-out details, Don almost lost his life, and Dough and Victor were hardly recognizable after that night. My sister was lost amongst the entirety of the moblike crowd, and in all honesty, I panicked, and could only think of what my parents would think of me if my sister was hurt. I believe I made the choice of being called a coward amongst my street family or being called a coward by my father. I chose the latter instead and went to find her and call for help—serious help.

I've been apologized to by many men since then—some who understood my plight, some who thought it was stupid to hold a grudge toward someone that was only trying to protect his bloodline while obtaining help for everyone who needed it. I've thanked them, and they've done the same in return.

Don shook off the notion that someone was plotting to kill us all one-by-one—although that's what Sam told him he believed. Could that be possible? Or was he just stretching it a bit too much?

At that moment, he called his assistant to ask for the mail, as well as for some help with an ingrown gray hair he'd been chopping off every time it decided to show back up.

"Mirror. *Mirror!*" he shouted to Tiffany. She wordlessly obliged and he snatched it off her, sighing. "Thank you, my dear. Now get the fuck outta here and call up Friday Night Lights; I haven't seen her in a few weeks."

Don then began leafing through his mail, after a few minutes finding one in a hand he didn't recognize. It also looked a lot more appealing than the others for reasons he couldn't put his finger on.

It was not addressed to anyone in particular, but it did have a return address: P.O. Box 13152. *What the hell is this? Niggas really use PO Box addresses?* Don thought to himself, shaking his head. Should he even read it? He wasn't sure if he'd be able to take anymore crazy shit right now.

After a few minutes, his curiosity got the better of him: he shrugged his shoulders and decided to open the envelope. Inside was a small card, and he read its contents slowly. Aloud.

*To the Don...*

He smirked a little acknowledging that he kinda liked how this asshole was addressing him.

*To the Don:*
*You are cordially invited to the biggest event of the century on: May 19th, 1996. Everyone who is everyone will be there—I've even invited Bruce Wayne. That guy is batshit crazy. Let's hope he shows up this time! Be there or be killed. Ciao!*

*—The Curse*

*The Curse?* Don thought incredulously. *What kinda Witches from Eastwick shit is this? Sounds like he takes it up the ass.*

Regardless of his thoughts, he knew full well he'd be going to this event, ignoring the impact this would eventually have on his life by rummaging through the rest of his mail. After discarding that month's water and sewer bills, he found a letter from Joseph Stylez's mother. A quick scan of it informed Don that Stylez had been locked up for the last few weeks, for various undisclosed reasons. She also mentioned that he was checked into a rehab facility for heavy usage of illegal substances—again, also undisclosed.

She ended the note by saying that his address was the only one she had in her little address book, and that she felt if anybody outside of blood family should know what was going on with Stylez, it should be him.

She left her home phone number on the bottom of the card and signed it delicately.

Don felt he was in a different kind of headspace, a mental level he was unsure he'd ever experienced before: an advanced placement of utter disbelief. He read the letter not once, not twice, but four more times to ensure he'd registered its contents.

He closed his eyes, a pressure headache building up behind his eyes, and sat all the way back on his black leather chaise chair. He reminisced on the hell they'd raised together and the incredible times he'd shared with Stylez.

Don couldn't wrap his head around how this could have happened. He thought about how differently Joseph had acted after Remington passed away. Sam and the rest of his family were right: Don just hadn't wanted to believe it, but at this junction, he had to.

He waved over to his assistant and whispered to her, "Tell Friday Night Lights her presence isn't needed after all. Maybe tomorrow."

Joseph Stylez had a serious problem, and it had to be dealt with for the betterment of him—whatever that was.

It was at that moment that Don decided to go upstairs for an afternoon nap, and, just as he mounted the first step, he received a call from yours truly.

"Yo, Don! What's poppin', Slime? I just learned some new shit about Stylez."

"Word? How coincidental: so did I."

"I'm out here in Paris, and I'm feeling refreshed. My mind is clear, and I have a plan on how to approach Stylez about this conflict of alleged business between us." I paused. "Well, that is, until I received a mysterious email from Brilliant Bobby Bushetta. He has some information about Stylez."

"Well, what did he say?"

I paused. "Brilliant Bobby has been monitoring certain areas with that new technology we used to trap Jake Solomon, and, believe it or not, he stumbled across some footage of Stylez coming out of a lounge on Scotland Road. He hopped into a little Nissan Sentra and drove right up a hill for about half a mile up before getting out. He was being greeted at the curb by none other than Dukeland Orange."

"Dukeland Orange?" Don echoed. "That fake producer motherfucker who's stole more dreams than The Sandman? Are you fucking kidding me?"

"Exactly my point, brother. You thinking what I'm thinking?"

"Always," Don affirmed without hesitation. "Call me the minute you're back in town."

# CHAPTER 44

CELO HAD RECENTLY BEEN having a conversation with his grandmother, Peachy the Great. She told him that one day, he'd recognize the actual reason that God put him on this earth; indeed, although Peachy never condoned any of the suspicious MentallyOrganizedBusiness activities, she instantly chose to take favor in the family ties and loyalty we had for each other. I can only assume that is the reason why she kept making us her amazing biscuits and allowed us all to call her Peachy, which is what only her relatives were permitted to called her.

Celo had been gone for a few weeks now and had already made an impact on his new community in Raleigh, NC. He loved his new home as well as the atmosphere it created, and, although he felt alone at times, he was sincerely appreciative of the fact that he could finally see his kids at beck and call; that was a fulfilling enough.

Over the past month or so, he'd been reading up on The Good Book—the one where The Most High speaks to us and we listen because we are natural-born sinners.

I remember him telling me a while back that he'd been thinking about doing God's work, and—and I mean this in the most respectful way possible—I'd told him I already thought what we were doing—getting rid of the trash on these streets—*was* God's work. He assured me it wasn't, and so I of course called him a liar. It was then that he Ric Flair chopped me across the top part of my chest for his troubles; indeed, most of us were big wrestling fans, and would often play out a lot of what we saw on TV into our everyday lives. I'm pretty sure Celo and Reeeno Nevada took turns Super Kicking some loser from Chancellor Avenue until he literally choked on his own teeth. It was a gruesome sight, but nevertheless impressive.

He said he had a greater purpose. I knew that he didn't know what it was exactly, but I knew that whatever decision he ended up making, I was going to support it 1000%: Celo Gaston had been my brother for quite some time, and we all often laughed about how his jokes were so corny, as well as about how he was the butt of most of our clowning around in and of itself. The man would even try to sing, and I believe I put a hit out on him at one point because I couldn't stand to hear another blasphemous note seep out of his esophagus. His voice literally sounded like a ghost getting raped—or perhaps a bag of forks being scraped across a chalkboard. Or, better yet, a ghost being raped with a bag of forks.

I spoke to him a few days after he left and he told me he was joining a local non-denominational church; he'd just felt compelled to do so, and so he had. Week after week, he reported feeling more and more alive, more and more needed. He started to realize he had found his calling. It was true: Celo Gaston had officially become a Deacon. Gone were the many sins he'd committed in the lonely streets of Ghost Town, NJ; forgiven were the many transgressions he had engaged in. Celo Gaston was ridded of what he felt had held his spirit down for so very long. He was out.

He called me and told me he was out of the family business, but he was never out of the family. I obliged his wishes and, with Don and Sam's blessings, Celo Gaston was no more. Out was Celo, and in was Poppa.

He was then introduced to a man who would later become his spiritual dad, a man that told him Celo had a very nurturing yet protective demeanor about him. This father figure possessed the same kind of love for Celo that one would normally possess for his newborn infant—and yet somehow on a grander scale. He nicknamed him Poppa because of it.

This was a man that held no boundaries on telling you how it is or was but was spiritually bonded to the Holy Spirit. Celo often spoke highly of his spiritual dad, and he told us that soon enough, he'd find his queen— but not before he was finished finding himself. Once self-clarity was established, self-redemption could commence.

I had no qualms with Celo deciding to do this; from a selfish standpoint, I needed my brother, and I didn't want him to go, but from a more understanding perspective, I later took heed and comfort in the fact that my need for him in my life was lesser than the need he had to discover himself. When you think about it, the two really don't compare, and I was happy enough to know he was enjoying his life—and, perhaps most importantly, helping people along the way.

Two days ago, he called me and shared the fact that he'd been seeing someone recently, and that he believed she might be a keeper. Either waym he was going to take it slow and see where God took him from there, which I agreed was the correct approach.

Celo Gaston is a man's man, a man of integrity and compassion. He's one of my best friends in this entire world, and I'm elated to call him by brother. Thus, it was around this time that I called him up and asked him to come back home on May 19<sup>th</sup>, even if it was just for the weekend. He agreed without hesitation.

"Why that date, though?" he asked curiously. "Is it someone's birthday I'm forgetting?"

"We're all invited to a gala of some sort," I responded casually. I'd already decided not to tell him exactly what it was: I was fearful he wouldn't come. Once again, I chose forgiveness instead of permission—something we do often as humans.

Celo walked into his backyard, where his dad and his brother Eduardo were starting a campfire. He loved those nights where he could just sit amongst the men in his family, talking about anything and everything in life. Life is a beautiful thing if you treat it with the respect it deserves. The moment a person starts to dishonor the gift that Life indeed is, is the same moment that person's life begins to end faster than it was destined to.

As I've told you before, Celo Gaston has always been a different kind of guy—very much so a twin of mine when it came to most things. Chances are very high that I would've probably chosen that path myself if I wasn't an O3 member: my responsibilities to the organization and that number of people that were just too heavy to neglect. Maybe one day in the future, I'd make that move to a calmer setting with my wife and children—perhaps let the younger kids attend high school within a better system. Maybe we'd join him in North Carolina. My wife had always been a Tar Heels fan, so at least she'd fit in. Saying this, I've always favored Georgia, personally. But we'll see. I just knew that right now was not the time.

# CHAPTER 45

"ESCOBAR! WHERE THE HELL are you, man? I haven't seen you since the Mets won the World Series!"

"Real funny, Al," I sighed through the phone. "I can't stop laughing. Can you hear?"

In case you haven't noticed, Al Gebra is an absolute prick—and also one of the smartest guys I know. However, the worst part about him is his lack of acceptance that I'm just as smart. He isn't a fan of this: he always likes to get the last word, the last laugh. I can't tell you how often and how long our hiking sessions have been: I believe we went back and forth for almost an hour one time, just me and him. I believe it went a little something like this:

"Yo!" he had greeted. "I'm about to try this rap shit out."

"You don't know nothing about that rap shit, son," I'd shot back. "What's your rap name gonna be? Tap Money?"

"*No*, you fuckin' Ren-and-Stimpy booty-juice-sippin'-ass nigga!"

"You sure, you fuckin' Ladies-Love Cool-James vodka-slippers-wearin'—"

"Ahh, you big Weehawken-cupcakes-baking—"

"Whoopty-whoopt ass nigga, slip-and-slide-music-subscription-havin'—"

"*We Are The Titans* herringbone-coat-wearing—"

...And so on. I kid you not, this would go on and on and on and on and on. We were two absolute fools, and we knew it. We physically couldn't stop competing with one another: it was quite literally the foundation of our relationship—and I loved my brother for that.

"Yo, when are you coming back home?" Al asked me now.

"We're actually on the way back now. I should touchdown by early morning. Everything good?"

"Oh, yeah, Sara is doing much better." The genuine happiness in his voice was contagious. "Obviously she's not medically cleared for any real business activities, but my queen will be back to full health in no time. Luciano is here now. I wanted to reach out to you about some new business."

"What's on your mind?" I asked.

"Sam, you tell him!" Al called.

There was some muffled static on the other end of the line before Sam's voice rang through.

"Brother, did you guys have a good time away?" came his warm tone.

"Absolutely! Just what we all needed. I'm ready to get to work, though. What's up?"

"Good to hear. Ol' Al Gebra is up to his 'take over the world" shit again is all."

"What's new? That's what drives the man, and that's all love right there." I paused. "Al, what's on your mind, man? Tell me."

Al took a moment to speak. "I think we should start that record label we always wanted to do and sign that local group—Krome 45—as our first act."

I grinned. "You know I've always wanted to do that. Every time I wanna pull the trigger on that move, we end up having to pull the trigger on some fool!"

"I know, trust me."

"Sam, what do you think about this?" I asked.

"I think it's a great idea," Sam said apprehensively, "but we gotta smooth this shit out with Stylez before anything—and then there's this stupid Curse shit that's reared its ugly head."

"Curse thing? The fuck you talkin' 'bout?" Al demanded.

Sam's sigh crackled down the line. "That's the reason I came over here, Al. Don told me he's been trying to call you, and for some reason you were the only Great 8 member he couldn't contact. So I opted to pop up at your house to tell you myself."

"Damn. My bad Sam; I've been really caught up in my work these past couple of months."

"I don't doubt it, Al."

"Well, what *is* this Curse shit, then?" Al asked again. "Sounds like a disease."

Sam addressed me again. "Escobar, you wanna tell him, or should I?"

"I got it, Sam," I responded. "Al, The Curse is simple: I'm pretty sure it's your moms trying to play a hoax on us because she used to hate when we turned any lights on at your house." I grinned as memories came flooding back in quick succession. "Remember when it was mad dark at Al's house when we used to go chill over there, Sam?"

"How could I forget?" he answered, "I lost my jeans over there once, and I didn't even take them off."

"C'mon, son, the electricity bill was *mad* high," Al reasoned. "We had to keep the lights off. At least my moms was conservative with her day-to-day operations and not hustling niggas for their money, like *both* your mothers!"

"Excuse me?"

"Oh, so now you gon' front and not admit that your moms use to run niggas pockets playing dominoes? And Sam, don't laugh over there; we remember when Mrs Luciano was running a Pitty Pat ring from the basement at your house!"

"He's got a point, Sam," I pointed out.

"Alright, alright, but can we get down to business?" Sam sighed. "You fuckin' Theo Huxtable dress-shirt-wearin'-ass niggas."

I sighed. "Al, in all honesty: we don't know who or what this Curse shit is."

"Apparently, he's sent notes to Hak and Jay's crib and Dough's ranch, too," Sam added. "We honestly don't know what the hell is going on around here."

"Me, Sam, and Don all received invitations to Galloping Hill by The Curse for May 19th, and that's the extent of the information we have," I continued. "I guess he wants us all there. I don't give a flying fuckstick about this dude; I'd rather be watching *YO! MTV Raps*, or some shit." I exhaled. "It's a few weeks away anyway, but we'll deal with it as we always do: once that stupid shit is over with, we're going to go full throttle with the record label."

"You sure?" Al checked. "Do any of us have anything to worry about? Are we going into this blind?"

"Nah, I don't think so," Sam said. "We're always prepared; we just gotta make sure everyone is on their a-game that night, that's all."

"Alright, man; if you're confident, then I am, too." Al seemed lost in thought for a moment. "So, to get back to what I was saying earlier: I'm telling you, Krome 45 is the truth. Have you heard their song *45 Ways to Die*? Or *Havoc*? That shit is sick."

"I have, actually," I mused. "I picked a mixtape up downtown a little while back, and I love their shit. I like Necessary Ruffness too, but I believe Karl Kani picked them up on his new music label."

"That's that bullshit," Al fumed. "I would've loved to have had the two hottest groups coming out simultaneously on our label."

"Agreed," I seconded. "If I had my choice, I would've picked Necessary Ruffness, though; plus, I heard one of them can sing, too—and not some rinky dink shit, either. Like, sing for *real*." I sighed. "Overall, their sound is more seasoned, but Krome 45 is going to be special."

"Al, have you thought of a name for the label?" Sam asked.

"What do y'all think about Foul Mouth Recordz?"

# CHAPTER 46

*Location: Used Car Dealer; St. Georges Avenue; Avenel, NJ;*
*May 1; 8:15 pm*

THERE REALLY WAS NO ill intent, but of course, things ended up that way: Harry Horrendous was in a celebratory mode because he woke up yesterday and could speak clearly again. His new teeth were fitted nicely. It's not like everything was 100% yet, but at least you could tell what he was saying now.

Harry, Johnny Sliver, Lexington Arms, and Billy DrumSticks wanted to buy new whips; it was a spur-of-the-moment decision, and they knew the dealership was closed for the remainder of the week because of some bogus hours they had. Thus, they decided to go check out the many used car lots on the strip, eventually finding one that was still open. It was after 8pm, and Harry pulled up and saw they were closing thirty minutes later.

"We got some time," he informed the crew. "Let's look around."

The boys parked the hooptie they were in—really a getaway car—and hopped out, Lexington having brought a big duffel bag with him. Only Harry knew what was in there.

They saw a Mercedes, Audi, Volkswagen, and even a Porsche—the latter of which Harry instantly gravitated to. He told Sliver to go into the little lobby and grab the guy in there: he had a few questions for him regarding the purchase of that vehicle specifically.

While Silver was doing so, Harry felt the beautiful finish of the car's hood. It was a 4.6-6cylinder engine motor—he'd done his homework. He would have normally favored a brand-new one, but a one- or two-year-old used one would serve just fine.

Meanwhile, Billy DrumSticks was admiring a classic tan Nova with manual transmission; it was considered a muscle car, which was more his style anyway. Lexington tagged along with Harry as h didn't have a car of his own—or a license, for that matter. I never knew how he'd been successful without one, but he certainly managed.

Suddenly, the lobby door swung open and there was Sliver with the guy from inside; he had the guy by the back of his collar, and there was blood dripping from the side of his mouth.

"Sliver, what the fuck are you doing?" Harry demanded. Meanwhile, Billy was inconsolable with laughter.

"This guy sucks," Lexington muttered.

"What do you mean, what am I doing?" Silver echoed, eyes wide. "You asked me to get the guy from inside!"

"As in, ask him to come outside so I can speak to him about potentially purchasing this car!"

"Well, you should be more specific next time."

"You gotta be kidding me," Harry exclaimed, burying his face in his hands. He turned to the bruised, bloody representative. "Sir, I'm so sorry about this: we didn't mean no harm. We all apologize for your pain. I'll pay whatever medical bills you have."

The car guy was writhing in Silver's grip, his swollen, bloody lips making his words nearly unintelligible. "Stupid fuckin' niggers."

Harry froze. "Excuse me? What did you say?"

"He called us some stupid fuckin' niggers!" Silver hissed.

"Nah, I don't think he'd do that. Would you, Sir?" Lexington said. "Could you be that dumb? You realize there's four of us and only one of you, right?"

"Why are you people here?" was all the representative apparently had to say.

"'You people'?" Billy echoed incredulously.

"I wasn't bothering nobody!" the guy continued. He was digging himself a deeper and deeper hole here. "I've been here on this lot for thirty-five years and never had problems in this neighborhood 'til this moment. I helped gentrify this entire area, and I see that time is changing!"

"Yeah, like, thirty years ago, you damn fool!" Harry spat.

"What are you people doing here?" the representative said again. "What do you want? I don't have any cash on me; I don't carry cash on my property here. I don't have any drugs, or any bootlegs of any kind. Can you just leave me alone?"

Harry eyed the pathetic man levelly. "Sir—and I say that loosely—, we came here to buy a car. That's what people do here, right? At a car dealership? I understand that my friend here acted out a little impulsively, but I want to extend my apologies, and I will leave you my card so you can send me the bill to cover for the obvious medical expenses."

"I don't want your stupid fuckin' card!" the man yelled out. "I'm going to press charges on *all* of you! I've already jotted a mental note on the license plate you rolled up in here on. I've got friends in high places, so this should be a breeze for me!"

Billy sighed and turned to Harry. "Can we just kill him now? I'm bored—and hungry."

Harry ignored Billy, instead addressing the car dealer again. "Sir, again, I assure you we were here to buy a car— this Porsche right here, more specifically. How much are you selling it for?"

"I don't sell to criminals," the car guy spat, "especially stupid nigger criminals! That Porsche costs more than a year's worth of education at Harvard University; you couldn't afford it anyway!"

"I think he's delirious," Lexington reasoned. "He doesn't know what he's saying. Let's get the fuck outta here; there's plenty of used car lots along this strip."

"Maybe you're right," Harry admitted. "Besides, this racist asshole ain't worth the third bullet in my chamber. I actually have it on reserve for someone already."

"You do? How thoughtful of you."

"Boys, let's bounce," Harry declared.

"I thought you'd leave after I threatened to sue you and call my cop friends over here!" the car dealer said triumphantly. "Oh, what do we have here? Just in time."

Sure enough, a cop was pulling up, blocking the group from exiting the lot. An officer swiftly emerged.

"Excuse me, Sir, are you okay?" he asked, addressing the dealer. "We got a call from a civilian who saw there was some kind of disruption going on here. Is that true?"

"Yes, Officer!" Harry could've slapped the fucker. "I want these niggers arrested! They came in here with no intent to buy anything and ransacked my lobby and stole the money out of my drawer!"

"This fool is lying on us! Wow!" Billy laughed.

"I can't believe I'm hearing this," Harry muttered. "Ya'll stay in the car; I got this."

Thankfully, the group obliged. The officer swiftly walked over and addressed Harry.

"Sir, please roll your window down all the way. Sir, this gentleman says..." He then halted mis-sentence, recognition sparking. "Harry?"

"Hilltop?"

"Holy *shit!*" the officer laughed. "How long has it *been*? Ten, fifteen years?"

"Sounds about right." Harry motioned to the rest of the crew. "Look who's in the car!"

The officer scanned the group and, sure enough, his face lit up. "Billy? Arms? You gotta be kidding me! Is that Sliver back there?"

"It's me, Hilltop!" Silver affirmed. "What's poppin', homie?"

"I can't believe this!"

The car guy, meanwhile, was unimpressed, to say the least. "Hello?" he called, waving an arm. "I'm still bleeding, and I haven't seen you take them into the back of your cop car."

The officer ignored the dealer, instead handing Harry a piece of card. "Here's my number; don't lose it. Let's get together for drinks next week sometime. I'm gonna make an excuse to leave right now." He shot the dealer a look of disdain over his shoulder. "I hate this fuckin' guy: calls us every time someone of color comes onto his property." He grinned mischievously at the group. "It's the first time I've seen him bleeding, though. Good job!"

With that, Hilltop turned to the dealer and made up some far-fetched story about a mass murderer on the loose in Ghost Town, meaning he had to leave, and that he was sorry. Harry laughed to himself and briefly considered getting out of the car and just ignoring the little racist guy until he opened his big fat mouth again.

"You haven't heard the last of me! You people are all the same! Just come around here, trying to take stuff that's not yours, things that none of you ever worked for! You're disgusting! I can't believe God even created you!"

The guy was really on one. Harry had been rolling towards the exit until he had heard that last sentence, after which he made the almost instinctive decision to put his car in reverse, turn around, and use the rearview mirror as a perfect visual assistance. He then floored the gas and ran the racist car guy down to the ground. He put the car in drive, moved up some, put the car in reverse, moved back some... and repeat.

After a few moments, the boys in the back started high-fiving one another, Harry getting out of the car to survey the damage. As it happened, the tailpipe was lodged inside the guy's throat. Harry kneeled down and closed his eyelids, whispering delicately in his ear, "If only you would've kept your mouth shut."

Harry headed back to the car, asked Lexington to pass him the black duffel bag, and, with it hand, walked inside the lobby and found the matching tag information on the key for the Porsche he'd wanted. He took $15,000 out of the bag and threw it down onto the carcass.

"If you were nicer, I would've given you the whole thirty thousand— hell, if you were nicer, I may have thrown in more to sweeten the deal." He surveyed the gruesome. "You may have still been alive."

He felt vilified. It was a certain kind of joy that was emancipating over him at that moment. His original plan to foil Jake Solomon had gone to hell when he and Snugglez had got into that accident, and it had been eating away at his soul that he wasn't around to help with the plan, or the aftermath. However, as he proceeded to hop into the Porsche, calling the rest of the crew to hop inside, he felt good.

They sped off into the night like the automotive prowlers they were.

# CHAPTER 47

*Location: Maplewood Diner; May 3; 8:00 pm*

SARA, WHISH, MULA, AND Yelly met at one of the town's best diners for dinner, Whish and Sara arriving together—as usual—, while Mula and Yelly drove in separately. Sara was finally feeling up to being back out in public; she couldn't drive yet, but could definitely get around on her own, which was obviously a very good thing.

They swiftly ordered everything on the menu: a feast fit for queens only.

Yelly and I had just returned that morning from our two-and-a-half-week vacation: it was like a massive burden had been lifted from our shoulders and whisked away into the deepest part of the ocean, never to be found again. We both returned rejuvenated and ready to make our next moves in life, having discussed the issues with Stylez and if she was ready to make a geographical move. Nonetheless, we spent great quality time together, and that's what was most important.

The waitress didn't bring back the lasagna Mula had ordered, but Mula was, thankfully, in good humor and let the young lady off the hook. This waitress didn't know how damn lucky she actually was.

Mula Madison then ordered drinks for everyone in the house. The other ladies eyed one another suspiciously: they didn't know what to make of Mula's exceptionally good mood. It was then that a young lady came over to the table, greeting everyone warmly, as though she had been invited.

"Well look who finally decided to show up!" Sara said good-naturedly. "You're late, girl!"

Yelly and Mula eyed one another in complete bewilderment. Sara noticed this and beamed at them both.

"Yelly, Mula, I heard you've already made acquaintance with Ms Jordache Blu?"

Yelly looked like she wanted the ground to swallow her up. "You know what, we have."

Mula was fuming. "*Really*, Sara? And just when I was in a great mood tonight..." She started looking around. "Where's that waitress that fucked up my lasagna order? I feel like smacking her right about now."

Whish, utterly confused, said, "What's going on, ladies?"

Sara smirked. "Well, our trusty counterparts here decided to pay Ms Blu a visit at her workplace not too long ago."

"And?"

Sara seemed very amused by this whole ordeal. "Well... Let's just say they almost shot a gun inside of a school."

"*What*?!" Whish said, the whites of her eyes showing.

"They locked this teacher up in her own classroom and interrogated her for fifteen minutes straight while scaring the living bejesus out of her."

Whish shook her head in dismay. "And why would they do something like that? C'mon, these are our contemporaries, our equals. Surely they had good reason to?"

"Oh, they had good intentions, yes," Sara affirmed, nodding solemnly. "Just not solid reasonings."

"What do you mean?"

Sara turned to the two women. "Who's gonna answer that one for our sister, then?"

Yelly was gripping the sides of her seat so hard, her knuckles were going white. "Mula and I here got the drop on Ms Blu," she said through clenched teeth. "As it turns out, a false lead was given to us by one of our street informants that Ms Blue had something to do with Sara's attack at the nail salon last month; so, of course, we went to check it out, and it turned out to be nothing. Simple."

"Nothing?" Sara echoed, raising an eyebrow. "You held a woman *hostage* in her own classroom, pushed her down to the floor, and, if I know Mula, you probably wanted to kill her right then and there, didn't you?"

Mula looked hurt. "How could you think I'd kill someone on school grounds? What kind of a monster do you think I am?"

"Well, when we spotted her alone in her classroom, you *did* offer to take her out right then and there," Yelly reminded her.

Mula whipped around to frown at Yelly. "Whose side are *you* on?"

Ms Blu sighed. "If I may, I was scared out of my mind; I'd never been in any kind of confrontation like that before in my entire life. I avoid confrontation as much as I can."

"We could tell," Mula admitted.

"How the hell were you guys so wrong, then?" Whish asked, looking faintly amused. "Where did you get your information from?"

"You know that new dark-skinned chick with the funny-looking wig? Been down Nye Avenue over by Slicks for about six months now."

"Slicks? That corny-ass strip club?"

"Yeah, that one!" Mula said. "Well, anyway, I've had a few informants around that way for the past few years, but this new one had me feeling a certain type of way: I felt like I was being looked at by a man the whole time we were getting our info because she kept looking down my shirt."

Realization suddenly dawned in Sara's eyes, her jaw quite literally dropping open. "Hold up; did you say Nye Avenue? By Grove Street?"

"Yeah, why?"

"Oh, Mula, Mula, Mula." Sara's eyes were sparkling. "I think you losing your touch, girl! You got *duped!*"

"What you mean?" Mula asked, panicked.

"You know why you felt like you were being watched by a man?" Sara laughed. "Because you *were*, fool! Remember Quiet Riot?"

Whish audibly gasped. "No, shut the front door all the way and then shut the fuck up!"

Mula frowned. "Sara Safebreaka, are you implying that I didn't recognize my own brethren?"

Sara was cackling. "I think it's safe to say there is clearly *no* implication going on here: you just didn't know!"

Mula held her hands up. "Okay, okay I get it, but I still don't understand: why would he be dressed up as a woman out on the streets like that? And why would he give me false information?"

Sara sighed. "Ladies, for those of you who don't know, Quiet Riot has played for the other team for quite some time now; I don't know if he always did, but he has for a very long time. He was a part of those original step teams with Reeeno Nevada, Celo Gaston, Harry, and Snugglez—oh, and Hilltop, Drumsticks, and Yelly's husband, Mr. PR Escobar himself."

"Yes, yes, of course," Whish said. "It's been so long since I've seen him; I knew he decided to walk out on the fellas a long time ago, but I didn't know it was because of *this* craziness."

Sara shrugged. "From what I know, the guys were beside themselves: they ousted him, but because he was family at one point, they decided not to harm him."

"Wow," Yelly breathed. "This is all news to me."

"I guess it kinda makes sense why he was dressed the way he was," Mula conceded, "but again, why single out your girl over here?"

Ms Blu began to speak. "I've been listening and while you ladies were talking, it dawned on me: Quiet Riot was a student of my mother's. I remember her telling me how he was the quietest thing walking, but he hated her, for some reason. He made my Mothers' Day a living hell; I couldn't forget that name if I wanted to. She's passed on now, so I can only imagine he tried to use you guys to get back at my mother through me."

"Makes sense," Whish muttered.

"Ain't that a bitch?" Mula said somewhat lightheartedly.

"Again, I want to apologize for scaring you like that," Yelly said quietly. "As you can tell, we're all very close, and we'll stop at nothing to fight back for one of our own."

"That I see," Ms Blu responded, "and I admire that; I admire *all* of you ladies for what you do for yourselves and your families. I never actually knew what Sara did for a living, but I guess I do now. Your secret is safe with me," she added, winking at Sara.

"Oh, it's no secret, Jordache," Sara shrugged. "Everyone knows me: one of Ghost Town's elite. I'm an original M.O.B. member; this is in my blood, who I am—who we are."

"And once again, my admiration is high," Jordache smiled. "Nice of you to ask me to join you here tonight, Sara. I'll be seeing you soon; I have to meet with Mr. Blu."

"Actually, I think we wouldn't have been able to get through the night without you. We thank you. Yelly and I will see you at the hockey game this Saturday, yes?"

"That you will. See you then!"

After she had left, Whish turned to the rest of the women. "She's such a nice girl. I hope you two didn't rough her up too much."

"Nah, I don't think so," Yelly said flippantly.

"She's cool," Mula said. "Not M.O.B. material, but cool."

"Agreed. Now where the hell are my lobster tails?" Sara demanded. "I ordered them shits, like, two hours ago!"

"By the way, Sara, I think you have some explaining to do yourself," Whish countered.

"Explaining?"

Whish leaned back in her chair. "How in the hell did you know the informant was Quiet Riot? You never go to those places in the 'hood."

Sara frowned. "What are you insinuating?"

"No insinuation. Just merely asking a question."

"Come to think of it, yeah; how the hell *did* you know that?" Yelly frowned, spearing some food with her fork.

"Okay, okay," Sara surrendered, flushing slightly. "Al was feeling frisky one night and I clearly had too much to drink, so I was going to pick one of those nightwalkers up."

Whish collapsed into giggles. "You nasty motherfucker!"

"You picked up Quiet Riot!" Mula squealed. "This is the greatest day of my life! Bartender shots for everybody on me!"

"Fuk ya'll, I'm out," Sara huffed. "And fuk these lobster tails, too!"

# CHAPTER 48

*Location: Escobar Residence; May 5; 8:30 pm*

I NEEDED A SHOWER—bad. I'd just finished having sexy time with my beautiful wife, and she was fast asleep already. Man, that woman drives me crazy; in a good way.

I stepped into my shower while playing Illmatic on the speakers—one of the greatest albums of all time by one of the greatest writers of all time, Nas.

I think I got to at least the third track by the time I was ready to get out. Don and Sam were on the way to meet up with me so we could go over the plans for the Stylez situation.

I leaned out to look over in my room from my master suite bathroom to check on my wife, who was out like Pace Won. I walked in and kissed her on her big Mother Africa forehead, something I kidded her about all the time; but hey, that's my queen, and I'm allowed do that—well, sometimes. *You* talk shit about it, on the other hand, and I'll kill you. Plain and simple.

I walked downstairs to the front porch and grabbed me a Corona with grenadine for while I waited for my brothers to arrive. I began thinking how our newest plan of execution was going to taste so good to so many people; see, this whole ordeal is a bit out-of-the-ordinary for us, as, believe it or not, we usually don't strike first. We're peaceful people, really; that is, until you provoke us. As Tony Victor would say: "Aww, they're adorable".

Truth be told, we didn't know a lot of these people who may not make it home in a couple nights: indeed, they don't know us, and we don't know them—although we know *of* each other, of course. Our issue lay in the effect they had on our brother, Joseph Stylez: the filling of his head with 100% garbage was a huge contributory factor to his wanting me killed. When someone is fed something long enough—especially when under the influence of something that won't render their regular thoughts and move patterns—, there's no direction: they become a pawn; a robot; a real-life puppet.

In my heart, Joseph Stylez never wanted me dead: he didn't know *what* he wanted, because he hasn't been in his right mind for a long time. When someone has crossed that line with themselves, it's awfully hard to detoxify their mind and body. There was no way Dukeland Orange wasn't going to pay for this. It was just a matter of time.

The doorbell rang and I let the butler get it, remaining comfortably seated on my recliner chair. There was a gorgeous plate of hors d'oeuvres my chef had put together for us. He's a good man; I think I'll invite him to my birthday party.

Don Corione and Sam Luciano entered and gave me two long hugs: brotherly love at its best. Sam then walked over to my kitchen closet and grabbed the broom, starting to sweep in front of me.

"Sam, what the hell you doing, yo?"

"Clearly someone didn't see the game this afternoon."

"Oh, come on!" I cried out. The Mets are gonna stink for the next five years or so!"

Sam shrugged. "Nevertheless, they got swept today by the Philadelphia Phillies. How do you feel about that?"

"Fuck baseball," Don muttered.

"Like I knew it. Like I prepared for that before the season started, when I saw we played them in a three-game series early in the year. But hey, thanks for the reminder."

"Anytime, brother," Sam grinned.

"I wish I could understand baseball, but it's so *boring*," Don moaned. "I'd rather watch grass grow alongside a wall I'm watching fresh paint dry on."

I turned to Don. "I can't thank you enough for being one of the biggest assholes in the history of all anal research and record-keepings."

"You're quite welcome, Sir," said Don, bowing. "Now, can we get to business?"

"Certainly," I responded. "So, how do we get onto the estate, or the land, or whatever the hell this jackass lives on?"

"We'll get Brilliant Bobby on that," Don shrugged, "but we already did the house trap. I was thinking about something bigger—something with pizazz. Something with brightness. Something—"

"Actually, I was thinking the opposite," I cut in. "I just wanna walk into that man's house, put a hot one through his heart, and call it a day."

"Sounds like a plan to me," Sam chipped in.

"Then it's settled."

"What? No! No! No!" Don protested. "That's unacceptable! He needs a slow, torturous ending."

"No, he doesn't," Sam sighed.

"Why's that unacceptable?" I asked. "It's quick and to the point. Does Dukeland Orange really deserve any more of our time, considering what he's done?"

"That's a negative," Sam answered before Don could respond. "That son-of-a-bitch stole our brother from us! That fuckin' guy destroyed the careers—and, more importantly, the *lives*—of countless aspiring artists, all so he could make a fast buck on their instant fame and then ultimately fuck them out of their paper by showing them the 'laps of luxury'." He shook his head, the tips of his ears going red as he got more and more riled up. "Don't get me wrong, Stylez is a man, and he made his own decisions and must reap them; but when is enough enough with this fuckin' guy? I've wanted him dead for a *long* time based off of principal, but never had a personal reason to justify it. Now, I think it's very warranted."

I let his words sink in for a moment. "Okay, I agree. So, what do you propose?"

Don shrugged. "I say we kill him."

"Well, no shit. But how?" We all elapsed into thoughtful silence before I shouted out "Wait a minute, I got it!"

"Got what? Milk? Gonorrhea? Five on it?"

"No, my easily-deterred, hip-hop-aficionado friend. We knock on his door and we let ourselves in. That's all."

# CHAPTER 49

**Location: Twisted Sins Bunny Ranch; May 6; 11:00 am**

A S A RESULT OF Salawicious Dough and Hak Hennesey holding "auditions" at the bunny ranch a few days before, there was work to be done: they saw sixteen women and narrowed it down to four. The job only required two, but Salawicious Dough figured he'd make a new special program—hey, maybe even building a new room at the bunny ranch for the other two. He just couldn't decide between the ladies.

There was Lexi Kisses, Trinity Glow, Rebecca Hinch, and Tish Paris, the latter of which being a beautiful, sultry young woman who fancied herself as a world champion in women's' wrestling in the early 80s.

In summary, these women were incredible, and would bring you to your knees—in more ways than one—if they needed to. It was safe to say their auditions were long and somewhat tasty—yes, tasty, like the chicken spot by the bus terminal down Ghost Town center. That reminds me I need to pick up a check from there: they pay us to promote their business because we've been long-term customers. At first, they refused to do business with us: they were cheap Arab fucks who only wanted to make money with their own kind—that is, until Tony Victor and Hak Hennesey went behind the counter one day and literally stuffed five Italian cheeseburgers up the owner's ass. I believe Tony told me the guy was shittin' fries for a week straight. Nevertheless, since then, it's been a great working relationship—although Frederick Linguini still threatens our new business partners from time to time.

Anyway, Dough figured he could make Trinity Glow and Lexi Kisses into independent acts down the road, they were that damn good. All his bunnies started out with tag team partners—it was much easier to satisfy the customer that way, as there was less pressure to deliver on your own as a new employee. Dough could be a considerate man... Well, for his bunnies, anyway.

Tish and Rebecca would work in the room Licki Bella and Tasha Banks used to use. Outside the room, Dough had made a shrine of them of sorts: not of their faces, but of imprints of each of their vaginas in a frame. This was rather normal for Dough, as you may have gathered by now: It was like collecting fingerprints for him. I'm pretty sure there were also actual sculptures of each of their vaginas sitting on his office desk; he had a custom molding company that could bring anything to life, in a sense, and then finish it off with a gorgeous gold coating of some sort. If you think about it, that's crazy as hell—but then again, if you're secure in your sexuality and open to art, then it's also pretty fuckin' awesome.

Twisted Sins Bunny Ranch was back and open for business, and Dough couldn't be happier: he had a new inventory available, as well as a full blow-up doll rendition of his new workers. Unfortunately, his happiness was only to last about fifteen minutes.

It was when he went out the back to get something from the flatbed of one of his company trucks that he noticed a really big black bag that he didn't recall putting there. He went to grab it before realizing it seemed a little heavy.

His curiosity getting the better of him, he climbed onto the back of the truck to get a better look and grip of the bag itself—in vain: he still couldn't figure out what was in there. However, it took a moments for him to instantly recognize an aroma in the air: the perfume Licki Bella used.

He knelt down and started frantically trying to open the bag up, wrapped heavily with what appeared to be saran wrap. He took his orange boxcutter from of his back pocket and forcefully tried to open it up, a million things rushing through his mind.

It took longer than anticipated, but he eventually opened one side, and, filled with impatience, decided from that point to just rip it upward from the initial tear. As the bag continued to open wider and wider, he saw them: Licki Bella's trademark socks, her name stitched into them, just as he remembered. They were her complete outfit on most occasions when she was entertaining customers—an absolute sight to see when you were in the room with her. Now, however, all he saw were her intestines sitting on top of her once-flawless stomach like a bowl of spaghetti. He almost threw up on her.

He hopped over the back of his truck and onto the concrete, refusing to look at her in that state. He just couldn't understand why someone would do this to a lovely flower such as Licki Bella: sure, he'd done some pretty gruesome shit in his time, but this was something completely something else. This hit home to him personally. He had a special kind of adoration for his bunnies; a superficial, skin-deep kind of adoration, but adoration, nonetheless.

At the end of the day, Salawicious Dough truly didn't give a fuck about any of them: they were his moneymakers, and that was it. He understood his choice of business had a revolving door reputation to it— but he also knew there would always be big money in it. He was very infatuated with these ladies' looks and all but was mostly concerned about his gross profits at the end of each night.

This *had* to be the work of the Curse guy, Dough reasoned.

Now he thought about it, where in the blue hell was Tasha Banks? He quickly scanned the rest of the truck—simultaneously avoiding making eye contact with the tragedy that was Licki Bella—, making sure there were no other bags stuffed in his back seat that he wasn't aware of. Finding nothing, he was a combination of both disappointed and disgusted—although perhaps not as disgusted as warranted, as, without thinking, he then pulled the socks off Licki Bella's corpse, deciding to keep them as a tribute to her legendary service at the Twisted Sins Bunny Ranch. They'd probably look beautiful draped across the vagina doppelganger of hers on his office desk.

Looking down at her still-perfect pedicure, he wrapped her back up, hopped into the truck, and proceeded to drive around town looking for the same guys that helped him throw the fat white guy and the stove in the Passaic river.

# CHAPTER 50

"**Y**O, DON, DID YOU hear that crazy shit that happened to Dough yesterday at his bunny ranch?" I asked Don. "What in the sweet cream on an ice-cream sandwich was *that* about?"

"Dough called me last night to tell me what went down; he was trying to explain himself so fast that I'm not even sure if I got the whole story." Even Don seemed to find this unnerving. "I know his worker Licki is dead, and then there was something about her socks being wrapped around the neck of the guy in the stove, or some shit." His eyes illuminated in remembrance. "Oh, yeah, and then he drove himself into the Passaic River."

"The Passaic River?" I echoed, shaking my head in disapproval. "He couldn't find a cleaner body of water to commit suicide in? I taught him better than that! Remind me to kill him the next time I see him, okay?"

We were outside Dukeland Orange's house, Sam Luciano being around the back keeping a close eye on the comings and goings of the estate's residents. This was all part of the plan we'd concocted—one I believed would work.

I got out the car, Don following swiftly. We walked up to the front door and knocked—and knocked again. The third time, we were met by a strange-looking kid we knew from the neighborhood named Cody; he was apparently one of Dukeland's producers and, if the look on his face was anything to go off, he knew who we were.

"Don Corione?" he said quietly, eyes widening. "PR Escobar? Does Dukeland know you're here?"

"What's up, youngblood," Don greeted jovially. "Nah, Dukeland doesn't know we here; we figured we'd drop by because we wanted to maybe pick his ear on some music business ventures, we may be looking into."

"Oh, that's dope," Cody responded sincerely. "Wait here, I'll go get him for you." And he disappeared into the house.

Once he was out of sight, Don and I walked around the house, checking out the bullshit life Dukeland Orange had built for himself: he had a taste for taste for fine arts, but it was clear that his maid/butler skills were not quite up to scratch.

"Don, do you hear that?" I snapped quickly.

"What, the music?"

"Yeah. Does that not sound like Joseph Stylez?"

Don listened intently for a moment. "Come to think of it, yeah, it does... Can I just murder this dude right now?" His tone was gentle.

"Really? And have Luciano miss this action?"

He sighed. "Yeah, you're right. He'd never forgive me."

"Gentlemen!" came Dukeland's voice from behind us. W both whipped around. "To what do I owe the pleasure of your acquaintance this evening? May I get your coats?"

"Dukeland Orange! We'll keep our coats, thank you. I'm sure the pleasure is all yours though." I smiled at him warmly. Dukeland looked a little annoyed, but I gave precisely zero fucks today, so it was swiftly onto the next question.

"You've clearly done such a great job for Joseph Stylez's career," Don countered, buttering him up, "that we were wondering if you'd do the same for this new hot act we're looking to sign to our new music label. We're in need of production, and maybe a consultant role we thought you'd be a perfect fit for." He offered a dazzling smile. "So, how about it?"

Dukeland looked caught off-guard. "Well, this is a surprise," he said, looking rather uncomfortable. "Where have you guys been? Stylez always talked so highly of you. We've flown across this country together making money moves, and you guys were nowhere to be found. Are you just trying to hop on his money train now? Is that what this is?"

My eyebrows went further north than Tony Victors' when it's fight time. Meanwhile, Don was looking over at me with the old, *Did this motherfucker just say that?* look on his face—all while maintaining his million-dollar smile.

I took a deep breath. "Now, Dukeland—if I may call you that..."

"You may."

The guy wasn't to be fucked with today. "Clearly, you don't know who we are. We are MentallyOrganiz—"

"Oh, I know exactly who you are," he cut in sharply. "You're the clowns who ran Joseph Stylez's career into the ground, and now you want to hop onto the gravy train."

"Now listen to me, you pompous son-of-a-bitch!" I exploded, all out of patience. It did the trick. "We have *more* money, power, and respect than you will ever be able to attain—so don't front like you don't know that. Secondly"—I nodded to Don—"he's Don Corione, and I'm PR motherfuckin' Escobar. If you got an issue with us..."

"Don!" came a familiar voice. "Oh *shit*, what are you doing here? I thought I heard your voice! Stay right there, I'm coming down!"

"Stylez?" I frowned. Don's superficial, plastered-on, moneymaking grin had spread into a genuine beam that lit up his whole face.

"Yo, my nigga!" came Stylez's voice again. "I ain't seen you in a minute! What's poppin'? And"—as he emerged from the house, his expression fell upon seeing me—"what the *fuck* is this backstabbing-ass nigga doing here?"

I closed my eyes and shook my head: I could only wonder how much longer I could last without laying all these niggas down right where they stood and just be done with the whole situation. However, I made myself hold back—and apparently just in time.

"Funny: I was just about to ask you the same thing, brother." Luciano. "What *is* this backstabbing-ass nigga doing here?" He strutted into the scene, looking ready for a scrap.

"Wait just one fuckin' minute!" Dukeland barked, turning to Sam. "What the fuck's goin' on here, and how the *hell* did you get in my house?"

Sam just sighed: people like Dukeland were just a daily inconvenience for him. "You know, they've made updates for those weak-ass locks you have on those doors. You might want to take care of that, or a nigga like me might come back." Dukeland had turned red with fury, but Sam just turned to Stylez. "Why are *you* here? Matter of fact, *how* are you here? Your moms wrote me and told me what happened, and that you were in some kinda rehab program."

"Yeah, I was." Stylez grinned. "Key word being 'was'. Dukeland checked me out yesterday, and I've been in the studio since. You niggas gotta hear what I'm cooking up in here; it's bananas! Y'all should come listen." He shot me a look. "Not pussy-nigga over here, though."

At that moment, I had had enough: it was either time to hash all of this misguided shit out with my brother, or one of us were going to die tonight.

With that, I casually shrugged off my coat off before pummeling Stylez down to the ground, knocking over some of Dukeland's cheap Walmart imitation shit in the process. I refrained from hitting him in the face, but I delivered some nice body shots to his frail frame. Saying this, Stylez was no slouch; rather, he was a ripped dude, and my ribs felt like they were touching after a couple of his blows.

Don and Sam eventually managed to wrench us off one another, Don noticing Dukeland smirking in the corner in the process.

Sam quickly spoke before anybody else could get a word in and add fuel to the fire. "Joseph, could you finally tell everybody here what the fuck your problem is with Escobar? Your brother and family for over two decades?"

Stylez spat some blood onto the floor. "Nah, fuck him! He knows what he did."

"Oh, so now I know what I *did*. Interesting." I wiped my bloody nose on my sleeve. "This keeps getting better and better."

"Enlighten us, Joseph," Don sighed, somehow sounding incredibly bored. "Please; we're all confused here."

"Yes, how about you tell them what your *brother* did to you?" Dukeland added, voice dripping with sarcasm. "Tell them how he stopped you from eating; how he was talking shit about you behind your back to the other music artists and producers because he wanted you blackballed from the industry; how jealous he was of your success. Go ahead, tell them."

His punches had hurt less. "Where the *fuck* are you getting your information from? The dollar store?" I demanded. "Because that's all that bullshit is worth!"

Stylez shrugged. "It's out in the open now, nigga! Just admit it: that you tried to sabotage my career, that you didn't want to see me succeed."

"Yo, Stylez, you're sounding crazy, man," Sam murmured.

"Sam, let him speak," Don ordered. "It's the only way we're going to get to the bottom of this."

"I'm gonna say this one time, and one time only," I said slowly. "I have *never* tried to stop my brother from eating; I have *never* tried to stop him from accomplishing his goals; and I have certainly never had him blackballed in *any* way whatsoever. I love you, boy, and I'd never do that to you. How the fuck could you believe otherwise?"

Stylez just shook his head, looking sad. "How can you guys not see he's lying?" he said to Sam and Don.

"No, Stylez," Sam responded simply. "Can't you see what *Dukeland's* done?"

"Who, me?" Dukeland said stupidly, prodding himself in the chest. "I ain't done nothing but bring this man's career to new heights! He's on a world-renowned label with major distribution and all the extracurricular activities he could imagine."

"Yeah, that's the problem," Don stated.

"How could you possible see that as a problem, little man?"

"You're cancer," Don responded. "We've known about you for years now and have always wanted to stop you, but something always came up that didn't allow us to." He sighed, shaking his head. "Little did we know that you'd directly affect us by destroying one of the parts that make up our nucleus."

"Don, you know how much you mean to me, nigga—as do you, Sam. But Escobar here?" Stylez cocked his head in my direction. "This nigga gotta go."

Thirty seconds of silence went by—each of which feeling like a year. Then, Joseph Stylez pulled out the hammer, holding it directly toward me, and I couldn't help but think of how Luciano must have felt in those two seconds before Jake Solomon shot him that night at the diner.

Don and Sam's eyes hit the roof of Dukeland's ceiling and both lunged toward him, rapidly throwing themselves into a struggle to rid him of the .45 in his hand. Dukeland stood back with his arms folded, content with the prospect of killing the M.O.B. family single-handedly from the inside.

As much as he may have planned for that little move, the next thing that happened was certainly not on his agenda.

The front door flew open and in came Blues Holloway and Brilliant Bobby Bushetta. I can't believe I'm gonna say this, but I think those two—of all people—are responsible for saving my life.

"Yo!" Blues called, seemingly surprised at the scene he'd entered. "Chill the fuck out with that, son!"

"Do you motherfuckers just come from *everywhere*?" Dukeland demanded, exasperated.

"I guess you could say that," Blues shrugged.

"Sam! Don! *Stylez!* You have to see this!" Bobby called.

Dukeland snorted. "What you got there, little buddy? A new porno by The Glowing Midgets?"

"No, asshole!" Bobby shot back. "A porno wit' ya moms getting that ass dusted by a gang of leprechauns!"

"Watch your mouth, nigga," Dukeland growled.

Bobby almost laughed. "Nigga, you watch *your* mouth! Better yet, *wash* your mouth. You brushed ya teeth today? The nigga's breath be smelling like he been sipping ass juice with a twist of lime."

"Yo, Bobby, what's poppin'?" Stylez grinned. "You just in time to see me oust this nigga!"

"Stylez, put the fuckin' gun down, you jackass. I told you, you gotta watch this!"

Brilliant Bobby Bushetta and Blues Holloway had done the impossible: they'd had Dukeland Orange under surveillance since that day Brilliant Bobby had told me he'd seen him go into Dukeland's house. Blues had used the wiretap system he and Dough had used on Polo Pasé while Bobby used the same visual technology as when they'd set Jake Solomon up. Together, they were bound to find something out—and that they did.

Bobby and Blues swiftly connected a wireless computer—which I later found out was called a laptop—with video footage of Dukeland Orange and his running buddies displayed on its screen. What we were all about to witness was incriminating, to say the least—but who gives a fuck? Dukeland Orange had it coming.

"Yo, what the fuck do you guys think you're doing? In my home, no less!" Indeed, Dukeland looked like he'd shit a brick: he was nervous at what he'd already seen.

"What you most certainly don't want us to do," Bobby shrugged.

You assholes got thirty seconds to get the fuck outta my house, or I'm calling the cops!"

"The *cops*?" Luciano repeated, laughing. "That's a pussy move if I ever did hear one."

Stylez sighed loudly. "Yo, Bobby, Blues: I love ya'll, but you're kinda disrupting something that needed to happen a long time ago."

"Yes, we are," Bobby responded matter-of-factly, "and that something is this."

With that, Brilliant Bobby pressed the Enter button and held the laptop up so everybody could see what was on display: the first ten seconds of the video were a little blurry, the audio also distorted, but soon thereafter, you could see and hear Dukeland Orange speaking to a few shady record execs in his home. There were also a few of his boys present we'd seen from time-to-time around town standing guard in the video. Indeed, I had a feeling we were all getting ready to find out what Stylez's issue was with me, hopefully finally putting an end to this madness once and for all.

Now, the audio was perfect, and we all could hear what was being said crystal-clear. Dukeland Orange looked like he was getting ready to shit his pants.

"So, how long has this charade been going on with Joseph Stylez?" the first executive asked casually. "Do you think he has an inkling of what's transpiring here?"

"Yes, tell us how you pulled this off," the second executive added eagerly. "It almost sounds too good to be true."

The Dukeland in the video grinned. "He doesn't have a *clue*. It was easier than I'd thought to convince him PR Escobar was out to sabotage him: I used a mutual producer I was working with—who's also working with a group Al Gebra wanted to sign to his label—, through which I met Al. They all had ties over at Seton Hall University, and it was after Al and I met one another's acquaintance that he introduced me to Stylez. He knew I had connections in the music industry and could probably find success for Stylez faster than anyone."

Both executives were leaning into every word that passed from Dukeland's lips. The image was extremely pathetic.

After a brief pause, Dukeland continued. "Now, don't get it twisted; Joseph Stylez is an incredible talent, and I wanted him to succeed. But I couldn't have him eating bigger chunks off my plate: I've been doing this for years now, and it's not my fault no one taught these artists the business. This is a cut-throat industry, and if you're not made for it, then fuck it: what do I need you for? I ain't here to hold no grown man's hand."

"But how did you have him convinced that Escobar was against him?" Executive One asked. My muscles started aching as I tensed in anticipation.

Dukeland sighed. "Well, Stylez may be smart, but I'm smarter. I did my research, and I knew he'd been having some personal problems and trust issues with his family at home—so I used that to tap into his psyche." He shrugged. "It may not have been the most popular approach but fuck it: I started spreading rumors throughout the industry that Escobar was trying to railroad him."

"But why Escobar specifically?"

"Me and the boys here grabbed straws, and Escobar's name came up. That's all: nothing personal. I think he's an asshole, but they're all assholes. Could've been either of them."

"And what exactly did these rumors consist of?" Executive One pushed. "Stylez wants to kill this guy!"

"I had everybody believing Escobar called record label executives and had Stylez blackballed from everywhere." Dukeland smiled lazily. "Told them he had everyone block his phone calls and show appearances. I mean, c'mon, that's the way the man makes a *living*: anytime someone threatens that of any man, there's going to be hell to pay. Oh, and I told him there were rumors in the 'hood Escobar was fucking his ex. And that was just to sweeten the pot!"

I could've killed the guy.

"When I told him that, the man flipped my chairs over! *And* I've been slipping him this angel dust, meth, and heroine. It's been like taking candy from a baby—or, in this case, giving candy to an idiot."

"You never cease to amaze me," Executive Two sighed. "That's brilliant: turn a family against one another from the inside and create residual profit." The guy was practically eating out of Dukeland's ass. "I guess my last question to you is, how much money have you made off Joseph Stylez?"

Dukeland looked like he was going to wet himself with excitement at this question. "Gentlemen, I can't begin to tell you: that man's contract is so fucked up for him, and so beneficial for me, I'm surprised people don't believe it's me on the songs or in the movies he's been in." He paused. "Of course, I've cut him a piece here and there, but he has no idea how much money he *should've* been getting. I look at it this way: without me, he wouldn't have done shit anyway; them M.O.B. niggas don't know shit about the music industry, so they would've fucked him over worse. Well," he reconsidered, "maybe not intentionally, as in this case, but he at least wouldn't have been known to the degree he is now. I'm telling you, that guy ain't going nowhere: I got him under contract for five more albums, and there's nothing he can do about it. He's my bitch now."

It was then that the video and audio started to distort, and, approximately seven seconds later, the screen faded to black.

The tension in the air was thicker than four dancers from *Breathless* after eating a slice of pound cake. Brilliant Bobby Bushetta stepped back fast, closing his laptop with a snap shut: he knew it was going to get violent at any moment, and he couldn't bear something happening to his pride and joy. What can I say? Techy dudes are fucking weird.

Blues Holloway glanced at Sam Luciano nervously, who had a smirk on his face longer than Cappadonna's verse on *Winter Warz*. Don glanced at me and nodded his head reassuringly: all was going to be okay—well, once we all took turns beating the everlasting shit outta Dukeland Orange, that is.

Joseph Stylez scrunched his eyebrows and flared his nostrils, reminiscent of a raging bull. He turned around and faced Dukeland Orange, who I quickly realized had less of a chance of winning a foot race than Pigleg himself. The ending was coming, and if his stricken expression was anything to go off, he knew it.

"I'm your bitch?" Stylez spat. "Really? That's what you think of me?"

With that, Stylez lunged for aa nearby lamp and, before anyone could register what was happening, smashed it over Dukeland's head, who fell to the floor, busted open. Blood spilled from the corner of his head and, sobbing slightly, he began crawling over toward the bear skin rug in the living area: there was a sharp samurai sword Dukeland loved hanging above the fireplace. Quickly realizing what was happening here, Stylez grabbed it and walked over closer to Dukeland's sorry-ass body: things were about to get interesting.

"Wait, wait!" Dukdland begged, holding his arms over his head in self-defense. "Let me explain!"

"*Explain?*" Stylez repeated, eyes lit with fury. "Sure, why don't we let you explain? Don, Sam: should we let him explain? Escobar?"

"Nah, that motherfucker ain't worth listening to," Don declared. "Don't you think he's done enough explaining?"

Stylez paused. "Point taken." He turned back to the bundl on the floor. "So, I'm your bitch, right? How's this sword feel right about here?"

And with that, Joseph Stylez plunged the weapon into the back Dukeland Orange's shirt, at the bottom of the neck to right above the lumbar part of his spine. To this day, I've never heard a man scream in such agony as Dukeland did in that moment.

We were all taken aback: not by the violence, nor by the potential for murder here, but at the precision of that sword. It was magical—some *Dungeons & Dragons* or *Masters of the Universe* shit.

We all saw the look in Dukeland Orange's eyes in that moment: raw, genuine, deep pain.

"Are you fuckin' insane?" he screamed, his voice breaking.

Don murmured, "I wonder if the Jets are winning their game today? I think it was 21-3 before we left to come here."

"You *know* they lost," Sam sighed. "That's what they do."

"You're a good man, Sam," I praised. "How about dem Cowboys? You and Ray Nathan going to next week's game?"

Dukeland's bloodcurdling screams of anguish still echoed across the small space.

"Good point," Don said.

"Why thank you."

Sam sighed. "I think Stylez would probably like our undivided attention at this moment, considering he's probably about to commit a homicide."

"We've been rude long enough," I reasoned. "You should probably apologize to the man."

Don's gaze, however, was fixed on the scene ensuing before us. "Ha! Look what he's got this nigga doing now!"

We both followed his gaze and, sure enough, Joseph Stylez had Dukeland Orange hanging from the flagpole Dukeland had had a handyman put up for him to the left of his mantelpiece. Every season, he'd hang up the flag of his favorite sports team—and I'd place my bets that he never anticipated he'd be hanging from it himself.

As blood continued to spill from his head and the length of his back, Stylez looked up to him, cocking his head and standing quietly for what seemed for hours. After an age, he finally cracked.

" I trusted you," he hissed, "and because of you, I have become less of a man. My family -don't even recognize me anymore—because of you. I can't believe I allowed this to happen; I can't believe I doubted my brother; I can't believe how much pain I've put my mom through. I can't believe what I've stooped to."

With that, Joseph Stylez kneeled to the ground and, with both his hands, covered his face and bowed his head. He cried: gently at first, and then inconsolably. The cries of a tortured soul.

Eventually, we joined him. It was a very surreal but touching moment that we shared with one another: Joseph knew he needed help and, for the first time, it appeared that he was willing to get it—but first, he had to do something, Something that's been long overdue and that we'd all wanted to do for a long time.

Stylez rose and gently asked me to hold the sword. I obliged, and, with that, he walked over and punched Dukeland Orange in the face so hard it almost swung him off the pole. Pausing for a moment to survey the damage, he hit him again, swinging some more in the opposite direction. I believe that second punch knocked out two of Dukeland's front teeth, and anybody who had been there would find that very believable. We all laughed as we wiped away the tears that had gathered on our cheeks a few minutes before, reveling in Karma in action.

After those punches connected, he asked me to pass the sword back to him, then instructing us all to take a few steps back: this might get messy.

Joseph then looked up to Dukeland Orange, who was now essentially just a silhouette coated in blood: the stuff had even run into his eyes.

"You took my life away from me; you took my love and happiness away from me; you took my belief in family away from me." Stylez's whispers were solemn, gentle—all the more blood-chilling. "Now, I take that all away from you—in a much more meaningful and lasting way."

Then Joseph Stylez plunged the samurai sword right through the chest of Dukeland Orange, the opposite end of the sword protruding through his already-pierced back and the flagpole he hung from.

His lifeless body dangled from the flagpole—an awesome sight, to say the least. Stylez then dropped the sword as if it had burned him, falling to his knees once again—only this time, we were met with saddening, melodic words: eerie yet beautiful.

After he had finished with his soliloquy of sorts, we all gathered around him and embraced one another: it was over. Joseph finally felt like his life was worth living, and that there was nothing but love surrounding him.

After God-knows-how-long, we rose from the ground and stepped back to give him some breathing room: it was clear that he needed a minute to get himself together. I felt emotional with love and relief: Stylez and I had reconnected our brotherhood.

Finally, he stood and turned to face me. "Escobar, I..."

I held my hands up in protest, stopping him in his tracks. "We won't be having any of that. Before all this, I needed a full fuckin' script of explanation, but that footage explained all I needed to hear." I rubbed him reassuringly on the shoulder. "I know you feel partially responsible or whatever, but I also know that that son-of-a-bitch over there didn't make anything easy for you."

Stylez exhaled shakily: he was emotionally drained. "And I thank you for being so understanding—but I ultimately make my own decisions, and I should've known better—better than to be coerced into thinking my family would do something like that to me. Especially someone like you; and for that I'm deeply sorry. You will never know how much."

"Apology already accepted," I smiled, emotion brimming in my eyes. "I love you, boy!"

"Love you too, homie."

"Now let's get this fuckin' Positive-K-lookin'-ass-nigga the fuck outta here!" I grinned. "I'm sure someone's going to come looking for him at some point or another."

"Probably," Don agreed, "but who? Who, who, who?"

"You're such an asshole," I sighed.

Don's eyes glistened. "Yo, Sam, you're not going to believe this!"

"What, nigga, what?"

"The Cowboys won!"

Sam looked like someone had died. "Oh my God... This is the time I need Tony Victor here, so he could slap the shit outta you for being so fucking *annoying*."

Don rolled his eyes. "What's he gonna do? Hit me with a Tupac CD?"

"Maybe."

"No, wait, I got a better one," Don said. "He's gonna slap me with a pair of Bugs Bunny slippers!"

"If he were standing here, I'm not sure you'd be talking this level of shit," I said.

"No, wait, he's gonna hit me with a Vin Rock action figure! Or maybe a rolled-up poster of Treach."

# CHAPTER 51

*Location: Baltimore, MD; May 10; 10:00 am*

BALTIMORE HAS ALWAYS BEEN a second home to me: I actually went to college there in the late 70s, and we had so much business out there for years that we found ourselves renting lofts in the downtown area by Eutaw Street. Those things were admittedly pretty expensive, but we didn't give a fuck: we were making so much money that those expenses were nothing to us. I guess it helped that we had some connections down there to keep business together and in ordnance when we weren't in town.

After all the craziness at Dukeland Orange's house a few days back, we all decided to take a few days to ourselves before we got together to address this Curse motherfucker. Being completely honest, I didn't want no part in it, and I believe I voiced this to my wife that evening: I'd told her we should pack up and just move to Africa on some Nas in *Belly* shit. Interesting enough, Yelly is black and is always talking to me about her motherland, so she actually started packing—that is, until I had to crush her dreams and tell her we weren't actually moving there: I was just talking shit, like I always do.

Anyways, Don, Sam and I decided to take a drive out to Charm City for the weekend, and, before we left, we made sure the family was intact— and that Joseph Stylez was back home with his bloodline, getting the help and support he needed after what had undoubtedly been the most stressful four months of his life. We told him we'd check in on him as soon as we get back in town.

It was Homecoming at my alma mater, and I wanted to get away and visit my extended family. Harry Horrendous and Lexington Arms were to meet up with us the following day after our arrival.

Man, I can't tell you the number of things we did on that college campus: they all used to come visit me on a regular basis, anyone from the outside probably assuming Harry was a student. There was a girl there that I'd been great friends with, who he'd also hit it off with when he travelled down. Don, of course, had one or two that he'd gotten attached to, too—but, as you know, he was just having fun, as were the rest of us.

We hopped onto 83 South off of the 695W toward West North Avenue before getting stopped at the very first traffic light. It was while we were waiting there that we saw a junkie trying to stand and lay down—at the same time. As sad as it was, I was a bit enamored with the fact that he hadn't made a definitive decision as to which one he was going to do so he decided to do. Thus, I thought this was amazing, but Jay BaDouche quickly put me in my place here: "Escobar, you're a dick."

Sam was driving his decked-out '93 Honda Accord, and it was then that I told him to pull over at the liquor store on the corner. He obliged and, the second he did so, I got out and deeply inhaled the dirty Baltimore air. *Home sweet second home.*

Don shouted out the car for me to bring him back a vanilla blunt, Sam then quickly shouting that he wanted a fifth of Henny. I opened the door to respond, only to be but met with a brushback by a towering figure who obviously hadn't been watching where he was going.

"Yo, you gotta watch where da fuck you going!" I shouted out, irritated.

"Don't make me slap you across the face with this bottle!" the guy yelled back. "I'm *beat*: my feet hurt, and I'm starved. You got a dollar so I can get me a hot dug?"

"A what?"

"A hot dug."

"The fuck is a hot dug?" I asked genuinely.

"A *hot dug*," the man repeated, getting frustrated. "You know, the long beef you put between some bread and kraut? Maybe some chilli or mus'tid or something?"

"Oh, a *hot dog*," I said. "Yeah, let me check." I fished in my pockets, coming out empty. "I'm sorry, man: I got exactly zero dimes for your country-speaking ass! And if you ever say you gon' slap me with anything at all ever again, I will personally take your hot dug, shine it up real nice, turn that sumbitch sideways, and stick it straight up your candy ass! Do you understand the words coming out my mouth?"

The guy looked on the verge of either having a breakdown or beating me to a pulp: I couldn't decide which. "Listen here, little nigga: I've been running these streets for forty years, and ain't no one ever talked to me like that. Who da hell do you think you are?"

"He's PR Escobar, Ralph," called a voice from around the corner. "One of the Original M.O.B. members from the origins based out in Ghost Town, NJ—and if you don't take heed to what the man is saying to you, I'm gonna be forced to rambunctiously take your life, right here, right now."

The guy looked genuinely scared. "Teddy, I'm sorry; I didn't know. I didn't mean no disrespect," he added to me.

"I know, Ralph. Just get the fuck outta here before you get physically dismissed. These guys ain't guys you wanna fuck around with. Got it?"

"Roger that, Teddy."

"Escobar, you really should watch the geographical direction you're taking out on these streets," Teddy said. "You could end up riddled with bullets *real* quick. I know we work for you, but these niggas out here don't know you by facial structure, and they won't give a fuck if you tell them: they're fearless out here. I'm surprised they haven't made a TV show about this slumlord of an area yet; HBO should do something." He laughed to himself. "Anyway, what in the calzone hell are you doing out here? You didn't tell me you were coming. I would've had some phat bitches and Everclear ready for you when you got here!"

Teddy Vocab was one of my HNIC brothers of Charm City: the intricate word speaker; the Victorious Honcho of Verbatim. He would use big words and configure them into long, drawn-out sentences when the simplified version would've done just as well—hence, his surname.

Alongside Victor Van Jigg, NativeTech, and Nappy Damous, they ran the M.O.B. chapter in Maryland—a very lucrative chapter, at that.

"Teddy, me and the fellas just came down here for Homecoming," I explained. "We just got here last night, and we needed something like this: something that showed unity and an atmosphere of people who want others to succeed." I grinned. "We've been so engulfed in feud after feud and beef after beef that we haven't had any time to just enjoy *life*. Plus, I heard Dru Hill was back off tour and performing at Druid Hill Park Saturday night—and that's my favorite group of all time, so I'm in there."

"I wholeheartedly understand your position, Escobar," Teddy responded understandingly. "It hasn't exactly been a 112 song down here for us, either. Do you know that rectal cavity "Lucky" Vaughn Masonry is charging people out here to walk in his studio just to see his platinum record from the 70's? He's *from* here, and that's how he repays his community." He shook his head sadly. "He could at least let the public admire his hard work and dedication for free, considering he's a byproduct of the neighborhood and all. That guy has always irked my bitter nerve."

"Damn, Ted, that sucks," I said sympathetically. "You want me to kill him?"

"Nah, he ain't worth the second bullet spinning in my chamber," he shrugged.

We laughed it off and made plans to meet later that night for drinks and a trip down Memory Lane with the other guys. It had been *forever* since I'd last seen them. I was genuinely looking forward to it.

After a warm goodbye, I got back in the car and, of course, Sam and Don let me have it.

"Yo, where they at?"

"Where what at?", I asked confusingly.

"Yo! You had *one job* buddy! One fuckin' job! Get me a blunt, and get Sam a fifth of Henny."

Before I could even come up with a bullshit reason for my forgetting what he and Sam asked for, a car pulled up, blocking the front of ours while blasting the new Tupac record. The driver then got out of his car and walked toward the front of ours, and all I remember saying was, "Oh, here we go again!"

"What's up, Loc?" the thug greeted sleazily, leaning against our passenger door and addressing Sam. "I never seen you around here. What set you claimin'?"

The guy was obviously confused, and we all sighed with irritation. Sam Luciano shot Don and I a glance—one we read immediately.

"Oh, my apologies, dawg," Sam said fluidly. "You right: I'm not from here, and neither are my brothers back here. Can we get out the car and allow you to pat us down for weapons? Just so we can prove to you and your homies here that we come in peace and mean no threat?"

"Yeah lil' nigga," the guy drawled, "why don't you and ya boys here go ahead and do that. *Slowly*, mind."

Obeying the guy's stipulations, Sam Luciano opened the door before closing it right away.

The guy crouched down beside the door. "Yo, what you doing in there? Y'all are supposed to be gettin' out."

"Forgive me, man; my seatbelt got caught in the door."

The moment Sam uttered these words, Don and I had our guns cocked and loaded: it was time for action. The guy was still crouched down and, in one swift motion, Sam banged the dude's head against the door with such ferocity it knocked the guy on his ass: he was out cold.

By the time his cronies even got around to attending to their fallen leader, Don and I had our guns drawn, aimed right at both their heads.

"Don't even try it," Don growled, getting out the car and leading one of the dudes against the wall, patting him down. He only had a frozen Snickers bar and a grand total of three dollars in his jacket pocket.

"What the fuck is this, dude?" Don demanded. "You out here trying to rob niggas and claim sets, and you walkin' around with less than five dollars and some ice cream on you!"

"And what do we have over here?" I said, having pinned the other guy to the wall in a similar fashion. "What the hell do you even have on? Why ya jeans so damn tight? You really out here stickin' niggas up, riding around to Tupac songs, lookin' like Toni Braxton?" After a thorough, somewhat invasive pat-down, I found the fruits of my labor to be a pair of socks in his damn pockets. I didn't even ask: I stuffed them each in his mouth and down his throat. "You two got to be the sorriest excuses of street criminals I've ever seen in my life: you lucky we ain't murking you right here. Don is feeling good today." I turned to Don. "You feeling good today, Don?"

"Yeah, I feel good today, Escobar."

"You feeling good, Sam?"

"Yeah, I feel tremendous," Sam answered back, grinning.

"Then it's settled," I said, turning back to the pathetic man before me. "Neither of us are going to kill you today."

"Really?" the guy asked stupidly. Meanwhile, the guy Sam had hit with the door—the leader of the "pack", if you could even call them that—was coming to.

"Yes. Really," I sighed. "We're not going to kill you. But that guy over there?" I pointed behind them. "I'm not so sure."

And with that, Teddy Vocab lit them up with a single shot to each of their heads in such a swift motion that I was envious for about seventeen seconds. Man, that boy was accurate: you may not have been able to understand half the words he was saying, but the boy could shoot with the best of them.

"Escobar; Luciano; Corione," he greeted. "I luckily stayed behind to finish some business in the liquor store, and the guy who manages came around the back to alert me that you three might need some help out in the front."

I'll be honest: for a second, I was speechless. "Well, I'm pretty sure we had this handled, but we do appreciate the assistance, Theodore," I eventually responded cordially. "Although I am a little besmirched by your actions: we just told these poor fellows we were feeling good today and that we were going to spare their lives."

"Oh. My bad," Teddy responded, smiling sheepishly.

"Good work nonetheless," Don offered. "Sam here doesn't really know much about the M.O.B. chapter of Charm City: we developed it while he was overseas on assignment with Hak Hennesey some time ago, but I believe he's impressed with your marksmanship."

"That would be correct," Sam agreed. "Teddy, it was a pleasure seeing you today: your skills are amazing, and I'm grateful that I got to see you in action—although I think we'll be leaving for home sooner than we anticipated."

"What? Why?" I asked.

He bit his lip. "I've got three missed calls and a two-way message from Whish: she said she received an express delivery to her home from The Curse stating he knows what she did to that woman at Dairy Queen a few months back. He said it's time she paid for her sins." Sam looked on edge. "He's threatened to kill her and those closest to her."

"Teddy, give my love to the brothers at arms. Looks like we're going to have to take a rain check on the happy hour specials and reminiscing memory train," I said apologetically. "That's our sister and his potential wife he's referring to. I'll hit you up soon!"

"Understood," Teddy responded. "Take care of home. We'll be here, waiting."

And with that, Teddy Vocab watched us speed off, knowing he'd missed a golden opportunity to learn from us all. He turned around and surveyed the three bodies on the ground, stepping over two of them and entering the store.

"Jose! Get somebody out here to clean up this mess! And bring some extra-large garbage bags—at least 3 of them!"

# CHAPTER 52

O F COURSE, A NORMAL three-hour drive back home turned into well past five hours: the NJ turnpike sucks ass. I do believe we've left a few bodies in between Exits 6 and 9 over the years, but if I give you any more details, I'd probably have to kill you—and I don't want to do that. At least, not now.

We stopped at one of those rest stops on the turnpike and waited in line for approximately eight years, just for some nasty-ass chicken from Roy Rogers. I don't even know how that place is still alive.

While we were in line, Sam noticed a fine thing with the fattest of asses walk up to the counter, asking if she could purchase one biscuit for her baby boy in the carriage. The manager promptly snuck her one and told her not to worry about it, and she took it gratefully, shooting him a silent *thank you.* Sam stood there, wordlessly watching the transaction transpire, and, when the time came for him to pay for his meal, he asked that same manager if he could get a free biscuit for *his* baby in the carriage over there. The manager cocked his head over and looked at him with an icy stare.

"Sir, that baby is not yours. That young lady was just here asking for the same thing for it."

"Yeah, I know she did: that baby is my *son,* and he would like another biscuit," Sam challenged. "So, can I get another one?"

The manager eyed Sam for a few moments before shaking his head, all politeness having gone out the window. "Sir, there is no way that baby is yours. It has blonde hair and blue eyes!"

Sam raised an unimpressed eyebrow. "We're from South Africa, and that's how the women and babies look down there. So, could you please get me my damn biscuit—or am I going to have to shove this chicken leg up your ass?"

The manager started trembling with anger. "Sir, I was not born yesterday, but if you feel like you must insert that chicken attachment up my rectum, so be it. Let me cash out my remaining customers and I'll meet you behind the counter."

Sam Luciano just stood there: he knew he'd lost that battle, and, with a last glare in the manager's direction, he walked away, defeated.

Thirty minutes later and Don had almost killed five drivers with his pistol alone, ultimately refraining from doing so. Such entertainment would have been good, but I was ultimately grateful he didn't commit any homicides when we arrived at Whish's: she was sure glad to see us.

"Brothers, I'm so glad you're here," she greeted warmly: indeed, her voice was laced with relief. "I hope I didn't totally mess up your trip, but this letter here is some bullshit. I wanna find this Curse guy *now* and beat the living shit outta him." She shook her head. "Threatening Whish Johannsen? Does this fool *know* who he's dealing with? I think not."

Meanwhile, I had Dixie, Laura, and Sunshine out the back, waiting to do anything I asked them them to: Sunshine even took her lollipop out her mouth to salivate properly, and you *know* she never takes that damn thing out.

Snapping back to the present, I asked, "Where's this letter, then?"

"I don't even know right now: I got so heated when I read it that I threw the damn thing and the piece of cardboard it came in across the room," Whish admitted. "I'm telling you, I was *this* close from tracking him down and ending this asshole for good." She's started scavenging across the room and, after feeling under one of the chairs, triumphantly held up a piece of paper. "Found it! Wait Here. Read it."

Whish handed me the special delivery envelope. It read:

*Dear Sisters of M.O.B.*

*How can you represent a "family" that stands for Money Over Bitches? Surely that's degrading for all women? What is wrong with you? How do you sleep at night knowing these men look at you as sexual objects instead of the delicate flowers that you are?*

*Anyway, please make sure you're all in attendance on May 19th at the Galloping Hill Inn.*

*Oh and, Whish, I know what you did to that young lady at Dairy Queen: she was my friend—a sister to me. So now, I'm going to have to kill one of your sisters—maybe a blood relative. I don't know. It depends how I feel when I wake up that morning.*

*Okay, lady. Love you! Bye, bye!*

*—The Curse*

"I just want to *scream* right now," Whish seethed, snatching the letter from me just as I'd finished reading it. "Threaten me? Say he's gonna kill one of my family members? I will *destroy* him! Does anybody know anything about this guy?"

"I don't know shit, honey; never heard of him," Sam responded. "But if he's going out of his way to invite us all to this gala on May 19th, then I think it's worth checking out. Besides, if we don't like what he has to say, we'll just kill him."

I wandered around the outside patio and back into Whish's spacious living area. She had great taste: her decor was amazing, as was her overall style. She was just awesome.

"Whish, I've never come across this guy," I said honestly. "He's been hiding really well in order to know us all and to be able to reach out to us seemingly without any issues. I believe I need to check in with The Great 8: this is beginning to get a little out of hand." I turned to the rest of the group. "Don, where are Dough and Tony at this hour? And Al and Hak? I know Celo isn't here, but he would be glad to chime in over the phone." I sighed. "This is something we need to handle as a family. Whish, call Sara and Mula; I'll also have my wife meet us here now."

There was clearly some real shit going on here, and, probably for the first time ever, it appeared as if we weren't ahead of the game: the more things happened, the more it looked like we were becoming the underdogs—an unfamiliar place for all of us. We'd been on top for too long, and ain't no faceless letter-writing motherfucker was going to get the better of us. You could count on that, or my name isn't Thom Foolery.

That's my fourth a.k.a. and, as per company policy, I'm supposed to kill you now—so if by some chance before you get to the end of this story of ours you drop dead, don't say I didn't warn you.

# CHAPTER 53

"**O**KAY, SO WHY DID you motherfuckers drag me outta bed again?" Sara demanded. "I was watching *General Hospital*."

"No, you weren't: *General Hospital* comes on at, like, one in the afternoon," Don pointed out.

"You never heard of a VCR?" Sara shot back. "I *record* my soap operas, okay? I may be a killer, gangsta, and married to a Great 8 member, but I'm also a girl and a mother, in case you niggas forgot."

"No, honey, none of us forgot," Al reassured her. "You tell me *all* the time. Anyway, I picked up eight pizzas from Bruno's and ten beef patties with cheese on the way here— so, unless we're stupid, I'd suggest we dig in before it all gets cold."

Bruno's Pizzeria was a staple in our lives: I tried to get a piece of that money for an entire decade, but couldn't do it. The actual owner was this big-ass Italian dude from Scotch Plains who had to be in his mid-sixties. He'd come in once a week, collect his profit, and then ghost everyone until the next week. He was a nice guy, and, outta respect and pure nostalgia, we let him continue making his money, figuring when he kicked the can, we'd go full-charge into controlling it. For now, we liked Bruno: he was a good man, and good men were hard to find in business—period.

Whish walked over to Luciano and expressed her concern for everyone's safety. It felt strange to see Whish Johannsen in a place of vulnerability, and it was kinda endearing, in a way. Ever since that night of my birthday party at The Black Box—the night Sam had been shot by Jake Solomon—, Whish has been on a high, and, secretly, I always wished that Whish and Sam got together. I just thought she was his counterpart, that she'd be the one to make him an honest man. Well, reality is starting to settle in with those two, so I'm either a prophet or a very lucky guy. Either way, my love for the both of them is extensive.

It was at that moment that my wife kinda came outta nowhere, asking if we should consider leaving the business. I responded that I'd never thought about that: I'd contemplated stepping down from my position on multiple occasions, but at the end of the day, I'm still PR Escobar, and I got a lot of responsibilities. However, if my queen was ever feeling that the time may be on the horizon, then I would at least have to give it some real thought.

Everyone was in the sitting area of Whish's home. And you could practically see the mental rolodex spinning in everybody's head: The Curse had our attention, and now was the time to figure out how we were supposed to handle this thing. But how do you prepare for someone you've never seen? This was going to be something really big, and it was killing us all that we couldn't figure it out.

I had noticed Don had been acting a little strange for a couple weeks now; he's a strange guy anyway, but I know my brother—something was definitely off.

Thus, I said, "Don, what's poppin' wit'cha? Don't tell me it's nothing, either or I'll call Sticks Morano over here to get it out of you."

"Chill, son; Sticks ain't getting nothing out of me. Do you understand me?"

"Yes, Sir, I do," I responded. "You're gay and don't want to admit it."

"Don't make me fuck you up, nigga!" he said lightheartedly. "I will castrate you via machete."

I shrugged. "And there we have it: *another* reference to another man's penis. Your issue with Sticks has really got you screwed up. You're fucked buddy; admit it. Go ahead! I'll wait."

"Sure. What do you want? Did you just come over here to fuck wit' me?"

"Nah," I responded. "All kidding aside: what's good? I know something's been fuckin' with you. You wanna tell me what's going on, or do I need to beat it out of you?"

"Whoa, whoa, no man is beating *anything* out of me!"

"You're an asshole," I responded simply.

"I know, but what do you want me to do? Apologize?"

"Hell no; then, I'd know you'd be lying."

"You know me so well," Don said sarcastically.

"That I do. So, what's the matter?"

He exhaled. "A few weeks ago, I got a call from somebody who was saying they was going to kill me."

My eyebrows flew up. "And why are you only telling me this *now*?"

He shrugged. "Because I knew you'd react just like this." He sighed again. "Listen, I've been getting those kinds of calls for years—as I'm sure you and Sam have, too. But there was something about that call in particular that had me a bit leery."

"What happened?" I asked.

"That's the thing: it wasn't exactly nothing out of the ordinary. It was more of a supernatural kinda premonition thing, maybe: just a very eerie feeling that I had when I hung the phone up." He bit his lip. "I wish I could tell you more, but I just can't."

"Yo, what you two whispering about over here?" Sam chimed in, swinging down beside us.

"Don received a call a couple weeks back from someone that said they were going to kill him," I explained.

"Yeah, I know. So what?"

I paused. "Wait, you *knew*?"

"Bruh, *anyone* in a position of power like we're in is bound to receive those types of calls," Sam answered. "Why you acting like you haven't?"

"I *have*, it's just been a while. Or maybe I just ignore the ninety-seven messages I have on my answering machine on purpose. There's probably a few life threats on there somewhere."

"If I were a betting man, I'd say that was a sure shot," Sam nodded.

"I don't *know*, yo!" Don burst out, evidently getting frustrated. "You think that call was from this Curse fucker?"

"It's very possible," I mused, "especially since you said it felt different."

"I don't give a fuck who it was from," Sam declared. "That person will be dealt with, one way or another; mark my words, gentlemen."

It was at that moment that Mula wandered over. "So, brothers, is there a plot in place for this May 19th disaster?"

"Yeah, I'm *dying* to wear this new dress from Natt Taylor to this gala," Sara chipped in.

"Sara, 'dying' was probably not the right word to use," Don pointed out sarcastically.

Sara pouted. "Sensitive today, are we?"

"Nah, just a little more aware than yesterday."

"Fair enough. I still wanna wear that dress, though."

"And wear it you shall, my love," Al smiled.

"So, are we going to get down to business here?" Tony cut in impatiently. "If not, I got these two Italian chicks waiting for me at home..."

"*Two*?" I repeated. "Why is there always *two*? Why can't you just have one woman, Tony? Just *one*. It makes us think you're lying; it can't be two *all* the time."

"Swear to God, yo!" Tony insisted. "I've been fuckin' with these chicks for a minute now. They're best friends, and they do everything together— and I mean *everything*." He grinned sleazily. "I can't help it if I'm that much of a man that one woman can't handle me."

"Really, Tony?" Mula snapped, looking thoroughly disgusted. "You're disgusting. I could've done without that image in my head."

C'mon, Mula, baby, don't be like that."

"Yo, I do got some ass lined up, so can we get this thing rolling?" Hak pushed.

"You too?" I asked.

"Yeah; only one, though. And it ain't Jay's mom, either."

"Well, that's a relief."

"For me, or for her?"

Don chuckled. "I love you, Hak. You always know how to make me laugh."

"I wasn't trying to."

"What did I miss?" came Dough's voice as he swung into the room. "I just left from the Bunny Ranch; business is *booming*."

"I'm happy to hear that Dough. I'll be over there soon," Sam promised. "Gotta see what Trinity Glow is all about."

"You gotta do what, Sam?" Whish challenged, unimpressed.

"Nothing, baby," he stammered, flushing slightly. "I was just telling Dough here that I have to check out that beautiful glow-in-the-dark vagina molding he has of Licki Bella. It's an art piece."

"Yeah, whatever!" she huffed, tossing a lock of hair over her shoulder. "You better watch yourself."

"Yes, ma'am."

"Family, we got a psycho on the loose out here," I stated, bringing us back down to earth, "who's hellbent on terrorizing us all. The son-of-a-bitch knows too much, which means he's been plotting to get us for quite some time. We're damn good at what we do—especially with being discreet with certain things—, so this guy must be equally as good to have this much information on us on an individual basis."

"He may be associated with Jake Solomon," Al mused. "Could that be possible? I mean, Jake was with Cocoa for a long time before he went apeshit; maybe Jake got some of our info from Cocoa at some point and saved it for a rainy day." He shrugged. "I know I'm clutching at straws here, but it does make a little sense, don't you think?

"Yeah, it does," Sam agreed. "But from my understanding, the first note was received by Salawicious Dough, and that was before Jake's death. So where's the correlation?"

"Good point," Al conceded, "but the letters continued even *after* his death. I'm just trying to make sense of all this bullshit..."

"Yeah, we all are," I reassured him.

"Babe, is there any way we could trace any potential fingerprints on any of these letters that have been sent?" my wife suggested, deep in thought.

"You know, I thought of that, but I didn't follow up on it," I responded. "Maybe we should investigate that a little further. Thanks for bringing it up, honey."

"You know it."

"Hey, family," called Don, "I got Celo Gaston on the line. I'm going to put him on speakerphone."

Celo's voice filled the room. "What's up, family!"

"What's up, fool?" Hak called back. "How's TarHeel Country?"

"It's beautiful out here," Celo said sincerely. "Just a better quality of life. I'm loving it."

"We're glad to hear that, brother," Don responded warmly. "We're happy for you."

"Indeed, we are," I seconded.

"Are Sam and Sara there?"

"We're here, bro!" both individuals in question affirmed.

"Awesome: I just wanted to tell you how happy I am that the both of you are okay. We all need you now, as do your families. You both gave us a pretty bad scare—although I knew Sam was going to be okay; I knew all along about the natural remedy we had access to." He paused. "But Sara... I wasn't aware of how much danger you were in with your head injury. I'm sure glad you made it through."

"Thank you, brother," Sara responded. "We're all good now; just trying to figure out how to deal with this new problem."

"What problem's that, family?"

I cleared my throat. "Celo, there's apparently a new threat to the family. He goes by The Curse."

"The Curse?" Celo echoed, voice dripping with irony. "What kinda Alfred Hitchcock meets Encyclopedia Brown ish is *that*?"

"Did you just say 'ish'?" Hak laughed. "As in, shit?"

"Yeah. Ish."

"You *meant* to censor yourself?"

"Yeah," Celo responded shamelessly. "I don't curse—no pun intended—anymore."

"That's the sound of when a DJ scratches the word 'shit' on a record so we don't hear the actual curse word on the radio," Sam guffawed.

"Ain't this a bitch?" Hak sighed.

"It's just the way of life I try to live now, that's all," came Celo's explanation. "I might slip up here and there, depending on if a situation calls for it, but I'm way more mindful now."

We all exchanged a glance but wisely remained mute.

"Anyway, tell me more about this Curse character," Celo resumed.

"That's the thing," I responded, "we don't know shit."

"And how has he communicated with you? No possible phone traces or anything?"

"Nope," Don responded. "This dick has only left us letters."

"Just letters?" Celo repeated, audibly surprised. "Definitely strange. And no one has *any* idea what he looks like, or even sounds like?"

"Negative," Sam said.

"Well, I'll be damned." Celo sounded genuinely stumped. "Looks like the mighty M.O.B. have been championed. We're stuck in reverse, and it sounds like we don't know how to get out of it."

"Sounds about right," Don muttered somberly.

"This is some crazy shit," Tony burst out, dragging a palm across his face. "Ain't no man out here gonna do this to us. We're M.O.B! I won't have no one thinking they got us figured out. We ain't The Great 8 and then some for no reason."

"I agree, Tony," I chipped in. "Any ideas?"

Tony thought for a moment. "You think Blues and Brilliant Bobby can detect anything off those letters? Like Mrs. Escobar over here mentioned earlier?"

"It's a possibility," Don reasoned.

"I don't know, man," Al stepped in apprehensively. "This asshole's got his tracks covered. But hey, it's worth a shot. Sam, do you have all the letters the family has received?"

"Yeah, over in my briefcase," Sam affirmed. "I'll get them for you."

"Good: I'll have Bobby look them over. Maybe there's some kind of software on that new technology he's been using that'll be able to pick up a trace of this guy."

"This shit got me heated," Tony fumed—and, indeed, he looked particularly wound up. He wasn't used to losing, and it was setting him on edge.

"I know; you've been walkin' around in the same circle for the past twenty-seven minutes," Hak muttered.

"Are you performing a seance?" Dough grinned.

"No, asshole," Tony bit back, unamused.

"Family, family," Celo cut in. "For real though, what are we going to do about this?"

"I was hoping you'd be able to help us with that," I responded.

"Right. Let me call Peachy the Great: we need prayer."

# CHAPTER 54

*Location: Breathless; Rahway, NJ; May 12; 10:00 pm*

S O, I'VE REALLY BEEN thinking about buying this place. I spoke to Tony Victor about going in on it with me, and we both thought it to be the most logical idea. The head bouncer always kept us in the loop about any impending sales, and it seemed like he would keep asking us about buying it every time we were there. Maybe he'd have preferred to have us as his bosses instead of the old man.

Anyways, the Champagne Room was off-limits to customers that didn't have any money—which clearly wasn't a category we fit into; more often than not, we didn't know what to *do* with the money we had.

Tony told me he wanted to open up an Army & Navy store—basically one that specialized in fatigue, sweatpants, sweatshirts, combat gear, thick socks, t-shirts, and any hat imaginable. He'd also spoken to me about a sneaker he wanted to develop—but not be any kind of sneaker: *the* sneaker for the dark-skinned individual.

"Escobar, remember a few months back when we were coming here and decided to take the backstreets instead of the normal route?" Tony asked me now.

"Yeah, I remember that. Why do you ask?"

"Well, do you remember that jackass we almost hit?" he continued. "The one that was not only walking in the middle of the street, but also had the nerve to wear all dark clothes? I think that block was experiencing some kinda blackout—which made it even harder to see him."

"Oh, yeah, I remember that fool! I almost hit him."

"Exactly!" Tony said excitedly. "So, I thought to myself: if a dumbass was going to do that again, what would increase his chances of being seen, ultimately avoiding his ass getting run down like Stone Cold Steve Austin?" He paused for impact. "Nigga Lights!"

"Excuse me? *Nigga Lights*?" I echoed, trying not to laugh. "What the fuck is *that*?"

"Plain white Air Force Ones by Nike—only with a crispy second white coating for extra brightness!" The guy was practically pissing himself with excitement. "If that fool would've had these on, we would've seen him coming from a *mile* away!"

Right at that moment, Danielle—an original Breathless stripper— came by and sat with us. This was nothing out of the ordinary: the girls always sat with us, probably because they knew we were the ones with bottomless pockets. If they had a moment or two before their next run on-stage, most of them came by us, basking in our presence. Can you blame them? We're M.O.B.—a good enough reason in and of itself, if you ask me.

I carried on speaking while Danielle wrapped her arm around my neck and sat herself on my lap. "Oh, shit, you gotta point there, buddy," I said. "Genius! Outstanding! Although I do have a question: how does this get you paid? Are you just trying to sell this sneaker in your store, or are you just wanting to develop it? You know you can't 'develop' something that's already been designed, right?"

"Of course, man; I ain't stupid," Tony brushed off. "While you fools been out on these streets using your *own* money to pay for this this and that, I've been using *other* people's money because of my credit. I'm probably at a 915 credit score right now: I could do anything I want." He shrugged. "So, yes, I'm going to take the original Nike design, but what's going to make my sneaker different is the patented second white coating for extra brightness."

The man sounded like he was reading out of a catalogue.

"Second white coating for extra brightness?!" I repeated incredulously. "Are you serious, son? That ain't gonna work! What kinda Richie Cunningham shit even is that? You put the Fonz leather jacket on and all of a sudden, you're the Fonz?" I shook my head. "No, you're still Richie Cunningham with someone else's jacket on!"

Meanwhile, the DJ was going haywire. "My name is DJ Arthur 'Radio' Fonzarelli, a.k.a.973, a.k.a get in my way and I'll have to move you! Thank you for all coming out tonight; we'll be here till three, so grab those asses and tell our dancers how much you love them!"

And with that, he started playing some dope shit. *This* was the kind of guy I'd want on my record label.

"You heard of this rapper? He's *dope*, yo!" Tony exclaimed, echoing my own thoughts. "But, yeah, going back to your point, if I put a second coating of black on that leather jacket and maybe put the words 'Nigga Lights' inside the swoosh, *boom*, new idea! No longer the Fonz jacket: it's now Richie Cunningham's jacket!"

"Okay, Tony, you're right," I surrendered. "Nigga Lights will grow big and strong, like you after a long day at Planet Fitness, you big motherfucker. What the fuck are you eating, anyway? People?" I grinned. "Secondly, yes $A^2$"—referring to the rapper the DJ was currently blasting— "is tremendous; I hear he's still unsigned. After this Curse fiasco shit is done with, I think we're going to start Foul Mouth Recordz, and I want $A^2$ and that other nigga Cheef Bali on there. Those fools are the fucking truth!" I took a swig of beer. "I just hope they're still available when we start this label. Imagine them two with Joseph Stylez! It'd be like a modern-day musical version of *Fight Club* in that studio. I'd see nothing but classic material coming from that equation."

"Oh, we'll make them become available," Tony shrugged. "If someone signs them, I'll just rub them out." He thought for a moment. "Matter of fact, I'm souped right now. Gimme my shoes: I'm gonna mow 'em down. Gimme my shirt; I'll rip 'em to bits! Gimme my tie!"

I was hysterically laughing: the guy was insane. "Did you really just reenact an entire segment between Bugs Bunny and Rocky?"

"Of course I did," Tony grinned. "Is there a problem?"

"Hell no! Do that shit again. Here, give me your shoes so I could give them back to you."

We were laughing our asses off for five minutes straight: I swear, if there was something the street and gangster world would want to know to hold over Tony Victor and PR Escobar's heads, it was our love for Bugs Bunny. That motherfucker was the *original* comedy gangster.

It was at that moment that none other than Jay BaDouche came sauntering over. We'd lost him about an hour before; I thought he got swallowed by that 54' ass we saw when we first walked in.

"Yo, where the hell you assholes *been*?" he exclaimed, eyeing the stripper still on my lap. "I've been looking for you since we got here."

"Man, no you haven't! As soon as we came in, I tapped Escobar to point out the Columbian chick on-stage, and then I turned around and you was gone!" Tony was still wiping tears of laughter from his eyes. "Escobar said he saw your long-head ass following Sensation toward the Champagne Room."

"Nigga, y'all buggin'!" he protested, throwing himself down next to us. "I've been sitting here the *whole* time, on this one stool at the bar." He shrugged casually. "Yes, maybe ol' 5"4 was over this way at some point or another, but I can assure you I haven't moved from this spot."

Right on cue, the bouncer strode over, ready to blow Jay's cover. "Woo, BaDouche! That ass is *amazing*, ain't it? I thought you'd never come out of there. How did her ass taste?"

"Who, me?" he said innocently. "That wasn't me, dawg!"

"Really, yo?" the bouncer frowned. "I walked right by, and you asked me if I wanted in. I'm almost positive it was you."

Tony and I had dissolved into laughter again.

"Nah, wasn't me, family," Jay insisted stupidly.

"Damn, I guess I'm trippin'," the bouncer responded. "The cognac got a nigga seeing things. I should probably get back to my post."

"Be safe out here," Jay said to the bouncer as he walked away.

Once the guy was out of earshot, Tony turned to the guilty man. "Yo, Jay, that *was* you, wasn't it?"

"Of course it was, dumbass!" Jay grinned, face lit up. "I sucked a fart out that girl's ass! It was *wonderful*. I can't help it, brothers; women are so fuckin' beautiful man." The guy looked in love. "Yo, I gotta question to ask the both of you."

"Lay it on us," I told him.

"Why do lesbians make the best rap group members?"

I was already smirking. "I don't know, Jay: why do they make the best rap group members?"

"Because they love to beat box!"

I'm sure there was a mental health facility we could all check ourselves into close by. We damn sure needed it.

# CHAPTER 55

*Location: Hotel Indigo; Brick City; May 13; 8:00 pm*

MULA MADISON WAS GETTING ready for the annual charity fashion event she hosted every year, receiving assistance from her little brother Gwop Madison for all the behind-the-scenes work. She'd always wanted to teach him the art of giving back, and so, by the time he was old enough, he'd known how to set all the tables up, formulate security in various places, manage all the overhead and allocation of funds, and speak to the hotel's reps like a real businessman should. She believed in hard work before play, and if he wanted to be a full-fledged member of MentallyOrganizedBusiness someday, he was going to have to show her how much he wanted it.

I noticed Gwop's interest in the family business early: he took a liking to me immediately, and, in some instances, he'd even mimic me and my style. He'd sometimes dress up like me, and calls from Mula giving me such updates became frequent. It was all very flattering. I liked the kid: he was a good kid. However, he was still just that—a kid—, and God knows what we do is *not* for the kiddies by *any* stretch of the imagination. Saying this, I'd be lying if I didn't say I'd told Mula before that, if he were shown the ropes properly, we'd potentially have a future M.O.B. leader. But time will tell.

Mula called Cocoa Butter, Pudgee, and Padlock Penny over to make sure the female talent was behaving; meanwhile, Frederick Linguini, Muscles Montana, and Snugglez McPherson had all been allocated the same task over at the men's talent area. Notably, Alexandria the Grape was set to perform as the intermission entertainment, too. The night was set, and the show was to start at 8:30pm.

It sure would've been nice if it never had.

Unfortunately, at approximately 8:11pm, there was a ruckus at the front door. Snugglez and Linguini were, of course, able to put that fire out rather quickly. The problem came during their dealing with that situation:

it was at that moment that a male figure with a Benjamin Franklin mask managed to sneak in, grabbing Mula Madison from behind with a knife to her neck. In hindsight, it seems to me that it was premeditated.

From this point on, mayhem reigned: there was a sudden rush of people trying to make their way to the front entrance, but they were also met by a gang of thugs who each held Snugglez, Linguini, and Muscles Montana at gunpoint. This was serious, and we suddenly found ourselves more vulnerable than we ever had been as a collective unit.

Whish Johannsen, who was in the front row, sent a two-way message to Luciano—or, at least, she hoped she had: it was as she was hitting the Send button that the two-way was snatched out of her hand by a man with an Abraham Lincoln mask.

Cocoa, Pudgee, and Penny had been tied up by three men—also sporting a past president's mask. They had been sat on three chairs, back-to-back, their wrists tightly bound, NY Giants Skullies placed over their heads so they couldn't see anything that was happening.

It was the man who had Mula at knifepoint—the one in the Benjamin Franklin mask—who decided to end the silence. "I'm going to make this as clear as possible, so even the slow ones in here will understand," he announced. His voice was deep; gruff. "We have direct orders to kill you, if need be, and trust me, there are a few faces I see already that I wouldn't mind permanently laying down. However, if you do as we ask, nobody gets hurt. Capiche?"

The man in the Abraham Lincoln mask called over to his associate, "Bring Mula Madison over here; I heard she cook her ass off! I can't wait to take her home and see for myself."

"Take me *home*?" Mula bit back. "If that's all you wanted to do, why didn't you just ask?"

The Abraham Lincoln guy paused. "Really?"

"See!" Benjamin Franklin said happily. "I told you she was a freak."

"Damn right I am! Why don't you come with us and I'll show both of you a time you'll never forget?"

Benjamin Franklin surveyed his prey for a moment. "Don't tempt me; I'm standing behind you right now catching a full-on woody."

"I know," Mula stated simply. "Let me move back a little closer so I can feel what I'm working with." Clearly thinking with his dick, the guy obliged, and Mula smiled. "Yeah, I like that. This knife to my neck business is a nice touch, too; brings an S&M kinda feel to it. You should bring it with you to my house."

"Yo, she wildin'," Abraham Lincoln grinned. "I know she want it." He sighed. "Fuck it, let's take her to the crib and give her what she wants."

Benjamin Franklin was clearly considering it. "I just might agree to that. What's this perfume you have on? It's delicious! Smells like new money..."

"You close," Mula praised. "It's called Brand New Money."

While she'd been speaking, Mula had managed to inch the back of her heel closer and closer, higher and higher, until she finally managed to get close enough to lift it right into Benji's family jewels.

He instantly dropped his knife to the ground as he withered in pain. Suddenly, everything descended into even more chaos: this change of plans completely put the other guys in disarray. It was an absolute domino effect of harmonious villainy: those few seconds that Mula took business into her own hands simultaneously created a string of events that all occurred in flawless fluidity. Snugglez, Muscles, and Linguini all turned the tables on their gun holders, instead holding the guns to *their* heads just like that. Whish arose and freed the girls from the chairs they'd been tied to, who all quickly took off their hats.

Like a deer stuck in headlights, the guy with the Abraham Lincoln Mask froze as all four ladies rushed to him and began beating the shit outta him. Don't ask me where my sister found a torque wrench at; to be honest, I'm not really sure why that was in a hotel to begin with, but fuck it: it served her well.

Padlock Penny literally had a bag of padlocks in her bookbag, which she hit Mr. Lincoln with a few times. I think she walks around with those things—for reasons unknown to everyone besides her.

Meanwhile, Whish walked over to the other three guys that our men were currently holding at gunpoint. She looked each of them up and down, smirked at the one with the Ronald Reagan mask, and swiftly pulled out her cellphone, calling Sara Safebreaka.

"Hello? Whish? This better be good; you're interrupting my soaps!"

Whish smiled to herself. "Would you believe this Curse guy tried to kill Mula at the fashion charity event today?"

Sara audibly gasped. "Are you serious? How do you know it was the Curse? Did you see him? What's that asshole look like?" Sara was equal parts horrified and elated: if she's seen him, we'd be that much closer to busting his ass.

"No, of course his bitch-ass didn't show up," Whish sighed. "He *never* shows up. But I know it was him: remember that letter he sent me the other day? About going after one of my blood relatives, or one of my sisters? Well, this was his attempt—but Mula is unfortunately too damn smart for their dumbassess, and she lured them into a trap and as soon as they let their guard down."

"Wow," Sara breathed. "Is the family is okay?"

"Oh, yeah; I just got some of our henchmen with three guns pointed at three heads right now. We're just wondering what we should do with them." Whish began circling around each guy, offering each a sickly-sweet smile.

"Are any of them cute?" Sara asked.

"I can't tell: they all came in with dead president's masks on. One had a Benjamin Franklin mask." She laughed. "Why do we call cash 'dead presidents' when the guy on the highest bill was never president? But, yeah, anyways, I don't know what they look like. We left their masks on."

"So, there's been no bloodshed?" Sara clarified.

"Nope; no bloodshed. I was a bit confused over the whole ordeal myself; that's why I decided to call you," Whish explained.

"And where's Mula at right now?"

"Oh, she and Cocoa Butta are at Mr. Franklin's shaken body." Whish gasped delightedly. "Oh, damn: Cocoa just dropped his pants and dipped his balls in the coffee pot! Go get 'em, girl! Imagine it's Jake!"

Cocoa turned around with a big-ass grin and went to work. The guy was screaming bloody murder—that is, until Cocoa got tired of his screams and sliced him across his larynx with the knife he'd previously held to her throat. Blood trickled down the lower part of his neck like a leaking faucet. It was a rather rich sight to see.

"Well, it looks like y'all got everything covered," Sara said down the phone. "I'm getting ready to get back to my soaps. Call me later!"

"But wait!" Whish protested. "What do we do with these three fools I got here?"

"Oh, just let them go," Sara waved off.

Whish hadn't seen that coming. "For real?" Her disappointment was palpable. Sara just laughed.

"Of course not. Kill 'em! All three of them! Love you guys. And drive safe when you're done." And with that, she hung up.

Whish wasn't one to ignore instructions: one-by-one, each thug fell right where they stood. It was a rather quick and painless death for them.

Once this deed was done, Mula walked over to Whish and the henchmen, Penny, Cocoa, and Pudgee following suit a few seconds later. All stood back and admired their work: the venue was dotted multiple dark, rich pools of blood.

They all looked at one another with silent acknowledgment of a job well done before all hugging each other and offering their congratulations.

It was at that moment that the double French doors opened up to the room where the event was supposed to take place—and in swaggered Sam Luciano.

"Whish! Family!" he greeted. "I got here as fast as I could. Where dem niggas at? I'll skin them alive!"

"Don't worry about it, babe," Whish smiled, planting a kiss on his cheek. "You're late, as usual. What's for dinner?"

# CHAPTER 56

*Location: The Glowing Midgets Shop; May 15; 11:00 pm*

QURTIS JENKINS HAD JUST arrived home from his latest porno film production. He walked over to his beautiful plush chair in his signature uniform: a straw hat, a robe—*TGM* inscribed in diamonds across the back of it—, bunny slippers, and a cigar imported from Sweden. He was a strange cat, but he was also one of my closest friends—and I'm sure he'd say the same about me.

His latest film was titled *Give It To Me Raw*, and was about girls with fascinations of men inserting uncooked vegetables into their vaginas. It was also hosted by Ol'Dirty Bastard—yes, the rapper. Don't ask me: people fuckin' buy this crap.

I called him too let him know that Don Corione wanted to do some business with him after we killed The Curse—something I'm sure would've left Salawicious Dough heated, but then again, he's gotta get over the fact that he and Q are in the same business—just on different spectrums. If he were smart, he'd stop trying to run Q out of town and capitalize on how much money they could make together; I mean, could you imagine films with Licki Bella—well, when she was alive—being in rotation forever? *That's* the kind of shit Qurtis Jenkins supplies; that, and a full inventory of adult toys. Meanwhile, what Dough has is a ranch where he provides a service for people to live out their lifelong fantasies in that moment. There's so much money to be made from each business, and Q is always open to partnerships of any kind, as long as his brand isn't compromised. Plus, his brand is M.O.B., just as Dough's is.

I'm sure Dough will get it eventually. After all, everything is eventual, right? Where have I heard that one before?

Anyway, Don called Q while he was puffing on the last bit of his cigar, who answered on the first ring.

"Don Corione, you fuckin' MC-Shan-fanny-pack-wearin'...! What's up, son?"

"Qurtis Jenkins! Ya fuckin' Leave-it-to-Beaver-sideburns-havin' ass-nigga!"

They—and we—could do this for hours on end—heck, for years and years. I don't know what it is, but we find laughter to be the highest form of pleasure, alongside any you can attain through a vagina.

"Q," Don continued, "my new porno is called *Giving It All Away And Getting It All Back Again,* starring Cravin Moorehead and his co-star Happy Endings. She's in all my movies, and I need you to direct it. What do you think?"

"What do I *think?*" Q echoed, somewhat insulted. "That's the dumbest thing I've ever heard, Theo! No wonder you get Ds in everything!"

"Theo? Like, from *The Cosby Show?*"

"No, Theo from *The Golden Girls.*" Q sounded irritated. "Matter of fact, my next porno will be Cravin Moorehead walking around town with a Gordon Gartrelle shirt on, swinging his penis around while the glowing midgets follow behind him singing *Beat It* by Michael Jackson. How's that for a great film?"

"That sucks," Don responded honestly.

"That's fuckin' awesome!" Q insisted. "I'm gonna call my brother Jack Lantern and see if he's open to doing it, since you obviously don't see art when it's right in front of you."

"Art?" Don echoed. "Q, I wanna do a porno film, not a fuckin' audition to the adult version of *The Wizard of Oz!* Not *one* time did you mention vagina... pussy... love hole.... gushy stuff. How can I make a porno without the main ingredient?"

"Of course, that's the be all and end all," Q reasoned, "but I make *films:* I must have some sort of plotline, props, and additional characters before the climax—pun intended—takes place. Don't you have any of that available for *your* projects?"

"Nah, not really," Don shrugged. "I was thinking more along the lines of: girl comes through; boy whips dick out; boy inserts dick into pussy; goes in and out repeatedly for six minutes the first time and thirteen minutes the second; and boom!—we're done."

Q sighed. "You'll never last in this business. What is this? 1946?"

"No, it's 1996, and the audience doesn't give a fuck about all that story shit."

"There's no way that's true, Don," Q stated simply. "I'm telling you; I've been doing this for fifteen years, and all my films have gone on to be major successes. The story is what initially piques their interest, but it's the characters and the way the act is presented that keeps them coming back for more. I know what I'm talking about."

Don thought for a moment. "I guess I never thought about it that way before," he admitted. "Give me a couple days and I'll be back in touch with you; I think I see where I could go with this."

"No doubt, Don!" Q said warmly. "Oh, and by the way, Escobar tells me you juggle three chicks back home— something about the days of the week? You should let me do a film with them: we'll call it *Menage a Twats*. You like it?"

"Q, you need to get help."

"I know," Q grinned, "but I refuse to do so. I'm having too much fun out here. I'll see you at the gala in a few days; I'll be in my TGM robe and bunny slippers. I hope there's no dress code."

"Who cares?" Don shrugged. "He's lucky we're even entertaining his punk ass. I'll see you then, brother."

"See you then."

With that, Qurtis Jenkins hung the phone up and went over to the East Wing of his shop, brushing past the award he'd won for Best Film Director at the Adult RawClub the year before. It always made him feel a sense of accomplishment, also making him think back to the good old days when he and his brother Jack Lantern would shoot these films on 118th Street in Brick City. If I remember correctly, the first film Qurtis Jenkins made was called *Smackdown*, and was about slapping hoes to the ground and then letting them pull themselves up by your penis—on purpose. It was a Pimp movie featuring Mr. Fantastic from The Fantastic 4. After all, who else's penis would allow you to pull your entire body weight up on it?

It was as he began to close shop that he heard a knock at the door. Q was equal parts irritated and intrigued: who the hell would be calling at this hour?

"Hold up, I'll be right there," he called out, swiftly grabbing his rifle and walking over to the front of the shop: you could never be sure. He opened the door, rifle in hand, and was pleasantly surprised.

"Q! Let me in! Hurry up! These little glowing bastards keep chasing me around."

"Dough?" Q grinned. "Well, I'll be fucked by a candy apple till the crumbs expire. The fuck you doin' here?"

"It's time to bury the hatchet," Dough shrugged, stepping into the shop, shivering. "It's time to make business moves—to invest in each other. I believe we could do amazing shit together."

Q raised an eyebrow. "Who paid you to say that, then? You'd never say that shit."

Dough smiled lazily. "Yeah, but I had you goin' for a few seconds, didn't I?"

"Not for one damn second," Q retorted. "What d'ya want, Dough? You're a pain in my ass, you know that?"

"Thank you; that actually makes me feel better," Dough said solemnly. "Escobar sent me over here to check out your shop, since our initial encounter a while back."

"Yeah, and why would he do that?"

"I don't know, man; why does he do anything that he does? The man's a certifiable genius, and a certifiable maniac, all at once." Dough began wandering around, checking out the place. "He apparently wants us to try to settle our differences and do business together. *I* think it's a horrible idea, personally; I think that—"

"Yes, I'll do business with you, Dough," Q interrupted. "It only makes sense to do so; I've been waiting to get your girls in my films for forever." He paused. "And the things your girls could do with my toys... You could charge your clientele double or triple with some of the shit I got. We should've done this a *long* time ago."

"You think so?"

"*Hell* no!" Q burst out, pushing Dough toward the door. "Now get the fuck out my store, asshole!"

# CHAPTER 57

*Location: Jay BaDouche & Hak Hennesey's House;
May 16; 8:30 am*

"**A**ND DON'T CALL HERE no more, bitch! I'm warning you!"
Jay's voice had reached a high-pitched frenzy as he addressed the chick on the other side of the phone call. He didn't give her the time to finish her protests: he slammed the handset down.

Meanwhile, Hak was finishing up a bowl of cereal—his third, to be precise—, which he quickly set down upon Jay's sudden silence: he walked into the other room to find out what the commotion was all about.

Tony Victor was at the house, too, as was Sam Luciano: the former was trying to figure out which pair of Nigga Lights he wanted to wear to the gala the following night—as if anybody would be able to tell the difference.

Hak saw Jay sitting out on the patio, looking like a sad puppy dog.

"Yo! What's the matter wit' you?" he called, standing in front of Jay. "You good? I know ya moms is good, because I just dropped her off last—"

"Nigga, say some shit about my moms right now and I'm gonna take each pair of Nigga Lights Tony got back there and shove 'em up your ass!"

Hak was taken aback. "Each? I believe one would suffice."

Jay pressed on, tense with frustration. "Yo, you know what this bitch had the nerve to say to me?"

At that moment, Sam Luciano walked onto the patio to check in on Jay BaDouche, as Hak had done a minute before. Jay continued: "Yeah, you know what this bitch had the nerve to say to me?"

"What she say?" Hak asked.

"Was it, ♪'Is it on my face'♪?" Sam piped up, and, to Jay's and Hak's horror, started gyrating on the back of the patio chairs. Jay and Hak cried for about three minutes straight with laughter, and Tony... Well, Tony was always late to the party: later, he could only go off what the guys had told him.

When he could finally talk again, Jay wheezed, "Sam, what in the douche-baggery-fuck was *that*?"

"Brother, I have no clue; it just came to me," Sam hiccupped. "It was almost like this masterpiece I've been waiting for the perfect time to unveil. It was kinda like my magnum opus... Yeah, that's it, my Magnum Opus."

"Your Magnum *what*?" Hak laughed. "You mean, like, Magnum PI?"

"*No*, fool; you don't know what Magnum Opus means?"

"I think you're making it up, to be honest," Hak shrugged.

Tony—having entered the patio a minute before—explained, "Hak, Magnum Opus is a person's greatest work—a sense of personal achievement in its greatest form possible."

"Oh, so it's a real word?"

"Yes, sir, it is," Tony confirmed.

"I don't give a *fuck* if it's real or not: what this man—one of our 'leaders'—just did was *the* funniest shit I've ever seen in my whole fuckin' life!" Jay declared, still laughing. "It was definitely not leader-esque, but when the time comes for us to vote for our new leader, I'll be voting for you." He was starting up again: the tears of hysteria were trickling down his cheeks. "That's the gayest shit I've ever seen since Sticks Morano licked his own index finger up and down over and over again toward Hak here, clearly indicating that he wanted to Schlong Dance with him via saliva assistance."

Tony snorted.

"That's not funny," Hak retorted.

"Yes, it is," Tony cackled. "That's funny as *hell*. I was there; I remember that."

"Okay, okay, I think we've talked enough shit for the moment, fellas," Sam pointed out, still smirking. "There was a reason we all came out here to see Jay. What's really good, bruh?"

Jay's expression darkened. "Sam, I've been fuckin' with this ghetto bitch over by the Palisades; I know it's a horrible neighborhood and that a man of my status shouldn't be over there, but Sam, her pussy is *so* fucking good. I physically can't help it."

"Okay, I get that," Sam assented. "Vagina should have its own star on the Hollywood Walk of Fame. I understand that, as do all of us."

"Yeah, he's got a point," Hak agreed.

"But then again," Sam countered, "what in the sour ass juice does that have to do with anything? You said the bitch had the nerve to say something to you, or something like that."

"Family, can we just go play a little ball in the backyard?" was all Jay said. "Me and Hak just got this new hoop installed. Let's go check it out."

"Yo, stop *stalling*," Hak cried out. "You don't even *play* ball!"

Jay ignored Hak and instead began descending the steps toward the basketball area. Realizing that they'd lost this fight, the guys wordlessly followed him. Jay then grabbed one of the fresh balls off the rack, then going to shoot his shot. He took careful aim before shooting—and missing by about three feet to the left. This guy couldn't put the ball in the hole if that shit was the size of a jacuzzi.

"Man, gimme that!" Sam demanded. "You don't know nothing about this."

"Yeah, he don't know *nothing* about our times on Chancellor... Temple... Linden... Kean... Seton..." Sam listed. "We played ball *everywhere!*"

"Word; I loved those times," Hak sighed. "We gotta get back out there, get back into shape. Anyway, are you gonna tell us what this chick said, or are we gonna have to beat it out of you?"

"I don't wanna talk about it," Jay muttered.

"Man, if you don't say something now, I'm gonna—"

"I'm having a baby." Jay's voice cracked upon saying these words.

Tony looked like his eyes were going to pop out of his head. "A *what?*"

"A baby." Jay had never looked so disturbed.

"As in, a person who looks like you? Who's gonna have your DNA running through its veins?" Hak countered. "As in, your sperm met an egg and decided to create a human out of it?"

"*Yes*, motherfucker!" Jay snapped.

"Whoa. I didn't see that coming," Sam murmured.

"Well, she didn't see it coming, either, you know!" Jay burst out. "I just bussed her ass and came inside of her, so neither of us 'saw it coming'."

"Let me get this straight," Tony cut in. "This is real? Jay BaDouche is going to be a father?" He shook his head in disbelief. "Nah... Sounds like a setup. This can't be real."

"Well, it is, Tony, and I don't know what to do."

Hak bit his lip. "How you know she's telling the truth? How do you know it's even *yours*?"

"Being honest with you, brother I don't," Jay responded, "but I just know; I ain't never felt this way before. There's gotta be something to it."

"Well as long as you want to find out what's real and what's not, we'll take care of this full steam ahead," Sam offered. "You want me to send Whish over to see her?"

"*Whish*?" Jay repeated incredulously. "Man, hell no! Whish hates me."

"She doesn't hate you, Jay: she doesn't hate anyone. She's too kind-hearted."

"She put a bullet in the brain of a chick she didn't even know!" Jay reminded him. "At a Dairy Queen, at that—a fine family establishment of joy and laughter."

"He's got another point, Sam," Tony said quietly.

"Okay, so she can be a hothead at times," Sam conceded, "but so can all three of you! You're all killers!"

"Whoa, whoa, whoa," Tony said, "that's where we draw the line, Sam. I ain't no killer; I just crush a lot."

"Oh, come on, Tony," Hak sighed, "that sounds like a rap line some fat guy is gonna use in a song in the next ten years."

"Oddly specific, but yeah, maybe. That'll be dope. But anyway, I ain't no killer: I just end people's lives when those lives don't deserve to be lived anymore."

"I second that," Hak chipped in.

"I can't fuck with any of you niggas right now," Jay said. "I *knew* neither of you were going to take this seriously."

Noting the look of hopelessness in his friend's eyes, Sam sighed and clapped his friend's shoulder affectionately. "Look, Jay, we got you; we *always* got you. We'll get the truth ASAP, trust me. Until then, you might wanna evacuate the premises."

Jay frowned. "Why?"

"'Cuz I just bussed my ass, and that shit smells *awful*. Clear the court, fellas."

# CHAPTER 58

S ARA HAD BEEN HAVING a tough time ever since her head injury and, considering I know Sara as well as I do, I'd bet my next million that she was angry that she couldn't kill the person herself who had hospitalized her: she'd always been a "take care of it herself" kinda gal—it was one of the many traits we loved about her so much when we decided to make her an original leading lady of the family and business.

Don, Sam and I never hesitated when making that decision, and I'm sure glad we didn't.

Padlock Penny was in the family room visiting her big sister, her nephew balanced on her knee. That boy was about six years old and could answer any math equation you gave him. I guess that's what happens when your Dad is a mathematical genius.

"Where's my brother-in-law's big-ass head at?" Penny asked, looking around the room. "I feel like every time I'm here, I never see him."

"Girl, I'm *married* to the man and I feel like I never see him!" Sara sighed.

"That must suck."

"At times," Sara admitted, "but I've been busy making these glasses over here."

Since her injury, Sara hadn't really been out on the streets conducting business much; instead, she had to preoccupy herself elsewhere—so had she started designing and customizing cups, glasses, and any other kitchen piece you could think of. She hadn't really thought about how much she'd missed simply *creating* things: her time as an adult consisted of being a mom, a wife, and a gangster for a super crazy faction known as M.O.B. so, on the whole, the whole let's-sit-down-and-make-shit thing had been off the cards for her.

"Do you like it?" Sara asked her sister, grabbing one of the glasses: this time the with her husband's name on it.

"Do I like it? Where the hell's *mine*, bitch?" Penny demanded. "I love it, though; these are so cool. Can you make two for me and Pudgee? I'd like to get her a gift for her birthday next month; I haven't really seen her lately, since she's been seeing ol' boy."

"Ol' boy? And who exactly is that?"

"Jackson Devereux," Penny stated, a mischievous glint in her eye. "He used to be a small-time dealer on South Orange Avenue, but later decided to leave that life alone and instead joined the church and never looked back. He's a deacon now, like Celo Gaston is in North Carolina."

"Is that right?" Sara mused absently. "Pudgee done found herself a church boy. Ain't that something? I wouldn't have believed that if I'd seen it with my own two eyes." She paused, seemingly lost in thought. "Is she happy? Like, for real?"

"I don't know," Penny admitted. "I'm assuming so. Like I said, I haven't seen her much in the last few weeks, but I've spoken with her, and she seems happy. I hope she is, anyway. I miss her, though; we'll see her tomorrow at the gala, though. I know she'll be there."

"Good; I can't wait to see her myself. What are you wearing? I got a few dresses here that you might like." Sara pointed toward the bed. "I just got these in from Atlanta by Natt Taylor. I love them, but I don't know which one to pick. Why don't you be a doll and take one, and that way my choice can be less painful?"

"Uh, you know I don't really do dresses, sis," Penny reminded her, sounding somewhat uncomfortable just at the prospect of wearing one.

"Yeah, I know, but get over it," Sara said bluntly. You're wearing a dress and you're wearing heels, so let's go: get your ass in that closet and pick out whatever you want. It's yours."

"Why you gotta be so pushy?" Penny huffed, still obeying her sister's wishes.

"Because if I'm not, you'd mistake me for one of your little friends out here, and then I'd have to smack you up."

"That's a good point," Penny admitted. "Where are your shoes? In this closet, or the other one?"

"*Closet*? Are you crazy? I have *way* too many shoes to put them in a closet," Sara reminder her. "They're in the room that used to be yours down the hall; the dresses are in that closet over there."

It was as Penny leafed through the articles of clothing, her back to her sister, that Sara felt a sudden rush of love and nostalgia toward her little sister, and she told her so. "You know, Penny, I don't think I've told you this in a long time, bit you've really blossomed into a beautiful young woman—and that body is to die for." Penny turned and eyed her sister suspiciously, expecting some kind of punchline, but Sara's expression was sincere. "I'm very proud of you and all the hard work you've put into climbing the family ladder. I just wanted to tell you that I see it and appreciate it. I love you!"

"Don't make me *cry*," Penny whined, and, indeed, her eyes were filling up. "I just put this stupid eyeliner on. Now it's all over my face." She looked in the mirror closest to her and groaned. "See? That's why I don't do this dress-up shit."

"Oh, stop it; you're a woman now, and this is what we do." Sara shrugged. "Besides, how you gon' make the boys go crazy when you're wearing the same jeans they got on?"

"I'm not interested in boys right now."

Sara rolled her eyes. "You've never been a good liar and you know it—well, not to me, at least."

"Now I see what Whish is always saying about you," Penny huffed. "You're so... *motherly*. I guess I can appreciate that, but it gets annoying sometimes."

"Yeah, you're right, and I don't care," Sara responded simply, "so hurry the hell up and pick what you want and get up outta here now: Al's on his way home, and I'm thinking about making another baby."

"Really?"

"Yes, really. I know my husband, and he's not gonna try his best to lay that seed if he knows you're here lurking in the house somewhere." Sara examined a nail. "Now, you've got five minutes, and then you gots to go, baby girl!"

"I'm just gonna take this red dress and black pumps," Penny sighed, showing her sister. "Simple yet elegant, don't you think?"

"The solid red dress," Sara sighed. "It'll do."

"And what about the black shoes?" Penny insisted, making her way to the front door.

"The solid black shoes with the solid red dress. You're gonna kill them. Now get on outta here; I think I hear him pulling up in the driveway, and I'm ovulating."

# CHAPTER 59

*Location: Casa de Escobar Original; Union, NJ; 6:00 pm*

POPPA AND MOMMA ESCOBAR have always been the set of parents most of the M.O.B. family considered to be their parents too. Don't get me wrong, Peachy the Great and the House of Gaston were the places of orientation, origin, and establishment of our family, and nothing will ever take that away, but my parents were also very down-to-earth: very in-your-face, and very real. The apple clearly didn't fall far from the tree.

My parents were from Brooklyn and the Bronx respectively, and I distinctly remember one time when my father told me a story about throwing his sister's cat out the window because she threw his GI Joe toys away. I remember saying to him, "Damn, Dad, the toys were replaceable, but you threw her cat out the window!"

If you're paying attention at all, you'll know that's the same woman who threw her husband out the window; apparently our window stories are consistent and hereditary, so if you're ever talking to me while we're standing next to one, you should perhaps move. Just a friendly suggestion.

"Brother, are you really going to eat all of Mom's pork chops again?" my sister asked me, shouldering me out the way. "I mean, could you at least leave some for the kids?"

"And why would I do that?" I asked, sucking some of the flavoring from my fingers. "They shouldn't be eating pork, anyway; their organs can't handle that type of food."

"Where'd you get that stupid shit from, then?" Pudgee asked.

"I don't know... I think I seen it on the opposite side of a Snapple cap, or something. Or maybe it was a *Looney Tunes* episode."

"Special Ed."

Pudgee had liked calling comical idiots like myself "Special Ed", so instead of retaliating, I whipped out the weapon I'd been waiting to use for what felt like forever.

"So," I countered, "who's this fool you're seeing? Or did you not think I'd find out?"

"I knew you'd find out," she shrugged casually. "You're PR Escobar. What *don't* you know?"

"I don't know who The Curse is, and that really boils my blood," I reminded her.

"Well, I'm sure we'll find out tomorrow night. On that note, are you prepared for what might happen?" She seemed unnerved at the thought of it. "I think I'm a little scared."

"There's no need to be scared, little sister," I reassured her firmly. "I won't let anything happen to you. Am I curious? Yes. But am I worried? No; I got this, as I always do. We're a group of men and women that cannot be stopped when we're together as a collective unit. There's absolutely nothing that can conquer us. So, because I know that to be the truth, I know that I have nothing to be worried about. You either pray or panic—you can't do both." I thought for a moment. "In terms of me being prepared... Well, the answer to that is, absolutely. There's no way I won't be: Don, Sam and I have decided to not have an elaborate plan-on deck, but to obviously be ready for anything. This Curse guy or gal—or group of people, potentially—can't be prepped for in any specific fashion; we don't even have a visual. The only way to combat that is to be ready for anything and everything: expect the unexpected, and don't expect the expected. In other words, don't think about anything due it being 'impossible'. Just be, then do."

"Better you than me," was her response.

"Well, thanks; that sure makes me feel good," I joked. "Although I'd wouldn't have it any other way, when it comes down to it."

With that, Pudgee made her way out the kitchen to bring over a massive plate of homemade biscuits: they were flaky and tremendously hot, but my mother knew exactly how I liked them. No butter for me; just the way they come out of the stove is just right.

"I didn't mean it like that, you blockhead!" came her voice from around the corner. "I *mean* you were built for this: you're a born leader, and were made to set trends and create paths for people to follow. That's who you are and, because of that, I know we're going to be just fine when tomorrow's over." She stopped to lecture somebody on eating too quickly.

"I, on the other hand," she continued, "would've never been able to handle this level of insanity. That's all I meant by that."

"Well, thank you for the clarification, but it wasn't needed," I assured her. "I'll always protect you. Now, you wanna tell me who this Jackson Devereux character is? He's not like that old fool that got into a tangle with, ending with the both of you ended up bleeding, is he? I don't fancy almost killing another one of your lovers."

"I don't know what you're talking about," she retorted.

"Sure you do," I insisted. "You're telling me you don't remember when Mom called me when that whole thing went down and me and Sam rushed down to where you were staying? Let's not forget the fact that when we pulled up, Sam went to the wrong house and scared the Holy Ghost out of this old woman sitting on her couch."

"Okay, yes, I remember. I guess I just tried to block that one out."

"Understood," I nodded. "But I did ask you a question."

My sister could literally avoid the plague, global warming and any act of terrorism if it meant she wouldn't be confronted about her emotions. She was a nice person but she didn't like talking about herself. Period.

"He's good," she eventually said. "I like him—a lot. And I think he might be The One."

"The One?" This was more serious than I'd thought. "Do Mom and Dad know about this?"

"*No*, so be quiet before one of them hear you," she hissed, placing her fingers across my mouth. "Please; I'm not ready to tell them yet."

"Well, how serious is this? How real?"

"Very." She took a deep breath and suddenly had what was unmistakably fear in her eyes. It was in that moment that I knew there was more to tell—much more. "I'm a few weeks late."

I could have collapsed in that moment, I swear to God.

"Holy *shit*," I breathed. I couldn't speak for a moment: I don't know what I'd been expecting, but it hadn't been this. "When were you going to say something? You want Dad to pull out the long snub-nosed one from the big box upstairs? If not, I might have to do it for him!"

"*No*, I don't want you or Dad to pull *anything* out! Damn!"

"So you're telling me you're serious with this dude and you might be with child, and yet your parents don't know and I've never met the guy? Yeah, that's out."

"I know, and I'm sorry." She looked genuinely emotional. "I don't know what else to say." And with that, her eyes brimmed with tears and spilled over, trailing down her cheeks.

I walked over to my sister and wrapped my arms around her: she always made me turn into a big ol' teddy bear.

"We good. Bring him tomorrow and I'll give him The Talk then. Is there anything I need to be prepared for? Anything at all?"

She rubbed her nose, sniffing up. "Well, he has this weird tendency to belt into a Stevie Wonder song outta nowhere. I mean, we were at the store the other night and this old lady walked by us with a very nice church hat on; I complimented her on it and, before you know, it here comes Jackson belting *Isn't She Lovely*." She smiled to herself. "I was so embarrassed, I couldn't get out that store soon enough. I stood out the front waiting for him for what felt like forever and, when he finally came outside, he told me that he struck up a conversation with the woman and that she'd be visiting his church next weekend. This fool could make friends at a funeral."

"That's actually pretty funny," I admitted. "Sounds like something I would've done. Okay, well, we'll see tomorrow; but for now, can you please bring the damn pork chops in already?"

My sister laughed while wiping the last tear from her lovely face.

# CHAPTER 60

*Location: Galloping Hill Inn; Vauxhall, NJ; 7:35 pm*

I WISH I COULD start this with "it was a dark and stormy night", like some kind of 1955 novel written by the Red Baron from *Peanuts Fame*, but no: it was a beautiful spring night, at approximately 68° with no wind chill—in other words, an absolute gorgeous evening. The ladies looked beautiful, and the guys were all dressed in their finest linens—that is, except for Qurtis Jenkins, who, as promised, really was just sporting his TGM robe, a straw hat, and some Timberland boots. At least he'd left the bunny slippers home.

I received a call from Poppa Vein last night, after I'd left my parents' house: he mentioned that he and Polo Pasé had both received invitations for this occasion, too. He was family to me, so I didn't mind this at all: in fact, it was reassuring to have someone else just as powerful as we were in the building. As I'd told my sister yesterday, I didn't have the slightest clue what to expect.

Frederick Linguini was accompanied by Alexandria the Grape. They looked good together. I didn't know if something was going on between them, but if it was, I'd be cool with it.

They walked in and sat down by Tony Victor and his two dates—and yes, we finally got to see the Italian chicks he was constantly talking about. As expected, they were fine as hell.

Don Corione literally walked in with Friday Night Lights, Saturday Night Fever, and Any Given Sunday all on his arm, quickly showing some love to everyone before heading right over to where Qurtis Jenkins was sitting. I'm not sure if I want to know what that conversation was about— at least, not then.

Sam Luciano and Whish Johannsen walked in, accompanied by Al Gebra and Sara Safebreaka. The Great 8 table was right in the middle of the dancefloor—something I think struck us all as odd, but something we all collectively ignored and kept it moving. All my brothers and sisters looked like $2,000,000: it was pretty astonishing.

My wife was in a beautiful gown, crafted specially by the good folks at Diakonos Designs. Whoever was the "eye" over there was a visual genius: Yelly looked beyond stunning, as she always does. Her hair was braided and draped over her left shoulder, caressing her bosom—a look she knows full well I like on her. I'm sure she did it on purpose. That's my baby; that's my queen.

Yelly and I made our way toward the double deck outside. This was a really nice place; we'd been here before for a wedding a while back. I forget whose wedding it was, but I digress.

I looked at my wife and I kissed her on the top of her nose—something she loves me doing—and delicately whispered to her that after tonight, I would give it some serious thought about getting out of this life—all she'd ever wanted. She was—and still is—a tough cookie, and will beat your ass if needed, but deep inside, she's a very delicate flower that needs to be nurtured and taken care of—a job I relished in shouldering. I would take care of and love her until God decided to call me home—and, even once I get there, I'd still ask how I could still go about loving and taking care of her on the other side. My love runs deep for my wife.

After about ten minutes, there was a sudden crazy, indecipherable sound coming from the front of the Galloping Hill Inn. *Well, I guess The Curse is here,* I thought, feeling pretty resigned over the matter at this point.

Sam and I went out to see what was going on. There was a big-ass Ford F250 pulling up that sounded like there was a leprechaun trapped in its muffler—or, better yet, a leprechaun having sex with a vacuum cleaner. It was rather horrible.

Twenty seconds elapsed, and we had all emerged onto the front. It was at that moment that the door of the car swung open, and there stood no other than Celo Gaston.

"What in the flying fuck is this?" I demanded. "Did you lose a bet, or something?"

"No," he frowned. "Why'd you say that?"

"Because the damn thing sounds like a terrorist attack!" Don yelled out to him.

Everybody on the steps started hollering and laughing hysterically. Celo, however, was not amused.

"I don't see what's so funny," he muttered irritably. "Let me introduce you to Betsy."

"Finally, we get to see this woman you've been clamoring about to me!" I said.

"No, Betsy is the truck," Celo clarified.

"What the everlasting *fuck*?" I burst out. "Are you serious? You *named* this hunk of shit?"

"Hey, she knows when you're talking about her," he scolded, "so cut it out." He turned back to his sorry excuse of a truck. "Now, I will introduce you to the future, Mrs. Gaston."

Celo continued to walk around to the back of the vehicle, opening the passenger side door for a young lady. She emerged looking pretty as snow on a January evening. He grabbed her by the hand to assist her out of the transformer—I mean, the truck.

Celo stared at his partner like she was a deity. "Family, I want to introduce you to Naija 'Nenee' Holmes—but you can just call her Nenee."

"It's a pleasure to meet you, Ms. Holmes," I said politely.

"Please, call me Nenee," she smiled. "And likewise; the pleasure is mine."

Celo turned to Nenee. "Why don't I bring you inside and away from these fools so I can introduce you to the rest of the family?"

"Okay." She dipped her head politely to myself and to Don, who had migrated to my side—no doubt to get a better view of the lovely lady. "It was nice meeting you, Escobar and Corione."

She looped her arm through Celo's and followed his lead into the house.

Once she was out of earshot, Don turned to me. "How did she know our names?"

"She's clearly done her homework," I shrugged. "I like her; she's in."

"Agreed." He began looking around. "Where's Jay and Hak? I haven't seen them yet."

Looking over his shoulder, I grinned knowingly. "Looks like you spoke too soon..."

Jay BaDouche and Hak Hennesey were rolling up together in Hak's brand new '96 Thunderbird. That shit was *bad*—and the dopest part about it was the music Hak would blast, as he was now.

"Yo, what in the hell is that you playing?" I shouted over the noise. "Sounds like Stylez to me."

"That's because it is!" Jay shouted back, leaning out the window and smiling widely—an overexcited dog.

"Whoa," Don responded, eyebrows shooting up. "When the hell did he do this?"

"It's been a minute; he left this tape at the crib," Hak explained through the open windows as he pulled up. "We just found it when Jay was looking for that new Black Moon album he had laying around. Luckily, we decided to give it a listen, and here we are."

"Yo, that dude's talented as fuck," I said, thoroughly impressed. "It's *ridiculous*! Have you heard anything about his status, Don? Because I haven't yet."

"His mom reached out to me last night," Don responded. "He completed the first ten days of the program and apparently already seems like a whole-ass new man. He's got a way to go yet, but our brother will be back better than ever, sooner than later."

"I don't doubt that one bit. I love that dude."

"Come on, let's get inside," Don suggested, Hak and Jay now walking toward us. "I'm sure this sugary motherfucker is getting ready to reveal himself sometime soon. Have you heard this gay-ass music that's playing in the ballroom?"

*

The fellas gathered around the Great 8 table, trying to figure out why it was in the middle of the room: clearly we were the center of the attention—or, at least, that's what The Curse wanted us to be, but that was all we had so far.

Salawicious Dough approached Al Gebra and asked him if he'd seen Brilliant Bobby yet, who answered that he'd seen him by the control room:

he was controlling the lights and the music for the evening. With that, Dough went to see him.

"Bobby, my man!" he grinned as way of greeting. "What's poppin', big homie? I can't wait for you and Blues to show me this new software y'all been working with. Man, the things I'll be able to do for my businesses and my bunny ranch... I'm happy as hell right now!"

"What's good, bruh? I gotta question for you," Bobby said. "Don't you hate when women say, 'Because you know I'm a single mother' when they're trying to make a point about something? That really gets on my damn nerves."

"Um, sure?"

"Well, this chick told me she was a single mother, so she couldn't do anything I needed her to do for me," Bobby pressed on. "Bitch, *I'm* a single father, and what does that get me? A thousand questions at the office when I'm trying to get assistance for my little one, that's what."

"Assistance? Bobby, you're a millionaire," Dough laughed. "Why the hell do you need assistance for the kids?"

"Why would I give up free money?"

Dough didn't have a response to that one: the man had a point.

"Anyway, women have it so much easier—well, through the system, that is," Bobby sighed. "Automatically, the father ain't shit, because that's how we've been labeled. I'm *sick* of that shit!" Indeed, the man did look at the end of his tether. "Plus, what gives them the right to talk shit about us as men? They won't and can't ever know what it is to be a man in this world."

"Yeah. Black Power!" Dough responded unhelpfully, throwing his fist in the air.

"*And,*" Bobby continued, "why do they always have to stress the point that they're a single mother? Maybe you're single 'cuz you won't shut the fuck up about your struggle, as if being a black man in America isn't a struggle enough!"

Dough remained silent for a moment before stating, "I think I'm gonna go now."

I don't think Bobby heard him, as long after Dough had left the room, he could still be found ranting and raving alone in the audio room: "And you know what else gets on my damn nerves about these...."

Upon Dough's return, he found Poppa Vein, Cocoa Butta, and Polo Pasé all in the ballroom together, all three of them dressed professionally and looking debonair. Vein walked over to Mula Madison and greeted her.

"Oh, hi, Vein," she responded. "I didn't know you'd be here today."

"I didn't know either," he admitted. "I received an invitation from The Curse himself a couple of days ago, and I figured why not; it's not like I have anything better to do tonight." He paused to survey the woman before him. "You look very nice tonight, by the way."

"Why, thank you, Sir," Mula responded smoothly. "I bet you say that to all the girls."

"Nah, just the Spanish ones," he corrected her jokingly, "and the ones with long hair." Mula's eyes sparkled. "The ones that, coincidentally, look like you."

"And I'm supposed to believe that? Really?" Mula challenged.

"No," Vein shrugged. "The only thing you're supposed to do is be Puerto Rican and die. That's it."

"Well, that's refreshing. Why do I get this overwhelming feeling that you want to go out with me but are too chicken to ask me directly?"

Mula's gaze felt like it was penetrating his soul. He swallowed—hard. "I'd say you were wrong," he said after a few moments, his voice catching slightly. "I like your look, and I do like how you smell, but I'm not the least bit interested. Okay?"

Vein wasn't a very convincing liar and Mula beamed, seeing right through his cool, collected façade. "Yeah, nigga, that's why you can't stop looking at my twin bags, huh?" She was enjoying herself. "Or what about my sultry lips? You know, the ones you can't stop wanting to kiss?"

"How've you figured that, then?" Vein queried, trying his best to feign surprise.

"Because you want her, brother! Damn!" Cocoa shouted out as she walked by the both of them. "Stop bullshittin' around and go get her, Poppa Lame!"

"Cocoa, I'm telling you now, if you don't shut your mouth, I'm gonna take my belt off and—"

"You ain't gon' do shit! Leave that girl alone," Mula snapped, and, unsurprisingly, Vein looked ashamed. "Why don't you come back around here, be a man, and grow some testicles?"

This last three minutes of Vein's life were probably the three minutes he'd gladly choose to block out, if given the chance.

"Mula Madison," Vein began, "I got an extra ticket for—"

"I'd love to go. Yes." Mula's smile lit up the whole room—or at least, it did to Vein.

"For real?" he said, unable to stop the smile tugging at his lips. "But you didn't even hear where it was... What if you hate it?"

"Vein, I've liked you for a long time now, so the fact that you've been putting up with me for the last five minutes while I've berated your character makes me like you even more," she stated simply. "So, in summary, I don't care where we're going, as long as I'm with you."

Poppa Vein was utterly dumbfounded: he didn't know what to say. He shook his head and said, "Spanish women: can never figure them out. I'm done. It's too stressful."

"Great. I'll see you tomorrow at eight," Mula said, twirling away.

Cocoa and Polo Pasé had been watching the whole ordeal unfold with delight: they were on the verge of looking for some popcorn. The game had been tossed right back in Vein's face, chewed up, and spit out... And yet he'd still got the girl in the end. Amazing.

Meanwhile, I had stepped outside for some fresh air, still awaiting the arrival of the mysterious Curse. It was while doing so that Harry, Swindel, Blues, Drumsticks, and Snugglez all finally arrived in a stretch jeep limo: stylin' and profilin', only like we could do. My brothers all dapped me up until Snugglez stopped and turned around in my direction.

"Escobar... I just wanted to apologize to you," he countered.

"Apologize for what exactly?"

"For that crazy shit I said to you that night at Vein's house," he said. "It's been a while since then, and I needed to say this to you: I was out of line, and for that, I apologize."

I shook my head. "Man, that's water under the bridge, son; don't you worry about it. I know you, and I believe you recognize your bad judgment or whatever, but I trust that your apology is genuine—and all I can do is appreciate that."

The guy physically seemed to untense: this had clearly been bothering him for a while. "You don't understand how much better it makes me feel to know you forgive me," he said sincerely. "Again, I'm sorry, dawg."

With that, we shook hands and embraced one another in brotherly hug that I felt was real. I must admit that I felt better, too.

As I walked back in to find Yelly, I ran into Al Gebra, who was coming out of the men's restroom.

"Al, what in the hell are we gonna do about this fool tonight?" I asked him quickly: the whole situation was making me feel restless, uneasy. "Did you ever find any whereabouts on this guy?"

"Nah, son; he has covered his tracks extremely well," Al sighed apologetically. "If me and Brilliant Bobby couldn't come up with nothing, then ain't no telling how good this motherfucker is. I personally wanna smack the shit outta him, pick him up again, ask him how he did it, and then smack the shit outta him again."

At this point, Al's frustration was comparable to mine—something that made me feel bad for the guy but reassured at the same time.

"Yeah, I know the feeling," I murmured before freezing. "What was that? Did you hear that?"

"Sounded like some kind of announcement from inside," Al mused, wincing. "Damn, the feedback is piercing through my ears."

The both of us quickly tried to take cover while putting our fingers in our ears in an effort to block out the crazy noise pouring out of the sound system. It was then that various bursts of smoke began to emerge from multiple directions. A cacophony of coughs started up from what felt like all directions, drowning out the serenity that the cool brisk air had given to us.

I then turned next to me to address Al—to find he was gone.

"Al! Where the hell are you!"

I had lost my Great 8 brother in the smog—something that unnerved me more than it probably should have. In the thick of the sensory overload surrounding me, I tried to find my way toward the front entrance of the inn. I'm lucky my mind made a mental track of the actual way we got there, or I would have been screwed.

When I finally found my way back to internal civilization, it became clear that the smoke was coming from outside. I coughed my way through a crowd over in the front lobby area and, to my utter relied, found my wife, who was also just recovering from the awful sound that has penetrated the air earlier.

"Babe!" I called. "Babe, are you okay?"

"Yes; it's just my ears are ringing," she said, her eyes darting around as they did whenever she was nervous. "They've popped like they do when we're driving at two-eighty on the highway—multiplied by the hundredth power!"

"That's actually a very good way of explaining it, honey," I said, smiling absently. "See, you're learning."

"No, asswipe, I learned already," she snapped. "I've been married to you long enough to know that I've inherited a high level of assholism from you."

"And how does that make you feel?"

"Shut up, fool!" she retorted, clearly irritable as a result of our circumstances. "Why the hell do you keep coughing so much? You've been hanging with Hak Hennesey too much."

Wisely deciding not to respond, I instead turned to the waiter, asking for two glasses of water. This smoke was thick, and it was hard to even see clearly; however, as it slowly started to clear, as did my vision.

"So, where the hell did all this smoke come from?" my wife asked. "Do we know?"

I shook my head. "Al and I were chopping it up outside when the feedback started from inside; the smoke started coming out of nowhere at the same time as whatever was happening inside started." The waiter arrived with our water and I took a swig. "It was almost as if a diversion was taking place," I continued. "It was strange. Is everyone okay in there?"

"Yeah, I think so," Yelly responded. "Frederick Linguini dropped a platter from Tasty's, that was catered in, so he was pissed, as you'd expect—but otherwise, all's fine."

"I love how you've adopted my sense of humor," I chuckled. "You're awesome. I believe—"

I never got the chance to finish my sentence: a voice boomed through a speaker, of course with the lovely addition of terrible feedback.

"Welcome, good people of Ghost Town, New Jersey. I need all of you to sit down at your assigned seats; The Great 8, I need you all to get to your specific table, right up front. O3, fall into the first three and the remaining five in the rear of the table ...Thanks! Please, get comfortable; all of you are in for an unforgettable night, so batten down the hatches. The show is about to begin!"

I shot my wife one last look of reassurance before all the lights went dim and a projector screen lit up the front of the bare wall at the center of the Great 8 table, which had clearly been strategically placed perfectly so we could see all the screen showed.

From there, the classic directors' countdown from 10 commenced. In that interval, I searched for my wife's hand under the table and squeezed it gently. She squeezed back.

After the countdown, an old film of 40th Street Park commenced, looking to me as though it had been filmed in the 1940s, or thereabouts. There was a sign that read "Welcome to Olympic Park - Camp Town's Favorite Amusement Area for Families!": Ghost Town was originally named Camp Town, but was later changed in the honor of legendary writer Washington "Ghost" Irving. That man was brilliant and an innovator in his own right.

From there, there was a short two-minute video on the history of Camp Town, which then faded out and was rapidly replaced with distorted images that became much clearer after a few seconds: street signs. However, these weren't any old street signs: they were Nesbit Terrace, Stuyvesant Avenue, Orchard Place, 40th Street, Irvington Avenue, and Park Place. These were the signs of the respective streets that we, The Great 8, each grew up on.

From there, old photos of all our family members started taking over the screen, one after the other, covering parents and siblings, grandparents and cousins, aunts and uncles. There was a very uncomfortable stench in the air, one of invasion and failure—the former being because these pictures and special moments were being visually administered without prior authorization, showcasing our lack of vigilance.

How had this happened? How had someone gotten so close to us that they'd been able to gain access to these memories of us—while still remaining far enough from any of us for none of us to know them?

I'd been doing this for a long time, and I'd never felt so hopeless—and, on a level, so embarrassed. We were all speechless: it was a very surreal, somewhat demoralizing experience.

The footage stopped and the voice boomed back through the speakers.

"I hope you're all enjoying yourselves right now. The big reveal is upon us. My apologies for this brief delay: there seems to be a little technical difficulty that we're experiencing right now, but rest assured, we'll be back up and running in no time—all before you could say, 'Fuck you, Curse!'"

The eight of us eyed one another apprehensively—and, to this day, I have never seen the faces of my G8 family, nor the faces of the rest of our family, look quite like that. It was like the ball of trust we'd built upon for our whole lives had been deflated in a matter of five minutes.

It was then that a stocky, largely built brother I didn't recognize approached me, asking politely if he could speak with me quickly. I nodded to him to meet me toward the back of the room.

It was so crowded that I had downed two screwdrivers before I'd even got to the back of the room to meet with the guy. He was waiting for me by the NY-style cheesecake spread that was beside the punch bowl—spiked punch, of course.

"It's an honor to meet you, Escobar," he greeted me politely. "My name is Diggz Omega; I'm from Murksville. I don't know if you've ever heard of it, but it's right between Brick City and Ghost Town. It's small, but it's real over there... And, well, I need your help."

"Yeah, I know where that's at," I responded, polite enough yet ensuring my tone asserted authority: if that speech just now had taught me anything, it was that I'd have to remain apprehensive of anybody outside my family unit. "I used to see a chick 'round those parts 'til I figured it wasn't worth my life going to fuck with her no more," I continued. "So, what is it you need? And why is it you think that I would help you to begin with?"

"That's a valid question, and I'm glad you asked." I couldn't help but warm to the guy. "There's this group—or, better yet, squadron—known as—"

"The Haitian Squadron?" I interrupted smoothly.

"Yeah!" the guy affirmed, eyes wide. "How'd you know?"

"Besides the fact that I'm PR Escobar and I know everything? Because I know them. So, what? What's the problem?"

"They kinda want to kill me," Mr. Omega responded bluntly.

"Oh, that's cool; you should let them. I heard it's a lot easier when you just let it happen—well, unless it's Polo Pasé providing the fatal blow." I grinned. "He's mean. Oh, and don't let Poppa Vein kill you; the man has no heart. Oh, and whatever you do, please do *not*, under any circumstances, allow Jake Solomon to kill you."

"And why's that?" the man challenged.

"Well, because he's dead—which means that if he somehow *did* manage to kill you, you'd have deserved to die." I sighed impatiently. "Now, are we done here? I'm sure my wife is looking for me."

"I guess we are, Mr. Escobar," Mr. Omega confirmed, somewhat irritably. "I'm sorry for taking up as much of your time as I did; please enjoy the rest of your evening, and safe travels to you and your lovely bride home."

I didn't respond, instead making my way back toward the front of the room without as much as a backward glance.

As I slid back into my seat, I started wondering if I'd perhaps been a little too hard on that guy; I was, of course, incredibly stressed out with this Curse situation, and had taken it out on the poor soul. It's been a hell of a few months.

It was then that I decided to find Diggs Omega and offer my apologies as well as my assistance in helping him in his situation; he had seemed like a perfectly nice guy—articulate and well-mannered—, and the least I could do was call my good friend Poppa Vein and maybe spare the man's life.

Yeah, that would rest my conscience.

However, this feeling of remorse was destined to be short-lived: the awful noise from the feedback came back from the dead and tore into all our eardrums, followed by that voice again—the voice of The Curse—through the speakers.

"Dammit! Is this thing working? Can you guys hear me? You can? Oh, good; that's awesome! I love when everybody can hear me; it makes me all fuzzy inside, and acknowledged, and wanted, all at the same time. It also makes me want to spare all of your lives." The ensuing cackle made the crack of the static almost unbearable. "Nah, not really. So, are we ready? Roll it!"

Right on cue, the lights dimmed down again, the distorted video coming back to life—this time to present an image even more disturbing than that we'd earlier: it was live footage of all of us. We were literally looking at ourselves on the wall through that projector, like some *Twilight Zone* shit I'd never seen before... and it only got worse from there.

The whole thing lasted about thirty seconds before the live feed switched to footage of me getting jumped outside the castle by Jake Solomon's goons. This was followed by footage of Tony Victor snapping the guy's neck at Breathless; then Sal Dough's girl Licky Bella being chopped up and put in the bag Dough had later found in the back of this truck.

There was a pause in the film, likely so the sick fucker who was behind this could watch all our faces as the gravity of the situation fell upon us.

Sure enough, the footage quickly started again, this time of Sam being shot at Don's Diner; an intimate moment of Al caressing his wife's face at her bedside in the hospital; Jay BaDouche's home, the same night we couldn't find Hak Hennesey after the shootout in Linden, Hak himself in a window pulling his pants up after coming from the upstairs apartment, then settling in at the table to play cards with Jay's mom. Celo Gaston leaving his home and packing his belongings before leaving for Raleigh; and, finally, a black fade, followed by a blood-chilling voice: "I'm gonna kill you. You're a dead man, Don. Watch your fuckin' back."

The following silence couldn't have felt heavier.

Now, the stage had been set, and the show was ready to start.

Don, making us all jump due to how on edge we were, suddenly gasped. "I *knew* it," he whispered to himself, before saying louder, "I know who The Curse is!"

"The Haitians?" Sam asked.

"No, you stupid fuck; we went down that road already." I swear I could hear the cogs working in his brain. "It all makes sense now. The Curse never had the audacity to show his face, right?"

"Yes..." we all responded dubiously.

"And we can all agree that that's a bitch move, right?"

Another chorus of agreement.

"And The Curse only chose to communicate to us through handwritten letters, right?"

"What you gettin' at, Don?" Tony cut in. "You're stalling here."

Don ignored him and continued with his musings. "Only letters... Never showed his face... And correct me if I'm wrong, but does his voice sound a bit bitch-made over these speakers this evening?"

"Yeah, you're right," Hak said slowly.

"By golly, Batman," Dough suddenly exclaimed, "I think you're onto something."

"Who are you thinking about, Don?" I pressed.

"It's... It's... It's gotta be Kane!" Dough said stupidly before smiling to himself proudly.

"Dough, I hate you," I sighed.

"I couldn't help it."

Don resumed. "It all points to that man right there! And not coincidentally standing by the sweet pie section!"

The entire room immediately looked over to where Don Corione was pointing to: a very tall and slender man who had enough makeup on to have been mistaken for IT. Don, for some odd reason, arose from his seat and approached the alleged culprit, who, visibly uncomfortable, began stepping back toward the exit—that is, until Don motioned for our henchmen to stop him in his tracks. Snugglez and Harry Horrendous quickly sprung into action: they bolted over to the man and quickly had him pinned by each of his limbs. Don then kneeled down beside the man—and proved to us that he was, indeed, the biggest jackass of all time.

"The man under this mask of gaydom is none other than Red Herring!" he announced.

"Red Herring?" I echoed. "Like the guy from *Scooby Doo?*"

"Yes; I've just always wanted to do that!" I could've hit the guy. "It was brilliant, wasn't it?"

"Did you really just put on this charade to make us all laugh? All our lives are being toyed with, and all you want to do is play around?" Tony fumed.

"Calm down, Tony," Al said, "I'm sure Don has an actual point here while holding this man here against his will."

"Don, what's going on here?" Celo asked. "Do you know this man or not?"

"Of course I do! We all do."

"Then who in the blue hell is it?"

Don looked ready to dissolve into peals of laughter again. "It's Sticks Morano!"

"Sticks Morano?" Hak echoed. "Ain't no fuckin' way Sticks could pull this shit off! Are you insane?"

"Really? Mr. Testicle Line Licker, The Curse?" Jay added, echoing everyone's thoughts.

"Uh, yeah?"

"Don, you should be ashamed of yourself," Jay scolded. "This man is not Sticks Morano: Sticks is standing right over there inside the kissing booth, probably getting anal-probed by a gang of Studio 54 goers as we speak."

Sam followed Jay's gaze and burst into laughter. "Holy shit, he's right! Don, what's the matter with you?"

"Harry, Snugglez, let this man go," I instructed firmly. "As always, we appreciate your dedication. Harry," I added, "I gotta quick question for you. Did you have sex today?"

Harry frowned. "Of course I did, Sir."

"Did you use a condom, and did you drink milk afterward?"

"Like you've taught me."

"You're a good man," I smiled. I turned to Snugglez. "And what about you, Mr. McPherson? Did you have any time inside the merry ol' land of Oz?"

"Nah, not today," Snugglez admitted. "I'm still recuperating from the night before."

"Outstanding! You're an even better man," I praised. "Good job to the both of you." I then turned to Corione. "Don, I can't believe you led us all over here for a revealing that was more of a discovery into how much more of a jackass you actually are."

"What time is it? I wanna go watch Monday Night Raw," was Don's remorseless response. "I can't even record it anymore: my stupid VCR popped the other night."

"That's awesome, Don; now, considering the fact that it's Friday, I'd shut your mouth and know your role right about now."

"I have a really, really bad feeling," Whish murmured, suddenly looking very small and vulnerable.

It was at that moment that the sound we all dreaded echoed around us: the bad sound system, yet again signifying The Curse's return. His voice quickly filled the room.

"For the first time in your life, I agree with you, Whish Johannsen: you shouldn't be getting a good feeling, because what's happening here is not *supposed* to be good." The voice was smug. It made me want to rip his head off, whoever he was. "Although it's not supposed to be bad, either; it's all open for debate, as it really depends how you depict what's happened here this evening and what's happened in each of your lives over the last few months. Allow me to re-introduce myself: my name is The Curse, and, if you will allow me to indulge your attention for a moment, I can explain everything."

"This guy is really starting to piss me off, ladies," Sara suddenly announced. "Whish, where the fuck is my gun at? I'm 'bout to off on this nigga, right here, right now. He's gotta show his face."

It was then that all the lights flickered back on and the projector that had previously showcased all our private lives was shut off. I could just make out Brilliant Bobby Bushetta walking out from behind the curtain, as if he was getting ready to tell us that he really couldn't give us heart, a brain, or courage.

As I was focusing on Bushetta's silhouette, the mini conversations began escalating to loud accusations before building to a shocking reveal.

"Bobby?" I breathed. "You're.... the Curse?"

"How is this possible?" Dough demanded, voice laced with betrayal.

"For the love of God, let him speak!" Whish burst out. "If he doesn't, I'm going use this hammer here on his ass in about ten seconds!"

"Oh, for God's sake; I'm not The Curse!" Bobby said. Despite his statement, he still sounded slightly unsettled. "Although I'm not innocent in all of this. However, I can assure you I'm not The Curse; he is."

Brilliant Bobby pointed behind us all and, of course, we all swiveled around.

The only person who stood behind us was Al.

"Hey, family!" he said, cocking his head to the side. "How's everybody doing tonight?"

"Baby?" Sara said hesitantly. "Have you been drinking?"

"A little, but nothing I can't handle." In that moment, I felt I didn't recognize him: he had an aura about him that just didn't sit right with me. "Have a seat, honey; I'm sure you're going to have to sit for this one."

"What the hell are you talking about?"

"Do I really have to spell it out for you?" he responded, eyes darkening. "*I am The Curse.*"

Suddenly, we all knew in that moment that this wasn't a joke: Al suddenly wasn't the man we all knew and loved.

"Now I *know* you've been drinking too damn much," Sara said, but too quietly: she was trying to convince herself.

"I haven't drunk enough to deal with all of you people," was Al's response. "As much as I love you men and women in here tonight, you guys got some serious holes you gotta fill in your lives."

"Whish, Mula, get me the hardest fuckin' drink in this bitch—and make it a double," Sara demanded. The pure hysteria in her tone was enough for both girls to oblige without question.

"Al, what the fuck is going on here?" I queried, turning from Sara to our perpetrator.

"You must be high on some shit right now," Sam reasoned, to himself more than anyone else.

"Nope," Al shrugged. "It's me, and now I could throw this stupid fuckin' voice decoder out the damn window. Makes me sound like Sticks Morano at a naked Lego workshop."

Oddly enough, this simple statement all seemed to make us relax a little: this was the Al we knew.

"Al?" Celo broached hesitantly. "What is the meaning of this? How could you do this to us?"

"I had to," Al responded. " Somebody had to be the one to prove to all of you that y'all are your own worst enemies."

Hak rubbed a hand across his forehead. "You gon' have to explain all of this from the very beginning—and *very* slowly. I just had an entire bottle of Henny, and I'm not even sure if what's happening right now is even real."

"Oh, it's real, my brother," Al murmured. He turned to Jay. "Hey, when you gon' tell our brothers and sisters here that you're the guy that Sticks has been fuckin' behind the scenes?"

"Wait, *what?* Nigga, you know I ain't no chocolate highway dweller!"

"I'm playing, Jay," Al grinned. We were all so on edge that we'd all have probably believed anything that came out that guy's mouth in that moment, and he seemed to be finding this particularly amusing.

"That's not funny," Jay huffed.

"Neither is you fucking with sixteen pregnant girls, not knowing if you're any of their baby daddies."

"Sixteen?!" Hak repeated, turning to Jay and arching an eyebrow. "You told me it was that one bitch and that was it, Jay!"

"He's tripping; it ain't sixteen," Jay corrected. "Maybe twelve, but not sixteen."

Hak went to say something, but Al smoothly intervened. "Jay, the last few days have been a real eye-opener for you, haven't they? Well, I'd say that you don't have nothing to worry about with eleven of those twelve women."

"How do you figure that one out?"

"Don't question me; I just know, okay?" Al said firmly. "The point here is that you're thinking about how you should operate better going forward now, aren't you?"

"I guess you could say that," Jay frowned.

"And Dough? What about you?" Al continued. "You've been trying to put our own brother, Qurtis Jenkins, out of business because you want all the money to yourself. You also take a much bigger cut from all of your girls than you deserve. I know it's your ranch, but *they* do the work, and from what I've heard, they're amazing at what they do. So, naturally, I had to hit you where it hurt the most: your pockets. So, I chopped up Licky Bella and sent her back to you."

Dough looked like he'd gone into shock. "You didn't..."

"I did," Al stated matter-of-factly, "but at least I kept her socks on; I know how you loved her socks."

"You have no heart," Dough said quietly. "You disgust me."

Putting two and two together, Celo suddenly asked, "Did you set me up with those women? The ones that got me in trouble?"

"I sure did, pal," Al confirmed.

"Why would you do that?"

"Again, I had to: it was the only way you were going to get out of your own way. Ever since Velma the Goddess passed, you've been different." He paused. "Don't get me wrong, outside of the tension we had with each other regarding Sara a long time ago, you've never done nothing but prove your brotherhood to me. Those women were all bad news for you, and I made them get you in trouble, so you'd get so fed up that maybe you'd pack ya bags and leave town. I knew that you had to make sense of your life and discover yourself first, and only then could you find true happiness with someone else—in being a father." He shrugged. "And it's not been for nothing, has it? The future Mrs. Celo Gaston is sitting at that table, is she not?"

Celo was silent for a moment. "That she is. Still, I can't believe you'd do something this extreme."

"The Curse is a made-up villain that we created in our own minds to justify the bad things that have happened to us," Al said. "What we don't pay enough attention to is what led up to those 'bad events'. I'd say eighty percent of bad things that happen to people could probably be avoided, if they just used their better judgement and not blamed everybody else for their fuck-ups."

"Then why would you put our lives at risk the way you did?" Sam asked. "I mean, Escobar could've been killed, I was two inches from dying or being paralyzed from that bullet, and your own *wife* could've died on that operating table!"

"No, no; I didn't do *any* of that!" Al said, shaking his head. "Jake Solomon was a son-of-a-bitch, and he deserved to die the way he did. That whole thing was a complete wrench in my entire plan: I didn't know any of that was going to come into play. I honestly only wanted to show everyone that The Curse is just your imaginary friend that you could kill over and over again and never have to pay the penalty. If you notice, I only sent notes to Dough, Hak, and Jay's houses—but not specific ones meant for everyone to see."

"You sent one to *me*," Whish pointed out.

Al sighed. "Perhaps I misjudged my method, but there was no possible way that I could foresee all the other things happening. I did question whether I should stop a couple of times, but the greater cause just seemed too important to just neglect." He looked troubled. "Whish, I'm sorry if I scared you when I sent you yours... Damn, I forgot that I did that. That was more to keep you on your toes: I didn't know if there would be any further retributions from that Dairy Queen situation. It kinda got outta hand, that whole thing."

"Yeah, it did," Whish snapped.

"But you whooped some ass at the charity event," Al reminded her. "You, Mula, and all the other ladies. I'm sure I speak for all of us when I say y'all are some tough bi-atches!"

"And as for me?" Harry asked.

Al burst out laughing. "Man, your shirt loks like ravioli!"

"Really?"

"No, Harry." Al paused. "Well, actually, yes, your shirt *does* look like ravioli, but regarding the night of your 'accident'... Well, I put an electronic device on the car so I could control your every movement for five minutes—ultimately allowing me to swerve you and Snugglez outta the lane and into the divider."

"You *what*?!"

Snugglez looked like he'd seen a ghost.

"Into the divider," Al repeated, as if Snugglez had really needed clarification. "So, you thought it would be cool to get behind the wheel of a car in the condition you were in—and Harry, you thought you'd go with him without your seatbelt on, huh? Hence why Snugglez emerged scratch free, but you didn't." He surveyed us all, and, noting the horror and disapproval on our faces, shrugged, "Again, I know I don't exactly do the 'popular' thing, but at the end of the day, my methods work. After all, Snugglez'll, think just a little more before doing anything crazy behind a wheel now. Won't you, Snugglez?"

"I guess so."

"And Harry, you got a more beautiful smile now, don't you?" he grinned. "Maybe you wanted one under different circumstances, but nevertheless, the both of you are way more careful when making life decisions, aren't you?"

"Forgive me," I cut in before Harry could answer, "but Al, you are one sick son-of-a-bitch." Once he opened his mouth to defend himself, I added, "But my brother, nonetheless."

Seemingly remembering my presence, he said, "Let me clear something up real quick, too: I never meant to do anything to any of you three. You're the O3, and I respect that."

"So who the hell's been calling me telling me that they're gonna kill me? Huh?" Don challenged.

"The last one was me," he admitted, "but all those other ones... yeah, Don, you got a long list of people who want you outta here. Permanently."

"I don't get it," Don said, looking genuinely hurt. "I'm a nice guy."

"You are," I reassured him. "I like you."

"No, you're not," Al corrected me. "Nobody likes you. I don't like you; he don't like you; ya momma don't like you."

"You don't like me, Al?"

"Of course I like you, fool," Al grinned. "I'm fucking wit' you. I only don't like you when we go to Six Flags together and we can't go on the rides because you gotta be this tall to ride and you're a little vertically challenged."

"Where's Billy DrumSticks when you need him?" Don huffed. "I think I need him to kill somebody for me."

"Oh, speaking of... Hak, you wanna tell them, or should I?"

Hak frowned. "Tell them what?"

Al looked at him like he didn't know whether Hak was being serious or not. "That you was fuckin' that Polish chick right upstairs in that apartment you broke into, upstairs at Jay's mom's house. Or how about the fact that it was you that almost killed Sticks Morano?"

"I don't know what you're talking about."

"Have you *seen* what I've concocted here, son?" Al reminded him. "I'd suggest you come correct."

Hak took a deep breath. "Okay, okay. Jay, I broke into your mom's tenant's apartment that night of the shootout so I could bang the Polish chick. Her parents were home, and she was hot and horny, so I reacted. I snuck her upstairs, gave her the business and snuck her down the back of the house and into a cab home afterwards."

Jay was instantly fuming. "What if those people came home while you were in their house fucking some chick?! Hak, are you *insane*?"

"Um... yes?" Hak said nervously.

"I can't win with this fuckin' guy," Jay mumbled.

"And what about Sticks?" Al chipped in, adding fuel to the fire. "Tell us all what happened there."

"I tried killing Sticks," Hak immediately admitted, "but he was shot at right when I pulled my trigger. I've been wanting to get rid of that guy since *forever* now."

"So why the hell does Billy think he did it?" Don pushed.

"He was the one that was shooting at Sticks from another direction— multiple times. He just missed each time," Hak explained, somewhat smugly. "It was mine that actually landed, but I knew he was trying to impress you, so I let him live."

"How nice of you," Don said sarcastically. "Billy, looks like I don't need you anymore; I have the actual shooter here now."

"How the hell did you know that, anyway?" Hak asked Al.

Al just shrugged. "I see everything from all kinds of angles before they even become one; it's what I do."

"Well, what about you, Al? You never done nothing wrong in *your* life?" Don demanded, mirroring my own thoughts. "Because if you think you haven't, then clearly your 'math' isn't up to par."

"Oh, I never said that," Al brushed off. "I've done plenty wrong, as we all know—like the time I went to the office to do some work and didn't brush my teeth, nor did I go home to do so. Or the time I had a drink before it was even evening."

Don rolled his eyes. "You know what kinda 'wrong' I mean."

"Well, I suppose I didn't marry my precious Sara sooner. That is definitely something I did wrong," Al mused.

"Whish, find me a room for the weekend," Sara instructed humorlessly. "This crazy motherfucker probably thinks I'm going home with him after all this!"

"Honey, you *are* coming home with me," Al said firmly. "That's the liquor talking right there."

"Oh, so you fuck everyone's lives up and now we're supposed to play happy families?"

"Actually, yes, Sara," I stepped in. "If we all learned something here, it's that the only way to kill something is to kill it from within." I turned to Al. "Brother, I commend you. Good work."

"I appreciate that, Escobar."

Sam appeared to be deep in thought, and, after a few moments, asked, "How the hell does Brilliant Bobby fit into this equation?"

Bobby took it upon himself to answer this question. "I've known about Al being The Curse since the beginning; you know I live in Colorado now, but I've been back home for the majority of the last three months helping Al with all the technology it took for us to pull this off. I didn't mean to cause anybody no harm," he added, looking somewhat apologetic. "I was given instructions by my higher-up, and was assured no one would get seriously hurt during the process, so I gave in to his commands. It had to be me, after all: someone 'brilliant' to man the boards when Al couldn't."

I had to give it to them: the amount of intricacy put into this endeavor was admirable.

"We used every bit of equipment from Operation Kill Solomon to Operation Save Stylez over the duration of this to obtain that footage we showed earlier tonight," Bobby continued. "Any of The Great 8 can gain access to all the things we touched on. When this computer software was created, Al and I had everybody bugged—not to invade anyone's privacy, mind, but to experiment and discover what we could do with this new technology." He briefly looked at me. "Luckily, that's how we knew who jumped Escobar: we saw it on the footage. We also knew who'd been destroying Stylez from the inside, and we had an up-close-and-personal look of when Luciano was shot. That was scary."

"The moral of the story is this: don't go looking for trouble, but if trouble happens to find you, then you deal with it." Al's words rung true for all of us in that moment. "But don't give trouble more credit than it deserves by pointing the finger at it when more often than not, you can control it."

We were all silent for a few moments, letting these words absorb, when Sam spoke up. "I believe, without a shadow of a doubt, that you have proved yourself to be one sadistic but maniacal genius. This was one hell of a plan you put together, and I think a lot of us got it—at least, I hope we did."

"Al, I just got one last question for you," I said. "If you're the big and almighty Curse sent to teach us all a lesson, then why is your wife leaving out the front entrance with another man?"

"*What?*"

And with that, Al ran through the crowd toward the front entrance like a complete madman, leaving the rest of us dumbfounded and attempting, in vain, to comprehend all we had just been told.

"Who's leaving with Sara, and why aren't we killing him?" Sam piped up.

"Chill son; it's Sticks Morano who's walking out with her," I grinned. "I'm sure Al will be relieved once he realizes it's not an actual man. After all this shit Al put us through with this Curse debacle, I at least could make him think his wife's leaving with another man, right?" I paused. "And besides, Sticks is like taxes: he's fuckin' everywhere, and you can't do nothing about it!"

Everyone laughed and, after a few moments of comfortable silence, Don said, "Family, it's been a long fuckin' day: Al Gebra, our treasured Great 8 brethren, has duped us all."

"You gotta give it to him, though: his plan was great, and it worked," I pointed out.

"Did it, though?" Sam contemplated.

"Absolutely," I insisted. "To realize that you're often your own problem is a very powerful sentiment to live by. I believe wholeheartedly that we'll all be better people moving forward, as we all now understand that it ain't always someone or something else's fault: it's usually yours. You get out of life what you put in it: plain and simple."

"I suppose so."

It was at that moment that Don, glancing around the room, asked, "Say, has anybody seen Vein and Polo?"

"I saw them earlier," Sam responded. "Why?"

"I don't know; they were telling me about this guy they were trying to off, and that they thought they'd seen him here tonight, dressed as a waiter."

"Oh, you must be talking about Diggz Omega!" I said, remembering my encounter from before."

"Diggz Omega?" Don echoed, surprised. "As in, the rap artist?"

"Rap artist? I've never heard of him, and you know I always got my ear to the streets."

"No, you do know him," Sam told me. "You know, the guy who sounds like Busta and that Darkman X guy. I think he's from Murksville, too."

"Oh shit, yeah, I do remember that dude now," I said. "I think Stylez maybe played me a record from him a while ago. Wow, he's dope." I won't lie, I felt a little starstruck in that moment. "That's the guy I met earlier?"

"Hold up, you *met* him?" Don parroted, eyebrows shooting up in surprise.

"Yeah: he asked me to help him out because The Haitian Squadron wants him dead."

"So, what did you tell him?" Sam asked, seeming to hang onto my every word.

"I told him, 'Whatever you do, don't let Jake Solomon kill you'."

"*What*?"

"I know, I know," I sighed, cringing to myself a little. "Sounds like I fucked up." Before anyone else could say anything more on the matter, I said, "Look, can we talk about this later? I wanna get my wife home."

"And I wanna get to at least one of my days of the week," Don grinned sleazily. "Although in order to prove that I learned the lesson Al wanted us all to learn, I'll maybe consider only having two days of the week instead of three from now on."

"Well, that's progress," Sam reasoned. "What else can a man ask for?"

It was then that Jay burst back into the room, cheeks flushed and eyes sparkling. "Yo, yo, family!"

"Yo, where the hell you been? You just missed Al kill Sticks Morano!" Hak chuckled. "All for the love of his wife. How touching."

"That's nice," Jay said absently. Without warning, the grown-ass man's eyes began to fill with tears. "Guys, it's a girl. I'm having a baby girl!"

*

That evening, we all celebrated Jay's news with multiple toasts in his honor. It felt somewhat unfathomable—the thought of Jay being a father—, but hey, babies—especially little girls—have a way of sitting a grown man down and restructuring his ways. It's been a long time coming for him and I'm happy for him; we all are.

You know, our story really could be a good book. Perhaps I'll take some time off at some point soon and write a book about all of this—if I can even mentally execute it, that is. I think such a story would be a bestseller, to be frank.

You know, I just might relocate down south somewhere—maybe Georgia. My wife and I have talked about it for a long time now, and it might be the time to go ahead and make a life-changing decision. How else am I going to find the time to pen a literary masterpiece?

# EPILOGUE

"**N**OW ARE YOU READY?**"** Pudgee checked. "I believe it's time. The people will be here in under an hour, so we need to get in and out."

"I told you I got this," Padlock Penny said, rolling her eyes, "and with plenty of time to spare. See, nothing to worry about. Now, where is that cute guy from earlier? Did you see what direction he went in?"

"Yeah, in the same direction my brother is going to put his foot up our asses in if we don't get in this damn store and get the books already!"

"Well, get your ass in there, then," Penny shrugged indifferently.

Pudgee hesitated. "You first. Please."

Padlock Penny and Pudgee Escobar slowly trailed into the retail bookstore. It had been approximately 7am when they'd broke into the store on the release date of *MentallyOrganizedBusiness*—the novel I eventually wrote.

I'll let you be the judge of what happened directly after that.

"*There* they are!" Penny hissed. "Your brother's books, stacked in a beautiful display, waiting for people to buy them. Too bad they'll be all gone when everyone gets here." She thought to herself for a moment as she admired the shrine. "It's a bit weird he wants to steal his own books, isn't it?"

"I've learned to not ask questions," Pudgee shrugged. "Just do, and ask questions later."

In the end, the girls managed to take over thirty books from the store: three boxes of ten. They weren't particularly heavy; the hard part was going to be finding a way to get them to fit through the small space they'd broken into.

It was just as they'd exited the building after some awkward maneuvering and were bringing the last box to the car that Penny froze in her tracks.

Pudgee whipped around and frowned. "What's wrong with you? You look like you've seen my brother, or something."

The expression on Penny's face said it all. Pudgee flushed. "He's standing right behind me, isn't he?"

Penny nodded her head up and down.

"And what in the fiery blue hell do you two think you're doing?" I growled.

"She told me to do it!" Penny snitched.

Pudgee's eyes widened. "I can explain," she said slowly. "You said to make an impact, so I took it upon myself to do what you asked."

"And what exactly was that?"

She bit her lip nervously. "Well, I thought it was obvious. You said your books needed to be stolen, and that they were going to be the talk of the town. Any publicity is good publicity, right?"

"Oh my God, Pudgee," I said, exasperated, "I said my book is going to be a steal because of what my publishing company chose to sell it for—and that it's so good that it'll be the talk of the town!"

Pudgee looked like she'd seen a ghost. "You're kidding me, right?"

"No, and I keep telling you two you're not ready," I scolded. "I appreciate your efforts, but you're just not *ready*. Now get my books back into that damn store; they're expecting a sell-out for book-signing!"

I should've slept in.

# ACKNOWLEDGEMENTS

To The Almighty: Thank you for providing me with life, and for shining your everlasting love onto me and my family.

For my parents: who loved me and my sister in their very Brooklyn-meets-Bronx kinda way. Your love is beautiful.

To my beautiful wife, Monique, and our incredible kids Kehlani, Malik, Jaden, Kanye and Amari: I can't do anything in life without the inspiration that is your individual lives. Thank you for loving me the way that you all do, and for putting up with me when I'm in my "creative space".

To my best friends in the world: Cory "Cheef", my favorite rapper, and his wife, Nytisha Davis; Curtis and Tamara Mitchell; Qais Johnson; Talib Winston—truly my God Brother and his wife, Aneesah Winston; Sal Bonet; Keith Bonet; Jason Pendleton; Nashawn "OX" Breedlove—only the best for you, kid; Sam Davis; Rasheed Guyton; Omar "Diggs" Jacobs; James Dixon; Barry Singleton; Sterling "SUG" Johnson; Andre Keith; Alex Ramos; Pete LiCausi; Larry Felder; Rich Tobin; John LaRocca; Holly Woods; Ilene Calderon; Jeremy Calderon; and Tish Johnson.

To my sister, Jessica Camacho-Moore, and my brother in-law, Tarik Moore; to Candy Garcia, Jamil Hooper, Reynaldo Osorio, Steve Buendia, Mark Anthony, Law Cunningham, and Eva Edmonds-Reid.

Added thanks to Katrina Baptiste; Denise Taylor; Aqeedah Ham; Dwayne Johnson; Harold Williams; Wendy and Kevin Jean-Louis; and Polo.

Special thanks to James 'The Cunning Linguist" Lewis: for your literary greatness, and being the inspiration behind my writing this book. Thanks, big homie!

And, of course, to everyone else who played even the smallest roles throughout our story: thank you.

# ABOUT THE AUTHOR

Rich Camacho is a songwriter and novelist. He attended Coppin State University in Baltimore, MD, and majored in English Communications.

He has released multiple rap albums with a number of groups, and recorded two solo projects from 1998 to 2013. He is also accredited for writing the majority of the song catalog for PGK, INC., a Law Global Enterprises company that provides children with a supplemental alternative: to desire knowledge through the power of music, books, and education.

He is currently working on creating the M.O.B. brand as an adult entertainment product with his business partners, advertising for comics, animation, paraphernalia, books, TV, and movie scripts based on the characters introduced in this book. He is an original founding member of M.O.B.

Originally from Irvington, NJ, he now lives in the beautiful suburbs of Lawrenceville, GA, with his wife, five children, and two dogs.

You can follow him on Twitter @RichSince78, as well as on Instagram via the same handle (RichSince78).

You can visit Rich's website for information and merchandising at www.themobshop.net.

www.ingramcontent.com/pod-product-compliance
Lightning Source LLC
Chambersburg PA
CBHW030531270626
47155CB00024B/2702